MUTINY ON THE POTEMKIN

Marcus Baxter Thrillers
Book Two

Tim Chant

SAPERE
BOOKS

MUTINY ON THE POTEMKIN

Published by Sapere Books.

20 Windermere Drive, Leeds, England, LS17 7UZ,
United Kingdom

saperebooks.com

ISBN: 978-1-80055-429-0

PROLOGUE

Lake Baikal, Siberia
June 1905

Marcus Baxter shoved his hands deeper into the pockets of his heavy wool coat and swept his gaze across the broad, calm, deep blue waters, the distant shadow of cliffs that looked like they had been pencilled onto the horizon. It was no longer winter in this part of the Russian Empire, but there was a bite to the breeze that blew across the ferry and whipped away the smoke from her four funnels.

"It feels good to be at sea again, does it not, Baxter?"

Baxter smiled slightly. It had taken him a while to convince the earnest young officer to drop the more formal 'Marcus Alexandrovic' in favour of what his friends called him. "This may be an impressive lake, Yuriy, but it is still just a lake."

Yuriy Makarovich Koenig, late of His Imperial Majesty's cruiser *Yaroslavich*, threw his head back and laughed. Baxter was glad to hear the sound — Koenig had been in low spirits during the journey, as well he would be. No sailor relished losing their ship, and as the senior surviving officer he would likely be court-martialled when the authorities got round to it. They would have many more illustrious personages to bring before a board of admirals before they reached a young officer who had served on an old cruiser that shouldn't have been there in the first place.

Koenig joined him at the rail, and Baxter caught a strong waft of vodka on the young man. *Well, that would explain his improved spirits.* "Well, true enough — but for sailors like us, a lake is better than nothing. And is this not a magnificent ship?"

That last was said with obvious pride. Baxter looked along the top deck of the SS *Baikal* from their post at the stern. "She is, indeed, a fine ship."

Koenig slapped both gloved hands down on the rail. "English built, you know, but assembled here."

Baxter smiled at the young man's enthusiasm and slightly awkward attempt at bonhomie. "Oh, I'd know a Whitworth ship anywhere. A clever design." He gestured over the back of the superstructure, down to the double doors through which he'd witnessed a line of train carriages being loaded that morning.

"And about to become obsolete," Koenig went on, his face falling. "They'll complete the line around the south of the lake later this year, I'm told, and there will be no more need for ships."

Baxter regarded the young Russian officer. Koenig was one of the good ones, who'd done his duty and well. Too many like him had gone to their ends in the bloody water of the Tsushima Strait. He deserved better than the way Baxter knew he'd be treated.

That took his mind in a dark direction. He thought of Juneau and the others on the old cruiser, the ones who'd stayed behind. Men he had trained and then fought alongside, even though he was not of their country or their Navy. No one knew what had become of any of them or their ship.

Koenig had survived, at least, and while he had been surprisingly quiet on the subject, he had confirmed that Ekaterina Juneau and young Tommy Dunbar had at least survived the journey into Vladivostok.

Baxter shook his head. Best not to dwell on such things. He reached out, clapped the much smaller, slighter man on the shoulder hard enough to rock him on his feet. "There'll always be a need for ships, and sailors to crew them," he said, trying to force some cheerfulness into his voice. Koenig's position and lurking bitterness reminded him of his own situation not so long ago. Unjustly cashiered from the Royal Navy, cast on the shore and struggling to find employment in the only trade he knew.

Looking back, it was hard to say if he'd been better off scraping by in Edinburgh. At least he'd had his liberty and hadn't been living under the shadow of a firing squad. He couldn't ignore that, even if he tried. The ever-present pair of nondescript men who watched him from a few yards away were a constant reminder of it.

He had to admit, though, that he'd lived more in the last seven months than he had for the previous five. Not least because of the woman he'd known and — perhaps — loved. Who may, or may not, have betrayed him.

It was all a little too confusing. At least now, though, he had something approaching his liberty. He'd been a bit surprised that the Tsar's police hadn't whisked him away to be kept under lock and key. It seemed that no-one quite knew what to make of him or, indeed, what to do with him.

If there was one thing a life at sea had taught Baxter, it was to enjoy what he could while it lasted. He took a deep breath, relishing the cold air in his lungs. "Enough of this talk," he said. "Let's go and get a drink."

The ferry's route took less than a day, in ideal weather conditions at least, cutting at a leisurely pace across the southern stretch of the long but narrow lake. That didn't stop it having a well-appointed lounge bar, and it didn't stop said bar being quite busy.

Most of the people in it were military, and most of those were soldiers. A small knot of sailors occupied a corner table, but Baxter knew he and Koenig wouldn't be welcome there. They were officers from the ships trapped in Vladivostok, not undefeated but surviving in the ongoing war with Japan. The reek of defeat clung to Koenig, though, and Baxter was regarded with nothing but suspicion.

Those sailors weren't as bad the Army officers, though. They clustered in two distinct camps, infantry and cavalry, at either end of the long, well-appointed room. The cavalry contingent in particular was surrounded by the detritus of their campaign against the bar's stock — empty champagne bottles upended in ice buckets and carafes of vodka for the most part — and were in full voice, singing loudly.

"What will you have?" Koenig asked as he and Baxter took a seat at a small table. The furniture was all dark wood and polished to a deep lustre. Brass fittings polished with, apparently, the same obsessiveness a Royal Navy crew might achieve, and glittering crystal decanters offset the other sombre furnishing.

"Vodka is fine," Baxter said, as a waiter appeared silently with a carafe of the clear poison and two glasses. He'd developed a taste for the stuff, which the Russians seemed to drink like water, during the long months at sea with the 2nd Pacific Squadron.

"I mean, what will you have with it?" Koenig demanded cheerfully, seeing away his glass. He cast a glance around the bar, seemingly oblivious to the hostility already manifesting amongst the Army officers. "I think a bottle of champagne will be most suitable."

Baxter briefly considered whether they should take the bottle and return to the upper deck. He'd spent altogether too long cooped up in a train carriage during the long journey from Vladivostok, and before that under house arrest in the Russian port. That had been tolerable, almost welcome, after a week or more at sea in an open boat. Of late, it had started to wear thin for him.

He noticed a young officer staring fixedly at Koenig. It wasn't hate. Anger? The icy glare turned on Baxter, then flickered away almost dismissively.

"Yes, champagne sounds like an excellent idea," he said. "And perhaps some caviar?"

He might as well enjoy his time, he thought, given how uncertain his future was. Particularly as Koenig was paying for everything.

"Any idea who the chap glaring at you is?" he asked quietly, after the bottle had been delivered and poured.

Koenig cast a casual glance at the cavalry officers. "Cossacks," he said dismissively. "Trans-Baikal Division — you can tell from the yellow flashes. No idea who that captain is, though."

Baxter immediately regretted drawing his friend's attention to the officer. The bar was too noisy for the Army officers to have heard him, but his glance and slight shake of the head had been clear, and just as clearly misinterpreted. The officer who had taken a particular interest in Koenig rose — more steadily than Baxter expected — and swaggered across the short stretch of deep red carpet towards them. None of his comrades rose with him, but directed their rapt attention to the scene.

It was a dynamic Baxter had seen a dozen times before, and he didn't like it one jot. The Cossack officer had a calm assurance that bordered on arrogance, and his flat dark eyes had little human about them. Although he was a Cossack officer, he was clearly an aristocratic Russian. Likely the sort of officer who was brutal to the men under his command — even by Russian standards. His uniform was well-tailored but disarrayed just enough to indicate it was deliberate.

In short, he was cut from the same cloth as any number of similar officers Baxter had had the misfortune to bump into in his own career.

"You are Koenig, of the *Yaroslavich*?" the cavalryman demanded. Like most Russian officers, he spoke unaccented French.

Koenig blinked up at the fellow, and Baxter realised the young lieutenant was perhaps drunker than he'd first appeared.

"Well, speak up, man!" the Cossack demanded. "Or has the thrashing you took deafened you?"

Baxter tried to keep his voice mild as he interjected. "Naval battles can indeed be very noisy things," he said, slipping easily into the same language. "Particularly if one is commanding one of the main guns, as my friend here did."

The officer feigned shock at being spoken to by someone he clearly believed inferior. "My God, the pet speaks, and speaks a civilised language. Not well, of course." Having dismissed Baxter, in his own mind, he turned his sneering expression back on Koenig. "So, commanded one of the guns, eh? Much good it did you." He turned with an expansive gesture back to his audience, inviting their participation in the ritual. "Why, I heard the entire fleet barely hit a Japanese ship, let alone sunk one!"

"A betrayal!" one of his fellows shouted. "If they hadn't dawdled, Port Arthur would not have fallen!"

Baxter could see the Vladivostok squadron officers stir uncomfortably. Koenig may have been a pariah amongst them, but they would not stand for a fellow sailor being so ridiculed.

Koenig found his voice suddenly. "Well, I heard you mostly turned tail at Mukden and ran!" he spluttered.

A sly smile crept across the officer's face, as his victim rose to the bait. Baxter knew, from what he'd read, that his friend was being unjust to the Army — mostly from ignorance and anger, he surmised. "Well, if our efforts had been properly supported…" the cavalryman began.

Baxter had had enough. He knew exactly how this would go, and he had to break the cycle if Koenig was going to salvage any sort of career. That's what he told himself, anyway, in the clear part of his mind. He could feel his anger surging, though, boiling up from where he tried to keep it tamped down. He'd been here before, been on the receiving end of it. Unfortunately for this posturing dandy, Baxter wasn't constrained by military discipline.

He rose, making himself appear casual, and then straightened to his full height. That gave him the satisfaction of seeing this cavalry officer blanche very slightly. Few people appreciated just how large Baxter was, until they saw him up close and standing straight. He'd used that to his advantage in the past.

"What's your name?" he asked softly, sticking to French.

The officer straightened as well. He was relatively tall, but couldn't quite muster Baxter's six foot five and certainly had none of his bulk. What he did have was the surety of the gentry that they were above reproach or consequence. "I am Rittmeister Yulian Danilovic Zubov, and you will address me as 'your Well Born'!"

"Will I indeed?" Baxter said mildly, then punched him in the guts.

It wasn't a hard blow, thrown straight from a relaxed posture, as much a shot across the bows as anything else. Zubov staggered backwards nonetheless, the wind taken out of him literally and figuratively, and was propped up by some of his fellow officers who rose in his support.

Baxter switched to Russian as he heard Koenig rise. Most Russian aristos barely spoke their mother language, but he and Koenig often conversed in it. "Stay out of this, Yuriy," he said. "I want this to be a fair fight."

"You dare!" the struck officer roared as soon as he'd caught his breath. He didn't quite know what to do with himself at that point, though. Men like him didn't use their fists — they used a riding crop or cane on their subordinates, and the troops under their command on the enemy. They didn't resort to brawling.

"But there's a dozen of them!" Koenig protested.

Baxter cracked his knuckles and grinned at the Army officers. "As I said. A fair fight."

CHAPTER 1

Baxter's head hadn't hurt this much since he'd been knocked out by Vasily Ivanovich, his one-time jailer and latterly friend aboard the *Yaroslavich*. His ribs felt tender, and he knew he'd be sporting a decent black eye.

His recollections of the fight, though patchy, suggested he'd probably got the better of it. At least until the two Okhrana men had intervened with the unfair advantage of having blackjacks. He guessed, from the difference in motion, that he was once more back on rails, which suggested a profound unconsciousness. A body and mind attuned to the changes of the sea would have noticed a switch of transport otherwise.

"My predecessor was unfortunately lax in allowing you as much licence as he did," someone said, just out of his line of sight. Baxter reckoned he should have been able to see the speaker, but his left eye was already swollen shut. "Not a mistake I intend to replicate."

He groaned as he sat up, trying to blink his eye clear. It was gummy but light finally made it through, bringing the other man in the train cabin into focus. As soon as that happened, Baxter knew that he was in trouble.

"While some of our betters may previously have interceded on your behalf, which may have given you a false sense of confidence, I would encourage you to consider that protection at an end."

The fellow wasn't much to look at, at first glance. Even seated, it was clear he was small, with iron-grey hair and a neatly trimmed beard. His eyes were a very pale blue, startling against his otherwise dark complexion. It was the eyes that let

Baxter know he was in a new world — appraising, sharply intelligent. Cold.

"I wasn't aware that anyone was interceding on my behalf," he said.

"Oh, apparently there are some who believe you are merely an innocent pawn in the great game." Scorn curled through the man's voice. Baxter was so disoriented that it took him a moment to realise he was speaking English, with barely a hint of an accent. "That you should be quietly let go, guineas put in your pocket to allow you to disappear off home."

"That's news to me," Baxter said, trying not to let anything show. He knew, instinctively, that this man would pounce on any hint of weakness, of human fallibility. He wasn't aware of having any friends in Russia. Ekaterina Juneau had apparently wanted nothing to do with him when he'd arrived in Vladivostok; indeed, he was not unconvinced that she had been behind his almost immediate arrest by the local authorities. Juneau himself was presumed dead, and Koenig certainly had no influence.

It must be Ekaterina, he realised with a stab of — what? Happiness? Joy? He knew she was in some way associated with the Okhrana, which had put her in a position to help him. Why she hadn't told him any of this, or just got him out, was a mystery to him. One his pounding head couldn't contemplate.

"You certainly present very well as being an idiot," the policeman observed mildly, breaking in to his chain of thought. "Your compatriot tells a different story, however."

Baxter stirred, but his anger had been spent in the brawl. "Arbuthnott," he spat. "I wouldn't believe a word he says."

He'd not seen the rogue British intelligence agent since Vladivostok. His own arrest had taken some of the shine off the triumph of survival, taking an open boat through the aftermath of a battle and enemy waters. He'd still taken some satisfaction in watching Arbuthnott being carried away under armed guard.

"Oh, I do not. This is not the way to survive long in my trade, believing what anyone says. Which is why I'm going to be spending a lot of time with both of you "

"Good job it's a long journey to St. Petersburg, then." Baxter stretched back out on the bench. He realised this wasn't the cabin he'd had on the Trans-Siberian train. That had been comfortable enough, even if his captors had not seen fit to acquire one of the more luxurious accommodations. This was bare, the train carriage itself smaller.

"Oh, we're not going to St. Petersburg," the man said, with a very slight smile. This confirmed what Baxter had come to suspect, that he had been transferred onto a different train. "You will not be permitted within the same city as His Imperial Majesty." The little man stood and fastidiously straightened his plain grey overcoat. "We are going to Odessa, where we will be able to spend much time together. Undisturbed."

The implications of that statement were clear. While Baxter may have friends in Russia, he was being taken somewhere they wouldn't look for him. He hadn't looked for help before, but now he knew none would be forthcoming.

"Look, why don't you just get on and shoot me, if that's where this is going?"

"Mr Baxter, we are not savages." He slid the door of the compartment open. "As we will be spending so much time together, I should introduce myself. My name is Bilyk. Kindly remember it."

Baxter knew he should be trying to ingratiate himself with this man. His continued comfort in captivity, not to mention his life, depended on convincing this Bilyk that he was what he appeared — an out-of-luck sailor run onto a lee shore. It did help that this was the truth, but Arbuthnott was working against him. That would complicate matters.

"It's not a hard name to remember." Baxter put an arm over his eyes — his head was throbbing tremendously and the light hurt. "What of Yuriy Makarovich?" he asked, almost unconsciously slipping back into Russian.

Bilyk replied in the same language, and even without having an ear for Russian accents Baxter thought it sounded as flat and unaccented as his English. "Lieutenant Koenig? He is of course a naval hero, one of the only officers of the Pacific Fleet to have made it through — even if it was without his ship. He is to take a prize assignment on the finest ship of the Black Sea Fleet — the battleship *Potemkin*."

Under other circumstances, Baxter knew he would have enjoyed a visit to Odessa. While he'd touched here once or twice in the past, as a young man learning the sea on one of his father's merchant commands, he hadn't seen much beyond the dockyard areas. Just a brief excursion up the grand Richelieu Steps to gawk at the broad, tree-lined streets and squares around the cathedral.

He didn't know where Bilyk had taken him in the city, though he doubted it was anywhere central. The secret policeman had gone out of his way to ensure Baxter was as confused as possible, moving him through the city in a closed carriage with the curtains drawn, despite the stifling heat. He couldn't say for sure, but he got the feeling Bilyk had also brought him by a roundabout route.

"You present something of a conundrum, Baxter," the dour Ukrainian said from the doorway of the small room where they'd deposited themselves the night before. He was speaking his flat, oddly accented English. "A problem. You and your friend."

Baxter fought down the urge to yell at this hard-eyed man. He knew it wouldn't do any good, would just be giving him what he wanted. A crack, an emotional response. He forced himself to look up and keep his voice calm, not put his head in his hands.

"I don't have to be a problem," he said. It was ... frustrating? Infuriating? To be back in this position, trying to convince a new set of Russians that he was no threat. That, far from being an intelligencer or criminal mastermind, he was merely a sailor who had found himself in over his head. "And I'm certainly no conundrum."

"What would you have us do, then? We cannot just deposit you on the street, here in Odessa."

Baxter shrugged. "I'm an experienced sailor who speaks Russian. I won't be there long."

"And the fact you do speak Russian with such facility is one of the problems with you." Bilyk was standing in front of the windows, and now turned to open them. Light flooded the small room, causing Baxter to wince and shade his eyes. "Mr Koenig, in his report, indicated that you learned it during the voyage from the North Sea. I find this ... unlikely. You people are not famed for your facility with other languages or willingness to learn them, and yet here you are. A fluent Russian speaker after six months on one of His Majesty's ships. No. It is unlikely."

Baxter rose, perhaps slightly faster than he'd intended. Bilyk's two shadows, stationed on either side of the single door to the room, stirred slightly, and he forced himself to adopt a relaxed posture. "What can I say?" he said, carefully sticking to English and injecting a touch of his father's Edinburgh accent. "A life at sea, it forces you to adapt."

"How very fortunate for you, that you can always fall back on that." Bilyk's gaze was suspicious, but then he was a secret policeman charged with propping up a crumbling autocracy. Suspicion would be his default mood.

Not for the first time, Baxter wondered what this little man had been told. He knew Koenig had provided a glowing report of his conduct during the voyage to Tsushima Strait and the battle there. From what Bilyk had said, Ekaterina had also spoken up for him. So why was this nasty, suspicious little man so concerned with persecuting him further?

"I can fall back on that, as that is all I am," Baxter said, trying to make himself sound as earnest and simple as he could.

"This is not what others have told me."

Yes. That was it. He'd not seen Mr Arbuthnott since he'd brought in his boatload of survivors from the *Yaroslavich* and handed him over to the relevant Russian authorities. Who knew what he'd been saying since then? He was, without doubt, the sort to say pretty much anything to save his own skin, let alone further his agenda. Baxter was starting to regret not just dropping the treacherous bastard over the side of the Japanese auxiliary cruiser they'd caught him on, instead of onto the deck.

"It is an attractive city, is it not?" Bilyk said, changing both his tone and the subject with a startling rapidity. He stepped aside from the window to give Baxter a proper look.

Contrary to what he'd expected, they'd brought him somewhere fairly central, rather than tucked away in the docklands. He was looking out over pitched rooves of red tiles towards a tall cathedral spire. They had him in a top-floor room, not unfamiliar from his life ashore back in Britain when he had often lodged in garrets. The last of those had been Mrs Dunbar's, and he didn't want to think about that; about how he had recklessly brought her youngest son along on his ill-fated expedition to observe the Russian warships passing through the North Sea. As far as he knew, young Tommy Dunbar had made it through to Vladivostok on the lifeboat Koenig had commanded. The Russian officer had told him as much, but could tell him nothing more; in much the same way as Baxter had heard nothing much of Ekaterina beyond what little Bilyk had mentioned.

"Do you not think, Mr Baxter?" the other man said now, breaking into his train of thought.

"Yes, yes, I suppose it is. I remember the steps as being very grand."

"Ah yes, built by the great governor Richelieu a few decades ago. A very beautiful city, the fourth largest in our glorious and ever-growing empire." Baxter could not quite tell from his tone how seriously Bilyk took that statement "And here, as with everywhere else, the rot of revolution, of social upheaval, festers just below the surface. I imagine it is the same across the world, the forces of revolution seeking to destroy the natural order of things."

No, no, he definitely meant it. Bilyk was a true believer.

"And it is the responsibility of the Tsar's loyal subjects to preserve this natural order. The sailor and the soldier, of course, are the most obvious. The peasant who toils in the field to feed the cities, and the worker who is fed and therefore makes the many modern things we rely on. But we of the Okhrana, we are the secret tool. We watch everything and everyone, and we must suspect everyone. On us rests the burden of protecting the very fabric of this society. And so you see, Mr Baxter, you are a problem for me."

True to his word, Bilyk spent a lot of time with Baxter over the next few days. The interviews, as he somewhat euphemistically called them, tended to follow the same pattern. Questions were asked, or more often inferred through statements. There was no violence, at least not yet. Baxter was under no illusion that this would follow if the secret police could not be satisfied. Bilyk always had the same two men in tow, one a big bruiser who looked like he'd be perfectly comfortable using his fists. The smaller of the two didn't look like much and could be dealt with reasonably easily — not that there was much Baxter could really do about his situation. Not yet, anyway.

They didn't allow him out of the little room, and he began to suspect that the choice of room had been deliberate. The house — and now he was fairly certain it was a house he was being held in, rather than a more formal government building — faced south and he could just make out the gleam of the sea. It was, to be fair, often lost under a haze of smoke and heat. But the ships he occasionally glimpsed meant a lot to him, and Bilyk knew that.

"It won't work," he told the night, standing in the little bay of the window and staring down towards the gleam of lights. They wouldn't break him, because he had nothing to tell them. Nothing of real consequence, or that Arbuthnott wouldn't already have said to save his own hide.

That was the real problem — he had no idea what the renegade Naval Intelligence agent had said. From what Baxter had picked up from his captors, Arbuthnott was spinning all sorts of tales in an attempt to exonerate himself and make Baxter out to be a villain of the first order. Or, at least, that was what Bilyk wanted him to think. For all he knew, Arbuthnott had clammed up as tightly as he had.

No. Arbuthnott wasn't the type. As much as he truly seemed to believe in his cause, of ensuring British naval superiority, he was clearly also driven by self-preservation. That was understandable.

What Baxter struggled to understand was why he couldn't bring himself to take the same approach. He could tell Bilyk everything he suspected, that Arbuthnott was a renegade determined to start another naval panic in Britain by bringing her closer to war with Russia. But even telling Bilyk that could be giving Arbuthnott what he wanted, assuming the Okhrana believed him.

It all made his head hurt; this was a life he wasn't cut out for, hadn't chosen and wanted nothing to do with. His problem now was convincing everyone else he was what he claimed to be.

"Just a sailor, down on his luck," he murmured.

The nights were close and hot, and increasingly noisy. "I know your people enjoy a drink as much as the next man, though perhaps not as much as my own," Baxter commented on his fifth morning in Odessa. "But it definitely seems like the natives are restless."

"It is good to see your appetite returning," was all Bilyk said in return. Baxter was polishing off the simple but substantive breakfast they'd brought him. The same breakfast he'd had every day, in fact. "You will need it."

Baxter looked up from the cup of hot, smoky tea, trying to work out if Bilyk meant that as a threat. The secret policeman seemed distracted more than anything else, standing in the window and silhouetted against the morning light.

"The night-time revelry keeping you awake?" he asked, allowing a certain amount of humour to creep into his voice.

Bilyk scowled at him. "These matters are not your concern. What should be of concern to you is convincing me that you pose no threat to His Serene Highness."

They stared at each other, Baxter once again feeling the familiar surge of anger at the situation he found himself in. His ribs were still sore, and his face felt tight and puffy around his left eye. He knew he wasn't in any fit state to attempt an escape. Even if he did manage it, he probably wouldn't make it far. No, best to batten down the hatches and ride this out. Eventually, Bilyk would realise this line of questioning was not fruitful, or his mysterious benefactors would catch up with them and see him freed.

Until that time, though, he knew he had to step carefully. He pushed away the tin plate. "So, Mr Bilyk. Tell me what you would like to talk about today."

"Tell me again, Mr Baxter, just how it was that you found yourself aboard a ship carrying a personal friend of the Tsar, and what it is you thought you might achieve by getting yourself into that position."

He fought the urge to rub his temples. This was going to become a very long day indeed. Seeing his response, Bilyk clearly decided to change tack.

"And tell me of the Countess Ekaterina Juneau," the policeman went on, his voice dropping to an almost conspiratorial whisper.

Baxter couldn't help it; he let his anger and pain flare briefly. "What the devil am I supposed to tell you about her?" he spat. "She's one of yours, isn't she?"

Bilyk smiled then, the expression that of a satisfied predator. "It is interesting to me that you should know this," he almost purred. "An odd thing for a simple sailor to know, given that I am sure she would not have revealed the information."

Baxter closed his eyes, realising he was no match for this interrogator. He could fall back on being a bluff, uncomplicated sailor as much as he wanted — because it was, after all, the truth — but Bilyk would find a way to rile him, get him to say things he shouldn't say.

But why shouldn't I say them and have done with this? he wondered, not for the first time.

CHAPTER 2

Within a week of having been brought to Odessa, Baxter knew he had no choice but to escape, and escape soon. There would be no waiting for Bilyk to tire of this crusade and release him; no hope of anyone coming to his rescue.

The secret policeman had finally lost his patience with what he perceived as Baxter's refusal to admit to any malfeasance; that, or someone further up the chain of command had become impatient. Even the reports of Baxter's conduct during the desperate fight against the Japanese combined fleet could not save him from the violence, and he knew that at the end of this they could not release him.

In the long nights and painful interrogation sessions, his mind kept coming back to the idea of giving in, of just telling Bilyk what he wanted to hear. Confirming whatever mix of truth and lies Arbuthnott would have been spoon-feeding him. Part of his resistance came from sheer bloody-mindedness, an inability just to do things the easy way. He also couldn't help the feeling that, once his usefulness was at an end, he wouldn't be quietly released.

"Explain to me the circumstances of the Countess taking you into her ... confidence," Bilyk demanded. He stood a little bit away from the small, uncomfortable chair they'd seated him on. No doubt he didn't want blood spatter on his neat grey suit. More than that, Baxter suspected that gulf of space allowed the Okhrana man to believe his hands were clean of the brutality he had meted out.

That question, slipped into the interrogation occasionally, was the real reason Baxter refused to divulge even the little he did know. He didn't know what Bilyk was after, exactly, with these questions. But he knew it wouldn't be good for Ekaterina. He didn't know where he stood with her and hadn't even seen her since the hellish last day on the *Yaroslavich*. He had thought she had turned her back on him, and had him arrested, but he was increasingly sure she was the protector Bilyk had mentioned.

Either way, he was determined not to say anything that would bring trouble to her door. He just didn't know how long he would be able to stick to that.

It had begun in a relatively restrained fashion. As Baxter had suspected, the big man was the muscle. He didn't speak, didn't ask the questions. He didn't even seem to need much in the way of instructions, though occasionally Bilyk would grunt 'Mieszko' and a blow would be struck. It took Baxter a few repetitions of that to work out this was his name.

All the while, the small wiry one watched from the corner of the room, his gaze a little bit too intent.

"I'm going to tell you this once, Mieszko," Baxter snarled in Russian as he righted his chair and sat back down. "Touch me again, and I'll break your arm."

"Mieszko doesn't speak Russian, or French, Mr Baxter," Bilyk said calmly as he very considerately shook out a clean handkerchief and handed it to him to dab blood from the corner of his mouth. "That and his apparent lack of imagination makes him very useful to me."

"Well, tell him in whatever language it is he does understand," Baxter snarled, cleaning himself up and throwing the bloody cloth back in Bilyk's face. "And, for the last time..."

He didn't see the wordless signal that the secret policeman gave the thug, so didn't see the blow before it connected with the side of his head. He rolled with it, but it still set his vision swimming.

"It does not do to threaten your captors, Mr Baxter. Come now, none of this…"

Baxter was already moving, though. He'd expected the blind rage he was used to, the fury that had driven his assault of the Russian officers on the Baikal ferry, and before that had thrown the punch that had finally ended his Royal Navy career.

Instead, it was a cold certainty that he wouldn't be made a liar. Mieszko recoiled, looking confused and slightly alarmed. He brought an arm up to defend himself and Baxter grabbed it, yanking it towards him and twisting with all his strength. Mieszko screamed in pain, a surprisingly high-pitched noise that only rose in volume as the bone went with a wet snap.

Ratface exploded out of the corner, moving faster than Baxter had been expecting. A pistol glinted in his hand. Bilyk seemed stunned by the sudden violence, poised in the corner of the room. That gave Baxter the second he needed as he closed down Ratface before he could bring the pistol on-target, slapping it out of his hand and swinging a blow at his head. Ratface danced aside, reaching into his coat and slipping a small, vicious-looking knife from its sheath. He actually smiled at Baxter then, the expression chilling on his narrow features.

A gunshot sounded before they could get into it, deafening in the confined space, and a bullet strike on the wall sent plaster dust into Baxter's face. He stopped, poised over Ratface, and the only sound he could make out was Mieszko's low sobbing.

"I should advise you, Mr Baxter, that I am a crack shot and that bullet went exactly where I intended. The next one will be in your liver."

It was the coldly certain tone more than the threat of a lingering death that made Baxter stop. He made a conscious effort to relax, opening his hands and dropping his shoulders as he stepped back, making sure he didn't go anywhere near the injured interrogator.

Ratface looked disappointed that he wouldn't be allowed to use his blade. He hadn't seemed at all worried about the thought of fighting a man at least twice his size, and that told Baxter that he was the dangerous one.

Bilyk said something sharp that he couldn't make out. The little man backed off, sidling around him with a hateful glare and moving to comfort Mieszko, who was now up on his knees and cradling his arm. The smaller man patted him on the shoulder and almost crooned comforting words to him.

Chaos erupted in the room a moment later, as other Okhrana agents tried to force their way through the door together. Bilyk was shouting something, but before Baxter could register it he went down under a flurry of blows to his head and other more vulnerable parts of his body.

"I really wish you had not done that, Mr Baxter. We could have conducted ourselves like civilised men, but you chose a … different path."

Baxter groaned as he tried to right himself on the low, uncomfortable cot he'd come to on. He winced as he sat up, a stabbing pain in his side telling him at least one rib was cracked. "Do you call what was happening civilised?" he spat. His head was throbbing and every breath he took hurt. He wasn't going to give this bastard the satisfaction of seeing that, though.

Bilyk had the good grace to look slightly discomfited. "Even cultured men must occasionally resort to less pleasant means, when confronted by dangers to the Crown and State."

"For the last time," Baxter ground out. "I'm just a sailor hired to do a job, who was in the wrong place at the wrong time. I will say no more on the subject or any other, and I demand to see the local British consul."

Bilyk smiled his thin smile. "You have no rights here, Baxter," he said, his level tone belying the cold fury in his eyes. "Not after you assaulted an officer of this department."

Baxter put his head in his hands. There was no point talking to this man, pointing out the hypocrisy of every sentence that came out of his mouth.

"What, no further protestation?" the secret policeman demanded, scorn touching his tone now. "No more demands to be released?"

Baxter looked back at him, imagining strangling the life out of the little bastard. He kept his mouth shut and just stared until Bilyk got up.

"Well, as you can see, you have lost the privilege of a room with a view," he said, voice betraying no hint of discomfort. "We shall speak again once you are feeling a bit stronger. Though, as poor Mieszko is in no fit state to assist me, Pavel will have to step in. And I suspect you will like that even less."

"How is Mieszko?" Baxter asked, just as his tormentor had reached the door to the small, dark room they had him locked in.

"Do you care?"

Baxter shrugged, winced as the movement sent slivers of pain through him. "I don't hold what he does against him," he said after a moment. He remembered the look in the big man's eyes, pain and fear and a weird sense of betrayal. "Yes, Mr Bilyk, I care. My quarrel is not with him. It is with you."

He lay in the darkness after Bilyk was gone, thinking. He didn't like the sound of Pavel being in charge of the beatings he would receive, though at a guess he was always the escalation from the relatively crude measures taken by Mieszko. He guessed it would go beyond just beatings, for one thing. Pavel — if that was indeed Ratface's name — was clearly the sort of small man who liked knives.

That all meant he really had to be away from here. Before, when he'd first been captured by the Imperial Russian Navy, he had had some sense of faith that these men weren't barbarians, that he wouldn't be killed out of hand. All such bets were now off.

He assessed himself and his situation. He was tired, and hurt, and his stomach ached for lack of food. There were no external windows in this room, and the cool dampness of the air suggested he was in a cellar. The door was wooden rather than barred, but wasn't thick oak or similar wood. So, a converted cellar, not a dungeon.

He would have smiled at that thought. Even a year ago, he would have thought it utterly bizarre even to contemplate being held in a dungeon. Now, it seemed almost like a normal notion.

Focus. His mind was drifting, beset by pain and thirst and hunger. He knew that if he was to have even the slightest chance of getting out of this alive, he had to go before he was too weak and damaged.

"Well, no time like the present," he told himself, pulling himself upright. He had a flash of memory, of his attempt to escape the Russian cruiser before he and the first officer Juneau had come to an understanding.

Long before he'd come to an understanding with the Countess Juneau.

He'd gone on the spur of the moment then as well, and would have had a good chance of getting ashore in Spain if he hadn't had the millstone of Tommy Dunbar around his neck.

Thinking about his young charge threatened to take the wind out of his sail. Having heard nothing more of Tommy other than the bare fact of his survival, he could only trust that Ekaterina had ensured his safe return to Scotland or was in the process of doing so.

He couldn't let himself worry about that now. He got off the low, hard cot. The cell was pitch-dark, but there was a smidge of light filtering in under the door — the weak, flickering glow of a candle. He listened as carefully as he could and thought he could make out the sound of running water.

He started hammering on the inside of the door. "Hey!" he bellowed. "Hey, you out there!"

Silence. It was entirely possible that the Okhrana officials just assumed their gaol was secure enough and didn't bother with a guard. He thumped the door again. Only an idiot would leave a candle burning, unattended, for no reason. "Hey, you!"

"Give it a rest, friend, I am trying to sleep," a muffled voice replied. It sounded as though it came from another cell, not the corridor. So, he was not the only guest of the Okhrana. "You should sleep too; you will need to keep your strength up."

Another double thump. "Come on, you Russki bastard!" he yelled, switching to English. He pressed his ear to the smooth wood of the door, heard someone muttering under his breath and the sound of approaching boots.

"What do you want?" a gruff voice demanded in Russian. "Can't a man take a piss in peace?"

"I want to talk to Bilyk," Baxter snarled back, and punctuated the statement by kicking the door. "Take me to him, right now."

"Don't do it, my friend," came the muffled voice again. "It will not make things easier for you. They will just take you out into the courtyard and shoot you in the back of the head."

The guard's voice came back, bleary with sleep. "Talk to him tomorrow, idiot. He has lots of time for you in the morning."

Baxter almost gave up, but thumped the door a last time. "Listen here, you little prick," he yelled. "So help me…"

"You are going to regret disturbing me," muttered the voice, and Baxter was relieved to hear the jangle of keys being sorted through. "I am going to beat you until your mother feels it."

Baxter stepped back, then to the side. Tension coiled through him as he prepared to strike. Then he heard Bilyk's voice, raised in anger. He guessed they were speaking Ukrainian; he certainly couldn't follow the conversation but could guess at the content. A moment later, a cell door banged open and he could hear his fellow prisoner's voice raised in protest, followed by the sound of a blow and someone's feet dragging across the flagstoned floor.

His own cell door was unlocked and flung open. His eyes stung as light spilled in — it came from a mere candle, but after the absolute darkness it was still dazzling. Bilyk's distinctive silhouette filled the space. "Get up," he spat, and turned away without waiting for compliance.

"But I've only just laid down!" Baxter protested, putting one arm over his eyes. He suppressed a wince as his forearm went across his left eye, puffy from where he'd been punched earlier.

"And now you must rise, Mr Baxter, as we are going on another journey." Bilyk muttered something over his shoulder, and two big officers came through. Baxter refused to rise, but did let them pull him to his feet without resistance, and he didn't struggle against the cuffs they put on his wrists.

The light and the speed with which they carried him meant it was all a bit of a blur as they hustled him out of the cellar. He saw a plain floor and whitewashed walls, then wooden stairs and similarly simple wooden floors with an occasional threadbare rug. He smelled boiling cabbage and piss, vodka and wood smoke. It was hot above ground level, a stifling humidity that was a shock after the cool dankness of his cell. Late afternoon daylight streamed in through the windows. That, more than anything, threw him. After the darkness of his cell, he had just assumed it was night time.

"Isn't it traditional to do this sort of thing at night?" he asked his captors.

Bilyk appeared by his side, a pool of icy calm in the disarray. "What sort of thing would that be, Mr Baxter?" he asked. He was trying to maintain his usual hard-edged urbanity, but Baxter realised something had the man rattled. "Do not fear, we're not taking you outside to shoot you."

Baxter knew he should feel relieved, but he didn't trust the Okhrana one jot. "Because you're civilised men?" he asked, trying and failing to keep the sneer from his voice.

"No, Mr Baxter. Eventually, your protector would find out, and even I would not like to see what would happen next." A pause as Bilyk stared hard at him, cold eyes unreadable. "Not until we have absolute proof of your criminality, and can proceed to a trial."

Baxter snorted. There didn't seem to be any point in protesting his innocence — not right now, anyway. Probably not ever. Bilyk seemed determined to find him guilty of something, somehow.

The Okhrana staff were in a state of organised chaos. Men scurried here and there, carrying bundles of files and valise cases. Baxter realised, as they marched him past the open door to a large parlour, that the smoke he could smell was coming from a roaring fire which was being steadily fed with papers.

"What the devil is going on?" he asked. Bilyk wasn't there, though, and all he got by way of response was a blow across the back of the head to keep him moving.

Everything was happening in a tense silence, just the occasional barked order and the startling clatter of someone dropping a box of files. In a way, it reminded him of a ship closing up for action. The same tension and quiet, fast efficiency.

What had stirred the ants' nest became clear as Baxter was prodded out into a closed courtyard. For a moment, he thought he could hear the sea. Then it resolved into the sound of thousands of voices, raised in anger.

He straightened slightly, heart rate quickening. In the distance, he could hear the pop of gunfire and the crackle of something burning. Black plumes of smoke marred an otherwise deep blue sky. The voices of the — what? Protestors? Rioters? — were much closer, though.

"That's right, my friend," a voice murmured at his side. "The revolution has begun."

He glanced sharply at the young man who had spoken, surprised he would sound so openly gleeful despite being surrounded by hard men whose job it was to suppress any revolution. He had spoken in English, though, and Baxter was sure none of the men guarding them would understand.

"Surely rioters would not attack a government building?" he asked.

"My friend, you have much to learn about *revolutionaries* if you think they would not attack a government building," the fellow said, the amusement glinting in his eye taking any sting from the statement. "Besides, this is not an official building. Everyone knows the secret police maintain a modest townhouse on Sjechenova Street, but it is not here *officially*. It is used for people such as you and I."

A plain carriage rattled into the courtyard, the horses' hooves clattering on the paving. "I'm not like you," Baxter grumbled as the carriage drew to a halt in front of them. One of their guards stepped forward smartly, threw the door open. Two others pushed Baxter and his new friend forward and into the dim, stifling interior.

"Of course you are not," the other man said as he slumped on the hard bench seat. Further conversation was prevented as Bilyk started to climb in. Baxter glowered at the secret policeman, unreasonably annoyed by the curtailment of his first opportunity to speak to someone who wasn't a captor.

Someone shouted from back in the house, and Bilyk scowled as he stepped back down. "A secret policeman's work is never done," the other prisoner said, venom in his voice as Bilyk hurried back indoors. "What is your name, friend?" he went on, gesturing expansively with quick hands.

Baxter bit down on giving his full name. "Marcus Alexandrovich," he said, accepting the hand that was thrust out at him, awkward in the cuffs.

"Kostenko, Ruslan Yaroslavovych," the little man said, then frowned. "Why the pleased expression?"

Baxter shook his head — there wasn't time for this now. "I knew a Yaroslavich once. It's a good omen."

"Ah, you are a sailor, I see." Kostenko had switched into English, and smiled when Baxter couldn't help but give away his understanding. "No one else is this superstitious. I find myself curious as to how a British sailor, who is not as you put it 'like me', should find himself a guest of His Imperial Majesty?"

"Long story for another time," Baxter said, voice short. He shifted, trying to get more comfortable. He was becoming increasingly tense. "Is it me, or are the rioters — my apologies, revolutionaries — coming closer?"

Kostenko tilted his head, squinting behind small, round glasses that reminded Baxter of those worn by Bilyk. "I do believe you are right, comrade," he said after a moment.

Baxter glanced around suspiciously. "Let's get one thing straight, mate, I'm not your comrade," he said. The last thing he needed was for one of the Okhrana to hear that suggestion. From what he could see of the little courtyard from inside the carriage, the policemen were distracted. They could hear the approaching mob as well as anyone else. One of the horses whinnied, and he heard the nervous stamp of a shod hoof, sharp on the flagstone. The driver called out something, asking where Bilyk was. Demanding to get moving. The response was testy, telling him to stay put. The speaker clearly didn't want to be here.

There came a sound of smashing glass close by, many voices raised in anger. One of the horses bucked in its traces. The driver had obviously had enough. With a shouted imprecation and ignoring the yells of his comrades, he snapped the reins. The carriage jerked forward. "Open the damn gates, you peasant!" Baxter heard the fellow yell. "I'm not hanging around here."

A second later, the carriage took a tight turn fast enough to sway Baxter and Kostenko. They'd left in such a hurry that no-one had closed the heavy curtains obviously intended to keep prisoners disoriented, and Baxter caught a glimpse of a tight mass of people moving along the street. Outside the high walls of the courtyard, the roar of the crowd was almost overwhelming.

"There must be thousands of them!" he exclaimed, just as a heavy *thump* indicated a thrown brick had hit the back of their conveyance.

"The people are angry, and justly so!" Kostenko declared, almost bouncing up and down with excitement. Another projectile clattered off the roof of the carriage, which seemed to put a dampener on his enthusiasm.

"Well, we might be about to become casualties of that," Baxter growled, just as the carriage pulled to a halt. They'd only made it a hundred yards at best — he thought it unlikely this was their destination. The noise was now a roar from which he couldn't distinguish individual voices. It was nothing like the all-consuming howl of a typhoon at sea, but it was still overwhelming. More rocks hit the carriage. Craning his head to see out, Baxter realised the mob behind them was only one branch of a torrent of angry people moving through the city. They were surrounded on all sides now.

Baxter saw the driver jump from the vehicle, landing next to it and staring about wildly. He made a terrible mistake, dragging a revolver from inside his jacket. A shot rang out almost immediately, but he hadn't fired. Baxter jerked back as blood spattered his face. The hapless policeman staggered back against the vehicle, turned and scrabbled desperately at the door. Seeking shelter anywhere, however fragile and temporary. His eyes met Baxter's, fear and despair in them, and then a second shot rang out and he slumped down.

"Well, we're for it," Baxter said, feeling surprisingly calm as the crowd surged forward against the vehicle and it started to topple over.

CHAPTER 3

The carriage tilted alarmingly as the crowd reached it. Baxter felt a surge of fear, but he got a grip on it quickly. It wasn't any different than being aboard a ship in a rough sea, he told himself.

"Except I'm not normally cuffed," he muttered, sliding along the bench seat until he was against the side of the carriage that was about to hit the ground; the mob seemed to have some sort of cohesion, at least, working together to topple the vehicle.

"Do not panic, my friend!" Kostenko shouted, just as their conveyance reached its balance point. "Our friends in the revolution…"

The rest was lost in a thunderous crash as it went all the way over. Baxter lunged forward instinctively, trying to brace the young idiot who obviously hadn't considered the real-world ramifications of what the friendly revolutionaries were doing. Kostenko still fell hard, but not as hard as he might have done. They lay against what had been the side of the carriage, the younger man gasping for breath.

"You're alright, you're just winded," Baxter shouted, then realised the noise from the crowd had abated. They seemed momentarily spent from the act of destructive defiance.

Light streamed in as someone wrenched open the door that was now pointed at the sky. A head and shoulders filled that square of light, and for a moment Baxter feared they would be shot like fish trapped in a barrel. *That would be rich*, he thought. Having survived a fleet action and the machinations of both

British and Russian intelligence services, only to be shot by an overenthusiastic revolutionary.

Then a voice shouted out, "Hey, comrades, we are in luck! It is Russie! Ruslan Yaroslavovych, and another poor soul in the clutches of the Third Department."

"See, I told you this would work out in our favour," Kostenko managed to gasp out, as eager hands reached in to help them out of the ruined carriage.

A febrile atmosphere hung over the city, as tangible and oppressive as the plumes of smoke that hung in the heavy, hot air. Sitting on the side of the toppled carriage, Baxter surveyed the slow-moving river of angry people.

At least they'd got his cuffs off. Kostenko, it seemed, was a useful man to know — as well as an inability to shut up, he also seemed to know his way around lockpicking. Baxter rubbed his wrists where the cuffs had chafed him, even after a short period of wearing them, and contemplated what the hell he was going to do next. Beyond the initial goal of getting free, he was at a loss. It didn't seem sensible to try to make his way through the crowd right now — it would be like trying to swim against a strong current, no matter which direction he tried to go. He certainly had no intention of joining it. He got the distinct impression the mob didn't really have a goal or a purpose, beyond random destruction.

It was late afternoon, and baking hot. He hadn't eaten or had anything to drink since … he'd lost track of time. He wasn't a stranger to privation — most sailors had experienced this, one way or the other — but that didn't stop his throat rasping as he tried to swallow or prevent his stomach from hurting. He squinted up at the sky, looking for a sign of cloud that would bring cover and, maybe, rain to douse the fires that had started.

The surface he was sitting on creaked slightly as Kostenko clambered back up to him. The lad had been huddled with some of those who had rescued them, talking excitedly. Baxter had expected him to be on his way and about his business, his fellow prisoner forgotten in the excitement of the brewing revolution, and was pleasantly surprised at his return.

"How's your uprising going?" he asked, trying not to sound too gruff as he saw Kostenko's glum expression. He shrugged in a characteristically Slavic fashion, his mouth turned down. He didn't speak for a moment, just handed Baxter a bottle of some murky liquid with a label he couldn't read, and a chunk of black bread.

Baxter didn't care what the liquid was. He just pulled the stopper and took a swig. It was cool, at least, and slightly fizzy. The slightest edge of alcohol to it. None of that mattered as he slaked his thirst with a long pull.

"Kvass," Kostenko said, then smiled thinly at Baxter's obvious confusion. "Beer bread. Bread, that is all the workers can have. To eat and to drink. Bread, and cabbage, and a bit of dried sausage if they are lucky."

"I've eaten worse," Baxter said, then shrugged. "Not by much, though," he admitted as he gnawed a corner off the chunk of slightly stale bread. It was true enough. A sailor's diet might still mostly be salted or canned food, but at least it was plentiful. "You didn't answer my question, though."

"It is ... not the revolution," Kostenko said after a moment. "It could be. It could be shaped into one. The people, though, they have no arms. A few pistols, here and there, maybe an old hunting rifle. But more importantly, they have no *purpose*. No goal to pull them on. Just anger, to drive them. This, my friend, this is not enough."

Baxter glanced sharply at him, eyes narrowed. "You don't sound like a working man," he said after a moment.

Kostenko's smile was disarming. "You would be surprised at how well-read, how articulate, some of the workers who come to the reading circles are," he said. "But you are right. I am a student, and like many students I cannot stand by while the peasant and the proletariat live under the heel of the Tsar and his nobles, while the song of the people is stifled..." He broke off, frowning in consternation.

Baxter fought the urge to burst the young man's bubble, but couldn't help it. "Your polemic needs some work," he said, and got another rueful smile in return. "So you actually had done something to warrant being held by the police?"

Kostenko nodded enthusiastically. "I was caught distributing pamphlets," he declared. "They thought me a low-level member of the local Social Democrat group and wanted me to implicate the others. I would, of course, not have done this."

Baxter grimaced, feeling it pull at the puffy skin around his eye. He didn't doubt Kostenko's sincerity, or indeed his mettle. He had willingly, if perhaps naively, thrown himself into a struggle that could lead to very serious injury, if not death. He knew, though, that the Okhrana had only just got started with him, and he found himself doubting whether he would have held out very long if he did have secrets to protect. He didn't want to get into a fight with the earnest student, however, particularly given he was Baxter's only friend right now.

"I should thank you, though," Kostenko went on, his voice more subdued — almost as though he'd picked up the thread of Baxter's thoughts. "I believe I was due to be interrogated when you arrived. You seemed to distract them from me. That does make me wonder who you are, and what *you* have done."

Baxter grinned. "Just in the wrong place at the wrong time," he said, and took another pull of the kvass.

"I'm sure this is something Mr Bilyk has heard before."

"He did mention that once or twice." Baxter sighed as he upended the last of the drink. "Without wanting to sound ungrateful, I fear that I may continue to be in the wrong place."

Kostenko shrugged. "Perhaps. Or perhaps the machinations of men and fate have brought you to this point *because* it is the right place for you."

"You still need to work on your speeches." Baxter grinned at him.

"What do you intend to do, then, if I may ask?"

Baxter scratched his chin, feeling the rasp of an incipient beard. "As you noted, I'm a sailor. I need to get to sea. Start working my way back home."

"This will be difficult, with or without funds. The docks are in uproar, and while no ships have been attacked, activity has ceased. Travel in and out of the city in general has become challenging. The military governor is trying to contain the revolutionary fervour by preventing travel. In this he has been assisted by some of our comrades, who have begun to tear up the rail tracks."

"Well, that's just bloody marvellous," Baxter grumbled. "Would it be possible to get a telegram out, at least?"

He didn't quite know who he would send a message to, of course. He had few friends, even in Britain, and they would be able to do nothing for him. Koenig? He would probably already be at his new posting. Ekaterina? The Russian Empire was huge, and she could be anywhere in it.

"The lines are open, but they of course cost money," Kostenko said. "I am quite sure our friends in the Okhrana will also be looking for you."

Baxter gestured expansively at the crowds that still surged past. Thousands strong, angry but aimless. "I think they may have bigger things to worry about," he said, but his mind was racing. He needed friends, or at least some sort of a crew. While he was normally quite capable of hitting the ground running in a foreign port, this was an entirely new situation for him. "But I feel you may have a suggestion for what I should do next. Out of the kindness of your heart, of course."

Kostenko blinked at him. "Out of kindness? Of course not. I think you may be of use to us."

Baxter stretched his legs out and sunk as far into the comfortable chair as he could manage. His whole body ached, from fatigue and exertion as much as the blows delivered by Mieszko or being rattled around in the carriage. But he had a glass of vodka, at least, and a cold repast hastily thrown together by his hosts.

He could hear them now, arguing with Kostenko. They'd been courteous enough, showing him to the small but comfortable drawing room and feeding him, but there had been a definite tension. A hostility, directed not at him but at Kostenko. He couldn't make out what was being said, but he guessed the young and enthusiastic revolutionary was getting taken to task for bringing a complete stranger into their home and their confidence.

He looked around idly, trying to keep himself awake. It wasn't a large house, but clearly middle class. That was at odds with what he'd expected, even though he knew Kostenko was a student.

"I clearly have a lot to learn about revolutionaries," he muttered around a yawn.

"As does Ruslan Yaroslavovych," a soft voice said from the doorway, speaking English. "Despite the fact that he *is* one."

Baxter craned his neck round, then started to pull himself to his feet as he saw who'd spoken.

A small man with iron-grey hair regarded him levelly from the doorway. For a moment, Baxter thought it was Bilyk come back to haunt him. The newcomer's eyes, though, were warm and good-humoured and his beard was longer and fuller. He waved Baxter back into his seat and then pulled a wooden chair round to sit opposite him. He moved briskly enough, but with a slight stiffness, and observed Baxter with bright blue eyes that weren't dimmed by age.

"He has strange and romantic notions of what a revolution should involve, and has a bad tendency to bring home strays he has convinced himself will be useful to the cause."

"If I have put you in a difficult situation," Baxter said carefully, "I can only apologise. Ruslan took pity on my situation and offered me shelter. If this is an ... inconvenience for you, I'll be on my way."

The thought of that, now he was comfortable and properly fed for the first time in days, filled him with dread. He just needed time to collect his wits and, perhaps, rest his head for a few short hours. The last thing he wanted right now was to be sent out into a city barely known to him, and one that was in the grip of civil unrest as night fell.

It had been bad enough getting there in the first place. It had taken them several hours, moving through the densely-packed mass of people, often against the flow, to reach this quiet neighbourhood. The gunfire had grown more frequent as the day wore on, and twice they'd had to duck up narrow, noisome alleys to avoid patrols of Cossacks who had clattered past with sabres drawn. They'd heard a bomb being detonated, somewhere distant, not long before they'd arrived at this unassuming little house. Ruslan had flinched at that. Having so recently experienced the world-shattering noise of a fleet engagement, Baxter had barely noticed.

The older man tutted to himself. "Where are my manners? It would be less than hospitable of me to turn you out at this time, or indeed leave you stranded on the street at all. Ruslan tells me you were also held prisoner by our Tsar's watchdogs, so at the very least helping you flee will spite them. There is a consul of your government here."

Baxter coughed into his hand. "I would, ah, prefer to avoid official contact with my government."

The old man, who had very pointedly not introduced himself, raised a bushy eyebrow.

"Nothing too illicit, you understand," Baxter added hastily. "There are entanglements I would rather avoid."

For all he knew, of course, the consul general would know nothing of Arbuthnott's activities. He couldn't take the risk, though, and had no reason in general to trust the British establishment.

"Very well." His host sounded only vaguely dubious. "Well, there are British merchantmen — and indeed those of many other nations — in the harbour. I am sure we can find a way for you to get aboard and book passage. In the meantime, we have made up a camp bed for you. I am sorry we cannot provide you with more comfortable accommodations."

Baxter inclined his head. "As I'm sure Ruslan has mentioned to you, I am a sailor. I can fall asleep anywhere."

Baxter did indeed fall comprehensively asleep almost as soon as he was in the camp bed, and he slept through until sunlight was streaming in through a gap in the curtains. He normally had a facility for coming awake quickly, but he was exhausted to the point that consciousness only trickled back slowly. He was aware of raised voices, but they didn't sound angry so much as excited, and he decided they probably didn't concern him. He lay still, enjoying the relative comfort of the bed and listening to the growing roar of the sea beyond the house. Where he wanted to be. Needed to be, in fact. He knew he should get up, get washed and dressed, and face the day. Start navigating this complex new world he'd found himself thrown into, in order to get back to his old familiar life.

"That's not the sea," he said after a few minutes of quiet contemplation. What he'd mistaken for waves in his half-asleep state was in fact the susurration of hundreds — no, thousands — of voices, rising. "So much for the revolution losing momentum."

A moment later, someone was banging excitedly on the guest room door. "Marcus Alexandrovich!" Kostenko shouted from the other side. "You must rise! Great things are afoot."

"Great things are always afoot," Baxter grumbled as he pulled himself up and hunted around for his trousers. His clothes were filthy, his shirt still stained with his own blood, but he wasn't quite sure what to do about that. He towered over most of the people he'd encountered here, aside from Mieszko. He doubted the Okhrana thug would be willing to lend him a suit.

"Are you awake?" Kostenko asked as he burst into the room. "You must come quickly, to the harbour. Such a wondrous sight, that you must see."

"Well, I needed to get down to the harbour anyway," Baxter said, then shrugged when Kostenko raised an eyebrow. "Best place to find a ship and get away from here."

"But do you not see? This changes everything!" the young man burst out. "Even Ivan…" He bit down on saying the full name of their host and the man who seemed to be in charge of … Baxter realised he didn't really know who he was dealing with here. Was it a single organisation, or one of many revolutionary gangs? Such matters normally weren't of interest to him, and he needed to get out of this city before his ignorance tripped him up.

"Well then, what are we waiting for?"

Kostenko ducked out of the room. "Where has Konstantin gone?" Baxter heard him calling. He didn't catch the words of the shouted response, but did understand the tone and Kostenko's apologetic response. The boy really wasn't cut out for this sort of work.

A brief argument followed, starting at a volume that rapidly diminished. A few minutes later, a chastened Kostenko reappeared. "I am to help you make arrangements to leave the city," he said, voice formal and constrained. "Though I am unsure of the best route to do so."

Baxter regarded the lad. Despite the fact they had only met for the first time yesterday, and that Kostenko knew nothing about him beyond the fact they'd both been prisoners of the Okhrana, he seemed to have become fixated on the idea that Baxter would be of use to the revolution. Even disabused of that notion by his superiors within whatever passed for this organisation, he and the others still seemed keen to be of some help.

Enemy of my enemy was their guiding principle, probably, even though they had no idea what Baxter had done. Or, at least, what the secret police thought he'd done.

Well, best not to worry too much about their motivations, if they could help him get out of Odessa. Preferably out of the Russian Empire entirely. Somewhere a long way away from the momentous events that seemed to be coming to a head.

"What is your preference?" Kostenko asked after a moment's silence. "Train, or ship?"

"When given the option, always take a ship," Baxter said. The student revolutionary brightened somewhat.

"Then we must, indeed, go down to the harbour!"

CHAPTER 4

Odessa's harbour was a broad, sheltered expanse lying some two hundred feet below the clifftop city, gleaming in the unrelenting sunlight. The port was crowded with people. From his previous visit, Baxter knew that in normal times it would have been noisy with the racket of industry and trade, the shouts of stevedores vying with ship's horns and the clatter of horses' hooves. Now, though, the entire seafront was a solid mass of people, the crowd thickest around an odd grey square of fabric. The roar of noise was that of thousands of voices engaged in angry protest rather than industry.

"See?" Kostenko exclaimed. "Everything has changed — we no longer fight alone!"

"Well, this crowd is certainly going to make getting a boat out to a friendly ship harder," Baxter said, sweeping his gaze across the mob before raising his eyes to follow Kostenko's pointing arm. What he saw, further out in the steading, made his heart beat harder.

There was no doubt she was a warship, a battleship of the Imperial Russian Navy's Black Sea Fleet. Not as big as the *Borodinos* he'd seen pounded into scrap and sent to the bottom of the Tsushima Strait, but modern. Unlike the vessels of the ill-fated 2nd Pacific Squadron, she was in smart peacetime colours, her hull and main guns a gleaming black and the funnels and upperworks a deep yellow.

Most importantly, she did not fly the St. Andrews Cross — the flag of the Empire — from her mastheads. Instead, red banners lifted lazily in the gentle, hot breeze.

"That's the *Potemkin*, isn't it?" he said after a moment. "And she's mutinied?"

"It is! They tell me she's the most powerful unit in the Black Sea Fleet, but I know little of these things. And yes, she flies the red banner of revolution. Some say the whole fleet has risen up, not in mutiny but in revolution. In common cause with the workers and the peasants, from whose ranks they are drawn!" Kostenko stopped, acknowledging with a diffident smile that he was launching into polemic again.

"That was better than yesterday's efforts," Baxter said, voice dark as he remembered what Bilyk had said about Lieutenant Koenig's plum posting to the ship that now lay before him. "And you're right, it does change everything."

Baxter picked up more details as he and Kostenko made their way down the grand, sweeping Richelieu Steps that ran from the centre of the city to the grimy heart of its wealth. The blue-green sandstone of the steps teemed with people, but not so many that they blocked his view.

It didn't take him long to realise a sleek and dangerous-looking vessel, also flying the red flag, was anchored near the *Potemkin*. Much smaller, it was designed to deliver lethal torpedoes at close-range. He shivered slightly despite the heat. He'd seen what torpedo boats could do at night, having fought them tooth and nail from one of the *Yaroslavich*'s steam pinnaces. He and Koenig, in command of the other small craft, had almost managed to foil the Japanese boats in their near-suicidal attacks on the cruiser — it was only as dawn broke that one had made it through to start her slow death.

"The whole squadron has mutinied, you say?" Baxter asked, keeping his voice low and speaking in English. Best not to be understood, if they could not avoid being overheard.

"That is what I have heard," Kostenko said, earnestly but mercifully quietly. "Others say it was just the *Potemkin*, that the men rose up against foul food while she was on a cruise to practise her gunnery."

"Well, that's definitely something your Navy needs to work on." Baxter couldn't help it, then shrugged at the oddly hurt look Kostenko gave him. "Though they fought well and shot straight against the Japanese," he conceded.

"Either way, the rest of the fleet must follow! The crews of the ships that lie before us have shown them the way. And even if they do not rise, surely there is nothing that those who remain loyal to the Tsarist oppressors can do to such a magnificent vessel."

Baxter kept his peace, though he knew most of what Kostenko said was at best naïve. He'd never experienced a full-blown mutiny, but they'd had trouble with a revolutionary cell aboard the *Yaroslavich* and other crews in the fleet had risen. From that experience and his knowledge of past mutinies, he could guess that some if not most of the sailors of the battleship weren't committed revolutionaries or even full-throated mutineers. They were men who had been driven to the edge by harsh discipline — probably excessively brutal, in fact — and poor food. When it had happened, whatever the trigger was, some would have lost their heads and pitched in; others would have gone through the motions to avoid the censure of their crewmates or just through peer pressure.

Many would just have tried to keep their heads down to see which faction — mutineers or officers — came out on top. Even now, most would be watching and waiting, and just hoping to survive one way or the other.

"She's a powerful ship," he conceded after a moment of expectant silence from his companion. "But she's just one battleship and a torpedo boat against…" He screwed his eyes up, trying to remember the strength of the squadron based in the Black Sea. In truth, he knew little of it except it was confined to this patch of water by international treaty, forbidden from passing through the Ottoman-controlled Bosphorus. "Well, against a fleet. She'll be outnumbered, and will the crew be able to fight her without their officers?"

Kostenko looked crestfallen, an expression Baxter was getting used to seeing on his face. His mood seemed resilient, though, and he bounced back quickly. "Well, it will not come to that. With the Navy risen, the army will follow suit — all but the Cossack scum, who are bought and paid for." He spat in the street.

"Calm yourself," Baxter cautioned, glancing around. The people on the steps, filtering slowly down towards the crowded port, all seemed to be protestors. Workers and students rubbed shoulders. The workers' wives were apparent; if they were anything like his old landlady Mrs Dunbar, they would be the backbone of the movement. Excited voices were everywhere, with much speculation echoing what Kostenko was saying.

Despite having only just been thrown into this world, Baxter already knew enough to guess the authorities might have people in the crowd. The police and the army — the feared Cossacks — were also in evidence around the periphery of the simmering mob.

"Now is not the time for calm!" Kostenko declared, switching into Russian and raising his voice. "Now is the time for deeds to give the truth of our words!"

That brought a few cheers and shouts of agreement. Kostenko seemed to be casting round for a higher place to stand, obviously seeking to take on the role of street preacher for his creed. Baxter had seen a few such people in the last couple of days around the city, often gathering small crowds who would listen for a few minutes and then move on to the next soapbox.

He briefly considered just walking away, as Kostenko started towards the massive granite blocks that delineated the steps. It wouldn't be much of a podium to speak from, but the best he could find. Baxter didn't owe the revolutionary student anything, although he had provided safe harbour for the previous evening.

He was also the only friend Baxter had in the city, as far as he could tell, and left to his own devices Kostenko would almost certainly get himself taken up by the Okhrana again, or just shot in the streets.

Baxter laid a hand on the lad's bony shoulder, just firmly enough to arrest him without causing him harm. He had a brief flash of a previous time he'd laid hands on another man, and the way he'd smashed the mutinying sailor's head in. He shook his head to dispel the memory — another time, and a great distance. Something in his look, though, stilled Kostenko's enthusiasm.

"Yes, we should get down to the harbour," he said, voice muted as his prospective audience dissolved into the wider mass of people. "And find you a ship."

"What word of the officers?" Baxter asked as they started moving again. He kept the question as offhand as he could, knowing that showing even the slightest interest in the *Potemkin*'s officer class could be misconstrued. He'd tried to hold off from asking it, but Koenig was on his mind. Surviving the bloodbath of Tsushima only to be killed by his own crew seemed … unfair, somehow. Assuming he'd even made it to his posting on the battleship before the chaos erupted on board.

Kostenko shrugged. "Killed, most or all of them. Running dogs of the Tsarist regime." He saw Baxter's look. "You may not have heard the stories of how harsh the discipline aboard is," he rushed on, voice defensive at how callous he had sounded. "Officers beating men without provocation, living in dreadful conditions afloat and banned from leaving their barracks when ashore. I am told the *Potemkin* mutinied because the men were forced to eat maggoty meat. Perhaps it is better in your own navy, how the sailors are treated."

Baxter knew exactly what discipline on Imperial Russian Navy ships was like, or at least under Captain Gorchakov of the *Yaroslavich*. He certainly wasn't about to mention that, though, nor admit that he was himself a former officer of the Royal Navy.

"Well, I'm sure that's true enough," he said, choosing his words with an unusual level of care. "But officers are like any other people — some good, some bad, some just indifferent."

"If any were good, I'm sure the sailors spared them," Kostenko declared. "They are just men, after all, fighting for a just cause."

"Well, I'm sure we'll find out soon enough," Baxter commented. They'd finally reached the bottom of the grand, sweeping staircase. Everyone seemed to be going in one direction, a flow of closely packed people heading in the direction of the tent Baxter had spotted earlier. He doubted many, if any, knew exactly why they were heading that way. He was none the wiser himself, but it was human nature to follow the crowd; even if he hadn't been curious, it would have been impossible to fight against the flow of people.

It was sweltering down on the quayside; redolent with the smells of industry and commerce familiar to him from ports the world over. Hot tar and pitch, coal dust and smoke. Fish threatening to turn rotten in the summer heat. Everything underpinned by the slight tang of salt water on the heavy air. Under normal circumstances he would find this invigorating, but this many people packed in so close, in this heat, rapidly frayed his nerves.

"Well, doesn't look like I'm getting onto a ship today," he commented. He was a lot bigger than most of the people on the docks, and while he hadn't been able to muscle their way to the front of the crowd he had at least managed to get them over onto the waterside. There were a few merchant ships tied up at the quayside, but they clearly didn't want to let anyone aboard and a few were already making preparations to depart. The only boats he could see on the harbour seemed to be going to or from the great steel beast that lurked in the far harbour, her main guns a very obvious threat even if they weren't yet trained on the city. It took him another moment to spot the accompanying torpedo boat, which was in the process of towing a collier alongside the coal-hungry vessel.

He gestured to her. "I'm surprised they're not sending men ashore to seize supplies."

"They are conducting themselves well," Kostenko agreed. They were not far from the little tent now and the crowd was thickest here. A voice was raised in the sort of passionate, angry rhetoric that the student obviously aspired to. Baxter could hear the sound of weeping women, other raised voices.

"We'll see how long it lasts." Baxter glanced out at the big ship again. He knew, perhaps better than most here, just how devastating the four 12-inch guns she mounted would be. Even her bristling secondary armament of 6 and 3 inchers could inflict terrible harm on the city.

Kostenko was prevented from replying when another young man, obviously catching sight of him in the crowd, shoved through. "Ruslan!" he cried out, seizing Kostenko's hand in both of his and shaking it excitedly.

"Konstantin! I missed you this morning!" Kostenko shouted, grabbing the other student by his shoulders and drawing him into a hug. "Is this not magnificent?"

Baxter examined the newcomer cautiously. He hadn't thought it possible that there could be another as loud and enthusiastic as his guide, but this man surpassed him. Slim, with intense dark eyes and a bushy moustache at odds with his youth, and a forceful manner.

"We have the first true martyr!" the young man went on, gesturing widely towards the pulsing heart of the crowd. They were close enough that beyond all the usual smells of the harbour and the close-packed people, Baxter could make out the stench of death. Of flesh starting to rot on a hot day. All of a sudden, he didn't feel a pressing need to make it to the front of the crowd to see the spectacle that had drawn the people here.

Nonetheless, morbid curiosity drew Baxter after the two excited Russians. He didn't have a watch on him, and couldn't remember the last time he'd even had a working timepiece. Glancing at the bright sun that hung in a cloudless blue sky, he guessed it was early afternoon already. Closer to the front, the angry voices became clearer. Podiums had sprung up around the modest centrepiece of the tent. A seemingly endless chain of spokesmen were taking their turns, berating the crowd, demanding action, putting forward resolutions. The increasingly fractious protestors roared back, mostly in approval, and already he could see placards and banners being hoisted as noisy gaggles of workers and students, united in their common purpose, started to push their way against the tide of people. Back towards the city.

Baxter could feel his temper starting to fray as he was jostled to the front of the crowd, trying to keep sight of Kostenko and his friend. "What are you doing, Baxter?" he muttered to himself. A few moments ago, he could have slipped away through the periphery of the crowd, tried to talk his way onto one of the ships. Now he was in too deep, the people pressed all about him. Sweat prickled his brow and ran down his back. He knew his battered and bloody appearance would normally attract attention and comment, but many here were in a similar state.

All of a sudden, there was a clear space ahead of him, a short stretch of cobble and then a tent improvised from a tarpaulin and a few spars. A coffin lay in the shade provided, the lid removed to reveal a dead sailor, his expression serene in repose. Sailors with rifles, bayonets fixed, formed an honour guard at each corner of the coffin, and another had clearly just finished his own harangue of the crowd. Baxter shuffled forward with Kostenko and some others, not wanting to stand out from the crowd more than he already did. He looked down at the dead man, trying to decipher the Cyrillic writing of the note pinned to his jumper. He'd become familiar with the language during the months he was aboard a Russian warship, but had never quite got his head round the written language. He was able to work out the man's name — Vakulenchuk, Gregori — and something about destroying their oppressors.

His eyes were drawn to Vakulenchuk's face, carefully arranged to match his new status as martyr. A typical Russian peasant, from the look of him, stocky and perhaps more intelligent than his officers had assumed. He could have been any one of the bluejackets Baxter had fought alongside barely a month ago. Men he had seen torn apart by shell splinters or burned beyond life and recognition by the raging fires set by Japanese explosive shells.

There was an angry muttering behind him, a queue of protestors wanting their moment with this rapidly-elevated symbol. Baxter stepped aside, seeing a woman shuffle forward to kiss the dead hands while her husband knelt and crossed himself.

Glancing around, he found Kostenko again. He was deep in conversation with his fellow student revolutionary, obviously strategizing over what to do next. After a moment, Konstantin hurried away, calling out to someone to procure them a boat.

Judging from the range of speakers expounding similar, but not always identical, philosophies from the impromptu podium, there were clearly a number of different revolutionary groups in the city. He had no idea which one these two students belonged to, or whether they were influential in any way.

Someone bumped against him. He turned, confronting the furious glare of a burly worker. "Why do you just stand there, like an idiot?" the man demanded. "Are you stupid, or a reactionary? There is much to be…"

The angry tirade trailed off as the fellow's eyes focused properly, or as close as he could manage given the amount of vodka he'd clearly drunk. He obviously realised just how big Baxter was.

It was not just the fact Baxter towered over him. The heat and the crowds were starting to erode the tight rein he was holding on his temper. For just a second, the sheer absurd injustice of the situation he found himself in threatened to unleash a blind fury. The worker obviously saw some of this in Baxter's eyes and backed away quickly, placating hands raised.

"Come, my friend," Kostenko said, appearing by his side and putting a restraining hand on his arm. "As our comrade here said, there is much to be done."

Baxter shook the hand off, knowing he appeared churlish. "How many times do I need to tell you?" he growled in English. "The only thing I need to do is get out of this city, and this piss excuse for a country."

Kostenko looked like he was about to respond in kind, then obviously thought better of it. "As you said yourself, it will be hard for you to find passage, *da*? And as for the state of the country, this is something we are trying to do something about."

Baxter blew out a breath. He knew he couldn't get involved here, couldn't make the mistake of liking this lad and his ilk. He'd done that before, getting too close to Ekaterina Juneau and her husband, Cristov, the first officer of the *Yaroslavich*. It had kept him aboard the Russian cruiser too long, and that had landed him in this mess. He could walk away, but he didn't know where he would go. He needed time to get his bearings.

He nodded. "Well, it appears I remain your problem," he said.

"Tomorrow, hopefully, things will be better," Kostenko said, beckoning him to join the people starting to flow in greater numbers back towards the city. "Seeing the strength of our sentiment here, the mayor may relent and the army retire, before anything violent happens."

Baxter glanced around, taking the measure of the increasingly restless crowd. "Things are going to get ugly, Ruslan," he said, his voice deadly serious. "And from everything I know of your generals, they are not likely to retire."

Kostenko sighed unhappily. "You are probably correct," he said. "But this is the price we must pay for freedom."

Baxter felt a growing tension as the crowd carried them back towards the Richelieu Steps. Back towards the city, with its military governor and his soldiers and Cossacks, and the mayor and his police. A knot in his gut told him things were about to go very wrong indeed. The protestors, the revolutionaries, were in an increasingly angry mood. The heat had made tempers wear thin. He'd seen this before, in the long months when the 2nd Pacific Squadron had lain in Madagascar. There, the will-sapping humidity was probably the only thing that had kept the sailors from rising en masse. This crowd seemed to have plenty of energy, crowding up the steps even as more people tried to come down, drawn to the martyred sailor's shrine.

They were drawn to the looting. He didn't know when the first warehouse had been forced open, whether it was the protestors or the sailors, or just opportunist criminals. Vodka was flowing freely, though, as was bread and meat and other foodstuffs normally beyond the average worker's reach. Smoke rose from at least one fire on the docks, though it didn't seem to be out of control. Yet.

Kostenko looked torn about the theft. "This will not cast the revolution in a good light," he said unhappily. "The Bolsheviks, they will be happy that the people's wealth is being distributed back to them, but others will look on this as nothing but spiteful crime."

"Sometimes, needs must," was all Baxter said. "Aside from this morning, I haven't eaten properly in days."

"Well, if we see a restaurant being smashed open..." Kostenko snapped, voice bitter.

"And a tailor, if you can manage it," Baxter replied, not rising to the bait.

Rumours ran like wildfire through the crowd. Regiments of Cossacks were descending on the docks; the police had sealed them in and were determined to let the protest burn itself out. Artillery was being deployed, against the protests or the battleship. The army had already risen in support of their worker brethren and the sailors.

No one knew anything for sure, and that was just adding to the tension in the packed space.

"Why hasn't the mayor done something yet?" Kostenko asked almost plaintively as they walked back up the long sweep of the Richelieu Steps, eating salt cod and sausage the young revolutionary had been handed by a young woman he'd spent some time speaking with, a contact within one of the other revolutionary groups, it seemed. Apparently his stance on the looting had shifted with his own growing hunger. Baxter had lost track of how long they'd been on the docks. The bloated red sun was low in the sky, though. At some point, he knew, they had to get away from the docks.

"It won't be the mayor who acts," he said, after a few moments' thought. "It'll be the military governor, and he won't be gentle in his response."

That was the other thing that had put a stopper over mutinous behaviour in the squadron. Rozhestvensky, the commanding admiral, had disappeared from sight for weeks. He'd taken a proper grip on the situation when he emerged from his cabin, though, instituting strict discipline. That had taken the form of firing squads and repression.

"I know, but it will galvanise the people. With the guns of the battleship, we will be unstoppable!" Kostenko said. "If the army masses, our revolutionary comrades will blow them to bits!"

The crowd of people going up the stairs was starting to slow, almost like a flow of water reaching a dam. The people packed closer and closer together, and Baxter smelled sweat and fear, the occasional waft of cologne. Many of the people on the steps were workers, men dressed in smocks and cord jackets, floppy caps pulled low over their eyes, everything in muted colours. More than a few women as well, in simple dresses that matched the menfolk. Children squeezed between the adults' legs, and here and there Baxter could make out students and others more finely attired than the workers, either local gentry who had come down to see what all the fuss was about and had become trapped, or liberals who supported the movement.

"Have you ever seen a 12-inch naval shell detonate, Ruslan?" Baxter asked, voice distracted. "I have. They're not the most … precise things, shall we say?"

"I'm sure they will send parties ashore to support us soon, or at least land arms."

Baxter could hear horses' hooves ahead. A lot of them. "Not soon enough, I fear."

CHAPTER 5

The revolutionaries were brave, Baxter didn't doubt that. It was a courage born of desperation and pent-up anger, and also the bravery that came from being part of such a large mob. The courage of people who believed they would receive miraculous assistance in the form of precise artillery fire, that they would win through, armed only with placards and thrown bricks, or the occasional pistol.

He and Kostenko weren't far from the top of the long climb when the Cossacks attacked. He heard shouting, the clatter of hooves rapidly advancing over flagstones. The *crack* of a pistol being fired.

The crowd recoiled, far enough that he could see the flash of steel in the sunlight as the mounted soldiers slashed at the front ranks. A horse reared, lashing forward with its hooves. The pressure from behind didn't let up, catching Baxter and Kostenko in a morass of bodies as people tried to flee the carnage while those further back, unaware of what was happening, demanded to continue onwards.

"Forward! Forward to City Hall!" someone bellowed not far below him.

"Back, comrades. Turn back, brothers!"

Baxter could barely move, but he knew trying to barge through would be fruitless. He felt his pulse quicken, a sort of fear that tornado or shellfire couldn't engender rising within him. He had faced a storm of steel and fire at sea without flinching, but this was different. Far more ... personal. He caught sight of Kostenko's wide, terrified eyes.

The mob further back finally started to realise what was happening when the Cossacks opened fire. There had been a few pistol shots before, but this was a sudden and furious fusillade, a rapid and unaimed fire into the packed crowd. Baxter couldn't tell how many shooters there were, but the stairs were only so wide. Bodies were falling, rolling down the steps and sending those not yet hit tumbling.

There was a breathless pause, the sound of boots clattering down flagstones as the Cossacks dismounted. He heard the whinny of nervous horses, smelled their shit, but couldn't see them. That was fine by him — he didn't fancy being subject to a cavalry charge.

Then he heard the unmistakable rattle of rifle bolts being worked. He dropped into a crouch as another ragged volley blasted into the panicking crowd. More bodies fell, and all of a sudden he was close enough to the front of the crowd to see the polished black boots, the smart white summer tunics of the light cavalry. The Cossacks surged on, the front lines on foot while others milled behind on horseback.

The panic had become a rout. Baxter felt the heat of a bullet's passage past his face, heard a woman's scream cut short in a choking gurgle. People were spilling back down the steps, some by their own volition, others tumbling. He went to the side, trying to drag Kostenko with him as he made for the granite blocks that separated the stairs from the steep gardens on either side. The Cossacks, obviously infuriated and cut loose from any semblance of discipline, waded into the crowd with rifle butts and slashing sabres. Men hardened to killing the Tsar's enemies, even when those foes were his own subjects, they seemed to have no compunction about the slaughter. Koenig had said the Cossacks were men apart, holding themselves aloof but also looked down on — a society within wider Russian society. The Tsar relied on them when all but his own Imperial Guard had failed him, trusting to their lack of connection with the people.

The rampaging soldiers surged onto the landing he was on, slashing around themselves with their sabres. Blood gushed as the wicked curved blades flashed in the dying light. The Cossacks were yelling their hate now, hacking down fleeing civilians or firing pistols into their backs.

Baxter heard Kostenko cry out, and spun round. The student had turned, charging headlong at a Cossack to try to stop him cutting down a young woman who cowered away from the raised sabre.

"Ruslan!" Baxter yelled, knowing it was too late. The Cossack may have been enraged, but he also clearly knew how to handle his sabre. The downward slash he was about to deliver to the woman's head became a cut across the student's face with a simple turn of the wrist. Baxter was close enough that he was hit by the blood spatter. Kostenko howled, hands flying to his face, then the return slash opened his throat and cut the scream off.

Kostenko fell, clutching his throat and jerking as he fought to breathe through a slashed windpipe. Blood spurted, dark in the sunset, between his fingers. The Cossack's humanity was lost behind a mask of bloodlust, of pent-up aggression unleashed, of the righteous rage their position as the Tsar's executioners granted them. Baxter cast a quick glance at Kostenko, but knew there was nothing he could do for the boy now. The young woman he had saved — Baxter recognised her fleetingly as the girl Konstantin had conferred with — sought the only safety she could, in the numbers and crush of the crowd.

Other violence-maddened soldiers were streaming past, and somewhere he could hear the furious bellowing of enraged officers trying to get their men under control.

The Cossack advanced on him, teeth bared in a feral grin. He was a much smaller man, whipcord lean and wiry, but he was also armed with a long blade and had a pistol in his belt. Baxter backed up, knowing that taking on this man who would have trained most of his life to fight with a sword while being unarmed himself was a poor choice. He couldn't just turn and flee as that would invite a sabre to the back.

The swordsman knew it, and grinned viciously as he started boxing Baxter in, ready for the kill. The cavalryman said something in a dialect Baxter didn't recognise. He could guess the content, though.

"Not today, mate," he shot back, glancing around for anything he could use. He'd even take a pistol right then.

A Cossack officer stormed down the steps. He was immaculate, taller than the men under his command and clearly utterly disgusted by their behaviour. A *hetman* trailed after him, translating his orders, snarled in French, to the troops he was bringing back under control.

The newcomer seized Baxter's opponent by the shoulder, demanding to know what he thought he was doing. Baxter backed up another step, felt the cold granite of the plinth against his leg. The Russian didn't seem interested in the people the Cossacks were attacking, didn't care that — ignored by everyone — Kostenko had kicked his last at their feet.

The officer glanced up at Baxter. The recognition was mutual and instantaneous; Baxter knew the elegant officer from the fading remains of the black eye he'd given him on the Baikal ferry, only partially concealed under cosmetic powder. He hadn't recognised him before, distracted by the chaos and the danger — if he had, he'd have made a dash for it sooner.

Rittmeister Zubov, the man who'd tried to provoke Koenig into a career-ending confrontation. The last Baxter had seen of him was his face twisted in fury as the Okhrana men broke up the brawl.

"*You!*" the Russian officer spat, hand flying to the gold-plated hilt of his sabre. The Cossack he'd been in the process of berating looked in equal parts confused and hopeful that there would be more violence. The non-commissioned officer trailing after Zubov asked a question, sounding a lot more plaintive than he should, and Baxter took the opportunity to hop onto the low stone plinths that lined the side of the steps, then over the barrier and into the tree-filled park on the other side. He didn't look back as he plunged forward into the darkness.

It was only a partial darkness, though; burning warehouses down on the docks cast enough flickering orange light that he could almost keep his feet as he plunged forward onto the steep, tree-lined banks of the formal gardens that flanked the steps. He concentrated on getting away, getting in amongst the half-seen trees.

A rifle cracked behind him, the bullet whining past and splintering a sapling. He stumbled, almost falling, but managed to grab on to the branch of something more sturdy and saved himself from a neck-breaking fall. He didn't have a moment to catch his breath or find his footing properly, though, as at least one rifle was spitting fire into the night behind him, the heavy rounds slashing through the foliage.

He kept going, moving away from the Cossacks and their angry officer. He could hear Zubov yelling at his men, trying to order them out into the darkness after Baxter, but he was obviously losing control of the situation. More rifles were firing, an uneven rattle that no longer seemed to be directed at him as he fled; no doubt other cavalrymen were shooting into the fleeing protestors again.

Baxter paused after another twenty or so paces, pressing his back against a tree as he caught his breath. The cool, smooth bark pressing through his shirt helped to ground him, calm his rattled nerves. He dropped into a crouch, realising now that the adrenalin had ebbed just how tired he was, how much his body ached.

At least some buildings in the port were burning, the flickering orange glow providing a deceptive illumination that cast jumping shadows from the trees around him. Smoke was billowing, threatening to blot out the light of the moon and stars. He could hear shouts and screams in the distance, the whinny of horses. The shooting nearby had died down again, but he could still hear occasional shots, punctuating the roar of burning warehouses.

A rustle in the half-dark alerted him to the fact that some of the Cossacks had come out hunting him. He dropped into a crouch, trying to control his breathing, as a twig snapped under a boot.

At least two, he decided, keeping as still as possible in the hope of blending in with the shadows. He heard one call out, a hard-edged language that was both familiar and yet incomprehensible to him. His comrade snapped back, a bit further away, and the nearer Cossack laughed coarsely.

It was that laughter, while his fellows visited death and destruction on the citizens of Odessa, that pushed Baxter over the edge. The fear that had coiled through him and settled in his guts when he'd been caught in the press of protestors turned into a seething fury. The Cossack had stopped nearby.

Baxter heard the rattle of his rifle being put down then the rustle of cloth and a flow of liquid. He rose slowly, a false calm settling over him. The soldier was pissing against a nearby tree, sighing with relief; his weapon was against another tree and out of his sight line.

Baxter picked it up, gripping the smooth polished wood of the stock. He'd once joked with Juneau that a gun less than 4 inches in calibre was of no interest to him, but he reckoned he could work this one out. He moved as slowly and quietly as possible. The Cossack must have been waiting a while to relieve himself, or had had a lot to drink, but eventually he rebuttoned and turned around, looking for his gun.

It took him a moment to find it, then another moment to focus on the big man holding it. "Alright, chum?" Baxter asked.

The Cossack raised placating hands, palms out towards Baxter. His dark eyes, almost lost in a sea of wrinkles, darted to the side, obviously looking for his mate. He wore a sabre and pistol on his hips. After a moment, he dropped his hands very slightly towards the weapons. Baxter could almost see the calculations happening behind his eyes. The man was a hardened soldier, a killer. As far as he knew, he was facing a civilian. Not used to combat, even if he did know how to use the gun in his hands.

The short, tough-looking man obviously came to the conclusion that the worst he would get out of this was a reprimand for almost losing his weapon.

Baxter smiled thinly, tightening his finger on the trigger and shifting his feet for better balance on the steep surface. The Cossack's eyes widened, filling with fear as he realised his calculations had been off. Baxter almost pulled the trigger. He knew he would have done, if he could be sure this was the soldier who'd cut down Kostenko.

Instead, he smiled as he took his finger off the trigger. He gave his opponent the barest moment to start feeling relieved, then drove the rifle forward with savage force, putting the muzzle into the Cossack's midriff and doubling him up. Then he brought the butt up and round in a powerful strike that lifted the fellow clean off his feet and dropped him into his own puddle of piss, knocked out cold.

Baxter almost lost his footing and stumbled a few steps further down the slope, using the rifle as a crutch. He thought about pulling himself back up to the Cossack, unsure if it was to finish the job or just loot him of his weapons.

"Don't get involved," he muttered to himself. He'd made his point with this fellow, who at the very least would be going back to his barracks stinking of his own piss, and probably had a broken jaw. He threw the rifle away into the darkness and started stumbling down the slope.

Dawn came hesitantly, the sun not so much breaking through the pall of smoke over the harbour but tinting it a different red to the night-time fires. Baxter sat alone on the quayside, staring out to sea and trying to plan out his next move.

A lot of the merchant skippers, sensible men all, had cleared out the previous day or overnight. Those that could, anyway — a Russian collier was still in the harbour, under the *Potemkin*'s guns. He could make out the burned skeleton of at least one other ship that had been tied up at the quay, blackened wooden ribs rising up out of the water. The air tasted of smoke and a fine layer of ash was settling over everything, including the bodies that dotted the quayside. A few fires still burned, crackling merrily as they consumed thousands of roubles' worth of goods and adding to the pall over the city.

There were fewer dead than he'd been expecting. He couldn't imagine, after the chaos and shocking violence of the night, that anyone had been able to organise a proper collection of bodies. Perhaps people had taken away their friends or loved ones. Or perhaps, despite their furious killing rage, the rampaging Cossacks hadn't inflicted mass casualties.

"Still too many," Baxter murmured, watching a kneeling woman silently weeping over the body of a man barely older than Kostenko. He realised that he'd been too busy trying to stay alive, to get away from the horror on the steps, to think about the young student. He'd been a brave lad, no doubt. Last night obviously wasn't the first time he'd put his life on the line for his cause, and he'd died defending an unarmed civilian. Baxter couldn't escape the feeling that the whole thing was utterly futile, though.

There was certainly nothing he could do for Kostenko now, or for the woman weeping over the body nearby. For any of the people who were still trapped inside the police cordon, smoke-blackened figures with tired faces moving disconsolately through the aftermath.

A speaker with a cracked voice started up, but couldn't rouse much enthusiasm. It was still too early. The anger would come later, Baxter knew, or the people would disperse when they were allowed, lesson learned. Cowed by the establishment's superior force, crushed by the Cossack boot heel.

"Not my problem," he told himself. He was bone-tired, dirty and bloody. While the Okhrana had other problems right now, he guessed they would come after him eventually. He needed to find a way out of here. Given his worldly possessions were the clothes on his back, he'd be forced to rely on his charm —

and the fact merchant skippers always needed experienced hands.

He just needed a bloody boat. The merchant ships may have cleared out, but he reckoned a number would either be making for nearby ports or would be standing out in the offing in the hopes of being able to coal for their onward journeys.

He smiled grimly. He had plenty of experience coaling at sea — all he needed to do was get out to one of them and convince the captain to take him on.

He looked back at the carnage, sweeping his gaze across the quayside. Somehow, the little improvised tent under which the martyred sailor's bier lay was still up, still under guard. What was his name again? Vakulenchuk, that was it. So much death and destruction, set off by this increasingly ripe body. There was nothing any of them could do against the Tsar's security machine, though.

"Not my problem," he told himself again.

As he turned away from the odd little vignette, a hand lashed across his face. It was so unexpected that he just blinked in surprise.

He looked down to see a small young woman, drawing her hand back for another blow. He tilted his head back, moving his stinging cheek out of her reach, and her nails caught his chin. He caught her wrist as she came back for another go. She glared venomously at him, swinging with her free hand. He caught that, painfully aware of how thin and fragile her wrists felt in his big hands. Not weak, by any means, as his face could attest.

"Madam, I do not know who you are or what I have done to occasion this assault, but I must ask you to desist!"

His formal mode of address seemed to astonish her as much as her attack had surprised him. She stepped back, as far as she could with her wrists still pinioned, and raised an eyebrow at him. He released her warily, stepping a little further away as he examined her. His first impression of 'small' was certainly accurate, but she wasn't delicate. She still glared furiously at him. He realised that she looked slightly familiar, someone he had met recently. Her hair was up under a scarf, a few dark locks visible on her forehead, and she wore a simple blouse and skirt. Then it clicked — the woman from the steps, who Kostenko had saved from being horribly injured, if not killed. He had seen her again just a few moments ago, weeping over a body. Tears streaked the grime on her face.

He opened his mouth, not quite knowing what to say. She certainly didn't have that problem.

"A big strong man like you, and yet you ran when your friend was dying!" she spat. "I'm surprised you're not afraid of me!"

"You're not armed," he said bluntly, finding his voice and a faint stirring of anger. "That I know of, anyway."

"The worker fights with the tools of his trade, the peasant with the tools of his farm. It seems the middle classes fight only with their words."

He knew he should just turn around and walk away, particularly as her tirade was starting to draw attention; a small crowd gathered around with curiosity that could spill into hostility at any moment.

He stepped forward instead, towering over her. She didn't back down, just crossed her arms over her chest and glared at him. He was careful to keep his hands by his side as he looked down on her. "Kostenko fought with more than words," he said. "And all that earned him was an opened throat."

There was so much more he wanted to say. About how he felt bad for Kostenko, although he had only known him a day or two — how he grieved for the loss of potential, if nothing else. About how he'd already seen enough men die for nothing. About the realities of combat and the absurd notion of going into battle against trained, well-equipped soldiers armed only with tools. He knew it was pointless, though, and needlessly cruel. He let his shoulders sag. "Go home, when the cordon is opened. Alive is better than dead."

She opened her mouth, but now it was her turn not to find the words. A slim young man slipped through the crowds and laid a hand on her arm. "Mashka, enough," he said quietly, as her eyes started to fill with tears. Baxter turned away, ashamed of himself and sickened to his stomach by this place. The small crowd parted in front of him.

He started to walk away, wanting nothing more than to be away from here and back where he belonged. Odessa, it seemed, was not done with him, though. The man who had intervened caught up with him and fell into step. It took Baxter a moment to recognise him as Kostenko's fellow student agitator, Konstantin.

"I understand from Mashka that Ruslan is dead?" the Russian asked, not put off by the dark scowl Baxter gave him by way of a greeting.

Baxter hadn't quite grasped that Kostenko knew the woman he had died saving, and was surprised someone from the workers' quarter would know the middle class students. "He is. Killed by the Cossacks."

"Mashka says he died well."

Baxter couldn't help but laugh at that. "There's no such thing as a good death. Not in battle." He turned on the other man. "What do you want from me?"

Konstantin looked up at him doubtfully, obviously debating with himself whether to speak further. Eventually he sighed.

"Ruslan was ... given to romantic notions, and had more interest in matters spiritual than was really healthy for a Social Democrat. As much as we took heart from the appearance of the battleship, not many would have seen it as a sign from God. Ruslan..." Seeing the look of amused incredulity spreading across Baxter's face, Konstantin broke off, flushing. "No, no, he did not think you have been sent by God. But he had convinced himself that the coincidence of your meeting in the Okhrana's custody, at this time, was perhaps a..." He trailed off, obviously struggling to explain what he meant.

"Look, Konstantin," Baxter said, struggling to maintain his patience. "Stranger things happen at sea."

The student looked nonplussed, and Baxter found himself at a loss to explain exactly what he meant. "Look," he said again. "I want no part of your revolution or your politics. I'm pretty sure I want nothing more of Russia or Russians."

That was only mostly the truth. There was one Russian who he desperately wanted to see again, though he had never worked up the courage to read her letter to him so he had no idea whether she would welcome that prospect. The letter was gone now, he remembered with a pang, lost with his overcoat and other meagre possessions when Bilyk had taken custody of him. That also reminded him of Koenig, the man who had delivered the letter, a few weeks ago in Vladivostok.

He had been in the process of turning away from Konstantin, but now turned back and caught his shoulder. "I think you made it out onto the battleship?" he asked gruffly. "You boarded the *Potemkin*?"

"I did, yes," Konstantin said, with a slight puff of pride.

"What are the conditions? Are the mutineers maintaining some form of naval discipline?"

Modern warships, Baxter knew, were fiendishly complicated machines. They were also packed full of highly explosive material — the last thing this city needed was for the ship to suffer a magazine explosion due to ill-discipline. He'd seen a battleship go up like that at Tsushima, and it wasn't something he wanted to be close to.

"They are. I am no expert in naval matters, but everything seems … shipshape, I believe you would say?"

Baxter forced a grin at that. "And the officers? I'm told they were all killed during the mutiny."

"The dragons were, yes, including the captain and the first officer. Many remain alive — indeed, the sailors' committee has elected an ensign to command." He spoke of the murders in a nonchalant manner that chilled Baxter. He knew mutinies could be bloody things, from the history of his former service, but it was disconcerting to hear a civilian be so blasé about it. "Why do you ask?" Konstantin said after a moment's pause, a note of suspicion creeping into his voice.

Baxter looked along the quayside. He guessed he had to be careful here, more careful than he had been. No sympathy for the aristocracy could be shown, and in truth he had none, not for it as a class anyway. He noticed a boat was pulling in, a launch from one of the merchant ships that had put to sea from the look of it. Obviously on an important errand, if they were taking the risk of coming in. Probably a last supply run, or looking for a mate who'd been left behind.

His pulse quickened as saw the men in front of him. Sailors from a merchant steamer in need of crew. This could be his opportunity.

"No reason," Baxter said quickly, realising that Konstantin was pressing his previous question. "Just good to know how angry the rest of the fleet will be when it arrives."

That seemed to mollify the revolutionary somewhat. "We are reliably informed by the sailor's committee that the rest of the Black Sea Fleet will mutiny, if it has not done so already. You will have nothing to fear from rampaging Tsarist forces on the high seas."

Indeed. Just ashore — all the more reason to get out of here. Baxter didn't offer an opinion on the likelihood of the fleet rising. He'd seen the state of morale in what had ended its days as the Pacific Fleet; he also knew the Imperial Russian Navy had some very capable officers in amongst the 'dragons'.

"I'd hardly call the Black Sea the high seas," he said instead. He noticed, for the first time, that Konstantin had changed his student clothes for the uniform of a common sailor, a white jacket and trousers with the familiar blue-and-white striped shirt and a cap bearing the battleship's name stitched neatly on the band. "Which you'd know, if you actually were a sailor."

Konstantin smiled briefly, obviously not taking offence. "A handy subterfuge." He pulled at his lower lip, staring penetratingly at Baxter. "Your name, I think, is Marcus Alexandrovich? That is what Ruslan said."

The first mate from the steamer — the *Liverpool Star*, was it? — had seen Baxter, and raised a hand in greeting. That looked promising. The launch crew were hurrying towards one of the intact warehouses. "Yes, that's it," he said absently.

"Ruslan said you are no friend of the establishment," Konstantin went on, voice slightly uncertain. "He did, after all, find you a prisoner of the secret police."

"He did." Baxter squinted into the light as the sun finally broke through the banks of smoke. A couple of the launch's crew, including the friendly first mate, were walking towards him. He took a half step away from the revolutionary, suddenly desperate to be away from the earnest young man.

Then Konstantin said the thing he'd been dreading. "It seems to me that an experienced sailor might be of great value to our cause. To provide us with advice as to whether our comrades aboard the *Potemkin* are ... being realistic, shall we say?"

Baxter looked back at him, chewing his lip. He knew he should walk away, be done with this whole sorry affair. There was just that one loose end to tie off. He didn't even know if Koenig was aboard the *Potemkin*, whether he'd made it to his new posting. He was without doubt not a 'dragon', a hard horse as Royal Navy sailors would describe them, but a crew cut loose from all bounds of discipline would not always be able to make that distinction. He knew some truly dreadful tales from history.

But he couldn't leave until he knew, and his gut told him he couldn't just come out and ask the question.

"There is likely to be pay, of course," Konstantin said after a moment, obviously misreading his hesitation. "The battleship is well-funded, at least, and the sailors' committee is determined to pay a fair price for everything."

Well, not misreading his hesitation too badly. Getting paid wouldn't hurt one bit, assuming he lived through the experience.

Baxter sighed, looked back at the merchant sailor and gave him a polite nod, raising his hand in both greeting and farewell. "Very well," he said to Konstantin, trying not to let his weariness show. "What do you want me to do?"

CHAPTER 6

Baxter wasn't surprised but he was annoyed when Konstantin explained what he had in mind. He desperately wanted to be afloat again, and certainly didn't want to be venturing closer to the heart of power in Odessa.

"And yet here I am," he said in English, speaking under his breath so as not to attract the attention of the revolutionaries clustered around him.

It seemed Mashka, who had somehow attached herself to this madcap enterprise, had sharp ears. "What is this you say?" she demanded in Russian. Her accent had an odd lilt to it, and he guessed she was a native Ukrainian. He shot a glance at her, wondering again about her. She had sharp features, dark intelligent eyes, and in her workers' clothes and headscarf he found it impossible to pin an age on her. Young, certainly, but her small stature and narrow frame could be a matter of malnutrition rather than youth.

"Just wondering what I'm doing here," he replied, dropping back into Russian. He risked a quick glance out of the alley in which the two of them sheltered to peer towards the military headquarters.

"Not fighting for the good of the working classes or the peasants, that is for sure," she spat back, standing as far from him as possible while still being able to observe the menacing building into which Konstantin, a priest and a delegation of sailors had disappeared. The headquarters of the military governor was an imposing affair some distance up from the grand statue of the duc de Richelieu that overlooked the steps down to the harbour, a granite monstrosity with a tall iron-bound gate that looked out of place surrounded by the elegance of the city.

"You're bloody right I'm not," he said, darting a glance up and down the street while doing his best to appear casual, and not keeping watch. There were Cossacks and policemen everywhere, which once again made him question both his own sanity and the point of this. It wasn't as though he and Mashka, unwillingly thrown together, would be able to rescue the delegation from the fortress-like building. That wasn't their job, of course — if it became apparent to them that Konstantin and the others had been seized or indeed summarily executed, they were to return as quickly as possible to the harbour and warn the *Potemkin*. It was hoped the threat of the ship's guns would prevent any such behaviour, and failing that would avenge any deaths.

He should have stepped away as soon as Konstantin had described what the plan was. It was foolhardy of him to come this far into the part of the city that the unrest had yet to touch. By that time, though, he had lost sight of the merchantman's launch and he had no other option but to sail the course he'd rashly set himself. The only other path would have put him right back at rock bottom, alone and on foot with no resources. He wasn't ending up there.

"I'm just surprised he trusted me for this," he went on, trying to keep his tone conversational as he risked another quick glance up the street. "I assume he belongs to some kind of organisation…"

"Ha!" Baxter glanced back at Mashka, surprised by the vehemence expressed in that exclamation. "There is no organisation here, Marcus Alexandrovich, there are just parties. Konstantin is a Social Democrat, as was poor Ruslan. I am told the mutineers are primarily Social Democrats. But there are

Bundists, and Marxists, and Mensheviks here. Right now we are all in agreement, though we will see how long *that* lasts. But no, there is no organisation and we take help where we can get it."

"And you?"

Mashka looked slightly startled, as though she was unused to men asking her what her affiliations were. "I am a Menshevik," she said at last. "Though I am not unsympathetic to the Social Democrat viewpoint. I often attend their reading circles, though some of my comrades do not approve. I am sure the workers in your country are fat and happy and do not worry about such things, but in the Russian Empire we must be active in these matters."

Baxter thought of the slums he'd seen — lived in, occasionally — around the docks in Glasgow and Liverpool; the grimy tenements of Edinburgh. He was prevented from further discussion of political theory, though, by the attention of a policeman. The fellow, a bit sharper than his colleagues, had obviously caught sight of the pair of them and come to the conclusion that they were up to no good. Which was only slightly unfair, he decided, as he ducked back into the dim space.

"We should go," he said, as the officer started walking towards them.

"Yes, we should. You were too obvious." Mashka said that over her shoulder as she turned away

"Well, I'm a bloody sailor, not a spy," he snapped irritably, turning to follow her. He briefly thought about stopping here and trying to subdue the irritatingly astute peeler, but thought better of it. While he had no doubt he could manage it, he couldn't be certain of managing it quietly. There were too many armed and extremely hostile people around the place to risk that.

Just as he was turning away, though, the policeman was distracted by the party of sailors — Konstantin and a priest they had found somewhere in the lead — emerging from the barracks. They looked cheerful enough, and a big man with the look of a peasant farmer was actually calling out cheerfully to some of the Cossacks who had escorted them out of the gates.

"Seems to have gone well, then," Mashka commented.

"For them — we're not out of the woods yet." Baxter started hurrying her back up the alley, guessing that the policeman's attention would only be held so long by the spectacle of bluejackets and revolutionaries emerging apparently triumphant, from a place they should never have ventured into.

"I'm still waiting for someone to explain to me what they were even doing there," Baxter said.

"Konstantin wants to be able to bury the martyr Vakulenchuk, with due ceremony and without interference from the Tsar's forces. He has gone to the general to seek his agreement."

"That may not be such a bad idea," Baxter had to admit. He could hear the policeman calling after them, demanding that they halt — he was still at some distance, though, and he put a hand on Mashka's waist to chivvy her forward before bullets started coming their way. She jerked away from him with an angry glare, but it had the desired effect of getting her round the corner and out of sight.

He felt the pressing need to break into a run, but that would draw too much attention. The streets were busier than he'd been expecting but quieter than they would normally be. A lot of those on the streets were obviously hurrying to leave, joining an exodus from the city. Here and there, gentlemen and ladies in their everyday finery promenaded through the elegant avenues as though nothing was wrong with the world or their city; shopkeepers and other businessmen were out cleaning up the mess around them. That mess, the boarded-up windows and sections of cobbles that had been torn up to be used as missiles, gave the lie to the brave face the wealthier residents of the city were trying to put on things.

That, and the sheer number of soldiers and policemen on the streets. They far outnumbered the civilians, and Baxter could see what he guessed were regular infantry and artillerymen, not just the Cossacks who had run wild the previous night.

Baxter hurried along, trying to stoop his shoulders. This was one of the few times he ever had cause to curse his size. He would curse his father, but he didn't get it from him.

He did get some odd looks from people passing by — he would certainly look like an outsider here, even if he wasn't dressed in borrowed and ill-fitting clothes. The noise of a *troika* rattling past made him jump slightly, and that only drew more attention.

"We should get back to the harbour," he said to his companion as they hurried along.

"You have a facility for stating the obvious," she shot back irritably. "As well as attracting unwanted attention."

He could hear a policeman shouting now, another joining in. The noise was some distance behind, and he got the impression the shouts were queries rather than a demand to assist in a pursuit.

They were moving quickly past a café that was just opening back up, the smell of freshly brewed coffee and baked pastries making his stomach growl. No time to stop, though, even if they'd had the money for it.

He glanced back over his shoulder, knowing he shouldn't show any interest but unable to stop himself. That was almost his undoing, but not because he caught their attention.

He jostled against someone just coming out of the café; someone almost as big as he was. He kept his head down, didn't make eye contact, and mumbled an apology in the hopes of being able to keep going without any hassle.

"Hey, watch where you're going!" someone snapped at him. "And your damn manners, at that."

It was a nasal, grating voice, and one he recognised. He mumbled another apology, keeping his head down and moving quickly. A hand — surprisingly strong for such a small man — grabbed his forearm. "I'm talking to you, you big oaf!"

He was forced to turn, facing Pavel, Bilyk's shadow. He loomed over the small, vicious man, hoping to intimidate him into backing down before he would be recognised.

Small hope of that. Ratface — Pavel — did in fact step back quickly, as though realising Baxter's size for the first time. Then his eyes widened in surprised recognition that rapidly became hate and anger.

"*You!*" he hissed.

"Aye, I get that a lot," Baxter said. He acted without really thinking, without giving Ratface time to think, his fist connecting with the secret policeman's jaw and sending him sprawling. Baxter didn't hang around to finish the job, as much as he might have wanted to. He turned briskly on his heel, but the men he saw coming out of the café almost stopped him in his tracks.

The first was Bilyk, which didn't surprise him in the slightest. He doubted Pavel was ever far from his chief. The head Okhrana man was just turning back from saying something over his shoulder to a third man. It was all very casual, friendly even, and that really wasn't right.

Because the last man out of the door was Arbuthnott. The rogue intelligence agent looked pale and was walking on crutches, but he was dressed in new, well-cut clothes and was very obviously not a prisoner.

Baxter met Arbuthnott's stare, and had the satisfaction of seeing a look of unmitigated panic come over the other man's face before he awkwardly turned and tried to get back into the café, stumbling into some customers coming out.

He felt the urge to pile forward into the pair of conniving bastards, or at least take a moment to enjoy Arbuthnott's undignified fall to the pavement, but his slight pause had already been too long. Bilyk had recognised him and reached reflexively for the pistol he wore under his jacket; Ratface was scrambling back to his feet and pulling a narrow-bladed knife.

Baxter took off at a sprint, glancing around to see where Mashka was. Like a sensible revolutionary, she had cleared out while Baxter drew far too much attention to himself. He couldn't blame her for that.

It did mean he was alone, again, in a hostile city. He ducked round a corner into a narrow side alley just as someone fired after him, the sharp *crack* of a pistol. He didn't know where the bullet went, beyond not hitting him, but he didn't hear any shouts of pain — just panic and consternation. He clattered along the alleyway, breathing hard, and didn't attempt to slow down this time as he came out into another avenue. Instinctively he turned towards the sea, charging headlong away from his pursuers.

His leg muscles started to burn and his lungs felt like they had iron bands around them. Curious civilians and alarmed soldiers watched him thump by. He heard someone — he was pretty sure it was Bilyk — yell something behind him. Someone else yelled a response. He ducked round a corner and pressed his back to the stone wall, sweat pouring from him as he tried to catch his breath. A full blown argument seemed to be happening behind him, loud even at this distance.

It took him a moment to work out what was happening. It seemed the patrolling soldiers, as much as they had been alarmed by Baxter sprinting by, had taken considerably more exception to the armed but not uniformed men chasing him. He could hear Bilyk's normally level voice raised in increasing fury, joined by at least one of the police officers who clearly wasn't happy about the military invasion of his city.

Baxter grinned, but knew it wouldn't take them long to straighten this out and for the whole lot of them to be on his tail. He started off again, walking fast rather than running. He needed to save his strength for when they came after him again.

Working his way back down through the city towards the harbour, there was no sign of pursuit, however. "With any luck, they shot the bugger on principle," he murmured, pausing in the shade of an Orthodox church and leaning against the cool stone.

It was hot again, the sun beating down on the tense city from a cloudless sky. It almost felt like the city was hunched up in expectation of more violence. Either from its own people or the soldiers flooding in, or from the battleship that still lurked in the outer harbour. Baxter wasn't far from the cliff edge here, giving him a grand view of the port. The jagged, blackened remnants of burned-out warehouses and ships were a stark reminder of the previous night's horror.

The floating steel castle, in her bright peacetime colours of yellow and glossy black, promised more horrors to come. The *Potemkin* sat quietly with her small flotilla around her — a torpedo boat and an armed auxiliary seized when she came into harbour the previous day — and with her turrets pointed fore and aft rather than at the city. The sense of her power, the threat she posed, was palpable, however. The army would bring in artillery eventually, he guessed, and if they had to they would shell her to the bottom, just as the Japanese had with the ships trapped in Port Arthur. *Though if they did manage to hit her, it would make them the laughing stock of the world.*

Baxter straightened and wiped the sweat from his face. He knew he had a decision to make. He didn't know what Arbuthnott was up too, how he'd managed to leverage his position from 'prisoner' to visiting a tea room with his Russian captor. It could be Bilyk had just been playing nice to get him to open up, though he found that unlikely. Arbuthnott wasn't the sort to stand up to the kind of beating Baxter had taken.

No. The intelligence officer was, without doubt, up to something. What Baxter had seen back there had not been prisoner and gaoler. He expected to feel the old familiar rage creep through him, but all he felt was tired. Exhausted really. It had been a day or more since he'd last slept, and his eyes were gritty. His clothes smelled of smoke and he felt filthy. He knew he could probably still get away from here. The sea might very well be closed to him, but there were obviously still trains leaving the city, if he could scrape the money together for a ticket. If nothing else, he could walk, though he did not know to where. He could disappear into the vast expanse of rural Russia, rather than the sea.

There was still the matter of Koenig, though, and what fate had befallen him. He also couldn't shake the memory of

Kostenko, who had shown him kindness and then shown courage, and been cut down for it. The lad hadn't deserved to die, let alone like that.

More than anything, though, Baxter realised that he needed to deal with Arbuthnott. No – *wanted* to deal with him. It wasn't any of his business, and it wasn't his world. But the slimy intelligence agent had derailed his life, and indeed had tried to kill him.

"That won't stand," he said quietly. "Not anymore — time to stop trying to run."

He felt a new surge of energy as he came to that decision, and he surveyed the harbour and the area around it with new determination. He had to stay in Odessa, and right now it seemed to him that the safest place was the one with thick steel armour and heavy guns.

He had to get aboard the *Potemkin*.

CHAPTER 7

The main problem with his plan, Baxter realised, was getting back to the docks. Well, that was the first problem — talking his way onto the rebellious battleship was probably going to be an even more significant barrier.

"Worry about the first problem," he told himself, shoving his hands further into his pockets and trying to lower his shoulders as he surveyed the top of the Richelieu Steps. The city was still crowded with soldiers and Cossacks, and there were fewer and fewer civilians in evidence. The police cordon around the harbour seemed to be there still, although it was obviously leaking — the steps themselves were being guarded but there were people coming and going.

Baxter couldn't escape the feeling that Bilyk would have people watching the steps; the Okhrana probably had men at the train station as well, blocking that route out even if he could have afforded it. He didn't think he'd be top of the secret police's agenda right now, with the riots and the threat of a battleship in revolutionary hands. Bilyk and the others had put effort into chasing him, though, and it seemed likely they'd be happy to collar him if they could.

He turned away, trudging further back into the city. He was starting to get a proper feel for the centre of Odessa now, even though he couldn't read the Cyrillic street signs. He'd identified a number of landmarks — the statue of Richelieu at the head of the steps, the cathedral, the military governor's forbidding headquarters. He drifted towards the cathedral now — he had to keep moving and stay alert. He'd rather do anything but slip back into the aimless funk that had characterised much of his time since he'd escaped the Okhrana's custody.

Baxter could hear raised voices ahead, a lot of them; they were far enough away that they almost sounded like the rumble of waves onto a beach. As he drew closer, he realised they sounded almost festive. He started to be able to pick out individual shouts and slogans, demands for freedom and an end to the Tsar's reign.

"Trust the Russians to turn a funeral into a protest," he muttered as he caught sight of the crowd. It was the most civilians he'd seen in the city so far, a mix of workers and middle classes pressing through a line of soldiers into the cemetery on Chumka Hill. He saw a number of banners and placards, and when he hopped onto the base of a streetlamp he had enough elevation to see white-uniformed sailors beyond the crowd.

It was Vakulenchuk's funeral, he guessed, and that meant this was an area he probably didn't want to be in. There were soldiers and Cossacks everywhere, trying to hem in the increasingly fractious crowd. As he watched, he saw the sailors being hustled into waiting carriages under armed guard. Though it was hard to tell at this distance, they seemed to be going willingly enough — there was no prodding with swords or bayonets and they weren't being held at rifle-point.

The atmosphere was starting to get the same powder-keg feeling he'd experienced on the Richelieu Steps and down in the harbour. The crowd seemed good-natured enough and the security forces were being restrained for now, but he guessed it had been decided the sailors' presence was becoming intolerable. As he watched, the carriages started towards the harbour, clattering past him across the cobbles. They weren't under heavy guard, but Baxter's gut told him something was entirely wrong with this situation.

Most of the Russian officers he'd known were honourable men, and there was no reason to suspect that if safe conduct had been given for the funeral, it would not be adhered to. But these men *were* mutineers and revolutionaries...

Baxter was moving before he'd given himself a chance to think about it, plunging after the carriages as fast as he could while trying not to give the appearance he was chasing them. He guessed they would be going along Preobrazhenskaya Street back towards the staircase down to the harbour. Trusting his intuition, he ducked into a side street that he guessed would bring him out onto the city's main thoroughfare. He slowed from his trot to a fast walk as he realised there was a company of soldiers waiting at the head of the street, looking very much like they were preparing for an ambush.

"Daft bastards," he panted, and turned into a noisome and cramped alley running parallel to Preobrazhenskaya, heart hammering in his chest with more than just the exertion.

He arrived on the main street just in time to see the soldiers he'd almost crashed into forming up behind the Russian sailors, rifles shouldered and ready to fire. The Russian sailors were huddled into a circle, finally realising the danger they were in and utterly exposed as the carriages clattered away.

Baxter opened his mouth to shout a warning, pointless though that would be. At that moment a bugle sounded, drowning out his voice, and the Russian infantry fired a ragged volley. Baxter ducked back into the alleyway as bullets smacked into the stonework of the building next to him. He risked a glance round the corner as the distinctive sound of bolts being drawn back preceded the tinkle of ejected cartridges hitting the cobbles. He expected to see torn bodies lying in pools of blood, and was astonished to see the majority of the mutineers sprinting away from the ambush site.

Baxter didn't hesitate. He didn't run after them, but instead turned back into the grid of side streets, trying to get ahead of them or at least keep pace. The Russian soldiers were shouting and more bugles sounded; he could hear the thud of boots on cobblestones as they gave chase.

He caught a flash of movement, a file of infantrymen with a burly sergeant moving to cut off the mutineers. They hadn't seen Baxter, though, and if they had they wouldn't have any reason to think he wasn't just a passer-by running in blind panic.

The soldiers formed a ragged line just as the mutineers came round a corner, on the opposite side of the assembling firing squad. Baxter had the briefest moment to see the look of horror spread across the lead sailor's face as he realised he'd led the others into a massacre. There was no way even the apparently poorly trained Russian soldiers could miss at that range in that tight, narrow space.

Baxter slammed into the sergeant's back, sending him sprawling before he could give the order to fire and careering into the five-man file, knocking them over like skittles. A rifle fired, but the round went wild. Baxter recovered himself and kicked the sergeant in the crotch before he could get up. As their leader doubled up around his offended parts, wailing and gasping for breath, the Russian soldiers scattered. They obviously didn't have much of a stomach for this work.

Baxter realised his hands were shaking and he was gasping air in great gulps. He bent forward and put his hands on his thighs as he recovered his breath.

"My friend, I cannot thank you enough," he heard someone say, and looked up into the face of the lead sailor. He saw a small man with characteristically Slavic features — currently flushed with exertion — and intense eyes almost lost behind busy red eyebrows. "I and my compatriots cannot hang around, but I must know how I can repay you?"

Baxter straightened up and thrust out his hand. "Friend," he said, keeping his Russian as basic as possible — no point giving away his hard-won facility with the language. "All I want is to get onto a ship and away from this reeking city."

He knew it was a hell of a gamble; he saw it in the way those eyebrows shot up in surprise. He'd judged his man right, though, seeing his impulsive nature in the way he'd even come to this place for a funeral. He burst into laughter. "Well, you're a direct fellow. You'd best come along with us, then! We'll soon get you afloat. Though I should warn you, it will be dangerous!"

"I had worked that out before I attacked these soldiers."

The sergeant had rolled onto his knees and was now puking into the gutter. Baxter tensed as one or two of the sailors looked like they wanted to make a move on the soldier, which was not something he would stand for. Before that could develop further, however, the lead sailor waved them forward. "I know we are tired, comrades, but we are not out of danger yet."

The streets around them were noisy with the tramp of boots, rattle of equipment and the clop of shod hooves on the streets. The sailors didn't need any more encouragement than that, following their leader at a tired trot away from the town centre.

It took them most of the remaining hours of daylight to get back to the harbour. They ran until their legs were dead and all of them were gasping like landed fish. Baxter came to the conclusion that the main benefit of being afloat was the limited distances over which he'd have to run.

They approached the docks by a roundabout route, skirting through the industrial slums to the north of the city and then following the rail track that ran down there. The police cordon here was thin or non-existent, and at around five in the evening the tired sailors walked down onto the harbour front. The sun was creeping down towards the horizon, casting long shadows across them as they made their slow way down. The battleship and her consorts were still in the light, safe haven for all of them. They hadn't been pursued since they had made it into the warren of side streets, although the noise of the searching soldiers and Cossacks had haunted their steps for some time.

They weren't out of danger yet and wouldn't be until they were aboard the *Potemkin*. Baxter knew their position would be precarious even there, but the Russians he was walking with seemed reenergised by the sight of their ship. Her apparent invulnerability was infectious.

"All we have to do now is get back to her, and we will show that treacherous bastard Karkhanov what we think of him!" the leader declared. None of the sailors had been introduced, but Baxter had picked up that he was called Afanasy Matyushenko. While he was a small, wiry man, he seemed to be a natural leader who the other mutineers deferred to.

A tired cheer of agreement came from the other men. Baxter kept his silence. Gunnery had been his speciality, back when he'd worn a uniform, and he had a good idea how difficult it would be to land shells on specific targets in the densely packed city above them. He also had a good idea just how devastating a general bombardment would be.

He'd got the impression, as they'd made their way here, that the men in the funeral party were probably some of the core movers of the mutiny. Perhaps not all committed revolutionaries, some of them at least were malcontents. Baxter understood Matyushenko bringing them with him, but he wondered how much of a risk that had been. Crews were rarely fully committed to a mutiny, and some sailors would just have gone along with it in the heat of the moment or because their messmates were already rioting. Anything could have happened to this revolutionary beacon if they'd been killed or captured.

"Let us find a boat and return, then," one of the party said. Baxter glanced across at the man, a stocky fellow with clean-cut features. He sounded more educated than the others, positively middle class in fact. The others seemed to have accepted him in their midst, and he was clearly one of the more motivated revolutionaries. Seeing Baxter's attention, the mutineer gave him a broad grin and offered his hand. "Beshoff, Ivan, at your service."

"That may be easier said than done," he pointed out after a moment. That earned him a warning glance from Afanasy and sour looks from some of the others. He shut his mouth, reminded that he was on dangerous ground here and that he would have to earn the right to speak in these groups.

"Never fear — we Ukrainians are resilient people," Ivan Beshoff said, clapping him on the shoulder. "Life will continue despite the oppressions of the Tsarists."

As they walked further down onto the docks, it became clear that the situation had indeed improved somewhat. The fire brigade had finally been allowed to pass through the police cordon, although there was not much for them to do beyond dousing down smouldering ruins. A cart was passing through the area, pausing occasionally to let the two men following it pick up a body and toss it, with the bare minimum of ceremony, into the back.

The harbour area was still pretty empty, though, particularly compared to the throngs that had crowded it to see Vakulenchuk's body. People were moving here and there, looking for the wounded or looting the dead. A few knots gathered, and he heard an occasional raised voice. It seemed the debates about the future course of this uprising, if that's what it could be called, were still ongoing.

Baxter saw that the impromptu shrine to the martyred sailor was still there, still with its honour guard of mutineers. Afanasy deliberately steered clear of them, leading his little party towards a gaggle of tied up fishing boats. Baxter was struck by how out of place this everyday scene was — weather-beaten, tough-looking sailors working on their single-masted boats, readying them for the next day's fishing. If it wasn't for the devastation around them, this would be a familiar sight the world over.

It made him think of the Hull boats, the flotilla the Russian 2nd Pacific Squadron had ploughed through and bombarded with great fury and little effect on its passage through the North Sea. There would be little difference between the boats, and the fishermen would probably have more in common with each other than with their respective governments.

That incident had almost precipitated war between Britain and Russia, coming close to achieving by accident what Arbuthnott had sought to achieve with his rogue operation that had got Baxter into this mess in the first place, almost a year ago now.

"That has to be what he's up to," he decided, thinking out loud. Still trying to start a naval panic, ratchet up tensions between the two countries. But what was Bilyk's involvement in all this?

"What who is up to?" Ivan asked. Baxter glanced at him in surprise, thinking for a moment that the Russian sailor spoke English. Then he realised he'd become so used to speaking Russian that his private musings were in that language.

Matyushenko saved him from having to answer, striding up to the quayside and adopting a broad stance, thumbs hooked into his belt as he looked down at the fishermen. "Comrades, the revolution requires your assistance!" he declaimed.

Only one of the fishermen glanced up at him with a sour expression. "And how much is the revolution paying, friend?"

After some negotiations and a final agreement on an over-inflated price, Baxter and the Russian sailors piled into the little boat. The fisherman and his small crew — Baxter suspected 'family' was probably more accurate — worked around their passengers with a minimum of grace despite the *kopeks* that would soon be jangling in their pockets.

Baxter took a deep breath as the fishing boat was poled away from the quayside and oars were run out, feeling himself ... well, not relax exactly. He was back where he belonged, at least, surrounded by familiar smells — pitch and canvas, saltwater and fish. Even if they weren't exactly pleasant, they were a comfort along with the movement of the deck under his feet as the boat set across the choppy water of the harbour towards the waiting behemoth.

A sudden bellow of laughter from a knot of sailors caught his attention. Afanasy was bending over to put a finger through a hole in the bell bottom of his trousers. When he straightened, a look of mirth mixed with delayed fear crossed his face. "Well, comrades, it seems I at least came closer to death than I previously imagined!"

"Remarkably fine shooting," someone else commented. "True marksmanship."

Matyushenko seemed to sober slightly. "That was a close shave, it is true," he said seriously, looking round the circle of sailors. "And I believe we only survived because many of the soldiers did not shoot, or deliberately missed. And this gives me hope — it seems what we have been told, that the army stands ready to rise as soon as we have disposed of their dragons, is true!"

"Not all of them missed," Ivan said, voice dark. "We were twelve when we were ashore, and only nine now."

The revolutionary party sobered again. During the mad, chaotic dash of their escape it had been hard to keep track of everyone.

"I do not know if they were shot or captured," their leader admitted. "And if they are dead, we will mourn them. But we must also honour their sacrifice, and pay the general back tenfold for his treachery! As soon as we are aboard, we will go to quarters and prepare to bombard the city."

Baxter had been about to point out that he'd seen at least one body in the street, but Matyushenko's blunt statement about unleashing the *Potemkin*'s fearsome arsenal on a crowded city stunned him into silence. The threat had been there all along, he knew, and the mutineers had been using it to cow the Russian general trying to maintain order in Odessa.

It seemed this general, Karkhanov, had either decided to call the sailors' bluff or had decided that the risk of massive civilian casualties was worth trying to bring the mutiny to an end by force.

"What the devil have I got myself into this time?" Baxter murmured to himself, leaning his hands on the fishing smack's low railing and gazing at the battleship as they crept closer. The *Potemkin* had seemed like the safest place for him, earlier, a base from which to wage his private war against Bilyk and Arbuthnott. He wondered if he was going to regret not just washing his hands of the whole damn situation.

Baxter wasn't quite sure what he'd been expecting of the ship, but it didn't match what he found when they finally got aboard. The first thing that struck him was that there still appeared to be some semblance of military discipline. The decks were clean and everything that should be tied down was. Casting a professional eye around, he noted that some of the equipment wasn't as well-maintained as it could be — there was more rust than he would have tolerated, for one thing — but that could just as easily have been a result of a poor maintenance routine before the mutiny. Despite that, he could almost have stepped onto a naval ship on a normal day. He could feel the throb of the engine, deep below, as a vibration through his boot soles. Not the full-throated thud of the boilers and pistons driving the ship onwards through the waves, but the gentler hum of harbour duties. A wisp of coal smoke came from her yellow-painted funnels.

There were far more sailors on deck than would be normal, though, taking their ease in the sunlight or gathered in groups heatedly debating politics or their next course of action. Everyone was still in uniform and there was little sign of disorder or damage from the mutiny, barring one or two bullet scars evident in the woodwork. He was surprised to see one or two petty officers — the professional sailors who served as intermediaries between the officers and crew. They were not generally the sort of men to join a mutiny, as their positions afforded them more benefits and therefore more to lose if the officers were overthrown.

He was surprised to see no evidence of dockside harlots, most sailors' first order of business when they made harbour. He could only see one civilian, a burly bearded man who was holding forth to a group of sailors, educating them on Social Democrat principles. His voice rasped but it did not detract from the passion of his delivery — Baxter guessed what civilian agitators there were aboard were working themselves to the bone trying to get the sailors on side and keep them there.

"Something's afoot," he commented, nodding to the groups of sailors who were starting to mass around the capstan, the great wheel that would be used to bring the bow anchor up.

Ivan Beshoff, the mutineer who had been most welcoming to him, grinned. "Time for our evening debate!" he said cheerfully, and joined the flow of sailors going forward.

Baxter drifted along after them, earning a number of curious glances, although the crew would be used to unknown civilians wandering around by this point. He noticed a couple of more hostile glares. Ships' crews could be a close-knit community, and not overly fond of outsiders. He knew he would have to tread carefully here.

One of those outsiders, the burly man he'd noted earlier, was on the capstan now. Sailors formed a semicircle around him, the front row sitting on the deck and the others clustering around. Yet more sat on the fore 12-inch gun turret or the barrels of the guns themselves, and others sat on the upper decks with their legs dangling down. It could almost be a normal, if slightly informal, crew gathering, if it wasn't for the agitator who had started speaking.

He spoke well and passionately, this representative of the Odessa revolutionaries, telling the sailors of the oppressed and downtrodden masses yearning to rise up against the Tsar, if only someone could light the way. The crew was quiet through the speech. Baxter was familiar enough with the common Russian sailor to recognise they were sceptical to say the least. Even though most of them would come from peasant backgrounds and would still have family ashore, they were severed from the land now. These concerns were distant to them.

A sailor stood up next as the speaker finished. "Here, lads, is a good man who wants to say a few words to you," he said simply, then gestured to a slim young man who hopped up onto the capstan.

It took Baxter a moment to recognise him as Konstantin, Ruslan Kostenko's friend and apparently an influential revolutionary in the city. The man who had dragged Baxter further into this mess. He looked out across the crowd, sweeping the sailors with his piercing and intelligent gaze, and paused briefly when he saw Baxter. Then he started to speak, fluidly and confidently. Baxter had known officers with this same gift, the ability to hook in their listeners purely through their voice, the cadence of their words. It wasn't a talent he had in abundance.

Konstantin kept very much to the same themes as his predecessor, painting a grim picture of life ashore for the worker and the farmer. He worked from that premise to their current situation, how they had to strike and strike now before they lost the initiative.

"Now is your time to choose!" Konstantin insisted. He wasn't someone who yelled from his pulpit, rather trying to bring his audience along with him. It was only as he approached his final point that his voice rose in volume. "Ahead of you is the glory and honour that are granted to fighters for the people. Behind you is the yoke of your former torturers. You choose which one you want. What we must do is to open fire on the city now!"

Those closer to the front were cheering, caught up in the speaker's fervour. Those closer to Baxter, who hadn't really joined the congregation, looked unhappy. They shouted their objections, that shelling the city would only hurt the oppressed people they were supposed to be liberating, that they shouldn't be getting tangled up in the affairs of landsmen. That cry was taken up. It was as Baxter had felt when he'd come aboard — although the crew wasn't marching with a single purpose towards the revolution, they closed ranks when an outsider tried to tell them what to do.

"Away with the landsmen!" someone shouted as Konstantin jumped down from the capstan and disappeared from Baxter's sight. The shout was taken up, becoming a chant. That was the last thing Baxter needed, as he'd finally got himself out of the city and into at least vaguely familiar territory.

Matyushenko bounded with enthusiastic energy onto the capstan, raising his hands for their attention. After a moment, the crew quietened down, all eyes turning back to their leader. Where the two landsmen had been good speakers, the leading mutineer almost immediately had his comrades hooked. Baxter half-listened to him, watched the way he moved around on the capstan more like a performer than an orator, drawing the men in and including them in his performance.

Mostly, though, Baxter was watching a petty officer who was standing a little further back from the body of the kirk, watching events with a sour expression. He kept glancing to his left, to the lookout position on the main mast. As though he was waiting for something to happen.

Baxter drifted towards him. Matyushenko had the crew completely hooked now, warning how their actions meant the noose for them all, unless they won through and brought about an end to the Tsar's regime. Telling them that they could not betray and abandon the people of Odessa who had risen up, that they would be damned by the people of Russia if they slunk away.

Baxter went and stood next to the petty officer. He was clearly unhappy with the current turn of events, one of a silent faction of the crew who'd gone along with the mutiny for their own safety but who would be looking for an opportunity to seize control of the vessel.

The fellow glanced at him with narrow eyes. "Piss off, landsman," he growled.

Baxter knew he should. He had enough problems of his own. He was tired of running and hiding, and right now this ship was a safe haven for him. Just as long as reactionary forces didn't manage to seize back control. "You know, I'm surprised the crew didn't throw you lot off the ship or put you in the brig," he said, keeping his voice mild.

"What would you know about it, landsman?" the fellow spat. He wasn't big, but he looked like he could handle himself in a fight. He reminded Baxter of Arbuthnott's minions who had stranded him on a disabled yacht at the mercy of Russian gunners; the act of treachery that had landed him in this mess last year. The Russian's hand shifted towards the belt of his trousers.

"Interesting that you should assume I'm a landsman," Baxter said quietly, managing to keep his temper in check. "But we'll worry about that another time. What I'd like to know is what you think is going to happen when you pull that gun, or your mate in the lookout nest takes a shot at Afanasy?"

The eyes narrowed down to dark slits. "Matyushenko is the ringleader. There will be chaos when he's removed."

"Think about it, man, look at how worked up they are. If something happens now, there'll be a frenzy. The best you could hope for is getting over the side and swimming to shore. And that's a hell of a swim."

The man swallowed hard, suddenly looking doubtful.

"And I'll make damn sure they know it was you," Baxter went on with a vicious grin. "Self-preservation, you understand? I'm a newcomer here, they'll turn on me. I'll have to offer them you — you know, the one with a revolver in his trousers."

He made it sound so reasonable that the petty officer just stared at him, hand dropping away from the grip of the Nagant revolver he'd been about to draw. His eyes flicked over Baxter's shoulder to his supposed sharpshooter ally. Baxter didn't follow the look, didn't let himself worry about whether he was about to be shot in the back; whether whoever was up there would act independently. He guessed the man above them was waiting on a signal.

The cheering behind them had become deafening. He could make out individual voices promising to follow Afanasy Matyushenko to death, that they would all die together. The excitement was palpable, and the petty officer subsided, knowing it was too late.

"I imagine you'll turn me in anyway, you Marxist scum."

Baxter shrugged. "I thought about it," he admitted. Mutinies were dangerous things to leave unchecked, and the habits drummed into him at the Royal Navy College at Dartmouth were hard to shake. Even if he found himself sympathising with the mutineers, having seen first-hand the conditions in which they lived and fought, he couldn't fault the man for doing his duty. "But really, none of this is any of my concern. Just try not to do anything stupid for the next few days."

"Well, brothers," Afanasy was shouting, having wrung agreement from the crew to commence a bombardment. "Now stand steady. Go to your places."

CHAPTER 8

The following few minutes were utterly surreal. The sailors went to their stations with a familiar rush and clatter of activity, as well as any crew under normal naval discipline would. The activity was accompanied by the rattle of drums and the calls of a bugle, and a normal amount of shouting and cursing from petty officers.

The hatch into the nearest 12-inch turret clanged open to admit a stream of men, all of them moving with an excited purpose. Other sailors ran to the second armament, the 6-inch guns mounted along each broadside and the smaller weapons that bristled along the upper decks. If it came to a real battle, the crews of those 3- and 1.7-inch quick-firing guns, mounted with shields but without the protection of an armoured turret, would be horribly exposed to shell splinters and raging fires. Commanding one of the *Yaroslavich*'s broadsides at Tsushima, Baxter had seen a lot of men he'd come to know and like torn apart by Japanese fire in just such a manner.

"No fear of that happening here," he muttered as the battleship prepared herself to inflict devastation on the city. The Russian Army was bringing heavy guns, he knew, but the danger right now was entirely one-sided.

"Get out of the way, you landsman!" someone bellowed at him. Baxter bridled at that description, having heard it a few too many times already, but he was just getting underfoot here. He stepped smartly to the rail as a file of sailors trotted by. He'd been on many warships in his life, and normally when they prepared to action he'd have a station of his own to run to. During the first months on the *Yaroslavich* he'd been relegated to his cabin when the crew drilled, and when he'd become an informal part of the crew he'd gone to the 4.7-inch guns. Here he was just in the way.

The capstan that, until a few minutes ago, had been a podium was turning now, dragging the massive anchor up from the silty seabed. Thick black smoke was starting to belch from the stacks as the engines were stoked to their full contained fury.

Sluggishly at first, as she was a great weight to thrust through the water, the *Potemkin* began to move.

Someone bumped into Baxter, and he spun, ready to unleash his temper on whatever clumsy oaf of a sailor hadn't looked where he was going. He relented when he realised it was Konstantin, the agitator. The slight, quick man looked both confused and excited by the rush of activity that must seem utterly arcane to a civilian.

Surprised at seeing another man out of uniform in front of him, he bowed formally. "Konstantin Feldmann, at your..." he began, falling back on proper forms of address as a form of defence in the suddenly alien world. "Oh, Marcus Alexandrovich!"

"The same," Baxter said. He was obscurely relieved the revolutionary remembered him — it occurred to him that having an ally like this (assuming he *was* an ally) would be helpful in finding out what Bilyk was up to.

"Mashka was sure you had been taken," Konstantin went on, sudden suspicion in his eyes.

He shrugged as nonchalantly as he could, realising he was in dangerous waters indeed. All it would take was the accusation of being a Tsarist collaborator and things would start to go very badly for him. "It turns out the real police and the army don't take kindly to men running around waving guns. I managed to escape in the confusion."

Dark, intense eyes glittered as Konstantin assessed him carefully. It was a good job that was the entire truth, Baxter reflected ruefully — Ekaterina had often teased him about being a terrible liar.

"Well, you're either an extremely well-practised deceiver or an honest man," Konstantin said at last, his expression relaxing into a smile. "I think you are the latter."

Glancing around, Baxter saw that the ship was almost closed up for action — it had taken them far too long to get there, though. Sailors were hosing the decks with seawater to prevent fires being set by enemy shells or the blast of their own weapons firing, and Baxter realised their shoes were about to get wet.

"I think it is better if we are on the bridge," Konstantin said, looking at the tide of water. "One hopes there will be less of this running around enthusiastically."

"I wouldn't bank on it," Baxter replied quietly, but followed along anyway. He found himself quite curious about the command arrangements on this renegade ship. Not to mention how they were going to manage this in the day's dying light.

The bridge was a bit quieter, certainly. The *Potemkin* was a considerably more modern vessel than the last Russian warship he'd been on, the venerable *Yaroslavich*. The bridge therefore had a number of modern conveniences, such as being enclosed and armoured. There were more enlisted men there than would be considered normal, but what surprised Baxter was that there were a number of men wearing officer's uniforms but with their epaulettes and other rank insignia removed. A young man who barely looked like he was shaving occupied the captain's chair, fidgeting nervously and glancing around.

"That is Ensign Alekseyev," Konstantin said quietly. "The sailors' committee elected him to the captaincy — the men do like a proper officer to be in command, even if the real decisions are taken by the committee."

An eerie silence fell over the bridge and the ship beyond it. The noise of the engine, the rattle of ammunition hoists, and the lap of waves against the solid metal hull were almost subliminal. Looking to starboard, Baxter guessed they'd moved about half a mile further out and turned the ship's broadside to the city. It was deep dusk now, the silhouette of the city melding gradually with the night; here and there fires still burned on the long docks. They didn't provide sufficient illumination to shoot by, and the smoke further added to the worsening visibility.

"All stop," the young man officially in charge ordered, the effort to keep his voice steady obvious.

Afanasy Matyushenko conferred briefly with the 'captain', then moved forward to call up to the appointed gunnery officer on the deck above. They kept their voices down, as though they were respecting the hush that had fallen.

A bugler played three staccato notes. Baxter, despite that warning and his long association with naval artillery, almost jumped out of his skin when a gun fired, the tongue of flame bright in the gathering darkness. He mastered himself quickly as he waited for the fall of shot, then realised they must have fired a blank as a warning to the civilians. Two more bugle blasts and blank rounds followed. He pursed his lips.

"Not a bad rate of fire. Not a *good* one, mind, but not bad." With all the talk of the city being bombarded, he expected the big guns would be brought to bear; the *Potemkin* was well within range of her secondary batteries as well. Instead, after another discussion between the figurehead captain,

Matyushenko and the gunnery officer, the 6-inch gun that had fired the blanks was brought to bear on what Baxter could only assume was a specific target.

A moment later, it fired again, a brief flash of yellow and green fire and a stunning clap of noise. Baxter felt his pulse quicken. A few short weeks ago he had been subject to the fire of guns not unlike this one, and had helped the Russians give … well, not as good as they got, but they had fought back with courage and spirit. Even the noise of a single gun firing brought memories of the battle surging back.

The bridge was silent, everyone straining to hear both the sound of the shell detonation and the results of the fire. It was a light shell, though, fired at a target several thousand yards away.

"Overshot!" the gunnery officer called down. Baxter saw looks of horror and stunned surprise on the sailors' faces, and he realised that far from seeking to unleash carnage they were shooting at specific targets. They all knew those targets were surrounded by civilians homes and businesses, and they'd probably just killed or at the very least wounded innocents.

"Get it right this time, Vedenmeyer!" Afanasy snarled up to the spotter's station.

"What are they even shooting at?" Baxter whispered to Konstantin, aware that they were intruders on the bridge and not wanting to draw any attention.

"We received word from revolutionary soldiers that General Karkhanov and the other senior commanders are meeting in the city's theatre. They are the target — though the warning shots would have given them time to find cover — along with the barracks and the headquarters."

Baxter suppressed a low whistle. "They're mad if they think they can land shells that precisely," he said, voice rising slightly.

A chorus of voices this time. "Overshot! Overshot!"

Aside from the bugle, the gun, and the hushed orders, silence reigned over the ship. Now it was broken by the sound of men shouting in anger, cursing the gun crew that kept missing the target, hammering bulkheads in fury and frustration.

"A white flag!" Vedenmeyer, the gunnery officer, yelled. "They're waving a white flag!"

"I don't see anything," one of the young former officers on the bridge called out, staring intently into the gloom through a set of field glasses.

"Well, it's there!" Vedenmeyer shot back, a note of desperation in his voice. No doubt he wanted to distract the sailors from trying to blame him for the missed shots.

Afanasy's shoulders seemed to slump very slightly, though he was such a wiry man it was hard to tell. "We have sent a message, at least, in the form of shells. Now we shall see how they respond."

"We should convene with the committee," one of the other mutineers said. Matyushenko only nodded in response.

"And what should the ship do, while you debate?" the young man in the captain's chair asked, a touch of frostiness in his voice. The question highlighted the real power dynamic on the bridge.

"We shall stand down," the real commander said tiredly. "And anchor here."

Konstantin Feldmann, the student revolutionary, sighed heavily. His expression spoke of deep disappointment, of a man who had been on the verge of seeing his dreams realised. His revolution finally supported by this fearsome beast of the sea.

It was a pity, for him, that the beast had turned out to be ineffective. Perhaps not a pity for the people of Odessa, Baxter reflected.

"So, Marcus Alexandrovich," Konstantin said with the air of a man turning to a small problem to avoid dealing with bigger issues. "You are an interesting fellow. You must tell me your story — all of it."

They retired to one of the officer's staterooms along with another revolutionary named Kirill. The furnishings were far more opulent than the small room in which Bilyk had interrogated Baxter, but he had no illusions that this was any less of a dangerous interview. The stateroom was without doubt one of the most luxurious spaces Baxter had ever seen afloat, matching even the suite Captain of the first rank Gorchakov had occupied aboard the *Yaroslavich* until he had lost his grip on reality and been transferred to safer but less grand accommodations on a hospital ship.

Konstantin got straight to the point once the door was closed. "Mashka tells me you and the secret policeman Bilyk are known to each other."

"I'm glad she made it back in one piece," Baxter said by way of reply as he settled onto a settee. "And of course I'm known to Bilyk — he personally oversaw my interrogation." He gestured to the bruises around his eye. It was still tight, though starting to fade already. He'd mostly forgotten about it, running as he had been on adrenalin for the last day or more. Something struck him. "You know this man Bilyk as well?"

"He is known to us, yes. We have been looking for an opportunity to assassinate him."

The cold-blooded way in which it was said chilled Baxter. Konstantin seemed too young — barely into his early twenties — to take such a pragmatic approach to murder. It spoke volumes about the repression in Russia. He'd had a glimpse of it in the squadron on its way to the Far East. His friend Cristov Juneau, who had risen to command of the *Yaroslavich* during Baxter's time aboard, had run a tight ship but not a brutal one. Despite that, it wasn't unknown for some of the older officers to have struck sailors, often with little provocation.

It seemed this approach was taken by the Tsar's state apparatus in civilian life as well.

Konstantin tilted his head to one side as he regarded Baxter. "You are something of an enigma, my friend. I think you are British, perhaps, but your Russian is excellent. You are hunted by the Okhrana, and Mashka is quite certain they are working with a British agent. Not only that, but at least some of our local secret policemen seem to have a personal grudge against you."

"He knows his way around a Russian battleship as well," said Kirill. He seemed more rough and ready than Konstantin, a worker or peasant revolutionary, and far more suspicious of Baxter than his compatriot.

Baxter forced himself to relax into the deeply-upholstered seat, untensing muscles that had coiled ready for a flight attempt. Just as he had said to the petty officer earlier, escape would be challenging, even for a strong swimmer — assuming he even got as far as the water.

"All of these things are true," Baxter said. "Would you believe me if I told you that all I am is a sailor who looked for work in the wrong places, and took it from the wrong people?"

"I would say, if it was true, that you are the unluckiest sailor," Kirill said flatly. "And this somehow led you to being familiar with our newest battleships?"

Baxter sat forward and stared at the stocky revolutionary. He couldn't fault the man — he assumed paranoia was quite literally the way of life for revolutionaries — but wished he'd just shut up. "I'd say the unluckiest sailors of recent years were those who died at Tsushima," he said flatly. "And I know Russian ships because I was with your Pacific Fleet there."

It was something Ekaterina had told him once, as they'd lain together in the cramped confines of the little steam pinnace they'd taken in pursuit of the traitor Yefimov. *Stick to the truth, Baxter, always. You cannot lie, and you will be a better man for not trying.*

He'd been trying not to think about the Russian noblewoman, the wound too fresh and his feelings about her too confused. He looked away from the two revolutionaries, not wanting them to see his discomfiture, the conflict in him that the memory stirred. Desire, still. Guilt about betraying his friend and her husband, Juneau. Anger that she seemed to have betrayed him or at the very least left him to the mercy of the Tsar's thugs when he'd made landfall in Vladivostok. He could only assume that she had also tried to protect him from afar, if what Bilyk had said was true.

He regretted, deeply, not opening the letter she had sent via Koenig; lost to him now. But regret was something he didn't have time for, particularly not in his current position.

"It has the ring of truth," Konstantin finally said.

"And only a madman would claim such a thing without truth," Kirill added. "While I would like to hear this story, I am more curious as to why you have chosen to come here. To join with our revolutionary comrades?"

Baxter stared hard at him. He didn't trust these men enough to ask about Koenig, but he knew he had an enemy in common with them.

"Bluntly, I'm not interested in your revolution. Not any of my business. But I do want a piece of Bilyk, which I think we can agree on. And Mashka's right, he seems to be working with a British agent. I don't know what they're up to, but I'm guessing it won't be good for any of us." He paused, another issue occurring to him. "And I think there had been mention of being paid."

That last sentence left a bad taste in his mouth. But then, why shouldn't he try to get paid? A fellow needed money for food, passage away from this fracturing land. He'd sailed into mortal danger with the Tsar's navy and he'd been arrested and beaten for his trouble. His own service had cashiered him, unjustly, and the black mark against his name had made it impossible for him to find work in civilian shipping.

Konstantin actually laughed. "Revenge and greed. These may not be my motivations, but they are ones I can understand."

"And if Bilyk offers him more money?"

Baxter was getting a bit tired of this man's carping attitude and the way he kept talking as though Baxter was an exhibit to be discussed. "I doubt Bilyk would offer to pay me, and I'll say this just once and clearly. I'm a man of my word."

That was all he had left in the world, he reflected, as he stared the revolutionary down.

They let him retire after that. He'd lost track of how long he'd been on the go, and couldn't even say how many days ago he and Kostenko had escaped from the Okhrana. Could it only have been yesterday, or was it the day before? He hadn't slept since then, and his limbs were leaden as he dropped, still fully dressed, onto the cot. His eyes, gritty for being open so long in a smoky atmosphere, closed as soon as his head hit the pillow.

It felt like he'd only been asleep for only a few minutes when he was shaken awake. He had the sailor's normal capacity to come alert quickly, particularly in response to the racket of a ship being got underway, but he clambered slowly out of the clutches of a dream that seemed to involve trying to save someone — Ekaterina, perhaps, or Tommy Dunbar — from drowning. Waking almost felt like coming up from deep water; like returning to the surface off the coast of Africa when he had saved Vasily from drowning.

A young man in an officer's uniform — like all the others, stripped of rank — stood over the cot. It wasn't Alekseyev, the pretend captain.

"We have found fresh clothes for you," the newcomer said without any preamble, gesturing to a neatly folded sailor's uniform as he turned away. He had a similar accent to Konstantin, Mashka and Ivan Beshoff.

Baxter swung his legs over the edge of the cot with a groan. "We're under way?" he asked, voice and mind thick with sleep. The deck was rolling slightly, and the engines' vibrations could be felt even through the carpet.

"My, you are astute."

Baxter surged to his feet before he could think things through, the sarcastic edge in this pup's voice cutting right through both his sleepiness and his patience. The young officer obviously hadn't been expecting him to move so quickly either, and had only just begun to react when Baxter lifted him by the front of his jacket and pinned him against one bulkhead.

He took two deep, shaky breaths and then put the sailor down and patted the front of his jacket straight. "What's your name, lad?" he asked, trying to keep his voice calm. He didn't step back to allow the young man to leave.

"Lieutenant Kovalenko," came the stammered response, with no hint of contempt this time.

"Judging from your accent, you're an actual officer, not a mutineer playing dress-up. You also seem to be going along with them willingly."

That seemed to put stiffness back into Kovalenko's spine. "I am Ukrainian," he said, as though that explained everything, but he had the good grace to expand on it further. "When the Tsar falls, not only will the workers and the peasants be liberated, but Ukraine will be free."

Baxter successfully fought the urge to snort at that, stepped back instead. "Well, in that case, you and I may not have a cause in common, but we're on the same side."

"You are here to get paid," Kovalenko said. "You're a mercenary."

Baxter gave him a grim smile, remembering something Juneau had said to him. "Well, there's a fine tradition of that in naval services," he said. "I mostly have a debt to collect. Now, why don't you explain to me why we're underway?"

"The squadron has been sighted, and we are sailing out to meet it."

Baxter stared incredulously at the enthusiastic young officer. "We, as in this battleship and a torpedo boat, are sailing out to meet ... the squadron?"

Baxter didn't know, off the top of his head, the Black Sea Fleet's order of battle. He guessed it probably included a fair few battleships, though he knew the *Potemkin* was the newest and most powerful ship in these waters.

"Well, I can only assume Matyushenko knows what he's about," Baxter continued.

Kovalenko's triumphant expression faltered slightly, allowing a brief glimpse of the anxiety that every sailor must be feeling. "We shall soon find out."

It was a sunny day, though the sea breeze was keeping things cool as Baxter got on deck. He guessed it was mid-morning, from the height of the sun. He didn't often sleep that long or deeply, undisturbed not only by the sound of the anchor being raised and the engines being woken, but also the drums and bugles that would have sent men running to their battle stations.

The sea was running short and choppy, the battleship's bluff bows shouldering the waves aside as she picked up speed. Leaning over the rail and staring astern, he could see they'd only just cleared the breakwater. The harsh noise of steel grinding against steel drew his attention towards the front of the ship. The fore gun turret was turning, the long barrels of the two lethal modern 12-inch guns swinging away from the city they had been menacing to point over the bows. Moving forward across an eerily empty deck, Baxter could make out the plumes of smoke — already visible to the naked eye — that marked the oncoming Russian battleships.

Enemy battleships, as far as these mutineers were concerned.

"I should get to the bridge," Kovalenko muttered as he brushed past Baxter.

Baxter just grunted a reply, eyes fixed on the approaching vessels. He dearly wanted a pair of field glasses to get a better look at the onrushing warships. He thought he counted three, possibly four plumes from big ships, though the fourth might have been haze from a number of smaller vessels sailing in close formation. Still more than the *Potemkin* should be able to handle, he thought, under normal circumstances — though that would depend on the quality and morale of the crews.

The reality of the situation finally sunk in. The dispassionate part of his mind had been analysing the situation without any real consideration of the danger he was in, and he was surprised when that finally did percolate through his sleep-addled mind that he wasn't too worried. He had sailed into battle before, of course, scant weeks ago. That had been on a ship he had become familiar with, under a captain he trusted and a crew he had helped sharpen to battle-readiness. While he had been surprised by the level of discipline maintained aboard the *Potemkin*, he had no idea how well the crew would handle going into battle against overwhelming odds.

"Best keep an eye on the boats," he told himself. He briefly considered petitioning to be put ashore. This was no fight of his. His business was with Bilyk and Arbuthnott, and he'd done his fair share of going into battle on Russian ships. *Too late now.*

He followed Kovalenko's path, going in through a hatch and up several flights of steel steps to the bridge. He passed a few sailors on the way, most of them pale with suppressed fear. He couldn't criticise them for that — no sane man was cheerful at the prospect of going into battle, particularly not against such odds. He didn't see anyone looking to shirk his duty; but then, Baxter had long since learned that loyalty to comrade and ship was a far more powerful motivator than anything more abstract like country, king or deity. These men also knew that, as mutineers, they had nothing to lose.

Afanasy Matyushenko was the only one aboard who seemed relaxed about the situation. As Baxter entered the bridge, taking up an out-of-the-way place at the back once again, the slight revolutionary leader was laughing and joking with the men around him.

"Tell the admiral," he was saying as Baxter entered the bridge, "that if he wishes to know our demands, he can come aboard to discuss them. We guarantee his safety." Matyushenko clapped his hands together, a sharp noise on the otherwise quiet bridge that actually made one of the sailors jump. "If he takes the bait, we wouldn't even need to hold him. Just by coming aboard, he will show his weakness and our brothers on the other ships will be further encouraged to mutiny."

"I thought you said they'd already risen?" a surly petty officer demanded. He flinched back when Matyushenko turned furious eyes on him.

"The dragons may still hold power on the other ships," he said. "But it is tenuous at best, just as it was for us. The captain and first officer certainly discovered how precarious their command was, anyway!"

A few men laughed at that, a high, nervous laughter. Baxter could see Matyushenko's intent, though, and why he was less anxious than the men around him. He didn't actually expect to fight a battle here, or rather he hoped not to. If the other crews mutinied, the nascent revolution would have a squadron of battleships. If they did not, the leader of the mutineers would likely be dead, and he at least seemed to be demonstrating a certain fatalism Baxter had come to expect from Russian sailors.

"He's quite mad," Konstantin commented quietly, arriving next to Baxter. The student revolutionary had himself under control, but was also clearly scared. He could face death at the hands of the army or police with equanimity, at least in the abstract. It would be a day-to-day reality for someone prepared to take up arms against the Tsar's regime.

This was a different kind of danger, though. The destructive power of these steel behemoths could awe even those well used to them; Baxter knew that many of the men aboard would be tormented by thoughts of their bodies being torn apart or horribly burned.

"No, I don't think it's madness," Baxter said after a moment's reflection. "I think it's a gamble, but it's a rational one given the position they're in."

"If the squadron opens fire…"

"That's the gamble," Baxter said, trying not to sound too dismissive. He was an outsider here, but he was at least a sailor, a man o' war's man, as his old instructors would say. He felt, obscurely, that he had more right to this piece of deck than the revolutionary. He doubted that the sailors, if they took the time to notice him, would feel the same way.

"That's the *Twelve Apostles* in the lead," Matyushenko said now. "I am sure of it. She will be the flagship."

"We are in range, I think, and outside their range still," someone pointed out. "We could…"

"Don't be stupid!" Ensign Alekseyev snapped. "We are well within range of their guns as well, and they have more!"

Baxter stared at the young man as he paced nervously across the bridge. While he didn't have access to a rangefinder or much information about any of the ships, Baxter knew that the *Potemkin* was more modern and there was still a great distance between the rogue battleship and her enemies — although the gap was closing. He doubted Alekseyev was right, though he couldn't tell if the former officer was just wrong or seeking to deceive the mutineers.

Baxter shrugged slightly — not his problem, and he would be quite happy if there wasn't an exchange of gunfire. He sometimes felt his ears were still ringing slightly from the terrible cacophony of the fleet engagement at Tsushima.

"What is he doing? Looks like he's turning," one of the lookouts at the front of the bridge said, his tone conversational.

"The whole squadron is turning!" Matyushenko almost whooped. Baxter stepped forward to get a better look, and could just make out the three battleships as they picked up speed into a turn and raced away from the closing *Potemkin*.

"Apparently they didn't fancy the taste of our guns!" someone joked, as cheers broke out across the ship.

"We should close and bombard the cowards as they flee!" Konstantin burst out. "Obliterate the forces of the Tsar while we are still within sight of the city, to give hope to the people and bring the soldiers out in support."

Matyushenko's expression soured. "What *we* shall do is return to our anchorage, and give *our* brothers on those ships time to consider what has come to pass. What *you* shall do, if you want to remain aboard, is stop trying to give orders on this bridge!"

Konstantin lapsed into a surly silence. Baxter clapped him on the shoulder. "Cheer up — sea battles really aren't all that much fun."

The *Potemkin*'s crew seemed to relax almost as one as the battleship turned back to harbour at a much lower speed. Baxter knew coal supplies would be a significant worry for the sailors' committee. As far as he could see, they'd already sucked up all the coal in the harbour and word was General Karkhanov had forbidden trade with the rogue ship. A big beast like this needed a lot of fuel just to stay functional in harbour, let alone operate effectively as a fighting vessel. The red battle ensign was furled and the ship returned to a peaceful anchor in the outer harbour.

Baxter leaned on the bridge railing and stared back towards the city, enjoying the warmth of the sun on his face. The fire brigades had finally been able to do their job on the docks, and a gentle breeze had cleared the remaining smoke. Despite that, the city was still a far cry from the hive of industry and commerce he had previously experienced. Even without the blackened ribs of burned ships rising from the water and the husks of warehouses, the sense that things were not right here was still palpable. There was a rustle of noise from the city, almost like waves on a distant shore but in reality the sounds of angry people. He could still hear the occasional gunshot, and once the deeper, flatter *crump* of a bomb detonating. Huge crowds could be seen anywhere with a view of the sea, civilians as well as soldiers had turned out to watch the outcome of the battle. They were starting to disperse now.

"I wouldn't go far," Baxter told them quietly. "I don't doubt the squadron will be back soon."

CHAPTER 9

The *Potemkin* sailors settled down to a lunch of bread and cabbage soup, which was usual enough. The men were in high spirits, having chased off (in their own minds) a superior force. There were ribald jokes about the courage of the Black Sea Fleet's commanders and boasts about how many hits they would have achieved if it had come to a shooting match. That was also perfectly normal for men who had just come close to a hot action — and, for many of them, for the first time. It was a release of tension and a celebration of still being alive.

What was unusual was the level of political discussion, often heated debates, going on. A lot of them were eating on deck, with their mess tins and hunks of black bread. The two civilian revolutionaries who had been allowed aboard were moving from group to group, speaking passionately with the men. What interested Baxter was the way the sailors clearly weren't just humouring Konstantin and Kirill — it was more a case of the agitators joining ongoing debates to add their thoughts and then leaving the sailors to chew them over.

Baxter mostly just tried to stay out of the way and avoid anyone's notice. Kovalenko had provided him with a sailor's uniform, at least, so he didn't stand out in his increasingly grubby civilian clothes, even if he wasn't known to the crew. They mostly seemed content to leave him in peace, those who even noticed him. He didn't think for a second he was blending in — even though the crew would be six hundred or more, they would know each other at least by sight. He was always going to be a stranger here, but a tolerated one, it seemed.

"Well, tolerated by most," he muttered, catching an angry glare from the petty officer he had interfered with yesterday. It seemed that hadn't gone down well, even though he had most likely saved the heavyset sailor's life. Baxter knew he was going to have trouble with him if he stayed aboard much longer.

He suppressed a groan as Konstantin stepped up beside him at the railing. "What's that you say?" he asked, without any sort of preamble. Baxter nodded to the knot of petty officers who kept their distance from the other men.

"I don't think they're happy with me," he said, keeping his tone conversational.

Konstantin pursed his lips thoughtfully. "They don't like anyone aboard. Some have argued that those Tsarist running dogs should all be imprisoned or put ashore."

Baxter shrugged, turning his gaze back to the city. "Hard to run a ship without them, dogs or not," he said casually. "Not my problem, though."

"It will be your problem if they manage to blow up a magazine," Konstantin pointed out caustically. "One of them was caught planning such a thing last night."

Baxter couldn't hide his surprise. He knew the petty officers often remained loyal to the captain during a mutiny, as they enjoyed better pay and conditions than the common sailors. Inviting not just death but complete annihilation through that drastic measure smacked of fanaticism, though. "I encountered some mutineers who tried to do the same thing, on the way to the Pacific. They had a couple of good goes at sending us to the bottom," Baxter replied.

Konstantin shot him an angry look. "I imagine you curtailed their noble struggle."

"No offence, old chap, but their noble struggle would have killed me, and a few people I ... cared about."

Konstantin sighed. "That is a reasonable position," he admitted after a moment.

"I'm so glad you agree." Baxter couldn't keep the sarcasm from his voice. "That incident, not to mention the sortie this morning, does make me think I should see about my business — our business — and then be on my way."

He'd been trying to work his way through this puzzle in the few quiet moments he'd had since he'd encountered Arbuthnott again. His natural instinct was to go at it head on, find Bilyk and Arbuthnott and kick their teeth in. He knew that inclination, and his training as a naval officer, would not be helpful here. The situation required a subtle touch, and patience. The sort of approach that had allowed Ekaterina Juneau to snare Yefimov and foil the traitor's attempts to provoke tensions if not outright war between Russia and Britain. Good God, even young Tommy Dunbar had more of an aptitude for these things than Baxter did.

He felt a pang of regret. He knew he should be putting both of them out of his mind. With any luck, by now Tommy was on his way back to Scotland and the capacious bosom of his loving family. He'd have some tales to tell, even if nobody ever believed him.

Baxter didn't know what had become of Ekaterina; whether her husband had been recovered, whether she really was his mysterious protector, or whether she had done the sensible thing and fled back to the family estates in ... wherever they were. He realised he'd never asked — it hadn't seemed important in that long, and at times dangerous, journey when they had often felt entirely cut off from the world.

Focus. Now was not the time for gathering wool. Yes, Ekaterina's help would be invaluable here, but here she was not. He'd have to make do with his own resources.

He realised that Konstantin was staring curiously at him, that he'd been staring at Odessa for a few minutes, lost in his reverie. Well, the frustrating Russian noblewoman may not be here, but he was not without allies.

He started to ask what the Social Democrat organisation in Odessa was capable of, and what it really knew of Bilyk, when a voice called down from above.

"Smoke on the horizon! It's the squadron!"

"Well, bugger," Baxter said. That was going to put a crimp on any plans to get ashore in the near future.

He was surprised when the lookout's shout didn't elicit immediate action. The bugles and drums didn't sound to send the men to their stations. A few sailors just looked up from their lunch. "Are you sure it's not just another merchantman?" someone shouted sardonically.

Matyushenko at least seemed to take it seriously. But then, as the real commander here, he had to. He hurried away from the group he had been speaking with and up onto the bridge. A tense silence fell as more and more sailors started to put their food aside or hurriedly gulped down the last of it.

Soon, all conversation had died down. Looking around at the men crowded onto the foredeck in the sweltering heat, Baxter could see a mix of expressions. Apprehension, certainly, and some fear. But also determination, and hope, and excitement.

From deep below came the drumbeat of the engines being stoked up; once again the funnels started belching their black clouds of smoke. "Prepare to weigh anchor!" Matyushenko shouted from the bridge. "The squadron has returned, and this time Admiral Krieger has brought friends!"

For the second time that day, the *Potemkin* made ready for battle. The massive anchor chain was drawn up into ship as she began to gather way. The movement seemed to attract some attention in the city, the remnants of the crowd being swelled as people returned to see the new developments. As the ship's screws started to thrash, driving her forward, the red flag of revolution once against broke out at the flagstaff. Some of the sailors started cheering as the huge red square — the ship's de facto battle flag — started snapping in the stiffening breeze. The cheers were taken up by others on deck, even those who did not appear to be full-throated revolutionaries.

Even Baxter felt a thrill as the battleship started shouldering the seas aside as she went out to meet her erstwhile comrades. He spread his feet to accommodate the increasing roll, felt the sting of salt spray on his face and breathed in the smell of smoke and sea air.

"I could ask Matyushenko for a boat to put you ashore," Konstantin said quietly, his voice almost lost in the cheering. Baxter glanced at him, wondering if the younger man wanted an excuse to vacate the vessel himself. The revolutionary had a determined look on his face.

Bugles and drums cut through the cheering. The sailors scattered, scrambling for their action stations. They moved with purpose, every man knowing his place and going to it without too much cajoling. Not all of them would be happy, but they went because their comrades were going or they didn't want to be seen as a counter-revolutionary.

"No," Baxter said after a moment. "No, I wouldn't want to distract them from the job at hand."

Konstantin gave him an odd look, as though wondering if he'd gone quite mad. Baxter questioned that himself. He had no obligation here, beyond a vague promise to get paid and help dealing with someone who had become his personal nemesis. Looking further out to sea, he could already make out smoke plumes from a considerably larger number of big ships than there had been earlier.

Friends indeed. He shrugged. "Well, whatever happens, we're living through momentous times," he said to Konstantin.

The young revolutionary didn't look happy. "As long as I get to survive them. To continue the struggle, you understand." He paused, then seemed to resolve himself. "I am going up to the bridge."

Baxter followed on, doing his best to stay out of the way as a stream of sailors came past clutching shells for some of the smaller guns. These were quick-firing weapons, the shells and cartridge a single unit rather than the system used for the big guns, which would have the shells and bagged propellant separate.

"Remember, wait until we are close," he heard a familiar voice whisper as he went into the superstructure. He paused just inside the hatch, realising it was the crew of one of the 4-inch guns mounted along the maindeck. "That madman Matyushenko thinks he can dare the fleet and provoke more mutinies; this is why he has given the order not to shoot. When the time is right, we will fire a shell at the flagship, and a deluge of righteous fury will send this cursed ship to the bottom."

"Yes, Vasya, but us with it," someone else hissed back.

"Do not be soft," the first man said. "We have sworn our lives to the Tsar. Besides, as soon as we fire and are certain the loyal ships are returning that fire, we will make our way to a boat and throw ourselves on the admiral's mercy."

Baxter was pretty sure the instigator of this mad scheme was the petty officer he had talked down from taking a shot at Matyushenko the day before. He should have known not turning the man in would just lead to trouble

He was tempted just to throw the leader of the counter-mutineers over the side. The last thing this crew needed, as they went out for the second time in a day to face overwhelming odds, was for there to be an altercation on deck. Despite their fervent cheering and expressions of support for the revolution when gathered in a crowd, that unity of purpose was only superficial for a lot of the men.

He glanced up the companionway to the bridge. He could hear Matyushenko's voice raised even from here, once again cheerfully exhorting his crewmates to the great and noble things he knew they could achieve.

Baxter turned away, stepping back out into the sunshine and heat. He deliberately didn't look at the rebellious gun crew as he walked forward, right into the bows. He put his hands in his pockets, and thought about whistling nonchalantly.

Don't overdo it, Ekaterina seemed to say in his head. He quirked a smile. That's why he'd never be any good as a spy — he always overdid things. Staring ahead, he could make out two distinct columns of ships now, at this distance bare specks below the horizon and identifiable mostly from their plumes of smoke.

It was glorious in its way, he thought as the bows rose and dipped beneath his feet, his legs flexing naturally to compensate. Wind and spray on his face, the air clean because the breeze was blowing their smoke plume behind them.

Baxter pushed aside his annoyance as a gaggle of mutineers, led by Kovalenko the Ukrainian officer, arrived around him to stare forward as well. The men had the look of stokers about them, their uniforms grimy with coal dust — normally they wouldn't be above decks at action stations. Many ships' officers didn't like them on deck at all, and only barely tolerated engineering officers in the wardroom.

"That's the *Rostislav* in the lead of the port column," he heard Kovalenko tell the others. "She's lean and fast, but she can't punch as hard as us. The *Three Saints* we all know."

There was a chuckle at that. Baxter guessed she was in the same category as the 'self-sinkers' that had been inflicted upon Vice-Admiral Rozhestvensky as he and his squadron had laboured around the world.

He wondered idly what had become of the irascible 'Mad Dog' admiral. He'd heard that he had survived the battle in the Tsushima Strait, although badly injured, and been captured as his loyal sailors had tried to ferry him to safety aboard a destroyer.

"Well, enough of this!" Kovalenko said, though the smile on his face and the lightness of his tone took any sting out of his voice. "To your stations, lads!" Kovalenko caught Baxter's gaze. "This may not be the safest place for you, should the shooting start," he said stiffly.

"Indeed, particularly as Matyushenko clearly intends to pass between the two lines," Baxter observed, nodding forward. The battleship's bow was pointed unwaveringly along a line that would bring her between the two lines of onrushing ships. Baxter guessed there would barely be two hundred yards clearance on either side, if that.

It was utter insanity. They were living in an age where ships could pummel each other from miles away. The battlelines at Tsushima had slugged it out at eight thousand yards or thereabout, and that had been knife-fighting range. The mutineers would sail their outnumbered battleship through a hostile formation at the sort of range wooden sailing ships fought at, despite being able to outrange anything the loyalist squadron had.

"Is this not glory?" Kovalenko breathed, an expression somewhere between fear and awe on his face. "The fleet is riven by discontent, just as the army is. When they see us coming on like this, the red flag of revolution at the masthead and not firing on our brothers, they *must* rise."

Baxter could think of a few other words for it, and a few choicer ones for himself for managing to be in this situation. He had to start doing something to make sure he came out of the other side alive.

"I overheard one of your gun crews," he said, keeping his voice low despite the now clear deck around them. "They intend to provoke a gun battle by firing on the flagship."

Kovalenko looked at him, surprised. For a moment Baxter wondered if the expression related to some of the crew betraying them, but he *had* to know there would be counter-revolutionaries in their midst. Then he realised that a necessary paranoia had set in deeply amongst the leaders of the revolution.

"Look, I've told you. I may not be one of your die-hard revolutionaries, but we've got a goal in common. Not to mention that I don't fancy getting blown apart in a pointless shooting match we can't win."

Kovalenko nodded jerkily, obviously thinking fast. For a few long seconds there was no sound except the sea and the wind and the grind of the forward turret coming to bear on the *Rostislav*. Then the flags on the bridge semaphore clattered into life, Matyushenko no doubt goading the Tsar's admiral.

The noise jerked Kovalenko into action. They were horrifyingly close to the loyalist ships now, barely a hundred yards. Baxter had to admit to a thrill of fear as he looked at the dull gleam of the opposing flagship's guns, even while the gunnery officer in him coolly assessed the weapon he was more or less looking down the muzzle of. *Ten-inch*, he thought, so less of a punch than the *Potemkin*. Not that it would matter if it hit anywhere near him. Assuming the *Rostislav* hit, of course.

"We should, perhaps, do something about the rogue gun crew," Kovalenko exclaimed.

"That would seem sensible." Baxter didn't know why he felt so calm, even elated, and could only guess that the utter preposterousness of the situation was getting to him. He followed Kovalenko back along the deck. "Three in gun on the upper deck," he said. "I'll point the bugger cut."

Kovalenko nodded. He'd pulled the service revolver he wore on his hip, but Baxter put his hand on his arm. "I wouldn't — even firing a pop gun like that could panic someone."

"We should try to do this without violence at all," Kovalenko concurred, putting the Nagant back into its holster.

Baxter shook his head ruefully as the two of them clattered up onto the upper deck, moving quickly enough to draw curious glances from the gun crews who sheltered behind bulwarks and gun shields while they kept their weapons trained on the other ships. He would have been astonished at their discipline, but he'd already seen how stoic the Russian sailor could be in action.

He didn't let himself worry about the fact they were now racing directly between two columns of five battleships. Every weapon that could be brought to bear on the *Potemkin* had been, gun turrets and broadside barbettes turning to keep the rebel ship in their sights. She was returning the favour, both turrets laid on the hostile ships in turn.

"That one," he snarled, spotting the burly petty officer crouched behind his 3-inch gun, one hand curled around the firing lanyard.

"Vasya Ulyanin," his new ally spat. "I should have known. We cannot startle him, though."

All of the gun crews ranged along the deck were tense; all of them must have known they could face death in the next few minutes. Ulyanin and his crew, however, looked utterly terrified as they knew they were about to provoke that death. The petty officer in particular was white as a sheet, sweat standing out on his brow.

Kovalenko was right. If they ran at the gun crew, startled them in any way, Ulyanin might accidentally fire. Even if the shot wasn't aimed and didn't hit, a round being fired would settle things.

Baxter slowed himself to a walk, remembering the number of times he'd gone careering around the *Yaroslavich* chasing mutineers and revolutionaries. He'd fought them in a magazine they were trying to detonate — killed one with his own hands, in fact. He'd run the last of them down as they'd tried to steal a boat to escape, and seen one of them dive into dark waters, choosing death over capture. Those moments, somehow, didn't feel as dangerous as these next few seconds would be.

He started whistling, a low mellow tune, as he walked past Kovalenko. A peasant song he'd heard more than a few times from the lower decks of the cruiser, during the long hot nights of the passage to the Far East. He smiled at Ulyanin as the fellow looked up, dropped his voice down.

"You understand that if you do this," he said, voice deadly serious and speaking as much for the rest of the gun crew as he was for their leader, "that you and many of your shipmates will die here. There won't be any stealing a launch to escape in the storm of fire that would come down on you."

"It would be worth it, to put this shame to an end," the fellow said, his voice a husking whisper that seemed at odds with his solid build.

"You'd be dooming men who feel the same way you do." Baxter fought to keep his tone calm and reasonable. If nothing else, he was distracting the counter-mutineers, keeping their eyes off the lines of ships that were going past on either side. They were almost at the end of the double column.

Ulyanin nodded uncertainly, dropping his hand from the gun's firing mechanism. He clearly didn't want to pull the trigger on this firefight, even if his sense of duty demanded it. Then he noticed they were almost through the gauntlet and decided perhaps the sacrifice was worth it, hand lunging forward faster than Baxter could move.

The breech block clanged as the loader released it, the unfired shell dropping out in his arms. The noise of the weapon being opened attracted glances from the tense sailors. "There goes Gosha being clumsy again!" the loader said of himself with a cheerful smile. "You know what Gosha's like."

"Bloody Gosha," another sailor was heard to mutter as the sudden tension dissipated.

Baxter relaxed once the deadly projectile was out of the gun. He rested his head against the metal of the superstructure, cool despite the warmth of the day, breathing hard. Kovalenko went past with a couple of reliable revolutionaries who quickly and quietly bundled the shamefaced Ulyanin into the ship's interior.

"You did well," Kovalenko said, voice slightly less stiff as he laid a hand briefly on Baxter's shoulder.

He nodded his thanks for the very slight unbending. "By the way, I've been meaning to ask," he said, deciding to strike while the iron was hot, "what became of Lieutenant Koenig? He was recently assigned to the *Potemkin*. He's a friend."

Kovalenko looked nonplussed. "Koenig? I don't believe I know him." He frowned slightly. "Ah, wait! I recall we were being assigned someone, a hero of Tsushima. No, no, he hadn't arrived before he put to sea. Quite safe, I assume — possibly even on one of the ships facing us."

Baxter just blinked at Kovalenko. He should have expected this, and had perhaps been naïve in staying around Odessa as long as he had. Long enough to get embroiled in this mess. The absurdity of the situation, of his own stubborn capacity to get himself in trouble, hit him and he started to laugh.

What started as a chuckle turned into a full roar of laughter that doubled him over. The men around him, not understanding what he was so amused by but finding the laughter infectious, started to grin and chuckle themselves. The whole battery was howling with laughter as the battleship scattered the flock torpedo boats that had been following the loyal battleships. It was a release of tension more than any real humour. Kovalenko just stared about, dumbfounded.

"You are all quite mad," he said at last.

Almost as though they were answering the laughter, cheers could be heard from the last two battleships in the line. Sailors were spilling onto the cleared decks, a flood of white across the polished wood, waving their caps and cheering for freedom, cheering on the *Potemkin*. The mutineers returned the salute, abandoning their stations to cheer and wave to their brothers across the water.

"Back to your posts!" Kovalenko barked at the nearest sailors. "Can't you see they still have guns aimed at us?"

There was little he could do to rein in the enthusiasm, though. The *Potemkin* was drawing away from her former consorts. The cheering and laughter died as the ship, still running at full speed, started a wide turn through the area of sea recently churned up by the fleeing torpedo boats. "He's going again," Gosha breathed.

"Yes, he is," Kovalenko agreed. "I am going back to the engine room."

"I think I might go to the bridge," Baxter said, his own mirth dying as Matyushenko once again put them against the squadron.

CHAPTER 10

The bridge was tense by the time he arrived. The mutineer leader was pacing around, almost bouncing on his feet with barely contained excitement. "It has to be today!" he exclaimed as Baxter ducked through the hatch and took up what was becoming his usual station with the two other civilians, Konstantin and Kirill. "Why don't they shoot? Why don't they rise?"

"What was the laughter about?" Konstantin asked. He seemed remarkably calm after the morning's jitters.

"Just sailors letting off some steam," Baxter said as nonchalantly as he could, as he took in the scene. The *Potemkin* had just finished her turn and was racing forward again. She must be doing sixteen knots or more, close to her top speed. The squadron had come about in line, the whole thing resembling some sort of monstrous seaborne ballet. The martial nature of the enterprise without firing reminded Baxter of the innumerable and tiring manoeuvring drills he had been part of with the Royal Navy.

Matyushenko was going for the same run as before, between the lines of the great steel vessels. Baxter couldn't fathom why they weren't firing. Did they want to avoid the embarrassment of firing on their own ship, even if she was in a state of mutiny? Were they worried about overshooting, the lines hitting each other rather than the target?

Or had the commanding admiral, Krieger, lost his nerve?

The admiral and the mutineer were exchanging rapid, increasingly caustic signals as the courses ran parallel again, the signal lamps flashing frenetically. More and more sailors were pouring onto the decks of the opposing battleships, men cheering and waving their caps. Their individual shouts were lost in the cacophony, but their meaning was clear.

Matyushenko burst out of the bridge onto one of the wings, waving maniacally to the sailors lined three deep at the railing on the battleship *Sinop*. "Arrest your officers and join us!" he bellowed, though whether he could be heard or not was impossible to say. The revolutionary was so excited, leaning so far forward, that Kirill had to lunge forward and grab him around the waist before he tumbled from the wing.

The sailors on the passing battleship threw their caps into the air. "Long live the *Potemkin*!" they roared as one and even Baxter, despite his practised cynicism, felt a stirring of something that wasn't quite pride but not so far removed from it.

"The *Twelve Apostles* is altering course!" a lookout called. "She's coming right for us!"

Everyone dashed to the port side of the bridge. Sure enough, one of the older battleships had come sharply around and was charging forward on an intercept course. "Signal her to stop!" Matyushenko shouted, as though that would make any difference.

"That's Kolands' ship — he's a hard horse," one of the other mutineers called.

"Where the hell does this captain think he is, the battle of Lissa?" Baxter commented, dredging up from his memory the last time there'd been a successful ramming attack.

"Maybe so," Kirill said, voice phlegmatic. "But I imagine he might detonate his magazines — I'm told some officers are that fanatical about their service."

"I really wish you hadn't told me that," Baxter replied, glancing out of a porthole to work out where the nearest ship's boats were. Not that it would make any difference if he did make it to one — he'd seen a battleship explode in the recent past, and it wasn't something he ever wanted to experience.

The *Twelve Apostles* was still coming, double-headed eagle on the bow looming larger and clearer as she came. Baxter braced himself, either for the tearing impact of metal on metal or, worse but faster, the annihilating shock wave of a magazine detonation.

Then the battleship lost way. Either something had happened to her engines or the all-stop had been signalled. Momentum battled the resistance against the fat hull in the water — resistance won when she was barely twenty yards away. There was chaos on deck, and Baxter could actually make out a furious-looking captain running off the bridge — no doubt on his way to detonate the magazines.

He linked his hands behind his back. Well, it had been a good run, he told himself, though he knew that was a lie. The *Potemkin* was hurtling away from the stilled battleship now, but he doubted that it would help much. A detonation like the one he expected would scour the upperworks of everything within a few hundred yards, and the blast wave through the water would compromise the hull.

The explosion never came, though. He could almost hear the impotent yelling of the frustrated captain as they left the *Twelve Apostles* in their wake. She hadn't fired, which suggested the crew weren't keen on killing their own comrades. They were obviously just as opposed to being killed by their captain.

"I don't know about anyone else, but that feels like enough excitement for one day," Baxter said to no one in particular. He felt oddly lightheaded. He was running on an empty stomach and a lot of adrenalin.

The squadron was on its way back out to sea, and the *Potemkin*'s bows were pointing directly at Odessa's harbour. It would suit him fine if the two forces could continue on their current courses with no further attempts to provoke each other.

"We are not quite done yet," Matyushenko declared. For a horrible moment Baxter thought he was planning to chase after the squadron, which showed no inclination of turning. The *Potemkin* was still well within range of her 12-inch guns, though, particularly as the *Twelve Apostles* was still wallowing and obviously out of her captain's command.

Another, older, ship was falling out of line. The wireless telegraphist was calling out a garbled signal from one of those ships, the *St. George*.

"The crew has risen!" Matyushenko shouted, sounding beside himself with excitement. And something else — relief, maybe? It was what he had been waiting for, what he had been trying to provoke since this engagement, if it could be called that, had begun.

"We must be cautious," Ensign Alekseyev said, his voice loud and brittle. Baxter realised this was the first he'd seen of the figurehead captain since they had left Odessa. He looked pale and wan, but was obviously recovering himself now the majority of the danger had passed. "Captain Guzevich could be trying to get us to come closer so he can use his torpedoes or ram us."

"Or not all of the crew could have risen," Konstantin pointed out.

This was born out a few minutes later. While the ship had slowed to a stop and dropped her anchor, her signalman flagged to the *Potemkin* that the *St. George* was in a state of chaos, the revolutionaries struggling to seize and maintain control.

"Still…" Alekseyev began.

"Enough!" Matyushenko thundered. "Signal the *Ismail* to come alongside and assemble a committee party. We will go aboard the *George* directly and assist in securing her for the revolution!"

Matyushenko ignored his supposed commanding officer's feeble protests and made for the hatch off the bridge. He stopped as he saw Baxter, eyeing him suspiciously for a moment before seeming to remember who he was.

"I'm not sure why you're still aboard," he said after a moment, a hint of suspicion in his voice. "But you're a big lad and will be handy if it comes to a bit of rough and tumble with any counter-revolutionaries."

Baxter stared at him. He knew it would be fruitless to object — or, rather, by objecting he would lose whatever good will he had built up aboard so far. He sighed. "I'm not using a gun," was all he said. "I'm no good with a gun."

"You won't need to," Matyushenko said with a grin. "I'm sure that by the time we get there, the sailors' committee aboard will have everything in hand."

It didn't appear that way as they approached the mutinying warship. The *Ismail*, the torpedo boat that had been captured on the first day of the mutiny and had been the Potemkin's faithful watchdog ever since, raced across the intervening water once Baxter, Matyushenko and a handful of trusted committee members were aboard.

Baxter wasn't too keen on the small number going with them, and the relative paucity of guns between them. As well as being a fast vessel, though, the torpedo boat was cramped and could only take so many — they'd have to rely on the threat of the boat's torpedoes to keep any counter-mutiny in check.

She was also, Baxter reflected as the boat jounced across another wave, a more than somewhat wet vessel. He was soaked through — none of them had thought to grab waterproofs before they went down the ladder into the waiting vessel. Kirill, who had come along to provide some immediate propaganda support, looked particularly miserable.

They were close now. The *St. George* was an old ship, not quite as venerable as those of the 3rd Pacific Squadron, but with a design that was already obsolete. Instead of having turrets, she was a barbette ship. She was also the strangest ship of her type that Baxter had ever seen, with a triangular central citadel that had a pair of old 12-inch guns with a very limited traverse at each corner.

"Wouldn't like to go into action on her," he commented.

"Who would we fight? The Turks?" Ivan Beshoff asked, a note of contempt in his voice.

"Each other?" Baxter suggested. Ivan bellowed a laugh but said no more, as the torpedo boat came up alongside the battleship.

Someone peered out nervously from the entry port, then raised a hand and called out a greeting to Matyushenko. They could hear raised voices — a lot of them — as they went up the ladder and tumbled onto the deck. The torpedo boat put away as soon as they were aboard, manoeuvring to point its tubes at the battleship's stern.

The revolutionaries stared around. The shouting had died down with their arrival, but they had stepped onto a tense ship. Everyone was waiting to see what these strange creatures who had cast off the shackles of oppression would do next. Some were obviously pleased to see them, but it was clear from the suspicious and surly looks that a large proportion of the crew wanted nothing to do with the revolutionaries.

Most concerningly, the officers looked down on the interlopers from the bridge. They looked scared and they were clearly not in control of the ship, but they were also not in confinement.

Baxter felt for them. His career in the Royal Navy had been short and he'd never reached command rank, nor had he ever had a mutiny occur at one of his postings. He understood how they would be feeling, though, losing their ship and not even to enemy action. Fear for their lives would almost be secondary to that.

Matyushenko was conferring with the sailor who had greeted them, obviously his opposite number amongst the *St. George*'s revolutionaries. Then the *Ismail* was summoned and one of the boarding party detailed to return to the *Potemkin* and bring across an armed party.

"That's not going to go down well with the crew," Baxter commented to Ivan. He felt somewhat at a loss now. He should never have agreed to come along; should never even have been aboard the rogue battleship. Well, nothing for it now, he supposed.

Matyushenko made his way through the crowds of sailors gathered on the old ship's forecastle. He called out cheerfully to men he knew, greeted those sailors who would meet his eye before he bounded up onto the capstan.

"Here we go," Ivan said with a grin. "Afanasy will soon get them onside."

In seemed, though, that the redoubtable mutineer had worn himself and his voice out after his exhortations of the last few days. His harangue of the sailors was a hoarse, cracked shadow of his usual vehemence. Some officers and petty officers had started to infiltrate the crowd of sailors, whispering that this was not a man to lead them to some bright new future; that perhaps it was better to return to the fold of the squadron that was rapidly sailing away. Matyushenko looked helplessly to Kirill.

"Perhaps now we're going?" Baxter asked Ivan. The two of them had taken up station towards the back of the crowd along with the other *Potemkin* crew members who had come across. Close enough to intervene if there was trouble. Not so close that they gave the impression of being a guard, that their leaders were afraid.

Kirill bounded up onto the capstan as Matyushenko stepped down, looking more tired than Baxter had seen him thus far. The Odessan revolutionary launched into his tirade with his customary vim, telling the sailors of the oppressed workers' struggle for equality and freedom, and for some of the wealth that their labours generated. He spoke passionately of how the crew of the *Potemkin* would no longer take part in the slaughter of their own fathers and mothers, sons and daughters.

The revolutionary spread his feet wide and turned his intense stare on the officers still watching from the bridge. Though he addressed them as gentlemen, he poured scorn on them and their rotten, lapdoggish adherence to the old corrupt order.

Astonishingly, he seemed to be bringing more and more of the sailors along with him. His presentation was different to Konstantin's or Matyushenko's, a slow build towards fury rather than the latter's energetic cadence or the rapid-fire way his fellow Odessan dispensed points. It was what was needed just now.

"In the name of the people," he roared at the officers over the swelling cheers of the *St. George*'s enlisted crew, "you are under arrest and will be taken to shore!"

There was shouting from the bridge, armed sailors corralling the officers and trying to herd them down to waiting boats. Looking up, Baxter saw a young lieutenant step out onto the bridge wing, backing away from the sailors trying to arrest him and strip him of his rank. It was too much for him, it seemed. With no hesitation, he put the muzzle of his revolver to his temple and pulled the trigger.

It was the only shot fired during the entire battle, a pathetic little snap of sound in comparison to the thunder that could have erupted, that preceded a body tumbling limply into the water.

"Well, that's that, then," Ivan said, and spat over the side.

Kirill cleared his throat and started speaking again. Baxter stepped away from the mutineers and looked over the side. There was just a trail of bubbles that marked the young man's passing.

"Silly bastard," Baxter said to himself in English. The pointless act of self-destruction drove home the need to get on with his business and get away from this whole unfolding disaster as quickly as possible. They'd been lucky so far, but that couldn't last.

He went back across to the *Potemkin* in the steam launch that transferred the *St. George*'s officers into captivity. Matyushenko, revolver in hand, kept them under guard. He needn't have worried — eyes downcast, their uniforms stripped of rank insignia and any trapping of grandness, they posed no threat.

"Konstantin tells me you have concerns that the secret police may be up to something," Matyushenko said over his shoulder to Baxter, disturbing him from the dark reverie he'd fallen into.

"Eh?"

"This man — Bilyk, was it? — and your fellow Englishman. They are up to something." He twisted round, teeth gleaming in his tanned face. "Do not look so surprised, my friend. A man in my position must keep track of everything."

Baxter shrugged, glancing at the officers who huddled as far away from them as they could. None of them gave any impression that they understood what was being said, or cared if they did. Matyushenko was, of course, speaking Russian and Baxter had to remind himself that the officer class often barely understood the men under their command. French was the language of nobility here.

"Well, I would not be too worried," the mutineer said. "With the *St. George* on our side as well, there is little that can be done."

"I thought you expected the whole Black Sea Fleet to have come across?" Baxter said, keeping his voice as mild as possible.

Matyushenko's expression became stormy, but only briefly. "This is the start, Marcus Alexandrovich. First old Georgiy, then the other ships. Soon we will no longer be a flotilla, we will be a fleet. Ha! What can the Okhrana do against that?"

"You would be surprised," Baxter said, thinking back to all the ways Arbuthnott and his man in the 2nd Pacific Squadron, Yefimov, had tried to cause trouble for them. "You don't want to leave men like Bilyk and Arbuthnott on the loose."

Matyushenko seemed to consider this. "Perhaps you are right. While the army and the uniformed police are the most obvious of the Tsar's boot heels, I am told the Third Department can be more dangerous. What is it you think they are doing?"

Baxter scratched his cheek, and realised he was close to having a full beard. "I've been puzzling over that. If it was just Bilyk, I think we could assume he's up to the usual. Working with a *rogue* British intelligence officer, though, doesn't seem to make a lot of sense."

"And what was it that Arbuthnott was trying to achieve when you fell foul of him?"

"Trying to bring Britain and Russia to the brink of war."

"That seems to me to be a foolish pursuit," Matyushenko said. "Why provoke a war, or even take your country to the brink of one?"

"I can't pretend to understand our betters, but in this instance I believe he wanted to create what we call a naval panic. The Royal Navy would be the first and main line of defence against the Russian bear, and increased tensions with Russia would lead to a clamour for the steel walls to be reinforced."

Matyushenko made a contemptuous noise and shook his head. "And all the while, the masses toil and starve for such … vanity. Well, if that was what he was about, then perhaps he is still trying to achieve this goal. Some men cannot let go of an idea once it is in their head."

Baxter held back from pointing out that he was in the company of one such man. Matyushenko was showing himself to be remarkably astute in these matters, which shouldn't have been a surprise given his highly political nature, and Baxter didn't want to insult the man. "Why would Bilyk be helping Arbuthnott, though?"

"Perhaps he has been duped?" When Baxter shook his head, the revolutionary shrugged. "But then, a war with someone closer to home — even the threat of one — would be a good distraction from our current troubles. Even those that have been caused by a conflict."

Baxter couldn't fault that logic. There was nothing like a threat to bring people closer together and to their leaders — particularly a threat from a country they had fought in living memory. "They would get what they want."

"The question is, then," the mutineer said, with another of his characteristic grins, "what are you going to do about it?"

Baxter sat back on the hard wooden bench. It was indeed time for him to do something. He'd been letting himself be carried along for too long now, responding to events rather than trying to get ahead of them. If he was going to stay here and bloody Arbuthnott's nose, it was time he started being proactive.

"What I'm going to do is talk to someone who knows the lay of the land, and then I'm going to borrow some of your sailors."

"Are you indeed?" Matyushenko asked, his expression turning serious.

"You said it yourself — whatever they're planning is going to work against you. It's in your interest to spike their plans."

"And what exactly do you have in mind, once I have loaned you some of my comrades?"

"Well, to stop them I first need to find them. That means going back to the last place I saw them."

CHAPTER 11

There was nothing Baxter would have liked more than a bath, some proper food and a decent night's sleep. He would even have taken those over seeing Ekaterina again, and finding out where he stood with her.

Almost.

He had to put these things out of his mind, though. He needed complete focus for this night's work.

The launch Matyushenko had loaned him, along with Ivan Beshoff and two of the more trusted members of the sailors' committee, cut through the dark waters of the harbour, the oars dipping regularly, the oarlocks muffled with rags to reduce creaking. As far as they knew, the docks still weren't being heavily patrolled by Cossacks or soldiers, but there were pockets of military presence and they were therefore taking precautions. Baxter felt a faint stir of excitement. This was the stuff of Royal Navy lore, the stealthy landing on an enemy coast to cause mischief.

The whole operation was not being conducted with the same rigorous planning as those raids in previous wars, however., He'd arranged the trip ashore in passing with Konstantin Feldmann while the revolutionary was preparing to lead an armed party to the *St. George*. Baxter didn't know how the revolutionary was planning to communicate with his compatriots ashore, and he just had to hope that the message had both got through and been obeyed.

Well, he'd find out soon enough. The launch was sliding through shallower water, the sailors lifting their dripping oars as the boat hissed up onto a small shingle beach. Baxter went over the side, the water barely above his ankles, Ivan Beshoff and the two other men following. Together they pushed the boat back out into enough water for it to float clear.

"Four hours," Beshoff ordered quietly. "Back here in four hours, no later. Don't hang around for us."

"You'll be dead or caught if you're not back, I know," came the reply from the receding vessel.

"Cheerful people, you lot," Baxter commented as they crunched up the beach. "Let's hope your revolutionary friends are also reliable."

They waited on the beach for a few tense moments. The sailors all had revolvers tucked into the waistbands of their trousers. One of them kept fingering the protruding handle nervously, to the extent Baxter was worried he'd fire the thing accidentally. Their immediate area seemed deserted, only the sound of the gentle waves lapping on the beach and distant singing disturbing the silence. The small but apparently growing revolutionary flotilla could barely be made out, a constellation of lights. The two battleships and the support ship were using their searchlights, and he guessed the *Ismail* torpedo boat was darkened for patrol. While Vice-Admiral Krieger had declined an open confrontation earlier, there was agreement amongst the crew that he would try something more underhand during the night, whether it was floating mines or torpedo boat attacks.

All in all, and despite the fact he'd been desperate to get afloat for days, Baxter was glad to be ashore this night. He could feel a change in the air, a heaviness to the humidity that suggested a rainstorm was coming. He'd prefer to have this done before that broke.

"Konstantin seems reliable, certainly," Ivan said eventually, voice doubtful. "Perhaps we should have had a signal, to make sure before we came ashore."

"Too late for that now. Could be we'll just have a long, quiet wait on the shore for the boat to come back." Baxter only had the vaguest idea of where he wanted to go, which is why they were waiting for a local guide. He had an even vaguer idea of what he wanted to do when he got there, but he had to start somewhere.

"You know I can hear you, yes?" a familiar voice said from the shadows. Familiar more for the acidic tone than anything else. Mashka detached from the shadow of a nearby burned-out warehouse and descended to meet them. "You know that this is madness?"

"It's the season for it," Baxter told her bluntly.

"Konstantin is a fool for trusting any of you, and I am a fool for trusting him. Come, quickly and quietly — let us be about this."

Baxter and his little collection of sailors followed Mashka. He'd been expecting more of an escort, but that either hadn't been possible or had been deemed unsafe. But then, given their lack of arms and training, it was perhaps better if there weren't too many revolutionaries along on the expedition.

They went up into the city, following the route the sailors and Baxter had used to escape after the failed ambush, moving quickly and without too much need to duck into dark alleys to avoid patrols. Mashka explained that the army and police seemed mostly concerned with protecting the centre of the city from ne'er-do-wells and rioters. Unfortunately, while they weren't going right into the centre, they weren't going far from it.

"We haven't been watching the house since the Okhrana abandoned it," Mashka said as they got closer to their target. "I did go past it on the way here, and it appeared to be closed up and dark. I do not know what you expect to find there."

Baxter wasn't sure about that either. He was still feeling his way through this world, relying on half-remembered lessons absorbed from Ekaterina and, to a lesser extent, Juneau's machinations. "I'm hoping to pick up a trail," he said. "I get the feeling they evacuated in a hurry, so Bilyk might have left some hint of what he was about and where he might have gone next."

"He has probably gone to his own headquarters or one of the garrisons," Mashka said dismissively. "Some men are cowards like that, they run to the safest place at the first sign of trouble."

Baxter didn't think Bilyk was any kind of coward, nor was he brave as such. More … fanatically dedicated to his cause. Which made him extremely dangerous, of course. Arbuthnott was another matter, although he was as dedicated as Bilyk in his own way. He was brave only when everything was going his way and he had expendable pawns between him and any harm. His sneering, dismissive courage had dissolved in the face of Baxter's violence during the last throws of Tsushima.

He didn't share any of his thinking in this regard with Mashka. "Perhaps," he said instead. "Though I think whatever he is doing, it's not with the approval of his superiors. I very much doubt they would have anything to do with a plot hatched with a rogue British agent. If Bilyk and Arbuthnott are actively trying to achieve something still, they'll be preparing it somewhere off the books."

Mashka didn't look convinced, making her disagreement known with a scowl of disapproval, but she kept her peace at least. "We are coming up to more patrolled areas, and must keep our wits about us. At least you idiots didn't come in uniform, so you will probably not be shot at on sight."

"At least you said shot at, not shot," Ivan said with a forced smile. Like the other sailors, the further he got from the sea and the safety of steel walls and big guns, the more nervous he became.

The small woman sniffed. "It is true that the army's shooting is even worse than yours."

"What's the situation in the city, anyway?" Baxter asked quickly. The last thing he needed was conflict erupting between the sailors and the Odessan revolutionaries. While he wasn't overly concerned with the long-term success of their endeavours — indeed, some residual sense of loyalty to Ekaterina and Juneau made him half think he should be attempting to foil them — his immediate survival relied on their continued co-operation.

Mashka made a dismissive gesture with one hand. "Most of the foreigners have already left, as have the bourgeois. The train station was a scene of chaos." There was a certain amount of satisfaction in her voice, then her expression soured again. "But they took much of their wealth with them, that which they could carry anyway, and only went because they expect you to devastate the city."

"We would never!" Ivan protested. "We tried only to hit the garrisons and kill the commanders."

Baxter felt a scowl developing. He felt like he was dealing with bickering children. He was saved from having to intervene again when Mashka hissed a warning that sent them all scurrying into a side alley just before a troop of mounted Cossacks trotted round a corner. They kept to the shadows, everyone staying still and silent as the soldiers passed.

"Good ears," Baxter said, once the echoes of iron-shod hooves on the cobbles had faded.

"A skill we have all had to learn in order to stay alive." At least she didn't spit the words at him.

They kept talk to a minimum after that, as they skulked through the eerily quiet streets. The quiet could have been explained by a curfew, but the buildings they passed were dark and boarded up. The streets had a desolate feel that came from abandonment rather than people simply keeping their heads down. One or two still had light leaking around shutters, but it was impossible to tell whether it was householders who couldn't or wouldn't leave or servants who had been told to stay behind and look after the property. Or, of course, looters moving in.

The house the Okhrana kept was no different to the others, dark and boarded up. Baxter almost didn't spot it — he'd last seen it in broad daylight and surrounded by a tide of angry people. It was only when Mashka tapped his arm that he realised he was about to walk past it.

"I will wait here for you," she said. It was understandable — despite its bland and nondescript exterior, the building would hold a special fear for Odessa's revolutionaries.

Baxter briefly considered ordering one of the sailors to remain with her, but he guessed that wouldn't go down well. He led the men across the street at a dash, knowing they couldn't hang around here. It had taken them almost an hour — according to the appropriated watch he now carried — to get here. Hopefully it wouldn't take two or more hours for them to ransack the place, and they'd be back on the beach ready for pick-up in comfortable time.

"Round the back," he hissed to the others, seeing the front door was barred and locked. At least that probably meant looters hadn't got in, unless they'd found the front of the building impenetrable and gone elsewhere.

They went down the narrow alley between the house and its neighbour. "This is probably our best bet," Baxter said, nodding up at the wall around the Okhrana building's courtyard. That was the only thing that made the house stand out as being in any way different. The wall was relatively new, and slightly taller than the others. The ironmongery along the top was also a bit higher and looked slightly sharper.

"Right, lads," Ivan said, holding his hand out for the line that one of his comrades wore wrapped around his torso like a bandolier. "Up and over."

Ivan swung the small grapnel at one end of the line a few times, getting a sense of the weight, and then cast it up. It didn't catch on the first attempt, clattering off the metalwork. Baxter lunged forward and caught it before it banged on the pavement.

"Well, at least the area seems deserted," Ivan said with a sheepish grin.

"Except for the Cossacks," Baxter bit out, squinting up at the iron railings as he tried to work out if there was a quieter way to do this. Probably not. "Second time lucky, eh?" he said, as he handed the grapnel back.

Ivan did indeed get it right the second time. Baxter led them over the top — it was his expedition, after all. He went up hand over hand, using his feet for extra purchase. The spikes at the top weren't quite as impressive as they'd looked from below and he was able to get over without too much trouble before shuffling along the top to make way for the others, then lowering the rope on the inside and shimmying down onto the cobbled courtyard.

Baxter paused in the shadow of the wall, the others crouching beside him. They were all listening intently for any sound of alarm from the house in front of them or its neighbours; for the sound of clattering hooves or running boots.

Silence.

"Back door looks a lot less solid," Ivan said, producing a chisel from inside his tunic. "And at least we won't be overlooked there."

"Quickly and quietly as we can." Baxter surprised himself with how calm he felt. It was the same feeling he'd got with the battle of Tsushima thundering around him, not so much detachment as a sense of complete control and confidence, markedly different to the black rage that could come over him when the violence was more personal.

Ivan jimmied the door open without too much issue. With a cheeky grin to the rest of the party, he placed the tip of the chisel against the doorframe next to the handle and wrenched, popping the lock with the sound of tearing wood that seemed deafening in the otherwise silent night. Baxter hustled them through and wedged the door closed as best he could.

They paused on the threshold of the building. The room they were in was a shade lighter than pitch black, only a faint glow from the streetlamps filtering around the closed shutters. From inside, the house seemed as silent and deserted as before.

Baxter fumbled out the lighter he'd grabbed from the officer's cabin he'd been sleeping in. The striker did its work first time, an orange flame casting a faint warm glow around them. In the jumping shadows cast by the flickering light, he could see they were in a small anteroom. He had even less idea about the internal layout of the house than he'd had about its location — the Okhrana men had moved him around as quickly as possible, often at night. There wasn't a lot of time to work things out, though, and the sailors were looking to him for decisive leadership.

"I think we can risk a bit more light," he said, nodding to the pair of lanterns that sat on a shelf. "This place is as dead as the proverbial."

Probably something he should have thought to bring, he reflected ruefully as one of the sailors shook the first lantern, checking it had oil. He nodded with satisfaction and Baxter awkwardly applied the lighter flame to the wick. "Keep them low," he ordered. No point advertising their presence more than they had to.

They moved quietly through the building, the two sailors with one of the lanterns excitedly exploring while Ivan stuck by Baxter with the other.

While it was clear from the lack of ornamentation that this wasn't a usual family home, it was also hard to imagine it was an adjunct building of a brutal secret police organisation. While there was furniture, it was worn, the stuffing protruding from split seams in a way that reminded Baxter uncomfortably of intestines coming out of an opened gut.

They moved aimlessly at first, just trying to get their bearings, to work out where Bilyk and his compatriots would have kept any records or notes. Anything that could tell them what they were planning, where they had gone. As Baxter had suspected, the house had been abandoned in a hurry, the threat of an angry mob chasing the policemen out. Loose sheets of paper, dropped from bundles either going to a furnace or a cart, were scattered here and there. A small round hat lay abandoned on a table that still had half-drunk cups of black tea on them. A hunk of black bread lay on a windowsill, already starting to go furry.

He winced as one of the sailors called out excitedly from further in, obviously finding the kitchen and attached larder. Food had clearly not been a priority in the evacuation. Ivan looked enquiringly at him. Baxter nodded, but put a hand on his arm before he could hurry away.

"Two things," he said firmly. "Take as much as you can for your comrades, and don't open the vodka until you're back aboard."

He knew he should tell them just to leave the vodka, but he hadn't been born yesterday and he knew what sailors were like. Ivan grinned and hurried away to join his comrades. He was rapidly lost in the gloom beyond the light cast by the lantern, feeling his way along the wall and calling out quietly to his mates.

"Right, enough of this," Baxter murmured to himself. Time to get searching properly.

The house started to feel more familiar as he moved through it. The mustiness of rooms that weren't aired enough combined with the sour tang of old sweat and too many men in one space. There was the slightest hint of dried blood as well, though there was no way of knowing whether that was from the prisoners who'd been shot or the ones who'd been beaten until they bled profusely.

He was just very glad he'd been considered valuable enough not to be shot out of hand when the Okhrana had exited the place. Best not to think about such things, though.

The uncarpeted stairs creaked underfoot as he went up, holding the lantern high in front of him. It was probably foolish to go to another floor unaccompanied and unarmed, but he was pretty sure the house was deserted. He couldn't imagine they'd station someone here just to keep an eye on the place or to wait in ambush for any looters.

The next floor seemed to be bedrooms for the policemen. He glanced into the first one, what would probably have been the master bedroom but had been converted into a barracks room with four cots.

"Did these people not have homes to go to?" he wondered aloud. He saw the same signs of a rapid abandonment as he had on the ground floor, personal possessions scattered in a hurry as the secret policemen cleared out what was most important or valuable. He guessed these rooms were for those working late or for the staff who guarded the prisoners overnight, rather than being a permanent residence.

He didn't bother going through the room in detail. The sailors would be up in due course, looking for any good loot. Matyushenko had impressed upon them the importance of the mission, or at least its potential to be important, but he suspected the main reason they'd come along willingly was to have the chance to indulge in some military acquisition at the expense of the hated Okhrana.

It was possible he should have been looking down rather than up, for any sort of record room or secure storage. He suspected the cellars had been put to other, less salubrious uses. While he'd been kept in a garret room and he suspected Arbuthnott had been close by, those were probably used for prisoners not being subjected to particularly aggressive interrogation or, indeed, murder.

He went along the corridor to the next room, starting to come to the conclusion that this whole enterprise had been a needless risk. Of course the Okhrana wouldn't have left sensitive documents lying around when they evacuated, and even if they had, it would take days to search the mess in here thoroughly.

Idly, he nudged the door of the next room open and stepped through, raising the lantern. He didn't know why, but he almost immediately got the sense that this was where Arbuthnott had been kept. It had a single bed and was much more comfortably appointed than the previous room. That could have made it Bilyk's room, but Baxter had the feeling the sinister policeman just found a convenient chair to sleep in when he got tired.

"Either that or he has a lair somewhere," he said to himself, then laughed. Wondering around this peculiar deserted building was making his mind drift.

He walked across to the dresser by the bed, and finally saw what had alerted his subconscious to the person who'd been sleeping here. It was the very slight, sickly smell of laudanum, emanating from an unstoppered bottle with the dregs of a dose left in it. Another, completely empty bottle had rolled into a corner.

"He's turning into a bit of a dope fiend," Baxter mused, moving the bottle off a sheaf of papers covered with handwriting. The bottle had left a ring-shaped stain on the paper. The writing was wild, unsteady, with just a hint of a proper copperplate hand. It was the writing of a drug addict, and best of all it was in English. He spent a moment trying to decipher it by the lantern light, then shoved it into a pocket. There'd be plenty of time for that later.

There wasn't much more of interest in this room, no sign of any further personal effects. He paused on the room's threshold, a noise from somewhere else in the building making the hairs of his neck stand up. He cocked his head, trying to work out if it was the creak of a floorboard above or the sailors getting increasingly rowdy in their looting. He may not have been in their chain of command, such as it was, but he'd give them hell if they'd already opened the vodka. The last thing he needed now was to try and sneak back to the ship accompanied by drunken singing.

He heard something break below, and a gale of rapidly suppressed laughter. "They're either already drunk or just overly excited," he mused, putting the noise he'd heard before down to their high spirits. He'd check another couple of rooms then go and gather them up. Better to be back at the rendezvous ahead of time.

It took him a moment to work out what the next room was. Smaller than the others, it might once have been a dressing room. It was certainly filled with clothing now, unceremoniously dumped on any available surface, piled in heaps on the floor. He realised after a second that this was where they stored items confiscated from prisoners. Even if they ended up leaving custody alive, he guessed they were put out with just the shirt on their backs as a final indignity.

He was really starting to dislike the Okhrana, he decided. He felt a sudden, irrational urge to leave this room be, and prevent the sailors from poking through the messy remnants of other people's time here. He paused when he spotted his own suit and coat on top of the pile nearest the door. It had been run up for him in Vladivostok, nothing special but at least it was cut for his frame. Everything else he'd worn since changing out of his bloodied clothes on the night of the massacre had been too small.

"Well, this expedition won't have been a complete disaster, then." He was careful to put the recovered papers to one side before he changed quickly, tucking them safely into his trouser pocket. Even in the middle of the night, it was too hot for the overcoat, which he folded over his arm.

There was that noise again, clearer now. Definitely the creak of a floorboard, and almost directly over his head. He froze, listening, but only for a moment. He finished pulling on the last shoe, lacing it loosely before heading out of the storeroom as quickly and quietly as he could.

The stairs up to the garret rooms were at the far end of the landing from where he was — he remembered that much from his brief captivity here. He didn't stop to summon the sailors, just ran the length of the house.

"Marcus Alexandrovich!" he heard one of them — Ivan, perhaps — call out as he went across the top of the staircase that ran up from the ground floor. He didn't stop, but hoped his speed would impart to them a sense of urgency. He took the narrow, bare wooden stairs three at a time. They were so creaky there was no point trying to creep up on whomever was skulking around up there.

Baxter went through the door at the top, almost taking it off its hinges, not knowing whether he'd be confronting a policeman with pistol pointed or a looter. Maybe just a vagabond looking for shelter.

The narrow landing was empty, and if there was someone up here they'd gone very quiet. He didn't fancy the idea of kicking in the door of each room in turn, in case someone was waiting in ambush.

He filled his lungs, raised his voice to the sort of pitch a sailor needed when the wind was howling and rain lashed the deck. "Alright, whoever you are!" he boomed. "I've got three armed sailors with me who are itching to shoot a policeman, so you'd better come out with your hands up!"

It was partially true — Baxter could hear Ivan and his two comrades making their way up the stairs behind him, but coming considerably more cautiously. With any luck, they'd arrive in time for any shooting.

Was that a whisper? He braced himself, either to try to shout whoever it was into submission or fight them if they came out swinging. Then another door was flung open.

"Mr B!" a familiar voice — one he'd thought never to hear again — piped in English.

"Tommy!" he exclaimed, so surprised that he forgot about the whisper he thought he'd heard. "What the devil are you doing here, you wee shite?"

CHAPTER 12

Before Baxter could say anything else, Tommy had raced up to him and thrown his arms around his waist.

"You're alive!" the lad blurted out as he stepped back, cuffing away what looked suspiciously like a tear. "We ... that is, I thought you'd bitten the bullet. Couldn't find you anywhere."

Baxter found himself oddly touched by the boy's concern and obvious relief at finding him alive. He stopped himself from yelling anymore, though that was tempting, knowing it wouldn't help and could serve to bring unwanted attention. "Well, I clearly haven't," he said, with as much patience as he could muster. "A more pertinent question, and one that you've yet to answer satisfactorily, is what on earth you're doing here?"

"Looking for you," the lad said simply, then his eyes widened as the sailors piled onto the landing behind Baxter, pistols waving wildly.

"It's alright!" Baxter told them quickly, then remembered to switch into Russian. He was honestly surprised his English wasn't horribly rusty at this point. "He's a friend, stand down." He turned his attention back to the boy. He knew they didn't have a lot of time, but he needed some answers quickly before they could leave. "Are you by yourself?"

Tommy nodded. "I ran away from herself, because she was going to send me back home an' I din' want to go and I overheard her sayin' that me ma had ... well, anyway, an' she was also worried sick that you'd been caught by some folks she works with but dunnae like, an'..."

Baxter put a hand on the boy's shoulder, trying to steady him. Tommy had turned fourteen during the voyage to the Far East, and was a far cry from the lad he'd agreed to take onboard for a day or two's sailing experience. That had been a fateful decision for both of them, one he still cursed himself for, but a couple of near-death experiences aside, young Master Dunbar seemed to be prospering. Even if his dialect was still incomprehensible when he got excited.

"I don't think we have time to go into the details," he said, sounding more severe than he'd intended. He made an effort to lighten his tone. "Exciting as I'm sure they are. You'll be coming along with us, and you can tell me all about it when we're back aboard."

Once again, he was putting Tommy in the position of being aboard a Russian warship that could be facing complete annihilation. Right now, though, he couldn't see any other options. The city certainly wasn't safe for a lad apparently running around by himself, and if it looked like the mutineers were going to challenge the Black Sea Fleet again he would most certainly insist on them both being put ashore.

"Marcus Alexandrovich, would you tell us who this strange child is?" Ivan asked, his voice uncertain.

Tommy dropped seamlessly into the rough, lower deck Russian he'd picked up during the months they'd been aboard the *Yaroslavich*. "I'm no child, and I'm not strange!" he snapped at the surprised sailors.

"It's a long story, comrades," Baxter said. "Too long for now. Do you have what you came for?"

He'd already noted the sailors had bread, cured sausage and bottles of vodka stuffed into their tunics. One of them lifted a sack stuffed with food, grinning happily. "And you?" Ivan asked.

Baxter patted his pocket. "Yes, I do believe I do. Let's get back afloat."

They went out the way they'd come in. The gate at the back was locked, not just bolted from the inside, and nobody had seen a key. Tommy went up and over the wall with the same speed and efficiency as the sailors, and without complaint. Ivan and the others seemed utterly bemused by the boy, but also oddly entertained by his facility with their language and apparent enthusiasm for mischief.

They found Mashka where they'd left her, or rather she found them. She'd moved an alley up to maintain her watch. "Over here, you idiots," she hissed from the shadows before they could reach the conclusion that she'd abandoned them. "It doesn't do to stay in one place too long," she added, glancing around nervously. "Particularly when the idiots you're waiting for are making so much damn noise."

She caught sight of Tommy as they joined her, and shook her head in disgust. "Ah, we are kidnappers now," she muttered. "I knew Konstantin shouldn't have trusted you. Come, we must away."

It was deep night now, the city quieter than Baxter had heard it for a while. They definitely had no legitimate excuse to be out and about at this time, and they felt a sudden need to be somewhere secure. The fatigue that came from being constantly on edge was starting to bite at all of them.

Tommy stared around with eyes like saucers as they scurried through the streets. Baxter dearly wanted to interrogate him as to what the hell he thought he was about, and how he'd even managed to end up in the Okhrana's house on the very night Baxter had decided to raid it. It was a big world, and coincidences happened all the time — a sailor knew that probably better than anyone. This was stretching belief, however.

It would have to wait, though. Mashka glared angrily at anyone who even looked like they might be about to speak, and had kept silent herself after her outburst. The streets were still being patrolled, though Baxter knew from bitter experience that this was the hardest watch and the men who rode or marched along the grand cobbled avenues would be dozy and inattentive.

They almost made it back to the docks undetected, or at least undetected by anyone who cared. The sailors weren't overly keen on long walks, much preferring to go any distance by sea as was only natural, and Baxter was inclined to agree with them. Glancing occasionally at Mashka, he was struck again by how slight and young she was, clearly undernourished. She was kept going by her fury and fervour.

Only Tommy still seemed energetic, but for all Baxter knew the lad was well rested and fed. Now that the immediate excitement of finding him alive had passed, the lad — a young man, really — had settled into a watchful calmness, greatly at odds with the wain Baxter had first brought aboard. It seemed life at sea really had done wonders for him, much as his mother had hoped.

That reminded him of something that had almost been lost in the babble of words that had come out of Tommy when they'd met — a mention of the redoubtable Mrs Dunbar that was one of the reasons why the lad had run away from Ekaterina's care. He was about to press that point in a low voice when Ivan, who was keeping an eye out behind them, shouted in alarm.

Baxter spun round, a curse on his lips unvoiced. Mashka was less restrained, attacking Ivan's parentage in a low urgent whisper. The sailor's shout wouldn't have made any difference, though, as there was no way to escape the notice of the four policemen who had emerged from a side street.

Mutinous sailors stared at policemen with mutual shock and surprise. Mashka was backing up, face pale. She had as much at stake here as the rest of them, perhaps more.

"Get 'em!" Baxter barked. A quick stride brought the first police officer's jaw within range of a haymaker that knocked him clean out. Taking their cue from him, the sailors swarmed over the hated agents of the Tsar with no further hesitation.

Fists and boots thudded into bodies. The officers were swiftly overwhelmed, before they could draw their weapons or shout for help. The only action Baxter needed to take was to catch one of the sailor's arms before he could drive a short, wide-bladed knife down into the chest of a cowering policeman.

The mutineer turned a furious glare on him. "What do you mean by this? They are the enemy of the people!"

Baxter squeezed just hard enough to send the knife clattering to the pavement. "Look at him," he commanded in a low, urgent tone. "End of the day, he's not so different to you. Killing him won't help."

He didn't add that killing a person up close wasn't something you wanted to carry around with you. God knew, he'd been a part of killing more than a few men, but at range. The ones that stuck with him were revolutionaries aboard the *Yaroslavich* who he'd killed up close — with his bare hands, in one case.

The sailor nodded. "Never take a life when you don't have to," Baxter added, suddenly overcome with fatigue. It wasn't a command as such, more advice.

The policemen were unconscious or dazed, overpowered without a shot being fired. The clatter of nearby hooves, however, told Baxter that the damage had been done anyway. He looked around, feeling a wild panic threaten to overtake him. No one wanted to be caught on foot by cavalry, particularly not the wild, hard men of the Cossack regiments.

"Run!" Mashka snapped. "We're not far from the docks."

Baxter was about to follow her lead, knowing it was futile but also that they had no other options, when he stopped, turning to face the cavalrymen as they trotted into view. There were six of them, Cossacks, but their sabres were still in their scabbards and their pistols were holstered. They'd been coming to investigate a disturbance, not expecting to charge into battle.

The sailors had started to follow Mashka, as had Tommy, but they slowed to a halt, looking at him uncertainly. "Tommy, follow the girl!" he snapped. At the very least they could buy some time for them to get away. "The rest of you, what the bloody hell were you issued pistols for?"

The sailors scrabbled for their Nagant revolvers. None of them wore holsters, the big clumsy weapons stuffed into the waistbands of their trousers. The sack of food hit the pavement with a thud, and a vodka bottle smashed as it hit the cobbles.

The Cossacks recovered from their surprise quickly, putting spurs to the flanks of their small shaggy horses and dragging their wicked curved swords out of their scabbards. "Shoot the buggers!" Baxter shouted, realising after a moment that he was both closer to the charging horsemen and unarmed. He turned and ran back to the sailors as they formed something approaching a line.

Ivan and his companions showed remarkable coolness, or perhaps foolhardiness combined with a commitment to their cause. They started shooting before Baxter had got completely clear, the sharp *crack* of the firearms almost drowned out by the clatter of horses' hooves. He heard someone shout in pain, the whinny of a panicked animal, and when he looked back he saw the cavalrymen milling in confusion, obviously unprepared to have come under fire. At least one was out of the saddle and motionless on the street, and another was fighting to control his mount with one arm hanging limp by his side.

"Don't just stand there, fire again!" Ivan shouted, before Baxter could encourage them to take the opportunity to run. The sailors thumbed back the hammers on their weapons, the distinctive click and grind of oiled mechanisms working. One of the Cossacks shouted something, seeing the sailors preparing to fire again from barely five yards away. Instead of running, those that could spurred forward. There were, after all, only three obviously untrained men with revolvers facing them.

Ivan managed to get a round off, ricocheting off a lucky Cossacks' metal scabbard. Another revolver fired, hitting a horse in the flank and sending the rider plunging as it reared. Then the horsemen were on them, the stench of frightened horse and unwashed human strong in Baxter's nose. He ducked a sabre swipe, hearing the whistle of the blade over his head, and staggered as a horse barged him. He could hear someone screaming horribly, and straightened in time to see his assailant expertly turning his mount to come back at him. A revolver fired, and men were shouting.

Baxter stumbled over the heavy sack of sausage and bread, and that probably saved him from death as the sword cut the air over him as he fell. He'd always been light on his feet and fast, despite his size, and he scooped the sack up as he scrambled back to his feet, turning and swinging it with both hands with all his strength, catching the man who'd tried to kill him in the back and sending him flying from the saddle.

A horse barged him, his head ringing as the rider's boot caught him with a glancing blow on the forehead. Lights exploded behind his eyes and he staggered backwards, falling over again. But as his vision cleared, he saw the Cossacks were withdrawing. No, scattering. Hot elation surged within him. They'd actually survived this!

Ivan looked anything but elated as he helped Baxter to his feet. "Danya is dead," he said, voice dark. "And Lev is badly hurt. As you appear to be."

Baxter realised blood was running down his face. He resisted the urge to put his hand up to probe the wound, and instead tried to stop the flow reaching his eyes. "I'm sorry about Danya," he said. He didn't feel pain from the wound as such, but his head was starting to ache and he felt ... disconnected from reality. "We should get out of here — those Cossacks will be back, and the shooting will have attracted others."

"Agreed," Ivan said shortly, taking the heavy sack from him and slinging it over his shoulder. He actually smiled slightly. "I will carry this, in case we encounter any more and you need your weapon back."

Where before they had crept as quietly as they could through the city, keeping to the shadows, they now ran pell-mell. Well, as fast as they could, given Baxter's gashed forehead and the slash wound across Lev's chest, neither of which they had the means to treat. The Cossacks didn't fancy their chances, at least, their withdrawal turning into a canter away, no doubt to inform their commander and organise more troops to surround the errant sailors.

"I'm sure by the time they've reached the command post, it will have been a full-scale rampage by a mob of revolutionaries," Lev commented, smiling weakly, as they paused to catch their breath. They'd made it as far as the docks, at least, the smell of the sea out in the darkness telling them that they were almost safe — by a given definition of 'safe', of course. The injured sailor was in a bad way, blood covering the front of his chest. When he took his hand away from the wound, Baxter saw that a flap of skin was hanging loose, blood welling from it and over his fingers.

"You'll have a good scar from that," he said, as he gently put Lev's hand back in place. The wound didn't look too deep, but he was losing a lot of blood. "You'll impress the ladies."

"I'll have to get them to the point where I've taken my clothes off to show them," the sailor said, his voice increasingly weak.

They caught up with Tommy and Mashka not long after that. The young local was guiding Tommy along, despite his protestations that he'd rather go back and help Mr B and his mates. She had a firm hand on his shoulder and kept having to turn him around to keep him moving.

The lad's eyes lit up when he saw them catching up. Mashka just put her hands on her hips and shook her head. "You have made a fine racket," she said. "And a mess of yourselves."

"I'm afraid we don't have time for that right now," Baxter snapped.

She flinched slightly. "We are almost there," she said in a more conciliatory tone. "If we go quietly, we might avoid further pursuit."

He nodded tiredly, the energy draining out of him. His feet hurt with every step on the hard stone of the dockside as they made their weary way down to the beach. He squinted at his watch, reading it by the moonlight. "About another twenty minutes," he declared as they crunched down the slipway and onto the beach. He wasn't bleeding much — it really had just been a glancing blow, otherwise his skull would have been crushed — but his head was hammering now. Lev sank down with a whimper, Ivan fussing over him. Without prompting, Mashka went to help, taking off her shawl to help stem the bleeding.

Behind them up in the city, Baxter could hear distant bugles alerting the garrison to the possible intrusion. Nearer, he could hear raised voices and the sound of running feet. His vision swam as he turned and he almost lost his balance.

"Everyone lie down and keep quiet," he hissed, deciding that being prone was probably the best option for him now anyway. He just hoped the launch crew, when they returned, didn't just wait offshore. Or, worse, raise a hullaballoo and attract unwanted attention. He couldn't remember if he'd told them to actually run the boat ashore. "Christ, I really am bad at this," he mumbled to himself, closing his eyes and trying to stop the stars spinning overhead.

When he opened them again, someone was applying something cold to his forehead. For a drowsy moment he thought it was Ekaterina, having come back to nurse him. His mind drifted further, to his recovery from a wound and subsequent infection in the town they'd come to call Nossibeisk on Madagascar.

While it was hot here, though, it wasn't the coast of Africa hot. And the hands weren't quite so gentle. Focusing, he saw Mashka scowling down at him. "You passed out," she said bluntly. "I have covered the wound, but I think you will need a surgeon."

A few things he could say in response crossed Baxter's mind, but there was no point in antagonising her when she was still being helpful. The fact that had even occurred to him reassured him that the injury wasn't that bad. "How long did I pass out?" he murmured, aware that there was still coarse sand under his back.

"Do not be so dramatic," she snapped. "You had a dizzy spell that lasted a few moments."

Baxter started to sit up with a groan, but Mashka pushed him back down. He realised she was recumbent next to him. The noise of running boots nearby told him why she was being so cautious. "What of Lev?" he asked.

"He lives, but he should definitely see a surgeon soon. But then, what do I know? I just work in the factories."

Baxter lay in the dark silence, gathering his wits. After a few moments the sound of running soldiers faded, and they were left with the noise of the waves on the beach and Lev's increasingly ragged breathing. It was so quiet that he heard a bottle being uncorked and the glug of someone drinking.

Well, they'd earned that.

"Where the hell is that boat?" Baxter muttered, deciding the danger had passed sufficiently that he could risk standing up. Pain swelled but he kept on his feet. He stared away from the muted glow of the city, slowly sweeping his gaze across the dark expanse of water. Looking for the tell-tale glint of the white boat hull, the noise of an oar dipping gently in and out of the water.

"I'm surprised they're not scouring the docks," Tommy said, appearing by his side. "The sodgers seemed to be running into town, though."

Baxter started to put his hand up to rub his forehead, then stopped himself. "We're in civvies," he said. "Could be they thought we were just revolutionaries."

That had been the point of changing out of the distinctive Imperial Russian Navy uniforms, and he certainly hoped it had worked. The few shells the sailors had lobbed into the city hadn't seemed to provoke much of a response, but an armed incursion like this combined with the Black Sea Fleet being put to flight might be the straw that broke the proverbial camel's back.

"Someone's coming." Ivan's low and urgent voice came out of the darkness. Baxter dropped into a crouch, pulling Tommy down beside him. He heard the *snick-snick* of a Nagant being cocked.

It didn't seem to be a patrol, though. If it was, there would be more men and a lot of running and shouting. That was Baxter's overwhelming impression of any army, anyway — they did like to run and shout. He realised, after a tense moment's waiting and listening, that it was someone approaching quietly and also uncertainly. He caught a brief glimpse of a soldier's cap against the light of a campfire further up the dock, but the fellow seemed more concerned about avoiding the notice of others rather than the sailors he was approaching.

This was confirmed a moment later by a voice coming out of the darkness. "Brothers, you are from the *Potemkin*?" The voice was rough, an accent he didn't recognise, but at least he was actually speaking Russian and not one of the many other languages of the Empire.

Baxter actually heard Mashka sigh with annoyance. He caught Ivan looking to him for guidance, and shrugged. It wasn't for him to advise the sailors' committee or any of its members. "If it is a trap, they've already found us," he said, relenting after a moment.

Ivan nodded. "We are, yes," he replied to the unseen speaker. "Who are you?"

"I am with you, comrades, as is the regiment. We were ready to rise yesterday, when you were shelling the city. We tried to signal you to keep shooting, but you stopped."

"We didn't see your signal, brother, only someone waving a white flag," Ivan called back. "If we had seen it…"

The soldier had crept a bit closer and dropped into a crouch. This had to be the strangest parley that had ever occurred. A mutineer and a would-be mutineer crouching in the darkness, on the edge of a city in turmoil, exchanging pleasantries.

Baxter scowled. It wasn't entirely true to say that they had seen a white flag, and hadn't seen the signal. The gunnery observer, the one watching for the fall of shot and directing the gun crew, had *reported* seeing a flag. *Not your problem*, he told himself for the hundredth time.

"Will you shoot again? Will you land?" the soldier demanded urgently.

"We have another battleship now," Ivan replied, a note of pride in his voice. "I think it is a certainty that we will bombard the city. You must all keep your heads down and be ready to rise when we land. Remember, do not follow orders and fire on the people — there must be no more innocent blood on your hands."

"We haven't!" the fellow replied, defensiveness creeping into his tone. "We may have fired, but we fired over their heads."

"I believe you, brother. Soon, I promise, soon we will help you shake off your own dragons and we can drive those still loyal to the Tsar from the city."

"Bring your shells down on the general's headquarters and kill him!"

"We will, brother, we will!"

"Will you two keep your voices down?" Baxter snapped. Their volume had gone up as they got more and more excited.

He also wanted to prevent Ivan making promises he couldn't keep. It wasn't that he thought the mutineers wouldn't fire, more that he retained doubts about them being able to hit anything they were actually shooting at.

A hoarse shout from the direction of the campfire caused the soldier to start up. "That is my sergeant — I should go. Never fear, comrades, I shall tell him I was out here making water."

With that, he slipped away into the darkness. Baxter contemplated sending Ivan out to intercept him, render him incapable of speech for a while, in case this had been a ruse to confirm their presence or the soldier spilled his guts when confronted with authority.

Too late, now, and the sailor had seemed genuine enough, and brave with it. Baxter was staring to get paranoid, he realised. He had good reason for it, but it was starting to poison his thinking.

"Where's that bloody boat?" Lev said suddenly, voice stronger. He was obviously becoming delirious with pain and shock.

Baxter was about to give up hope of being picked up. It wasn't a disaster for them — might even save their lives — assuming he could talk Mashka into helping them find somewhere to lay low and get medical treatment for Lev. That was going to be the hardest part of it. He'd already got one sailor killed, and didn't fancy adding to that — even if they *were* committed revolutionaries who had indicated a willingness to die for the cause.

"Hello the shore!" a familiar voice called out, making him wince at the volume. They clearly hadn't seen the campfire, or just assumed it was locals rather than local troops.

He was still trying to force his sluggish brain to deal with the implications of this, and how they were going to warn the crew without drawing too much attention to themselves, when one of the nearby troops started singing. It seemed to be a raucous drinking song, and was rapidly taken up by a number of other voices.

"Men and your drinking songs," Mashka muttered.

"Be thankful for the cover," Baxter said. He was pretty sure it was their brief visitor who had started the song, and that it wasn't a coincidence.

Ivan had waded out into the water, gesturing madly and calling out to his comrades in the boat as quietly as he could, trying to get their attention and get them to stop shouting. It would be beyond an absurdity, Baxter reflected, if they were caught now because of over-enthusiastic hailing.

The message seemed to get through, and Baxter felt an enormous wash of relief, a release of tension in his shoulders, as the launch slid out of the darkness.

CHAPTER 13

"Start talking," Baxter said to Tommy Dunbar as the launch shot back across the harbour towards the battleship. They were making no attempt at stealth now, the oarsmen putting their backs into driving the little craft through the water while Lev lay groaning in the sternsheets. Mashka had elected to come with them, which had surprised Baxter. She was obviously more than capable of making her own way around the occupied city, but she had decided that on this night it would be safer aboard the mutineering ships.

His tone brooked no dissent. Tommy didn't look happy, and clearly knew he was in for a hard time. He sighed theatrically, and opened his mouth to speak.

"In English," Baxter added, casting a cautionary glance at Mashka and the sailors. He was pretty sure none of them had much if any language beyond Russian and Ukrainian. Tommy nodded.

"Well, it's like ah said before," he began. "Herself was going to send me home, like you asked her to. But she'd also, well … she'd found out that me ma had died." Tears welled up in the lad's eyes, which he quickly cuffed away.

Baxter didn't quite know what to say to that. He felt guilt swell inside him at the thought of the redoubtable Mrs Dunbar dying believing that her youngest son and the apple of her eye had been lost as sea. It may even have contributed to her death — he couldn't imagine her succumbing to anything common or garden.

Well, nothing he could do about it now — something else to add to the ever-lengthening list of mistakes he'd made.

"There was nothing for me to go home to," Tommy went on, the words starting to tumble over each other as a pleading tone crept into his voice. "Rab's in the Navy and Alisdair's with the herring boats, and neither of them have time to look after a wain. Me da died years ago, or went off — Ma wouldn't ever say, and ma sisters all have wee ones of their own..."

"So why in blazes didn't you make the case to Madame Juneau?"

"I did!" Tommy protested. "But she was adamant, seein' as you ask'd her to see me home to Edinburgh. So I reckoned..."

"You'd come and find me and get me to look after you?" he asked, deeply doubtful.

Tommy actually looked affronted. "Are you joking? I wanted to stay with herself, in her palace. Wanted you to tell her that I should stay with her."

Baxter doubted that Ekaterina owned a palace, but she *was* a countess and the Juneaus had certainly given every appearance of being wealthy. If the more blue-blooded officers he'd served with in the Royal Navy had been anything to go by, she would have a large country house on a pleasant estate. To a lad from the tenements of Edinburgh, it would indeed have seemed like a palace.

"It seems like you do have some sense in your head," Baxter said, feeling slightly wounded at Tommy's reaction to the idea of staying with him. "And you managed to work out, from overhearing her conversations, that Bilyk had me stashed here? Right down to the address?"

Tommy had the good grace to look slightly embarrassed. "Not just by overhearing," he mumbled. "I did some snoopin' as well."

Baxter knew he should castigate the boy for betraying the trust of a woman who'd taken him in, but he was impressed.

He didn't know many fourteen-year-olds who would have taken it upon themselves to sneak information out from under the nose of someone in the secret police and then take himself halfway across a foreign country to look for someone in a large city. A combination of the sort of sneaky intelligence Tommy had started to develop under Ekaterina's tutelage, and a painful naivety that had made him think it was a good idea.

Either that, or he was lying through his teeth. From the look on Tommy's face, Baxter guessed he wasn't going to be getting much more from him today. "Any word on Captain Juneau?"

Tommy's face fell. "Still missing, last I heard," he said. "Nobody seems to know what happened to the *Yaroslavich*. Vasily's retired from the Navy; he works for herself, now."

That brightened Baxter's mood slightly. The solid, dependable *botsman* had probably been his first and firmest friend, in an odd way, aboard the old Russian cruiser. He was too good a man to have his life thrown away on another madcap enterprise.

Tommy tilted his head curiously. "You haven't asked about herself."

Baxter wanted to keep his silence. He told himself he didn't care, that he was better off not knowing. "She's well?" he asked, despite himself.

Tommy nodded after seeming to consider the question for a little while. "I think so. Sometimes she seems out of sorts, ya ken, 'specially in the morning. Think she misses Captain Juneau. She talks about you sometimes, seems to be worried about you."

Baxter's only response was to grunt an acknowledgement. He had more important things to worry about right now. He wanted to interrogate the boy further about how he'd got to Odessa and even found the unofficial Okhrana building, but they were all distracted by a searchlight being turned on them, dazzling eyes that had grown accustomed to the darkness.

"Who goes?" a voice called from beyond that painfully bright light. Baxter could just make out the *Ismail*, the battleship's loyal watchdog, as a dim shadow.

"It's us, you blockhead!" Ivan roared back. "Now turn that damn light off! We need to get to Dr Golenko."

They'd made good time. The battleships lay a mile or more out from the dockside, in the outer reaches of the harbour. Looking up, Baxter made out the harbour lights of the *Potemkin* and, beyond her, the slightly smaller shape of the *St. George.* The electric lights dotted around the ships picked out their hulking outlines, making them seem even more menacing that they did in daylight.

Tommy sniffed. "Not as impressive as the *Borodinos*," he said. Baxter caught Ivan giving Tommy a hard look, which told him the revolutionary leader had at least a smattering of English. He could understand Ivan's sentiments — it didn't matter what she was like, most sailors took an inordinate pride in their ships and didn't appreciate them being unfavourably compared to other vessels.

"Well, just remember that most of those are at the bottom of the Pacific," Baxter pointed out grimly, as the launch slid into the inky darkness in the lee of the *Potemkin*. He dropped his voice to a murmur. "And remember that we are in very dangerous waters here. Very dangerous indeed."

They didn't have time to talk more, as they and the sailors scrambled up the ship's ladder and spilled onto the deck. The battleship was quiet, but there were enough men sleeping on deck that Ivan was able to rouse a party to bring the groaning Lev up in a bosun's chair. "I will go and wake the doctor and tell him he has patients," he said.

Baxter touched his own head, and gently felt the blood that had crusted over the wound. "He's got one patient. I just need a wash and a bandage."

Ivan shrugged. "Suit yourself. You should find Matyushenko and tell him what has transpired."

Baxter shoved his hands into his trouser pockets, and felt the sheaf of folded paper. 'What had transpired' covered a lot, and he just hoped it had been worth it.

He glanced across at Tommy. He was adept at staying out of the way on ships, as well he should be after the number of months he'd been afloat. He had tucked himself away in a corner as Lev was swung inboard and gently laid out on a stretcher. Rescuing the lad, for him, made the expedition worth it, but he doubted the revolutionaries would see it in the same light.

"I am afraid my English is not good," Lieutenant Kovalenko said as he straightened up from his examination of Arbuthnott's scribblings. "It does seem to be the ramblings of a madman, though."

It had turned out, on investigation, that for once Afanasy Matyushenko was resting. The sailors' committee wasn't debating into the night and the leaders of the mutiny were taking the opportunity to sleep. All but Kovalenko, anyway, who Baxter found restlessly roaming the ship. The young officer had courteously offered Mashka his cabin, which she'd accepted after the briefest of protestations. Tommy was stretched out on a chaise longue in the stateroom they were using to discuss the night's events. He'd gone out like a light.

Kovalenko glanced at the boy and shook his head. "The things our children must go through," he said sadly.

Baxter tossed back the glass of cognac he'd appropriated from the sideboard in the stateroom, and almost immediately regretted it. It just made his throbbing head worse, and sat heavily in his empty stomach. "I was at sea when I was younger than him," he said, voice harsher than he'd intended. He turned back to Kovalenko in time to catch a sharp look. He stared back impassively until Kovalenko looked away.

"Mashka as well," he said at last. "Why, she cannot be more than sixteen, and yet her circumstances drive her to put her life at risk on a daily basis to fight the forces of oppression."

Baxter stalked back to the drinks cabinet to replenish his glass. His mood was turning darker by the second, keeping pace with his cracking headache, and all he really wanted to do now was sleep. He knew, though, that blessed state would elude him until he worked out if the expedition had really been worth one sailor killed and another seriously injured.

Kovalenko pushed the papers across the polished dark wood of the table. "You have read these already?"

Baxter stooped to look at them. He'd not really had a chance or the light to look at them since a brief glance back on land, and he felt a bitter surge of disappointment as he realised just how incoherent the rogue agent's ramblings were. He was about to throw the sheaf of papers away in disgust, when his eye caught one or two words that sent a chill down his back. "See here? He's talking about Dogger Bank and the incident there."

"Where our ships drove off Japanese torpedo boats hiding amongst British fishing trawlers."

Baxter glanced up, trying to work out if Kovalenko was being sardonic. He seemed earnest enough, though. "People still believe that?" he asked, then shook his head, realising there was no point arguing. Even if he'd been there, and he was pretty sure Kovalenko hadn't been with the squadron, he guessed the effort would be futile. "Doesn't matter — the point is that the incident brought our two countries dangerously close to war — achieving by accident what Arbuthnott had tried to do." Baxter had briefly explained the almost absurd set of circumstances that had brought him to this place already; something he was becoming adept at whilst managing to omit anything too incriminating about himself. Kovalenko had listened impassively to the sorry tale and had seemed to accept it at face value.

"He cannot hope to achieve something similar here. Good God, his first attempt failed miserably, if what you say is true."

Baxter rubbed the bridge of his nose, resisting the urge to probe the growing lump on his head. He hadn't seen himself in a mirror lately, but he could only assume with the bruises received from the Okhrana and during his escape that he wasn't a pretty picture. "Rationally, I don't think he can hope to achieve anything at all. Judging from these scrawlings and past experience, I think he's gone a bit beyond the rational."

"But why would the Okhrana be helping him, or even a clique within it?"

"I think Matyushenko was on the money with this," Baxter said. "A war in the Pacific, against an enemy you know little about even if he literally borders your Empire, merely stirs discontent — particularly when you're losing it so disastrously. Britain and Russia have fought within living memory, and our navy — the Royal Navy, that is — can threaten your very capital."

"As our navy can threaten yours!" Kovalenko put in, with just a hint of affronted pride in his voice.

Baxter acknowledged the point with a wave of his hand, though what he wanted to say was, 'What Navy?' "Either way you cut it, it seems to me that the threat of war between our countries will pull people together behind the Tsar far more than a losing war in the imperial sphere."

Kovalenko nodded, the ramifications sinking in. "It is a … breathtaking gamble. If the war was actually to start, and Russia was somehow to start losing…"

"We're dealing with committed believers who either think the gains are worth the risk or don't believe they could possibly get things wrong."

"Very well." Kovalenko extracted some of the sheets of paper from the pile. "I find myself convinced, Marcus Alexandrovich. I think it is a matter of urgency to find out what it is they plan to do, because whatever it is, whether they succeed or not, it will not bode well for us."

Baxter nodded. "Well, we've got a long night ahead of us, then."

As it turned out, Baxter didn't have a long night. Fatigue and his pounding head forced him to retire an hour later, just as dawn was starting to lighten the eastern horizon. Rather than the gradual spread of the day's glow over a cloudless sky, however, day broke as fingers of sunlight poked through a thickening layer of cloud that did nothing to alleviate the heat or humidity.

The problem of Kovalenko not being able to read Arbuthnott's scribbles was solved when Tommy roused from his slumbers. With an almost uncanny sixth sense, he came awake with the galley starting its work to prepare the enormous amount of breakfast required for a crew of more than six hundred.

"Run and get yourself some tea and bread," Baxter said in English through an enormous yawn. "Then get yer reading eyes on — Lieutenant Kovalenko here needs your help."

"I would be most grateful for your assistance," the Russian said in very heavily accented English.

To give Tommy his dues, the look he gave Kovalenko wasn't *too* disdainful. "I speak Russian," he said in that language. "I've even got a bit of French, if you're more comfortable in that."

Kovalenko smiled delightedly. "Russian is fine!" he said, then turned back to Baxter. "You must explain to me how you came by this one, at some point."

"Probably," Baxter said, his capacity for communication and patience for other people rapidly approaching an end point. He stumbled into the adjoining sleeping cabin and more or less fell onto the cot, asleep as soon as he made contact with the mattress.

Baxter woke to the quiet sounds of a ship in harbour — people moving around, the ever-present thrum of the engine and the gentle lap of waves against the massive steel hull. There was none of the thunder that came from a ship preparing for action, or even the multitude of noises that accompanied a sea voyage. The wind was picking up, he noted drowsily.

His headache was no longer intolerable, just painful, and he noticed he'd bled a little onto the pillow. It probably made sense to go and bother the doctor at some point, or at least one of his assistants, to get something for the pain and perhaps a stitch.

He lay still for a while, taking a rare moment to enjoy being at rest even if he wasn't at peace. After a while, his hunger overcame the waves of pain and he dragged himself out of bed and into the day cabin.

Tommy was still there, resting his forehead on his cupped palms as he stared intently at the papers spread out across the dining table. He looked up as Baxter came through. "You're awake then, aye, Mr B?"

"I am, and you remain an impertinent wee shite," Baxter replied good naturedly, making for the pot of tea. He discovered when he lifted it that it was empty and it had left a ring-shaped stain on the polished wood. He opened his mouth to make a comment about how Mrs Dunbar had raised Tommy better than that, but managed to stop himself.

Tommy was a sharp lad, and from the scowl that had already started forming Baxter guessed that he'd followed that sluggish thought process.

"Where's Kovalenko?" Baxter asked instead.

"Some lad called Dymchenko turned up and said there was trouble brewing on *St. George*," Tommy said absently, turning his attention back to the pages in front of him. "He went to do something about it."

The plate of bread and cheese next to the teapot, at least, had a morsel still on it. Baxter picked through it, improvising a sandwich out of the fragments Tommy had left. "He work out anything?" he asked, nodding at the papers.

The lad directed a vaguely hurt, vaguely contemptuous look his way. "The lieutenant? No, he couldn't work out much. Think I might be on to something, though. Just need to work out a couple of these references."

Baxter was struck, once again, by how different young Master Dunbar was to the boy he'd gone to sea with. Or, at least, how he'd presented himself. There was certainly a lot more to him than anyone had suspected, and not all of it would have been picked up through the hard knocks of being on a warship or learning spycraft at Ekaterina's knee.

"I'm going to need to keep an eye on you," Baxter said around a mouthful of sandwich. "You're too clever by half."

Tommy's eyes became veiled briefly. "Never understood why that's an insult," he mumbled. Then his gaze became clear and innocent. "You should go and see the doctor, Mr B, that lump on your head needs looking at."

"Well, if you've commanded it, then I'd best be about it."

He found the deck considerably busier than when he'd last seen it. Matyushenko, looking more energetic and cheerful than the last time Baxter had seen him, was overseeing a launch being swayed out while a party of armed sailors mustered under Kovalenko.

He stepped out from the ship's superstructure, taking in the scene, the darkening clouds, and the way the rising wind was starting to make the sea choppy. Preoccupied as he was, he didn't see Dr Golenko until the small man bumped into him.

"Get out of the way, you blundering idiot," the doctor snarled at him.

Baxter hadn't really encountered Golenko, though a few of the sailors had mentioned him. He appeared to be something of an oddity aboard the rogue battleship, along with Lieutenant Kovalenko, Ensign Alekseyev and a handful of other officers who had either chosen to remain aboard or who hadn't been given an option. Baxter gathered that Golenko was of the former ilk, though he'd also heard that the doctor had precipitated the mutiny by declaring maggoty beef fit to eat.

"And a good morning to you, Doctor," Baxter said, surprising the little man with both his cordial tone and his easy transition into French.

"Ah, yes, you are the … ah, well, no one has quite explained to me who you are or what your role is aboard. Though you have managed to get one of my charges killed, and another hurt."

Baxter was relieved to hear Golenko mention only one death. "How is Lev?" he asked bluntly.

"He'll live, though he lost a lot of blood and will carry a scar for the rest of his life." Golenko blinked at him from behind small, round glasses. "Not that it will make much of a difference, the way things are going here. Now, if you will excuse me…"

Moving remarkably nimbly, he sidestepped around Baxter and hurried away to speak with Matyushenko. Baxter scowled after him, debating leaving him to it and going to see one of his assistants instead.

There was something about the dismissive way he'd spoken that made Baxter follow him. As he got closer, he noted that Golenko's manner had changed entirely as he spoke to the leader of the mutineers, entreating him to let him go aboard the *St. George* and treat any injured or sick crewmembers.

"It would be a useful gesture," Kovalenko put in. "Demonstrating the bond of brotherhood and solidarity between our two ships."

Matyushenko nodded thoughtfully, then waved the doctor into the launch. "Ah, Marcus Alexandrovich!" he said cheerfully. "You are well and up and around I see, though the good doctor should really take a look at your head."

"Everyone keeps telling me that," Baxter said sourly. "Though I feel it requires a deeper examination than anything the *good doctor* has time for anyway."

"Well, as your sense of humour is intact, I doubt you are too badly injured — perhaps you should accompany the launch so the doctor can provide a cursory inspection," Matyushenko said, a caustic note creeping into his voice. "Take your coat, though. I think it is going to rain."

Baxter locked stares with the de facto leader of the ship. Every instinct he had told him to walk away from this situation, demand a boat to put himself and Tommy ashore (and anyone else with any sense). The *St. George*'s crew had clearly not been fully committed to the mutiny and the revolution they were supposed to inspire. Despite the high spirits on the *Potemkin* in the aftermath of yesterday's silent, almost bloodless battle, what happened next could break them. And, in truth, none of it was his problem.

"Good idea," he said instead. He knew he couldn't risk provoking this volatile sailor, given how he had been responsible for two trusted revolutionaries being put out of action, one of them permanently. Kicking up a fuss now would most certainly not be well received.

Matyushenko's smile was without humour. "I'm glad you think so," was all he said, before turning back to organise the party that he must hope would bring stability back to his squadron.

CHAPTER 14

Baxter went back to the cabin where he'd left his belongings, gathering up the greatcoat that had been cut for him in Vladivostok. It was too warm for it still, but the heavy wool would keep him dry at least. Tommy didn't look up from his work or even acknowledge him. He was shuffling the papers excitedly, obviously thinking he was on to something.

"Mr B!" he exclaimed, just as Baxter reached the hatch. "Ah think…"

"It'll have to wait, lad," Baxter said. Right now, keeping on the mutineers' good side probably outweighed whatever news Tommy had. "Stay here, stay out of the way. Maybe try and get on Mashka's good side."

The lad's expression deflated slightly, and he mumbled something about doing like he was told and never mind. Baxter could have kicked himself for the short tone he'd used, but it was too late now. He paused at the door. "If you have got something, Tomas'ka, it's damn good work," he said, trying and failing miserably not to sound too awkward.

Tommy smiled briefly. "You sound like herself," was all he said.

"But seriously — stay out of trouble, and stay out of the way."

Baxter went back on deck, shrugging on the coat, to see that the launch was in the water. It seemed, though, that they were sending a propagandist intervention rather than an armed party. He guessed that Kirill at least was carrying a pistol, however.

193

At Matyushenko's slightly sardonic invitation, Baxter went down the ladder with every appearance of enthusiasm and joined Kovalenko, Golenko and the two civilian revolutionaries at the back of the launch.

"Cast off, smartly now," Kovalenko called out to the oarsmen. The sailors were grim-faced but resolute as they got the launch moving, its prow turned towards the bulk of the wavering battleship.

Baxter's headache was starting to clear, though he didn't know if it was the freshening breeze or the prospect of action that had done the trick. He realised he didn't feel a lot of apprehension at the coming encounter; it certainly seemed to offer less threat than the last time he'd boarded a Russian ship from a small boat. The memory of that night at anchor in Madagascar, when he and the Juneaus had suppressed a mutiny, brought a slight smile to his face. Although he suppressed it quickly, Kovalenko caught the expression.

"Something amuses you, Mr Baxter?" he asked, speaking French to keep their conversation private from the sailors around them.

"I'm a gunnery officer by training," Baxter replied, not really knowing why he was being so open with this man but also knowing it didn't really matter. "Trained for a modern naval war in which ships will batter each other from ten miles or more away. And yet, in the last few months, I seem to have done little else but take part in boarding actions."

"Well, hopefully it won't come to an actual action," the doctor commented, voice quiet and miserable. "I am sure we will be able to talk some sense into those who are not fully committed to the cause of freedom."

Baxter glanced at the fellow. He'd spoken the right words, Baxter knew, and the revolutionaries all seemed satisfied with his … well, performance was not too strong a word. There was something just a little bit rote about the way he spoke.

The *St. George* was anchored close by and the launch was coming up fast on her. Looking beyond the odd, old ship, Baxter's eyes lit on the *Vekha* transport ship. The *Potemkin* mutineers, he had gathered, had tricked her officers into coming aboard when she'd sailed into harbour and thereby seized control of the vessel. She was by far the least of the ships in this ragtag little squadron, larger but less useful in a fight than the torpedo boat, and had reduced in importance with the arrival of the second battleship. He hadn't heard anything about how her crew really felt, though Ivan had told him they'd pleaded with the mutineers not to harm their officers.

Looking at the two ships, he couldn't escape the feeling that Matyushenko, Konstantin and Kirill's well-laid plans could be about to come unstuck. What he had to do, he knew, was decide what part he wanted to play in any of this.

Probably best to keep his head down and make sure both he and Tommy came out of it in one piece, he decided as the launch bumped up alongside the *St. George*.

The sailors, all of them trusted and true revolutionaries, went up the side fast. Kovalenko followed and, with less expertise or confidence, the two civilians. Baxter knew he had to show willing and followed them up, realising as he did that once again he was going into a potentially dangerous situation without a weapon.

Golenko followed on last of all, going up the side quickly enough but without the same enthusiasm.

They were met on the quarterdeck by a burly *botsman* who tried to block their way at the top of the ladder. "We don't want to hear from you *Potemkin* mutineers anymore," he said, voice surly. Baxter noted that he didn't appear to be armed, and none of his own party seemed keen on pointing their weapons at an unarmed comrade. "We're going to leave for Sevastopol, and make our peace with the admiral."

Baxter kept his face impassive, moving slightly away from the gang of mutineers and their civilian co-conspirators. It wasn't unheard of for Naval authorities to forgive at least some mutineers if they came in quietly and could demonstrate that they weren't ringleaders. He didn't know much about the admirals responsible for this fleet, but he guessed they were cut more from 'Mad Dog' Rozhestvensky's mould rather than the firm but fair leadership Juneau had demonstrated.

"Then let us hear this from the crew, not one of the petty officers," Kovalenko demanded, physically shoving the boatswain aside. The boarding party hurried towards the forecastle, where the *St. George*'s crew had gathered. Baxter followed a little behind, not wanting to subject himself to the harangues he knew were coming. He'd seen more than enough aboard the *Potemkin*, not to mention when they'd brought the *St. George* into the revolutionary fold in the first place.

Kovalenko and Kirill took turns calling on their comrades, both desperate to have an impact, to keep the momentum of their cause going. If they lost this second ship so soon after she had joined the squadron, the morale aboard the *Potemkin* would crash.

Most of the crew was focused on what these interlopers were saying, and the two of them seemed to be making at least some progress with resuscitating the necessary fervour. Baxter took the opportunity to explore a bit of the quaint old battleship.

He'd been on some obsolete vessels in his time, not least the *Yaroslavich*. That cruiser had been almost thirty years old when she was presumably sunk, a hangover from that odd period of warship design when the various admiralties and naval ministries still hadn't quite trusted steam power. Ships of her vintage had therefore carried sailing rigs, although by the time of his peculiar service aboard the rig had been cut right back. It still saved their lives, when the engines were sabotaged during the great storm halfway across the Pacific.

The *St. George* was slightly younger than that, and hadn't been afflicted with a pointless top hamper that wouldn't have been able to move her through the water anyway. Her odd armament layout and age meant he wouldn't want to take her into action against anything approaching equal strength, but she was a pleasant enough vessel in her build and fittings.

He encountered one or two sailors as he made his way through the corridors of the superstructure. They gave him suspicious looks while trying to appear as though they had actual duties rather than trying to avoid association with the mutinous assemblies. Nobody challenged him or gave him a hard time, though, probably because he was bigger than anyone he met and had long ago adopted an attitude that said he belonged wherever he happened to be.

He went up a companionway and out onto the broad sweep of the bridge deck, in front of the fat twin tunnels. Walking to the edge, he was surprised to see Dr Golenko jumping up onto the pile of wood that was serving as an impromptu stage for the political lessons. Even from up here he could see the shocked look on Kovalenko's face, one that bordered on panic. The sailors were staring with something like curiosity at this odd little man, the ripple of conversation dying down as he started to speak.

The doctor was surprisingly eloquent, moving even, as he spoke about how his father had been a peasant and how he had made good in the medical profession and the naval service despite everything stacked against him. He demanded to know what they would ask, when they got to Sevastopol. "Will you demand that the borscht be cooked better?" he shouted, his voice surprisingly strong. "Or that you be allowed ashore more often?"

A rustle of laughter went through the gathered crew. There were several hundred men packaged onto the forecastle, and Golenko seemed to have them hooked.

"Comrades, Russia is rife with injustice! I joined you to demand quality for everyone — we must eradicate the injustice to achieve that!"

The speech was short and to the point, and a lot of heads were nodding in agreement as the doctor climbed down and disappeared into the crowd.

"We must go to Sevastopol!" a petty officer shouted, his voice cracking slightly. "Enough of this madness! Vice-Admiral Chukhnin is a fair man; he will see we were led astray but have come back to the fold."

"Chukhnin's a madman, a tyrant!" someone else shouted, and that was taken up. "The doctor's right, even the simplest demands won't be met."

A sailor Baxter vaguely recognised as one of the leaders of the mutiny on this ship raised his arms for attention. "I promise you, lads, we won't do anything else until we've spoken more with our brothers on the *Potemkin*. How does that sound?"

Baxter stepped from the railing and headed back into the ship. It seemed the disaster had been averted, this time, despite his concerns. He didn't know how long it would last, but they'd somehow managed to stabilise the situation.

He was heading back down through the slightly labyrinthine interior when that view was abruptly altered.

"I can't stay on the *Potemkin* any longer. They'll shoot me one way or the other."

The voices were coming from the bottom of the companionway he was about to descend. Baxter paused, stepping back and listening intently to the low, urgent conversation. For a second, he thought it was Kovalenko who was speaking.

"And yet you put on a convincing performance just now, to get us to stay." That belligerent voice was most definitely the boatswain who had challenged them when they'd come aboard, and with the context Baxter realised it was the doctor who was busy betraying his shipmates.

"I had to convince them I'm still on their side!" Golenko protested, voice rising slightly. "They've been suspicious of me since I tried to stay on the *Vekha* before they sailed out on their damn fool challenge to the fleet."

"Who's there?" a new voice broke in, while someone else hushed the doctor. Baxter heard a foot thud onto the lowest step of the companionway, and knew they'd rumbled him somehow.

At the same time, he could hear a number of sailors talking heatedly as they approached on his own level, making it hard to try to sneak away.

Instead, he shoved his hands into his pockets and did his best impression of Tommy Dunbar when the lad was up to no good and didn't want anyone to know it. He came down the metal staircase as though it was the most natural thing in the world.

"Morning, gents," he said cheerfully in English. "Just stretching my legs."

Golenko's eyes narrowed. He at least knew that Baxter spoke French, but to the best of his knowledge that doctor had never heard him speaking Russian. It was a gamble, but all he could do now was play it out.

"Ah, doctor," he said, shifting into deliberately broken French. He lifted the cap he kept perched on the back on his head. "Do I need to make an appointment for this?"

Golenko's expression went from suspicious to sour. "Do not worry about this idiot … tourist," he said, still speaking Russian. "He has attached himself to the revolutionaries, I do not know why, but he is not dangerous. I'm surprised he's still alive."

"God loves a madman," the boatswain said, with a cruel laugh.

Baxter stopped in front of them, smiling around the group happily. Golenko switched into French and gave Baxter a patronising smile. "Mr, ah, Baxter, wasn't it? Why don't you go and wait outside and I will see you directly. I must finish my business here, you understand. Just making arrangements for the care of some of the sailors aboard."

Baxter nodded affably. He kept his hands firmly shoved into his pockets to keep them steady as he walked out of the hatch, not wanting the slight shake in them to give him away. He let out a large breath of relief once he was well away from the hatch and stared towards the impressive bulk of the *Potemkin*.

It was clear to him, now, that there were those in her crew who were working against the revolution. Ensign Alekseyev, the figurehead commander, clearly was one, though his resistance was passive. Baxter harboured suspicions about the sailor who had directed the gunnery on the night they'd shelled the city. Had he really seen a white flag, or had that just been his way of giving the mutineers a reason to stop shooting? Had he just ignored the signal from the soldiers ashore to keep firing?

Golenko was clearly a counter-mutineer, and actively plotting with his like on the *St. George*. The question in Baxter's mind was whether it was any of his business. If Tommy had really found something, he could be on the edge of resolving his business in this blasted city and would then be on his way. He'd have other problems, of course, such as how to get the troublesome youth back into the care of Ekaterina, and how to keep himself free from the Okhrana.

Problems to be resolved in the future, he decided. He had to tackle what was in front of him. Dr Golenko had emerged from within the ship, and directed a sour look in his direction.

"Right, let's have a look at your cursed skull and be done with you," he snapped. Baxter just smiled slightly. While it seemed that his skill at subterfuge wasn't up to Ekaterina's standards, or even Tommy's, it had been enough for the doctor and the petty officers plotting to take this ship back.

As the launch bobbed its way back across the bay towards the *Potemkin*, Baxter thought further about what he'd heard aboard the *St. George*. He had no way of knowing if what Golenko and the others had planned would work, or even what they had in mind — he'd been spotted before they'd got to the details. Tipping the leaders off about the mutiny could just cause increased chaos, but he knew from naval tradition that mutinies had a way of devolving into chaos anyway. There was nothing to guarantee that Matyushenko and the rest of the sailors' committee could keep control aboard their own ship, let alone their flotilla. And there was the constant threat of the carnage they might unleash on Odessa.

Necessity had driven him to help them, or at least that was what he'd tried to tell himself. Baxter was capable of enough self-reflection to realise that he'd also been drawn in by the revolutionaries' rhetoric. There was certainly truth in what they said, but once the bullets and shells started flying in earnest, the truth wouldn't matter anymore.

"Time to get a grip," he murmured quietly, watching the hypnotic rhythm of the oars as they dipped into the waters and drove the launch back towards the behemoth that lay at the centre of his web.

Baxter was still mulling over what to do about what he'd overheard as he headed back to the stateroom they'd been using. He'd never been more certain that this really wasn't his problem, but at the same time he felt he owed Matyushenko some sort of debt. They could have abandoned him to his fate, or shot him out of hand. As it was, he'd been shown some degree of hospitality and even received assistance.

He was so distracted that he didn't notice that the stateroom was empty for a few moments. "Tommy?" he called out, wondering if the lad was sleeping. The cabin felt deserted, and the short jacket and cap Tommy had been wearing weren't anywhere in sight.

Baxter spun round, almost knocking into Ivan Beshoff. "Ah, Marcus Alexandrovich!" he cried cheerfully. "You will be happy to know that Lev is still alive and seems to be gaining strength. I also have a message for you, from the boy you rescued last night. I can only presume, from his obvious anger towards you, that he is in fact your son."

Baxter stared at the man, unable to stop his mouth hanging open in surprise. Then he snapped it shut. "Well, spit it out, then," he said, more harshly than he meant to.

Ivan didn't seem to mind. "Now, what was it, yes…"

Baxter restrained himself, knowing that the sailor was almost certainly acting on instructions from Tommy. Despite the fact that he was still young, Master Dunbar had a way of getting adults to do what he wanted. It seemed to work on most people, aside from Baxter himself and Ekaterina. Even Juneau had been susceptible to the lad's wiles.

The sailor seemed to sense Baxter's tamped down impatience, and obviously decided he'd bought enough time. "He said he thinks he's found what 'that bugger Arbuthnott is up to', which is an exact quote, and has gone ashore with the girl Mashka in order to confirm his suspicions. He says not to worry, and not to mess things up by trying to follow him, and he will be back later."

Baxter clenched his jaw shut and balled his fists at his sides. He'd basically only just finished pulling the idiot boy's fat out of the fire, and Tommy was off again. With some young woman — girl, really — who he barely knew. It was beyond belief that either of them could have been that stupid. Particularly Tommy.

No, scratch that. Tommy could be and had been exactly that stupid.

Baxter didn't express any of this. "Might I trouble you for the loan of a small boat?" he said at last. "I shall row myself across."

"Do you have any idea where to go?" Ivan asked doubtfully.

"No, I'll need to think on that."

"You should be aware, as well, that there are more Cossack patrols on the docks. General Karkhanov has said there will be no more trade, no more discussions, with us. Anyone attempting to land is subject to arrest."

"I'll take my chances," Baxter said, as he ducked back inside the stateroom and hurried to the table.

"I'll make arrangements."

As he'd expected, Tommy had left the papers carefully and neatly laid out. Baxter could see his handwriting — still childish, but neat — on some of the pages. He shuffled through them quickly, eyes darting across both sets of handwriting. He may not have been as adept as Tommy seemed to be at picking out fine details, but he could recognise patterns and spot where the budding intelligence agent had made particular notes.

"Got it," he said with a certain degree of satisfaction, just as Ivan stuck his head back into the stateroom.

"I have a boat ready, and will row you across myself."

Baxter gave him a tight smile. "I can handle a skiff," he said.

"I don't doubt it, but I suspect you will need your strength for when you're ashore."

Baxter nodded gratefully. "There is one more thing I must trouble you for, if I may. A revolver, if you would be so kind, and ammunition."

Ivan grinned at him. "The former is no use without the latter."

CHAPTER 15

Ivan wasn't able to tell him exactly how long Tommy had been gone, though he and Mashka had wheedled their way onto a boat going ashore not long after Matyushenko had sent Baxter on his way to the *St. George*.

Baxter reckoned with the journey out to the other battleship and back, on top of the speeches and arguments and then getting his own landing expedition organised, it was at least four hours.

All in all, it was a lot of time for Tommy to get into trouble. Or cause some.

"I do not like the look of this sky," Ivan commented, as he sculled the little rowing boat in towards the docks. He was putting Baxter ashore well away from the heart of the district, where so much of the recent trouble had started. They were working on the theory that the army and the Cossacks would not be patrolling that far out. With any luck, Baxter might find some allies in these parts as well.

"I'm inclined to agree," Baxter said. The clouds that had been scudding overhead all morning were starting to thicken as the day made its way into mid-afternoon. "But then, we're sailors, you and I. What does some dirty weather matter to us?"

"Very little, though the men doing the coaling will complain bitterly." Ivan nodded back towards the *Potemkin* as an appropriated coal barge was towed alongside. Her coal bunkers would be dangerously low from the two sorties the previous day.

"Well, I imagine they will — though they're welcome to try coaling at sea off the coast of Africa and see how preferable *that* is."

Ivan gave him an odd look, but obviously guessed enquiring further into that statement wouldn't get him anywhere. "I was not always supposed to be a sailor, you know, but unlike many of my comrades I chose the life."

"Even less reason to complain about the weather, then," Baxter commented, keeping his tone amicable. He'd suspected since meeting Ivan Beshoff that he wasn't of the usual peasant or proletariat stock that formed the bulk of the Imperial Russian Navy's manpower. "What would you be, if you hadn't chosen it?"

Ivan looked surprised at the question, and then thoughtful. "A student, perhaps, like Konstantin Feldmann. Though perhaps less annoying than he is. Or I might have emigrated somewhere, maybe Britain, and opened a restaurant." He saw Baxter's dubious look, and laughed aloud. "I'm serious!" he protested. "Ask anyone who has sailed with me — Ivan Beshoff is a man who knows his way around a fish!"

Baxter could think of a few things to say in response to that, none of them polite, but they were getting close to the docks now. There were a few people, here and there, but nothing like the activity he would normally expect to see at such an important trading hub.

"No sign of any Cossacks," he said. "If you stretch out, you can have me ashore and be on your way before anyone spots you."

"I can wait for you," Ivan offered. Baxter wondered why the man was being so helpful, but he just seemed to be that sort of fellow.

"Wouldn't want you to get wet, old chap," he replied. He didn't want to add that he had no intention of returning to the *Potemkin*. His mind was made up on this point — he was going to find Tommy, take him by the scruff of his neck and find a way to get them out of the city. Preferably overland. If he could spike Bilyk and Arbuthnott's little scheme at the same time, so much the better. He doubted he'd ever see the promised payment from Konstantin, and had never really agreed anything with him except that there would be payment for services rendered. He knew he'd need money to get anywhere or do anything, but the risk posed by hanging around any longer far outweighed the possibility of a few roubles that wouldn't be worth much outside the Empire.

But the main thing, he'd come to realise, was survival. Whether or not the counter-mutiny worked, it was clear that things were about to take a turn for the bloody.

Ivan brought the little boat in against a pretty dilapidated-looking wooden wharf, and without any further discussion Baxter went up the slime-encrusted steps, pausing briefly at the top and nodding a brief farewell to the mutineer as he sculled out and began the long journey back to the *Potemkin*. The water's surface was beginning to be stippled with spots of rain, nothing hard or continuous. Baxter suspected Beshoff would be soaked by the time he got back to the battleship.

"Well, I'm going to get soaked if I stand around here," he muttered to himself. The temperature hadn't dropped much with the clouds, reminding him somewhat of the sudden and intense downpours he'd experienced off the coast of Africa. He went along the slats of the little structure that stuck out into the sea, the wood creaking underfoot, almost unconsciously stepping over or around parts that looked rotten through.

The air smelled of seaweed and brine, and rotting matter. He was used to these scents — they were as natural to him as coal smoke and burned propellant. The smell got a lot stronger as he reached the end, though, and he crouched down to lift a section of wood. It was so badly rotten it came apart in his hands, but that wasn't the source of the stench.

It took him a moment, in the dim light that filtered through, to work out what the pale blob floating in the water was. Then he realised it was a face, so bloated with decomposition and damaged by immersion he couldn't even tell if it was a man or a woman. Adult or at least a teenager, he thought, seeing for the first time the half-submerged body tangled with weed and old rope. He guessed it was someone who'd gone into the water during the massacre — three days ago, was it, now? The last few days had been such a blur of danger, activity and injury that he was finding it hard to keep track.

He straightened, feeling his face harden. "I definitely need to get out of here."

The neighbourhood he walked into was well away from the hive of commerce and industry that the heart of the docks would be under normal circumstances.

Odessa's harbour was broad and deep, though, and the northernmost side of it was crowded with smaller warehouses and wharfs for fishing boats. The rail line ran from the industrial slums in the north of the city through this area and then down to the main docks, but had passed this area by. Which wasn't to say that on a normal day the area wouldn't have been bustling, with smaller coastal vessels and the fishing boats tying up or putting off; the cobbled harbourfront would normally be busy with workers, fishmongers, and sailors come ashore.

It was exactly the sort of place, Baxter thought, people like Bilyk and Arbuthnott would use to get up to no good. Narrow, noisome alleys ran between teetering wooden warehouses and brick-built tenements. He was glad of the weight of the Nagant revolver he wore in a holster below his coat, even though the grip occasionally dug into his ribs.

So far, this area didn't seem to have been affected by the unrest that had rocked the rest of the city. He didn't see any sign of fire damage as he moved along the waterfront, and what looting there'd been was more opportunistic than evidence of a wrathful mob. Even with the threat of bombardment — somewhat more pressing than the impending rainstorm — he expected to see more people out and about. Instead, he caught the occasional flicker of a frightened face peering through barely-opened shutters.

Baxter had known a hundred districts like this. Occasionally, as a young officer in the Royal Navy, he and his fellow junior officers had gone looking for the sort of seedy fun you could have somewhere like this. More often, once he had been cashiered from the service, he'd had to go looking for work or even lodgings in similarly down-at-heel neighbourhoods around the world.

Ultimately, they were all the same. Different language, different food, different liquor. But those were just the trappings.

He stopped briefly to try to get his bearings. There was no point trying to read what street signs there were, as they were in Cyrillic. Tommy also hadn't been able to work out an exact address for whatever it was the conspirators were working on; nor had he been able to tell even what it was they were doing. Baxter had a nasty feeling he could take a guess, though, and he assumed Tommy had come to a similar conclusion.

He had a rough idea of the area, and he knew the sort of building he was looking for. After twenty minutes walking along the deserted harbourfront, he felt his heart sink. He'd come to the right district, but he'd underestimated the number of little shipwrights along it.

Every port city needed them, though they were not necessary for the big ocean-going vessels that were increasingly built in Britain, France and the US. The Black Sea Fleet's ships were, he assumed, all built in Sevastopol. But even a trade hub like Odessa needed coasters, fishing trawlers, possibly the occasional pleasure yacht.

He noticed an old man watching from the open door of a pub. He was clearly a fisherman, his long beard neatly groomed and his jumper and heavy trousers worn and patched, but clean. "Are you looking for something, friend?" the local asked congenially. "Perhaps you have come down from the city, looking to commission a boat?"

The fellow laughed uproariously at his own humour, giving Baxter more of a look at his mostly toothless gums than he was really comfortable with. A waft of sour vodka accompanied the laughter.

"The Lord alone knows, we need the trade," the fellow went on more soberly. "But with this damn rabble running around the place, cursing His Holiness and throwing bombs, I fear the city will never recover. And if those big beasts out there open fire…"

The fellow was clearly at least slightly drunk, though whether he was the proprietor sampling his own wares for lack of other custom was hard to tell. Baxter thought there might have been a few people inside the establishment, though it was hard to tell through the shutters and smoky atmosphere inside.

Baxter looked him up and down, weighing whether or not he should take a risk. He stepped closer, despite the fellow's smell, and dropped his voice to a confidential volume. "Well, I can tell you're a true and loyal son of the Tsar," he said, doing his absolute best to mimic some of the officers he'd heard when they'd tried to speak Russian with the men under their command. "Perhaps you've been keeping an eye on any comings and goings around here? Seen anyone, aside from me, who doesn't belong?"

What he really wanted to ask was whether any of the shipwrights were working right now. It would be hard to hide such a thing, particularly when everywhere else was silent as the grave. He didn't want to tip the fellow off as to what exactly he was looking for, though, in case he just told Baxter what he wanted to hear.

The old man tugged at his beard thoughtfully, casting a disturbingly astute eye over Baxter. Something about him seemed to inspire trust. "Well, old Oleh's eyes are getting worse," he said after a moment. "Why I had to give up the sea, in truth, that and the stiffness in my hands making it impossible to handle the nets. But my ears still work well, and I have heard what sounds like work going on in Andrei's shop. Half a mile or so along the front."

"You've done the Tsar a great service," Baxter said. Ironically, as far as he was concerned, he was telling an unvarnished truth. Bilyk might think this mad scheme would help the Romanoffs maintain their grip on the country, but it was clear that he was steering for a disaster. The Royal Navy had been ready to fall on the Empire after a few fishermen had been killed, and if this plot succeeded there would be a far greater provocation. He reached into his pockets to see if he had any loose change at all, but stopped when old Oleh gave him an offended look. It seemed doing right by his Tsar was all the reward the retired fisherman needed.

Baxter gave Oleh his best earnest smile. "Well, I'd best be about my work, then," he said cheerfully, trying not to show any relief as he stepped away from the pub and the particular odour of the old man. He felt his faked cheerfulness dissolve as he looked up at the sky, feeling the rain start in earnest on his face.

Well, he'd been out in worse. At least the surface he walked on wasn't heaving across massive waves, though the lack of movement put him off slightly. He'd become reaccustomed to being on land during the weeks since he'd brought his launch full of sailors into Vladivostok, but now he already had the feeling of the land being alien.

The rain, as it turned out, was more than just uncomfortable. It hammered down on him hard enough that he pulled his collar up and cap down, hurrying along with his hands in his pockets. That meant he didn't see the policeman who stepped out from a side alley until he'd almost barged into him.

Baxter was surprised enough that he pulled up short, then cursed under his breath — his only way through this would just be to keep going. He wouldn't be able to get to his gun, even to threaten the man out of his way.

The man facing him was obviously experienced, and wouldn't threaten easily. He had his own pistol drawn, a Nagant just like the weapon holstered uselessly on Baxter's hip, but he wasn't brandishing it wildly. He kept his distance, outside of easy grabbing range, with the gun held low and levelled at Baxter's guts. Water dripped from the brim of his cap and trickled down his drooping moustache. He smiled, but his dark eyes were flinty.

"Why don't you come along with me?" he said, voice surprisingly mild. He didn't need to be loud or threatening. The revolver in his hand provided the threat, and would be loud if it came to shooting. Baxter heard the click of boot heels behind him, and guessed the officer wasn't alone anyway.

He stood stock-still, weighing his options and realising he didn't have any. If the man was alone, if his pistol wasn't already drawn, if...

Baxter spread his hands, matching the policeman's humourless smile. "What's the problem, officer?" he asked. He briefly contemplated trying to bluff this out as an idiot British citizen wondering around where he didn't belong (which was true enough, on one level) but that would only last as long as they didn't discover the Russian service revolver he was armed with.

"You can discuss that with the captain," the policeman said, twitching the pistol's muzzle. "Come along now."

Policemen came up on either side of him, each taking one of his arms in a firm grip at the elbow. The first one stepped in and searched him quickly, tutting as he removed the revolver and tucked it into his own belt.

Baxter fought down the urge to lash out. It was too late for resistance now, and he felt a yawning chasm open up in his gut. To have come this far on his madcap enterprise, only to be foiled at the last by a trio of ordinary bobbies...

He took a deep breath, causing the men on either side of him to tense up, expecting violence. He relaxed into their grip. He wasn't done yet, though. Wind and tide were against him right now, but there'd be a way through this mess.

His optimism disappeared when he saw where the policemen were marching him. He'd expected to be taken to a local station, though what that would have looked like escaped him

— his contact with police services had mostly been confined to bobbies in Britain and the Tsar's secret police.

Reporting back to the local station, in fact, seemed to be the plan. The policemen, their uniforms and capes already soaked through by the rain, grumbled bitterly about having to be out in the weather.

"At least with an arrest we can be inside for as long as it takes to do the paperwork," the leader of the trio said.

"And we can get Bogdan to do the paperwork," the second offered. "He can barely write, he'll take forever."

"I would be offended by your words, Yefim, but I see the wisdom of your plan."

"You mean to say I'm being arrested purely because you wanted to get out of the rain?" asked Baxter.

"You are being arrested," the leader said, with a certain amount of satisfaction, "because you are an armed revolutionary. Oleh said perhaps you are a foreign spy, when he told us about you, but your Russian is too good."

Under normal circumstances, Baxter would have taken that as a compliment.

"Being able to get inside, though, is a bonus," Bogdan added, then his face fell. "Though I fear we may be out of luck — *khokhols.*"

Yefim spat in the street. Baxter didn't recognise the word, but when he looked up his heart sank. A troop of Cossacks blocked the street, looking every bit as sodden but less miserable than the police officers. Worse, he recognised the officer who sat at the head of the troop, a satisfied smile spreading slowly across a face that was still heavily bruised.

The Rittmeister dismounted, taking his time about it. He was more expensively attired than his men, and consequently drier, but his face showed distaste as his tall, gleaming boots splashed down.

He stalked towards Baxter and his escorts. The leader moved to intercept him, a bland smile on his face as he attempted to communicate with the obviously aristocratic officer. "This man is now my prisoner," was all the cavalryman said, before stopping in front of Baxter, the smile returning to his face.

"I don't believe I caught your name on either of the two occasions we met," Rittmeister Zubov observed, then lashed Baxter across the face with his riding crop. "And as you are unable to turn tail and run, this time, perhaps you'll have the opportunity to tell me. Well, speak up, man!"

"Bastard," Baxter said in English. His face stung from the blow, though he couldn't feel any blood trickling down his face. He wanted nothing more than to wipe the smug smile off Zubov's face, but he knew that would likely be the last thing he ever did.

The temptation was strong, though. He could break free easily enough, do *a lot* of damage to the slim young Russian and then dash for the buildings on either side. The Cossacks all had their swords sheathed and pistols holstered. At least one policeman had his pistol drawn, though, and he didn't doubt the capacity of the cavalrymen to charge into action at a moment's notice.

"Bastard?" Zubov feigned being nonplussed. "I do not believe I have come across that surname before, though it could apply to many of your people." He struck Baxter again, a backhanded swipe with the crop. Again, not hard. Just to show he could.

"Do you normally need someone to hold the people you beat?" Baxter responded in French, his voice grating even to his own ears. "It seems in character."

Zubov made a dismissive, shooing-away gesture to the police officers. They gratefully relinquished their grip on Baxter, obviously sensing the potential for violence here even if they didn't understand the language being spoken.

"There, is that better?" Zubov smirked. "Would you like to strike me now?"

Baxter nearly did, and damn the consequences. The Cossack hetman had his sabre drawn now, and had walked his shaggy little horse closer to the confrontation. Baxter breathed out, forcing himself to appear relaxed, and just smiled at his new captor.

Zubov looked briefly disconcerted by that expression, the last thing he would expect to see. "Hmm, it seems not." He seemed to tire of the conversation, and nodded to the non-commissioned officer. "Take him and bind him. We will retire somewhere dry to interrogate him."

'Somewhere dry' turned out to be a livery stable that the Cossacks appeared to have turned into their barracks. The men and horses obviously occupied the stable part of the building. Baxter, his hands bound before him, was hit by the smell of close-packed, wet humans and animals as he was dragged in through the open double doors at the front of the wooden building. It was overpowering, far worse than anything he'd experienced at sea. Even in the middle of a storm, with no one able to get on deck and half the crew laid out by seasickness.

The Cossacks led their mounts into the stalls. Baxter noted that the cavalrymen looked after the animals before themselves, getting their saddles and tack off and starting to dry and brush them down immediately. Zubov left his taller mount to a servant, of course, and indicated Baxter should be taken deeper into the building.

He was marched along narrow corridors and into a small, dark parlour. It smelled of tea and woodsmoke, the former from a samovar and the latter from the fire over which it hung. The rain drummed against a small window. The Cossack hetman lit an oil lamp and then retired to one corner of the room while Zubov seated himself and waited to be served tea by a shawled old woman.

At Zubov's nod, the hetman pushed him down into a low, soft seat that smelled strongly of horsehair. He sank right into it, well below the level of his knees. Zubov smiled in satisfaction. "I am told," he said, after taking an appreciative sip of the tea, "that you are some sort of British agent. This is what the men of the Okhrana told me after you were taken away. I find it hard to credit, myself, as you are obviously so incompetent."

Baxter sat still, feeling the wet cord around his wrists tighten as it dried. He focused on that pain, using it to control his anger. Zubov was clearly a man much in love with his own voice, so he didn't feel the need to join the conversation.

"I mean, from what the policemen said, you could not have been more obvious," the Rittmeister said after a pause. He looked at Baxter enquiringly, expecting him to rise to the bait and seeming disappointed by his calm manner. "I could just have you shot," Zubov went on, when he received no response. "Yes, we are supposed to bring people in for trial, but what is one more body in the harbour?"

Baxter thought of the floating, rotting corpse he'd seen earlier. He wasn't a man who worried too much about violence. He'd seen a bit of action in the Royal Navy, more so with the Russian Navy. He'd seen men die, and had himself taken lives. Yet the cold and casual way that this man talked about the murder of political prisoners chilled him to the core.

"It really is no wonder this country is falling apart," Baxter said, keeping his voice mild.

Zubov started up from his seat, reaching for this riding crop.

Baxter moved without hesitation. Hesitation had been his problem before, when he'd been held by the Okhrana and had got as far as breaking Mieszko's arm. He'd let himself lose momentum then. He wasn't ever going to be held prisoner by any damned Russians again.

He powered up out of the sear, rising faster and more smoothly then either of the Russians in the room expected. His legs were tired — his whole body was — but he'd spent most of his life at sea and he drew on the same reserves that had kept him going during the great storm in the Indian Ocean. His hands were tied in front of him, so he headbutted Zubov in the face. It made his own injured head ring, but he had the satisfaction of feeling the aquiline, aristocratic nose break.

"You don't learn, do you?" he snarled, bringing his knee up into Zubov's crotch and dropping him.

The hetman, surprised by the suddenness of the violence, recovered and ran forward. As his sabre rattled out of his scabbard, Baxter grabbed one handle of the battered copper samovar and, ignoring the pain of the hot metal, swung it round and hurled it blindly towards the Cossack.

The heavy metal object struck the soldier square in the chest, knocking him back and punching the wind out of him. Zubov, despite the solid blows Baxter had landed, had started to pull himself to his feet. That was a mistake, as it put him right in the path of the scalding liquid spilling from the vessel.

The officer screamed, clutching at his bloody and now scalded face. Baxter didn't hang around, didn't hesitate. He desperately wanted a weapon, but he could already hear running boots beyond the parlour. The window was small, but he'd squeezed through tighter spaces. He reached up to grab the narrow window frame, pulling himself up with a heave and curling his legs before going through the glass feet-first. He almost managed to get his feet under him as he landed, but slipped on the wet cobbles and came down on his shoulder, surrounded by shards of broken glass.

He didn't have time to lie around in the street feeling sorry for himself, though. Behind him, Zubov was still screaming and the hetman was shouting breathlessly. A face appeared in the shattered window, followed by a rifle. Baxter rolled to his feet and sprinted away while the Cossack was trying to get his cumbersome weapon through the broken remnants of the frame.

He heard the crack of the rifle firing, but kept running. Before the Cossack could work the bolt action and get another shot off, he skidded round a tight turn onto one of the narrow side streets that honeycombed the area.

He stopped at the end of that street, leaning against the side of a ramshackle warehouse and sucking in great gulps of air. He knew that he hadn't escaped yet. He had scant seconds before the Cossack pursuit began in earnest.

The rain was still coming down, but seemed to have eased off slightly. He'd lost his cap somewhere along the way and his dark hair was already plastered to his skull. He stretched his sore, tired muscles. It didn't feel like he'd suffered further injury, though he knew once the adrenalin wore off he'd hurt all over.

No time to worry about that now. He needed to get his hands unbound, not least because the cord that bound his wrists was starting to cut off the circulation to them. Then he needed a weapon.

CHAPTER 16

It didn't take much effort for Baxter to force his way into the warehouse, which surprised him. Given the current state of the city, he'd have thought any sensible merchant or proprietor would want their property well secured.

There was only so much one could do against an angry mob, though, he guessed.

As it was, he was able to kick his way through a back door, the wood around the lock splintering under his bootheel. The inside was dim and smelled musty, abandoned. That would explain why no one was taking particular care of the building.

He paused in the doorway, breathing quietly as he listened. Even if the building had been abandoned, there was nothing to say it was unoccupied. The only sound he could hear, though, was the scurrying of startled rats.

Baxter knew he didn't have time to hang around here. He groped his way forward in the half light, awkwardly feeling with his hands. He saw a few cases, from which the worst of the smell emerged, and bales of fabric. His search was lent urgency by the fact that he could already hear the clatter of hooves on the cobbles — he hadn't gone far before he'd stopped, and he guessed it wouldn't take them long to start searching buildings.

His questing fingers found something that felt a lot like a knife handle, left carelessly on top of a cask. He didn't want to risk knocking the cask over and potentially losing what could be the only knife in the whole damn place.

"This'll do," he said to himself as he held the blade up. It was a short, wide working knife, the metal a little rusty and the handle plain and worn. He tried to reverse the tool in his hands, but the loss of circulation had made him clumsy and he almost dropped it. Feeling his pulse start to race, he crouched awkwardly and wedged the knife point up between his knees, the edge away from himself. He hooked the cord around his wrists over it and sawed desperately at it, hearing the sound of horses coming closer. He could hear the Cossacks shouting now and the thump of boots, the sounds of doors being hammered on and kicked in when there was no response. Or the response was not quite fast enough. Voices were raised in angry protest, and the search party was getting closer and closer.

"Do or die," he grunted, redoubling his efforts. The Cossacks were not likely to be merciful, given what he'd done to their officer, and even if they didn't shoot him out of hand, Zubov would certainly give the order.

Running feet reached the big double door at the front of the warehouse, and someone battered at the smaller personnel door set into it. "Open up, in the name of the Tsar!" a guttural voice shouted.

"Come on," Baxter hissed, frantic now.

"Open up or we smash it in!" the voice shouted again.

"It's a warehouse, there is no one in there," a second, quieter and less excited voice said. "Let's just kick it in."

The cord was held together by a single skein of fabric now. One of the soldiers outside smashed his rifle butt against the door, causing it to shiver on its hinges.

The cord gave. Baxter launched to his feet then stumbled, crippled by a sudden burst of cramp in his thigh. The front door gave at the second blow and it was too late for him to run.

He turned the stumble into a lunge with the knife, catching the first man by surprise. The man hadn't managed to bring the muzzle of his rifle up. It was more luck than judgement that put the point into his throat. The blade wasn't in good shape, but it was sharp enough and had Baxter's weight and strength behind it. There was a slight resistance of skin and muscle, then the man was down, collapsing onto his knees and pulling the knife from Baxter's grip. The dying Cossack gurgled, clutching at the hilt that protruded from his neck.

Baxter looked up into the startled eyes of the second Cossack. He felt as astonished as the Russian soldier, but recovered himself faster. Moving lightning fast, he got one hand onto the man's Nagant revolver the soldier held. The other closed around the Cossack's throat and with the double grip he pulled the fellow off his feet and into the warehouse.

Baxter turned the movement into a throw, launching the man a few feet into the darkness inside. He took the briefest look outside, at the rain-slicked street, and realised that luck was on his side for once — there were no other pursuers out there.

He kept moving, knowing his only hope now was finishing this without more noise. Mercifully, the fellow had hit some of the baled fabric and fallen heavily, the wind knocked out of him. Baxter took a moment to drag the dead Cossack into the warehouse and dashed back to his comrade just as he dragged himself back up, trying to pull his sabre from its scabbard. Baxter kicked his hand, sending the weapon clattering away, and resolved the matter with a downward-angled haymaker to the side of the head that laid the horse soldier flat out.

Baxter knew he'd feel that later — it wouldn't surprise him if he'd broken a knuckle. No time to worry about it now. He left the cavalrymen's swords, as he didn't have the first clue what to do with them beyond knowing which end to hold. The policeman had left the holster attached to his belt and Baxter shoved one of the pistols into it, then took up one of the rifles.

He took a moment to look down at the dead Cossack, wondering if he'd deserved what had been done — whether he was one of the men who'd fallen on the essentially unarmed protestors with such savage glee. There was no way of knowing that, now, and it didn't matter. He left the knife in the dead man's neck, and went out the way he'd come in, pulling the damaged door closed after him as best he could.

He moved fast now. The sudden burst of brutal violence seemed to have woken him up, making him feel like he'd been drifting sluggishly until the moment he'd attacked Zubov. He had a clear task now, and by killing a soldier of the Tsar and injuring others, he had crossed a boundary that couldn't be ignored.

The truly unforgivable sin, of course, would have been injuring Zubov — he doubted the aristocratic officer and his ilk would particularly care about the dead man.

Baxter couldn't just walk away, though. Tommy, with all of his facility for getting himself into trouble, was still out there, as was Mashka. If nothing else, he wanted to give the young revolutionary a piece of his mind for going off with a child on such a madcap enterprise.

Most of all, he had to admit, the thought of letting Arbuthnott get away with what he was planning rankled him. More so than any outcomes of the plot.

The area was in something of an uproar now, though it seemed to be only Zubov's Trans-Baikal Cossacks out hunting him along with a few police officers who were going door-to-door. The heavy-handed tactics were bringing out the people, despite the foul weather and gathering darkness. At least one revolutionary had gathered a small crowd, shouting from the shelter of an awning. Baxter doubted the rabble rouser would get up much steam — he didn't have quite the same fire as the likes of Konstantin or Kirill, and the weather worked against him. The young, earnest man did provide a distraction for Baxter's own work this night, though.

He moved through the narrow alleys, dashing across wider streets when he had to. There was no trying to brazen it out — he was obviously armed, and as the last few hours had demonstrated he rarely succeeded in any attempt at bluffing. Night was also starting to fall, and the streetlighting here was patchy to non-existent, which worked to his advantage.

He had a rough idea where he was going now. The maze of streets threatened to confuse him, but he figured that if he kept going downhill and towards the gathering darkness to the east, he'd come to the dockside eventually and would be able to work his way back from there to the collection of small shipwrights that was his target.

Even when he got there, of course, he still had the problem of what he was going to do. He knew Bilyk and Arbuthnott would not have left their work unguarded. He didn't know how many of the local Okhrana were under Bilyk's command or what other resources he had to call on. Baxter was one man, with a rifle and a pistol he wasn't overly skilled with, against that unknown force. There also seemed to be a lot more Cossacks around now — he guessed the troops Zubov was commanding had sent out for reinforcements as the area became more restive.

A slow smile crept over his face as he finally reached the harbour. Night had truly come now, the rain driving down hard. Being closer to the sea made him happier — for one thing, a man of his parts could always find a boat to get himself out of immediate danger. He smiled, though, because he'd worked out how he was going to tackle the problems facing him.

He stuck to the slight shelter of the buildings along the front. By chance, he'd reached the dockside not far from Oleh's slightly dingy pub.

He worked his way along the waterfront, eyes and ears alert, straining to discern shapes in the flickering shadows, sounds of movement amongst the lap of the waves and the hiss of the rain.

It seemed Oleh had been right about one thing. Now it was dark, Baxter could see light shining around the closed shutters of only one of the shipwrights. It was a slightly larger shed than the others, which made him wonder what the hell they'd been getting up to in there. He watched for a few minutes, and didn't see anyone on patrol outside.

Baxter resisted the temptation to think this was going to be easier than he'd first imagined. He'd been overconfident before, and it had got him captured. He kept low as he moved forward cautiously, the polished wooden stock of the rifle a comforting weight in his hands. First thing was to work out an escape route. There were plenty of boats tied up along here, mostly fishing smacks. He needed something that he could manage by himself, though, or possibly with the assistance of Tommy. Something that could get them away from here, even if that meant just along the coast to a neighbouring country.

His search was cut short by the sound of raised voices from inside the shed. He'd just been examining one of the smaller fishing vessels which might do the trick, and froze on the spot, worried that he'd somehow been spotted.

"Get yer 'ands off 'er!" he heard quite clearly. A second later there was a shrill scream that could only have been Mashka.

"Well, bollocks," he said, hauling himself back up onto the dockside. It seemed like there was no more time for planning, and as usual Tommy had found a way to torpedo even the rough plan he'd tried to come up with.

Baxter dashed across the cobbled street that ran along the dock. Closer to the shipwright, he could smell oil and the acrid tang of coal dust — not a scent he would forget in a hurry, after months cooped up on a Russian cruiser where every spare space was filled with sacks of coal or just loose mounds of the hateful stuff.

He found a gap between the wooden boards of the shed, just enough for him to see a sliver of the interior space. It was immediately obvious that it was empty of any vessel under construction. He cursed under his breath — it seemed it was too late for him to interfere with the plan.

He had more immediate concerns, though. There was another burst of shouting, this time incoherent, and then the thud of something heavy hitting flesh. A second later he saw one of Bilyk's henchmen — the one he thought of as Ratface who was actually called Pavel, the dangerous one, rather than the big thug Mieszko. He was dragging Mashka into the centre of the space by her hair. Without her shawl and in this moment of absolute vulnerability, it was clear just how young she was. Realistically, barely older than Tommy.

As Baxter watched as Ratface, with a look of savage glee, forced her onto her knees and pulled an automatic pistol from inside his coat, checking the action.

Baxter didn't stop to think; he didn't worry about whatever came next. He was round to the front of the shed in a flash, desperately searching for a way in. A door presented itself and he booted it open. "Hey!" he roared, bringing the rifle's stock up to his shoulder.

Ratface had been in the process of pressing his pistol's muzzle to Mashka's forehead. He was clearly taking his time, savouring her terror as she realised she was about to die, enjoying the look in her eyes. The vicious little man turned as Baxter burst in, the slam of the door being forced open startling everyone.

The room froze for a moment in that tableau. Baxter took it all in with a glance — a couple of men he vaguely recognised, one of them with an arm around Tommy's neck. Ratface, a stunned expression on his face as he lifted the pistol away from Mashka's head, opening his mouth to speak.

Baxter pulled the trigger as soon as the pistol was aimed away from Mashka's brain. The sound of the shot was stunning in the confined space, and at that range even Baxter couldn't miss. The heavy bullet took Ratface in the chest and smashed him from his feet, even as the brass-bound butt slammed Baxter's shoulder.

The Okhrana man didn't die instantly, but writhed and thrashed on the stone floor, calling out in a wet voice for his mother, for his God, for Mieszko. Baxter, feeling calmer than he had any right to, worked the smooth oiled action of the rifle as he looked with cold contempt at the two other policemen in the room. The tinkle of the spent cartridge case hitting the floor and bouncing was startlingly loud.

"Anyone else?" he asked, his voice cold. The two men glanced at each other, then the one holding Tommy let him go as they gave Baxter wan smiles and backed away, making placating gestures with their hands.

In the distance, he heard a bugle and that could only mean one thing. Nearer, he could hear the thunder of running feet inside the shed. "See to Mashka," Baxter said, voice calm and controlled, as Tommy started to head towards him. He swivelled as an internal door was flung open and Mieszko burst through.

Baxter brought the rifle back into his shoulder. The big man — the torturer, Baxter reminded himself — wasn't carrying a weapon, though, and his arm was still in a cast. He stared from Ratface, who had subsided onto the floor but still breathed wheezily, to Baxter and back again. His face broke down into a profound grief.

"Tommy, get Mashka!" Baxter barked again. If Bilyk's two closest minions were here, then it was likely their chief was also in the vicinity, and Baxter had no way of knowing how many others he had with him. "We have to go!"

The tone of command in his voice got through to the scared lad. Tommy put his arm around Mashka and helped her to her feet. She was crying and shaking, but seemed far more collected than a lot of young people would be in the circumstances.

Mieszko had walked numbly to his compatriot, eyes fixed on him. He knelt and held one of his hands, saying something to him in that dialect Baxter couldn't understand. Tears streaked down his face.

Baxter kept the rifle on him. After a moment, though, he took his finger off the trigger and lowered the weapon slightly.

Mieszko stared up at him as Ratface breathed a last, rattling breath and went still. He spat furious words at Baxter, and although he couldn't understand them, the meaning was clear. "I've got no quarrel with you," he said, in the hopes that Bilyk had been lying or wrong about how much Russian Mieszko understood. "But if I see you again, I'll kill you. And tell Bilyk he's done."

Tommy had Mashka at the door now and Baxter stepped back towards him, not wanting to turn his back on Mieszko.

He didn't seem inclined to come after them, instead returning his tearful attention to the dead man. There were other people coming, though, and he could hear hooves now.

"Across the docks and find a boat" he snapped to Tommy, following him out into the rainy night. Another Okhrana man had emerged at the far end of the building. Baxter fired again, conscious that he didn't even know how many rounds were in the rifle. The muzzle flash was dazzling in the darkness, but while the shot didn't hit it was enough to send the secret policeman diving for cover.

Tommy and Mashka had made it across the short section of open ground and were hurrying down a set of slimy steps towards a boat. A few hundred feet away, he could make out a clutch of Cossacks trotting in the direction of the gunfire, which is exactly what he wanted. He fired another shot into the air, just to make sure they knew exactly where the altercation was happening.

He felt a surge of satisfaction as they kicked their horses into a canter and headed in his direction. The triumph he felt turned to alarm as someone fired at him, the round cracking past his head, and he ducked and followed the two young folk down the steps.

To his dismay, he saw that they had found pretty much the only rowing boat in the vicinity.

"What the bloody hell do you think you're doing?" Baxter roared. "We need a bigger boat to get away from Odessa."

It was only when Mashka turned fiery eyes on him that he realised he'd shouted in Russian. "We are not getting away from Odessa!" she said coldly, and he realised she had Ratface's pistol in her hands. It wasn't aimed at him, at least, though he found himself wandering if she'd actually shoot him. Her eyes said she would.

"Ah thought we were goin' back to the ship," Tommy protested, sounding hurt rather than scared.

"Well, no time to argue about it now," Baxter said. The Cossacks were getting close and the Okhrana were plucking up their courage. The little boat was tied by a painter to a larger fishing boat, and he was briefly tempted to transfer the two of them bodily if he had to. Instead, he untied the painter and with a great heave against the fishing boat's hull, he pushed them out into the water. "We will have words about this later, though."

"Aye, I'm sure we will," Tommy said truculently.

Mashka was staring at the two of them. "I do not understand what you are saying, but I know you are both quite mad." She was fumbling with the oars, having obviously decided that someone had to get them away from the dockside. She was still shaking, though, and Baxter just managed to get them away from her before she managed to drop one overboard.

He settled onto the strut that ran across the boat between the two oars, determined to scull them out of there. Then he turned on the bench, facing away from the direction of travel. "Tommy, lad, take the helm," he said, keeping his voice gentle. "And steer us back to the *Potemkin*."

There was a rattle of gunfire behind them, causing all of them to duck down in the boat, but if it was directed at them, it went wide enough that they didn't hear the bullets hit the water.

"Hope the bastards are shooting at each other," Tommy muttered. "Begging your pardon, Mr B," he added almost automatically.

Baxter just grinned at him as he set to and started the long row back to the battleship — the one thing he'd genuinely hoped never to see again.

CHAPTER 17

Baxter was exhausted, wet through, and various parts of his body hurt like hell. He was pretty sure now that he hadn't broken a knuckle on the Cossack's skull, but all of them on his right hand were swelling up.

There was no point complaining about it to this pair of errant children, though, and even less in feeling sorry for himself. "Are you both unhurt?" he asked instead, once he'd settled into a steady stroke back out across the harbour.

"Bit rattled, Mr B, but nay bad," Tommy said, his natural good humour bouncing back. Mashka just nodded, dark eyes in her pale face staring at him. Her wet hair was plastered to her skull, and she looked miserable.

"Why don't you see if you can find a tarpaulin or something to keep you both out of the rain," Baxter suggested. "Try not to fall in, or upset the boat," he added as Tommy got up. The lad scowled at him, obviously about to protest that more than half a year afloat had made him pretty comfortable around boats. Baxter's grin defused any incipient temper and he quickly unearthed a blanket into which both he and Mashka could fit.

Baxter watched them both as he settled into the rhythm — lean forward, dip the oars in, then lean back as he drew them through the water; raise them and lean forward. It had been a while since he'd rowed a boat, but it came back naturally enough. Unlike a lot of his fellow officers, he hadn't learned to row by fooling around in pleasure boats or on the river at Oxford or Cambridge. He vividly remembered his father's gnarled first mate who had taught him so much about the sea, including this particular skill.

"What were you thinking?" he asked Tommy in English. "You must have known how dangerous that would be."

"Aye, I did," Tommy replied from under the blanket. He had the good grace to look embarrassed, as well as slightly awkward about being huddled against a young woman. "But like you said, it was important and you were busy. I jus' thought we could go and see if I was right, but then we saw they were launching the boat, and we were trying to work out what to do when they caught us…"

Tommy's voice trailed off. The realisation of how close they'd come to a pretty ignominious death was obviously only just hitting him. Baxter had seen it before, during Tsushima and after the couple of other skirmishes he'd been involved with as a younger man. Sometimes, people only got scared after the fact.

He realised there was no point chastising the boy further — almost getting murdered by Okhrana officers was probably enough of a punishment, and the fact the pair were obviously still shaken served to dampen his own anger. And, he had to admit, they'd managed more than he had over the course of the day — aside from saving their lives, right at the end of it.

He sighed and switched into Russian for Mashka's benefit. "Well, you'd best tell me what you saw."

After his brief glimpse inside the shipwright, he already had a reasonable idea of the size of the vessel being worked on there. At least fifty or sixty feet long, probably more. It probably wasn't anything too dangerous or impressive, given the amount of time they would have had to work on it. Chances were it was a refit of something else, he reasoned.

"It looked a bit like the little ship with the *Potemkin*," Mashka said after a little while. "Maybe slightly smaller."

Baxter blinked at her in surprise. "The *Vekha*? The supply ship?" That was nonsense, of course; nothing of her size could have been built in that shed.

Mashka shook her head impatiently. "No, the other one. The toy ship, that takes messages around."

"You mean the *Ismhail*? The torpedo boat?"

She made an expressive gesture with her hands, one of which clutched a Luger self-loading pistol. The last time Baxter had seen the weapon, it had been in Ratface's hand. He marvelled at her presence of mind to have retrieved it, even when she'd clearly been scared to death. "Ship? Boat? What does someone of the proletariat know of such things? It looked very much like this torpedo boat of yours."

Baxter thought about that as he continued to pull back out over the water. It was approaching being cold now, with the wind and the rain, and the waters were getting choppy; their little boat was shipping water fairly frequently and soon he would have to ask Mashka to bail it out. He contemplated turning back and landing somewhere on the south of the harbour — not only was this little toy boat not able to take them away from Odessa, it seemed it wouldn't even carry them as far as the revolutionary squadron.

He rested on the oars briefly, breathing hard. At least the exercise was keeping him warm, and doing away with some of the effects of land-based living. He had to give it to the Russian authorities: they had fed him well — at least when he'd been under Koenig's guard.

He looked back to shore, then twisted around to find the little cluster of lights that showed him where the battleships were lying. They were closer than he'd thought, and despite the wind and current Tommy had managed to keep them more or less on course. He and Mashka had the tiller handle wedged between them and were sharing the effort, Baxter realised.

"I think one of the battleships is moving," Tommy said suddenly, sitting up straighter and letting the blanket fall from his shoulders. Mashka tutted and pulled more of the fabric around her.

"It's probably just the *Ismail* on its patrol," Baxter said, craning round again. The rogue sailors always kept the torpedo boat sailing a circuit around the rest of the squadron at night, for fear of a sneak attack. A squall of rain blocked his view for a second, and he started rowing out to sea again, keeping his muscles moving so they didn't cramp up.

"I know the difference between a battleship and a torpedo boat, Mr B," Tommy protested. "Even if the lassie doesn't. Besides, that's her over there."

Tommy pointed off to port, where a dim, low shape could just about be made out. Baxter happened to have been looking for starboard at the time, the sound of an engine attracting his attention. He felt a crawling sensation between his shoulder blades, the same sixth sense that had warned him of the presence of Japanese torpedo boats in the long night after the first day at Tsushima. "No, I'm pretty sure that's the *Ismail*," he said, gesturing in the direction of a second torpedo boat, slightly further away.

Baxter came to the horrible conclusion that he knew what Bilyk and Arbuthnott were about, and why they had built and launched their own torpedo boat. Tommy obviously reached the same conclusion. "We have to stop 'em!" he almost squeaked.

"What can we bloody do?" Baxter growled. "One man, one boy and a girl against a torpedo boat with … I don't know how many aboard. Even if we could catch up to..." He frowned, breaking off as another noise joined the beat of small, light steam engines on either side. Much bigger engines, accompanied by the rushing noise of a large hull picking up speed through the water. "I think you're right that the squadron is moving," Baxter said, craning round so far his neck hurt as he peered into the darkness.

Almost without warning, the blunt prow of the *St. George* loomed out of the darkness, heading at a tearing pace towards the inner harbour. "The attack has begun!" Mashka cried out, having obviously regained a lot of the fire that the near miss with death had knocked out of her.

Baxter was too busy to reply. "Hard to port!" he shouted at Tommy as he started rowing for all he was worth. They were only a few hundred yards ahead of the big beast as she ploughed onwards, and while she wasn't coming directly at them, they were definitely closer than he was comfortable with. She was throwing up quite a bow wave that could quite easily upend them, and her screws would smash the boat to matchwood if they got caught up in them.

He felt their boat start to rise, and his heart rose into his throat with it. All he could do was keep rowing, sweat standing out on his brow and his muscles burning. The wave didn't turn them over, though, and then they were being carried down the side of the ship into her wake, bobbing madly. "Lunatics!" Tommy yelled, while Mashka quietly threw up into the bottom of the boat.

Baxter fought to keep them stable and moving in the cut up water, pulling hard at a right angle to the course the battleship had taken. Only when they were well clear did he slow his strokes, staring into the darkness as he tried to pick out the *St. George*'s course. "I don't think it is the attack," he said, voice dark. "If they were going to shell the city they would want to be further away, and if they were landing sailors they'd go it by boat."

"Then what's going on?" Tommy demanded.

"Wish I knew, lad, wish I knew." Baxter had a distinct feeling that he did know, that Dr Golenko and the *St. George*'s petty officers had pulled off whatever it was they'd been planning. It had gone from his mind entirely when he'd seen that Tommy had disappeared off on a self-appointed mission, and he still wasn't sure if he'd told the mutineers about it anyway.

"They're going the wrong way to escape," the lad pointed out now.

Baxter nodded, still plying the oars gently. Looking over his shoulder, he could still make out the lone, low shape of the mysterious torpedo boat. It was idling, obviously as confused as they were about what had just happened.

If it stayed still just a little bit longer, and if the crew were as inattentive as lookouts at night usually were…

He thought about trying to signal the torpedo boat under the revolutionaries' command, but it appeared to be racing in pursuit of the rogue battleship. That meant it was up to them.

Just for a second, he considered rowing back to the city, or making a madcap dash for somewhere else. He was tired, though, bone tired, and that more than anything else decided him. More than the thought of finally clapping a stopper over Arbuthnott's antics, of doing his duty to king and country by putting a stop to this nefarious plot that could draw the two countries into war. He just couldn't be bothered to row much further.

They were close enough now that he could make out figures standing just abaft the little vessel's single funnel. He could quite clearly see the turtleback-style bow that would house at least one torpedo tube. The boat looked to be very similar to the *Ismail*, though perhaps slightly smaller.

He held his finger up to his lips, then rowed as gently as he could towards the vessel. The handful of men on deck were all clearly staring after the ship and conferring amongst themselves. For some reason, Baxter realised, a lot of them were in naval officer's uniforms. He would expect to see one or two junior officers on a vessel like that, and the rest of the men would be ordinary sailors.

He snorted. Was that really what Bilyk and the rest of the Okhrana thought of the navy, that it was crewed by nothing but aristos? Or was there something else going on here?

Someone aboard gave an order. There was more than the usual expected amount of confusion, during which time Baxter managed to creep closer, before the order was then clearly relayed to the engine room.

Baxter stretched out at that point, the noise of the steam engines being re-engaged and masking the creek of the oars.

"Steer us for the bows," Baxter ordered Tommy, as the torpedo boat started moving, slowly at first.

"We'll never make it!" Tommy protested.

"I know — now do as you're told!"

He pulled the oars as hard as he could, sending the little rowing boat surging forward. It was sluggish with the amount of water — not to mention vomit — now in the bottom of it. The torpedo boat was sliding past them, barely a few yards away, and yet somehow the crew still hadn't seen them.

Tommy was about to point out that they'd fallen well short of the bows, but Baxter had already abandoned the oars and stepped to the front of the boat, gathering up its mooring line as he relied on the forward momentum to bring him into range. For a horrible second he thought the excess water they were carrying was going to slow the boat enough that they would miss. He gathered himself, knowing he had no other option, and launched himself forward.

He didn't quite manage to make the slippery deck of the torpedo boat, crashing into the side hard enough to knock the wind out of him. He caught a hold of a stanchion and managed to drag himself aboard, fumbling the line after him.

"I have got to stop boarding ships," he gasped to himself, before rolling onto his front. From this vantage he could see the rowing boat was dangerously low in the water. He'd been so focused on the task of rowing, and so fatigued from his exertions, that he hadn't noticed it.

He dragged the bobbing rowing boat closer, hand over hand, wondering how long it would be before the incompetents crewing this vessel realised they were being boarded. Tommy and Mashka were both huddled in the bows and he was able to reach down and, with some effort, bring both of them aboard.

"Told you we'd miss the bows," Tommy said.

Baxter grunted as he pulled himself up into a crouch. "I never planned to hit them."

They'd managed to come aboard at the stern, mercifully ahead of the single screw.

"Stay — and I cannot emphasise enough how serious I am when I say this — here," Baxter said.

"You cannae storm a boat with just yersel'," Tommy protested.

"Surely you've had enough excitement for one day?" Baxter pointed out. He briefly considered pressing the point, but it occurred to him they'd probably find a way to cause trouble. "Alright, just stay back — and don't shoot anyone with that thing, Mashka."

The three of them crept forward along the cluttered, narrow deck, Baxter in front with a revolver in hand. He'd left the rifle in the boat, now bobbing around somewhere behind them, but he didn't have any more ammunition for it anyway.

There was definitely something peculiar going on here. He knew these sorts of vessels only carried small crews — little more than twenty men — but he could only see a handful clustered forward. The boat was a turtleback design, the bows entirely enclosed as far back as the small conning tower with a steep tumblehome along the rest of the hundred-odd feet of the hull. They were optimised for the waters of the Black Sea and wouldn't be great on the wider ocean, but the bows would provide a modicum of protection for the torpedo tubes mounted there.

Even with a handful of men below in the engine room and probably one or two more in the armoured enclosure forward of the funnel, the crew seemed to be understrength. Not only that, but Baxter's previous impression of men in officer's uniforms was confirmed. And the devil of it was, he was increasingly convinced these were genuine naval personnel, not people masquerading as part of some elaborate plot.

He would have to act soon, he knew. They were closing in on the *Potemkin*, which was still anchored. He contemplated trying to get belowdecks, into the cramped confines of the little vessel to do something about the engines. Even if the torpedo tubes weren't enclosed, he hadn't had much to do with the still relatively new-fangled weapons, and didn't want to risk blowing them all sky-high by interfering with them.

There wasn't anything else for it. "When I step out, start making some noise back here," he said to Tommy and Mashka. "Don't be seen, but make them think there's a boarding party back here."

He didn't wait for any sort of confirmation, and in truth he didn't expect them to achieve much. Mostly he wanted them to stay where they were but feel like they had something to do so they didn't go looking for trouble. He stepped forward, just as the helmsman set a course to aim the bows of the boat towards the *Potemkin*, still a mile or so away. Baxter kept his footing easily, the movement of the vessel on the choppy seas feeling far more natural to him than the steady, unyielding nature of the land.

The clutch of officers and petty officers were clustered around the conning tower and the hatch into the covered bows, which hung open. One of the junior officers was holding up a lantern and Baxter saw a pair of boots protruding from the hatch as he stepped forward into the pool of light.

"It's definitely been sabotaged," the man in amongst the torpedo tubes was saying, voice muffled. "We were right not to trust the enlisted men. I think it is a simple fix, though I will remind you again that I am a gunnery officer."

Baxter smiled slightly. Man after his own heart. He coughed politely and thumbed back the Nagant's hammer. "Gentlemen," he said in French, keeping his tone calm and reasonable. He hadn't even thought about what he would say, as he expected the situation to degenerate into a fight pretty quickly. He couldn't help but grin when it came to him. "You may now all consider yourselves prisoners of the revolution, and this vessel confiscated."

Behind him, Mashka actually laughed out loud, which wasn't quite the effect he'd been looking for as her laughter was clearly that of a woman. It seemed to disturb the cluster of men more as they backed away from this strange apparition that had come out of the night. Most of them were armed with revolvers, but none of them were drawn and everyone was keeping their hands well away from them.

"Could somebody pass me a spanner?" the voice from inside the torpedo compartment demanded. A hand flapped slightly comically, and then its owner backed out of the tight space when the tool was not forthcoming.

"What the devil do you..." he demanded as he straightened up, glaring around at his colleagues. His eyes widened when he caught sight of Baxter. "Baxter? What in God's name are you doing here?"

Baxter gave him a feral grin. This day probably couldn't get any more surreal. "Getting into politics, Yuriy Makarovich," he greeted Lieutenant Koenig. "I trust I won't have any trouble with you?"

Back towards the inner harbour, they heard a sudden crashing noise, thunderous even at this distance. It seemed to go on for a while. Baxter kept his attention focused on the Russian officers, all of whom were now looking in the direction of the tearing racket. Only Koenig remained looking at Baxter, a look of deep disappointment on his face.

"I think we both know what that was," Baxter said.

Koenig nodded glumly. "The *St. George* running aground, at full speed."

CHAPTER 18

Baxter had expected a bit more resistance from the officers, but his sudden appearance as if from nowhere and the debacle with the *St. George* seemed to have taken the wind from them.

The torpedo boat — named *Zataka* — was a *Yalta* class, and while it would normally have warranted a crew of eighteen it was running with ten. Of the five ordinary sailors aboard, three had immediately declared their undying loyalty to the revolution and the other two had retired to their tiny, cramped quarters and made it very clear they wanted nothing to do with the events that would follow.

"What were you even trying to achieve?" Baxter asked Koenig quietly. The other officers had been herded below by the three revolutionary sailors and Mashka. Baxter had taken the wheel personally and put them back on a heading for the rogue battleship but at a less breakneck speed. He wanted time to think, and time to confer with his friend and, it seemed, prisoner; not startling the crew of the *Potemkin* would also be a good idea.

Koenig shrugged uncomfortably. "A mad scheme, I admit. After the…" He seemed to be struggling for words to describe what had passed between the *Potemkin* and the Black Sea Fleet the day before.

"After the engagement," Baxter prompted.

"Yes, that is as good a word as any. After that, it became clear that another attempt would be futile. Not even Captain Kolands could guarantee the *Twelve Apostles'* crew would not rise again, having already prevented him sending the *Potemkin* to the bottom."

"And themselves with it, most likely," Baxter pointed out. "You can't really blame them."

If he'd been talking to another officer, he knew, he would get a lecture on the honour of dying for their father the Tsar and for God. Koenig had seen too much, though, and was a realist. He would be relatively rare amongst the officers of the Black Sea Fleet, having seen recent action.

Koenig nodded. "Oh, indeed. It was generally felt that not even the torpedo boats could be managed, the rot of revolution had set in so deeply. The squadron has therefore returned to Sevastopol, but some officers volunteered to take a boat in and try to sink at least one of the rebellious vessels."

Baxter kept his peace, both about the workability of the plan and Koenig's dismissive tone when he spoke of the mutineers. "Brave move," was all he said.

"Oh, utterly absurd!" Koenig actually laughed. "An old boat, torpedoes that may or may not have worked, an untrustworthy crew. A true recipe for disaster. I only volunteered as I hoped my experience fighting off torpedo boats might help and increase the chances of survival, if not success."

That was reasonable. Koenig had commanded one of the two steam pinnaces the *Yaroslavich* had used to defend herself against torpedo boats during the night action at Tsushima, and he'd done it well. Better than Baxter, even, as he'd managed to disrupt all the attacks that came from his sector. One torpedo boat had got past Baxter, as the morning broke, and crippled the old cruiser.

"I must confess, I still expected to die for the Tsar," the lieutenant went on phlegmatically. "Though I thought we would be blown out of the water, rather than being boarded by, well…" His voice trailed off. "I suppose we may still die," he said. "I understand that the mutineers are shooting all the 'dragons' who fall into their hands."

Baxter snorted. The battleship's lights were becoming clearer ahead, and soon he would have to convince her jumpy crew that this wasn't an attack. "I gather they shot one or two during and after the mutiny," he said, trying to sound reassuring. "Everyone else has been put ashore. And they certainly won't shoot any of you if I have anything to say about it."

Koenig cast him a curious look. "Why have you even joined them? And did I really see young Tomas'ka helping put my colleagues below decks?"

Baxter scratched his chin. "It's ... complicated. Would you believe I only stuck around here because I thought you'd been posted to the *Potemkin* and might require assistance?"

Koenig laughed again. "That I can believe, because you are one of the most ill-fated men I know," he said. "I had indeed received orders to join the *Potemkin*, but travel delays meant I only arrived after she had sailed for gunnery practice. I was going to remain in Sevastopol until her return, but got seconded to the *Sinop* when, well... But the last I saw of you, you were being hauled away by the police."

"I actually managed to escape during the riots in Odessa," Baxter said. He was amazed at how companionable it felt, standing talking with Koenig in much the same way as they'd occasionally whiled away some hours on the *Yaroslavich*, and more so during the train journey from Vladivostok. "And I should bloody well have kept going, as well."

"And Tomas'ka?"

That was too complicated to get into right now. "You know what he's like — he makes his own arrangements, even though I did my best to make sure he got home."

Koenig nodded judiciously. They were close to the battleship now, and unless discipline had broken down entirely they should be challenged by a lookout soon. "I should go below and see to my comrades. Reassure them that we are probably not headed straight for a firing squad."

"Probably wise." It would be better if the mutineers didn't see someone in an officer's uniform on deck.

Koenig started to go aft from the little conning tower towards the hatch that would take him down into the cramped interior. "I do not think you stayed around only because you were worried about me, you know," he said, voice oddly reflective. "I think you cannot help but involve yourself when you see something happening. After all, you could have gone ashore at any point during the last stages of our journey — you know the captain would have done as you asked."

Koenig was of course talking about Juneau, who had latterly commanded the *Yaroslavich*, rather than Gorchakov, who had been relieved of command after he'd lost his grip on reality. Baxter didn't want to think about that right now — he had bigger issues to worry about.

"Best be getting yourself below," was all he said, before filling his lungs to hail the battleship. "*Potemkin* ahoy! Don't shoot at us, we're friendly!"

Baxter found the ship in a certain amount of disarray when he got back aboard. Ivan Beshoff met him at the top of the gangway, a troubled expression on his face that only lightened slightly when Baxter greeted him.

"Marcus, I did not expect to see you again," Ivan said, gripping his hand. "I got the distinct impression that you had no intention of returning to us."

"That obvious, am I?" Baxter asked with a grin, returning the firmness of the handshake. "And yet, somehow, here I am."

"With a captured torpedo boat, no less. Unless you went shopping while you were ashore?"

"Long story," he said, reflecting that if he'd been a bit quicker or hadn't been briefly captured by Zubov, he might actually have been able to take the torpedo boat that Bilyk had somehow managed to acquire or refit. From what Tommy had said, they'd launched it only a short while before he'd finally made it to the area.

More likely, Baxter thought, he'd have found a way to burn it. He really shouldn't have been able to take the *Zataka*, let alone bring her alongside. "Speaking of which, you should send a party down to secure the vessel. There are a number of officers aboard, and they are *not* to be harmed."

Ivan frowned, rubbing his forehead. "Tempers are high right now," he said. "We were betrayed by Dr Golenko and the petty officers of the *St. George*. Some of our brothers are despairing and demanding we sail for Sevastopol, and others are ready to burn everything down."

Baxter put one hand on Ivan Beshoff's shoulder. He was a much bigger, stronger man, and he knew it. He applied just the smallest amount of pressure, enough to make a point. "Then I suggest you take charge of the party personally and take only steady men." Baxter hadn't wanted to take charge like that. This really was none of his concern, although he did feel some remorse for not having reported what he'd overhead Golenko discussing before. That was in the past, now, and he finally had a goal. A target.

Ivan winced slightly, then nodded with a placating smile. "I'll see to it immediately. I think we are leaving this place anyway, soon."

Baxter didn't quite know what he was going to do next, but something told him he needed to be aboard the *Potemkin* rather than seeing to the prisoners on the torpedo boat. He trusted Ivan Beshoff, though he didn't know why. The man had an honest face, he supposed. He did make sure that Tommy and Mashka came aboard. "You two stick close to me," Baxter ordered, and for once the boy seemed inclined to do as he was told.

They both looked exhausted, Baxter realised. As tired as he was, if not more so. They'd both seen things no one their age should have seen, and experienced things no one should ever have to go through. Mashka seemed to be holding up remarkably well, given that she'd been a trigger pull away from being shot in the head scant hours earlier, but she only spoke occasionally and then in very short sentences.

Baxter, with the two of them in tow, met Kovalenko on the upper deck. He could hear men elsewhere shouting about going to Romania — indeed, the country's name was being chanted. The young officer was as despondent as Baxter had ever seen a person, though that shouldn't have surprised him. Yesterday, they had been riding high on the success of bringing another ship on board, and had survived what should have been a suicidal charge against overwhelming odds.

Today, the ship that had given them so much hope had deserted them and, it seemed, ran itself aground. "Your torpedo boat is a consolation, but a scant one," Kovalenko said, voice low. "I take it you had a successful foray ashore, then?"

Baxter glowered at the fellow. "The capture was an accident," he said shortly. "A happy one, as it turned out, as we managed to intercept it as it was getting lined up to put a couple of torpedoes into you."

"Well, I was finding it hard to imagine that this day could have been any worse," Kovalenko said, brightening only slightly. "And this plot that concerns you?"

Baxter contemplated not saying anything further, as he didn't want to load any more worries onto the young, rebellious officer. Out of all of them, perhaps, he had the most reason to feel despondent. Each and every one of the mutineers aboard, certainly those who were committed and had made themselves known to the authorities, had gambled with their lives. As the revolution seemed to be in the process of unravelling, they looked to be losing that wager. As an officer, Kovalenko had thrown away far more than the others, for a principle that was now unlikely to be realised.

Well, perhaps he needed something else to think about. "I — we — weren't able to stop them, but I've got a better idea of what they're up to. I thought the torpedo boat we grabbed on the way back to the *Potemkin* was theirs, but it turns out your Vice-Admiral Krieger had developed a backbone — or some of his officers had."

Kovalenko's eyebrows went up. "Really? Well, I don't think that should be such a surprise. There are many good officers in the navy — it is a shame so many of them are wasted. What do you intend to do now?"

Baxter was feeling the day's exertions. "First I'm going to see the officers from aboard the torpedo boat put ashore, as has been done with the other ships."

"Unless any of them want to join us," Kovalenko said, with a faint smile that acknowledged the likelihood was low given the current state of the revolution. Even if any of them were inclined, a smart revolutionary wouldn't back an uprising that was looking more and more likely to fail.

Baxter acknowledged that with a nod. "Then I'm going to eat, and have a glass or two of vodka, and come up with a plan."

They gathered, later, in the stateroom where they'd spent the previous night. Kovalenko hadn't said who it had belonged to and Baxter hadn't asked, but he guessed it must have been a senior officer. He was surprised that Kovalenko or one of the other mutineers hadn't taken it over. The former officer was apparently content with his own cabin, and the mutineers seemed to be living by the Social Democrat principles they kept talking about. The wardroom and the admiral's stateroom — the largest private spaces aboard — had been taken over for the sailors' committee and other revolutionary business, but aside from that they'd stuck to their usual quarters.

Mashka and Tommy had both crashed out, the girl in the sleeping cabin and Tommy stretched out under a blanket on a chaise longue, so far out of it that even the quiet conversation didn't disturb him.

"So it's become pretty clear that Bilyk and Arbuthnott have either taken over a torpedo boat that was being built or refitted in Odessa," Baxter said, "or they've mocked one up well enough to convince someone who's seen the real thing before."

"Most of our shipbuilding for the Black Sea is at Nikolayev," Koenig put in. "Though they may have contracted a firm in Odessa for the hull, I suppose."

Kovalenko directed a cool glance at the newcomer. Despite his enthusiasm for other officers joining the mutiny — the revolution, as he clearly liked to think of it — he seemed suspicious of Koenig. Part of it was the natural paranoia that would come from any movement like this, but mostly it was because Koenig had made it very clear that he had no interest in the revolutionary cause. The other officers from the *Zataka* had already been put ashore, without even the ritual stripping of their rank insignia and swords — the mutineers had no time for such things now, and Baxter wasn't sure if the entire sailors' committee even knew they had added another vessel to their squadron, even as they lost one.

"This is true," Kovalenko admitted grudgingly. "You did your research after your triumphs at Tsushima, it seems."

Koenig shot him an angry look. "There was no triumph at Tsushima," he said, barely restraining his temper. "We were sent to slaughter, by men like this Bilyk."

He would have to get control of that, Baxter thought, if he was going to last in his chosen service. While a clique of Baxter's colleagues had worked to get him cashiered from the Royal Navy, he had finally had to admit that he'd made it easy for them through his often truculent behaviour. Koenig was in danger of making the same mistakes.

"And yet here you are, still serving the Tsar!" Kovalenko shot back.

Baxter cleared his throat before this could escalate into the first duel in the Imperial Russian Navy for ... probably only a few years, realistically. "Even if it's a mock-up, it could still serve their purposes," he said. "Remember, they're not trying to start a war between Britain and Russia — neither of them are that mad."

Bilyk didn't seem to be, anyway. He wasn't so sure about Arbuthnott. The others didn't need to know that, though.

"What are they going to do?" Ivan Beshoff asked. He was the only one of the sailors' committee in the stateroom. Matyushenko and the others were locked in debate only a short distance away from this cabin, deciding where to go next or even whether to surrender. "This still confuses me."

"I sympathise," Baxter said. Despite at least some association with intelligence agents and secret police officials in the last few months and a bit, the way their minds worked still mystified him. "I'm not entirely sure, and I don't think they even know. I suspect they'll either launch an attack against vessels in the Black Sea or at least make it look like they are. I suspect they'll sail under false colours, either British or Japanese. Either way, they'll stir up trouble."

"No one would believe British or Japanese torpedo boats could be here!" Ivan protested. "It is preposterous."

Koenig sounded almost apologetic when he spoke. "Enough people still think Japanese boats attacked us in the North Sea," he pointed out. "From what I understand, our local waters have essentially cleared of merchant shipping, though, as no one knows what the madmen in charge of this ship will do next. I cannot imagine our friends will be foolish enough even to fake an attack on our warships."

Baxter nodded. He'd considered whether the whole thing would be staged, that at least some of the commanders of the Imperial Russian Navy would be a part of this. That just didn't seem plausible with their attention focused on the war in the Pacific and unrest in the ranks, though.

"I agree," Kovalenko said. "More likely, they will assume that we will be brought to heel by the might of the Black Sea Fleet in due course and will act once things have settled down."

"Perhaps they will masquerade as revolutionaries?" Ivan suggested. "It would turn foreign feeling against us if people believed we had turned to piracy."

"What international sympathy could there possibly be for a group of rogues and mutineers who killed their own officers?"

Koenig asked with asperity. He obviously wasn't entirely comfortable conferring with Beshoff and Kovalenko.

Baxter rubbed at his forehead. The ache from the blow to his head was coming back, and he was reminded once again why he hated intelligence agents. "Let's not overthink this," he said, before the others couldn disappear down a rabbit hole of theories or start squabbling. "Whatever Bilyk and Arbuthnott's plan is, they're out there. They probably will wait, on the assumption that the *Potemkin* will no longer be a threat one way or the other. But they will act."

"So what will we do about it?" Koenig demanded, his voice still tight with anger.

Baxter realised they were all looking at him, including Tommy, who was peering blearily over the side of the chaise longue, obviously disturbed by the volume of the discussion. He didn't want this responsibility; he didn't want the others to look to him for leadership. He shouldn't even be here.

He looked down at the map spread out on the polished dark wood of the table. "We take the *Zataka* and we hunt them down," he said, voice hard. Here he was indeed, and he was there because of Bilyk and Arbuthnott and the fact they hadn't left him alone. That was what it came down to.

Silence greeted his pronouncement, then Koenig nodded. "I think the sailors who intended to join the mutiny can be persuaded to undertake this," he said. "And I know the boat at least a little."

"Will they follow you, though?" Kovalenko demanded.

"Yuriy Makarovich is no dragon," Baxter said, voice short, to head off another argument. "We will need more sailors. Ivan?"

The mutineer chewed his lip thoughtfully. "I will need to speak to Matyushenko and the rest of the committee," he said at last, as Kovalenko nodded his agreement. "But I think they will see the importance of stopping this diabolical plan. If nothing else, the thought of being able to do away with some secret policemen will appeal to some."

Baxter stretched. He was starting to feel the exertions of the day despite the carafe of vodka that sat half-empty next to the chart. "Well, it seems we're agreed," he said. The battleship's engines were starting to thump again, and he guessed that a decision had been reached amongst the mutiny's leadership. Ivan and Kovalenko looked keen to be away, but Baxter couldn't muster the energy to be interested. "Which is good, as I need to sleep."

"You may wake up in Romania," Ivan said, with an attempt at a smile.

"Well, I've been saying for a while that I'd like to get out of Russia."

And once he was out, he knew, he was never going back.

CHAPTER 19

Baxter didn't wake up in Romania. When he did finally struggle back into wakefulness, the *Potemkin* was on the open sea.

He'd done exactly as he said, the previous night, and gone straight to sleep after their conference had ended. At some point after that, it seemed, the revolutionary flotilla — the *Potemkin*, the supply ship *Vekha* and the recently doubled complement of torpedo boats — had put to sea.

Baxter was surprised it hadn't woken him. Like most sailors, his subconscious had a facility for stirring him when the state of the vessel he was aboard or the weather around her changed. It seemed, though, that he'd remained out for the count well into mid-morning.

As he emerged, bleary-eyed, onto deck he was struck by the complete … normality of the scene that confronted him. Aside from the three vessels travelling in company, the Black Sea seemed to be completely empty. The sun was beating down on them, and the forecastle in particular was crowded with men taking their ease. Someone was playing an accordion, a cheerful peasant song that some of the sailors were singing along to. Looking aft, Baxter could see a pod of dolphins jumping in the battleship's wake, the playful creatures obviously curious about the great metal beast that moved above them.

He rubbed his eyes, a particular fact slowly seeping its way through his fatigue-addled brain. There were only three ships here, and there should by rights have been four. The *Potemkin* was heading south by west at a steady crawl, the mutineers obviously intent on preserving their dwindling supply of coal; a brisk enough breeze was pulling her cloak of black smoke out to leeward. The two torpedo boats were still in company, their oil-fired engines producing less of a smog as they sailed on either side a half mile distant.

"Tomas'ka was worried that your snoring would bring the whole Black Sea Fleet down on us," Koenig commented as he handed Baxter a tin mug of tea.

"I don't snore," he said automatically as he accepted the mug, then remembered Ekaterina's gentle teasing on the subject. Not so gentle, in reality. He noted Koenig's uniform was now devoid of insignia. "Someone catch up to you with a knife?"

The younger man looked nonplussed for a second, then smiled as Baxter gestured to where the epaulettes should be sitting on his shoulders. "I thought it best to divest myself, so as not to stir up ill-feeling. Aleksei and I agreed it's best that I present myself as another officer who has thrown in with the revolution, and things were so confused last night that no one is sure of what happened."

Baxter blinked, trying to work out who Aleksei was. "Ah — Kovalenko? I'm surprised you're already on first-name terms."

Koenig shrugged. "We talked for a while after you retired — when we could hear each other over the snoring. We're not so different, and I find myself not unsympathetic with his views even if I can't tolerate how he has gone about trying to achieve them."

"Well, that's one less thing for me to worry about," Baxter said, after a swallow of hot, smoky tea. It was quite a risk for Koenig, as he could be denounced by any of the mutineers if they were ever caught by the authorities. "Next question — what happened to the *Vekha*?"

"I'm not too sure," Koenig admitted. "Not everyone believes my story, and even if they do I am a newcomer here so they are being tight-lipped. As I understand it, she parted company sometime in the night. I suspect the crew have followed the *St. George*'s lead and sailed for Sevastopol to try to seek clemency."

"I doubt they'll find any," Baxter said, voice dark.

Koenig nodded. "I'm inclined to agree. Vice-Admiral Chukhnin is known to be a fine commander, and a harsh disciplinarian. Even Vice-Admiral Rozhestvensky found him hard to swallow at times."

"And the *Zataka*?"

"A skeleton crew under the command of a petty officer from the sailors' committee. Aleksei and Beshoff are working to persuade the committee to accept your proposal. There are some on it who think the entire conspiracy sounds too far-fetched."

Baxter sipped his tea contemplatively. Here, in the sunshine and cooling breeze with the sleek grey dolphins jumping playfully in the battleship's wake, the plot didn't seem so much far-fetched as utterly lunatic. If Baxter hadn't known the people involved and how attached they were to their ideas of how the world should function, he would have dismissed it himself.

"We may need to stand ready to take matters into our own hands," he said at last. They were conversing in French — unlike many of his brother officers, Koenig did speak Russian, though he was more comfortable in the former language and it allowed them to speak with a certain amount of privacy. "Can I count on you?"

Koenig looked offended. "I am hurt that you feel you have to ask."

Baxter grinned and clapped him on the shoulder. "These are trying times, my friend," he said, then threw the dregs of his tea over the railing. "I'm famished — I'm going to rustle up some breakfast."

Later that day, the *Potemkin* neared land again, sliding past a small, mean-looking island that looked familiar to Baxter from previous voyages through the area. "Snake Island!" he declared. "That means we're in Romanian waters, lads!"

"Zmiinyi Island," Matyushenko corrected him, then raised his voice to address the men who had gathered to watch the island and its odd, stubby little lighthouse slip past them. "A gift from the 'barbarous Turk' to Romania after the last Tsar stole their land."

It was the first time Baxter had seen the mutineers' leader in a couple of days. While he looked haggard and his voice was cracked from overuse, Matyushenko definitely didn't seem beaten yet. He'd spent the day moving amongst the sailors on deck, reassuring them, shoring up their faith in the revolution and the committee that led them. Konstantin and Kirill were still aboard, though they both seemed deeply despondent and kept to themselves.

"I have been told of your escapades last night and your … theory, shall we say … about a rogue torpedo boat on the loose," Matyushenko went on, dropping his voice to a conversational volume.

Baxter eyed the smaller man, trying to determine whether he was being sardonic or whether Kovalenko and Beshoff had managed to make any sort of headway with him. It seemed that while the committee functioned as a true democracy, Matyushenko's opinion carried a lot of weight on the basis of his forceful personality and his status as a member of something called the Tsentralka. The man was giving nothing away, though, and Baxter decided to push him on the subject.

"Perhaps Lieutenant Koenig should be left in charge of the *Zataka*?" he suggested, keeping his tone mild and disinterested. "He knows the vessel…"

Matyushenko cut him off with a bark of laughter. "And he is a believer in this wild tale you have spun! No, no, it will not do. There are some who doubt this strange young man's dedication to the cause. While the sailors who joined us from the *Zataka* tell us that he is a good and humane officer, they have certainly given no indication of ever detecting sympathy for the revolution in him. No, he shall remain aboard, where he can be found and shot if it turns out he remains loyal to the Tsar and has been lying to us."

Baxter linked his hands behind his back to stop himself clenching them into fists. He seemed to be developing a long list of people he had put at risk through his ham-fisted blundering through the situation, including Tommy and now Koenig.

Matyushenko actually stepped away from him very slightly, perhaps detecting something in his expression that spoke to the anger he was trying to suppress. "Well, much to do before we make port," he said, before hurrying away.

Baxter watched him go with a sour expression on his face, then turned and went forward. They were still some distance from the coast of Romania, but the few hours' travel at a sedate pace intended to conserve their fuel supply slipped past until Costanza started to come into view. He saw the old lighthouse and the cathedral spire beyond it, then the low mass of the jutting promontory on which the ancient city was built. It had been many years since he'd been here last — it was, in fact, one of his father's stops on the way to Odessa when he'd worked the Black Sea trade — but like most ports he'd visited, he remembered the salient points about it. It wasn't as good a natural harbour as Odessa, but it was Romania's only port. The Ottomans, who'd ruled the area in living memory, had invested somewhat in the city, if he recalled correctly. After independence in the last century, King Carol I had continued that investment in the infrastructure but had neglected the navy in favour of land forces. And that was the extent of Baxter's knowledge about the city or indeed the country.

The port was lost to view as the battleship made her way towards the harbour, as a thick bank of fog rolled in seemingly out of nowhere. For a short while the *Potemkin* and her escorting torpedo boat were sailing through a white blanket, the temperature dropping off. Baxter put both hands on the railing and squeezed, remembering the foggy conditions on the first day of Tsushima. When the wind cleared the fog bank, though, the Japanese battle line was not there. Just the harbour, which the battleship nosed her way towards, and an old protected cruiser that still had her auxiliary sailing rig and was armed with a handful of small guns.

No threat to the modern behemoth, but the mutineers were at pains to appear as non-threatening and friendly as possible. The gunners of the starboard 6-inch guns were going to their weapons, but the ship was not closing up to battle stations. As the boat entered the harbour, the guns boomed out, long tongues of flame and smoke but nothing else as they delivered the twenty-one gun salute that courtesy required. As the echoes of the salute died away, the anchor splashed into the murky waters of the harbour and the sailors clustered along the starboard rail and stared hungrily towards the city.

Baxter wondered what sort of welcome they would receive here. There was an excited murmur as a launch left the port, men in the uniform of the Romanian Navy sitting in the stern. Excitement, and apprehension.

"Well, that's something," he muttered. "They're coming to talk and not opening fire."

The mutineers received the visiting dignitaries with all of the pomp and circumstance their station required, with an honour guard as they came aboard, trying to reinforce the idea that they were not wild pirates here to destroy everything. They'd even broken out the St Andrew's Cross, the flag of the Tsar, in addition to a red banner demanding equality and democracy.

Baxter decided it was politic to remain at a distance from the reception and subsequent discussion, though he saw both Feldmann and Kirill had appointed themselves to the committee. He'd already drawn too much attention to himself over the last few days, and was conscious that he cut the sort of figure that stuck in the mind.

Matyushenko and the others were below with the deputation from shore. There were two, probably the port captain and perhaps an officer from the cruiser, Baxter guessed. Everything seemed cordial enough, though the Romanians seemed taken aback at the lack of a captain or officer of the watch.

The sailors talked excitedly after the men went below. Baxter remained on the upper deck, enjoying the warmth of the sun and the relatively relaxed atmosphere.

Koenig joined him there, obviously keen on keeping a low profile as well. "Do you think the ship will be surrendered here?" he asked, voice quiet.

Baxter glanced around the few knots of sailors on this deck, and the others locked in discussions on the forecastle. "I think some would happily go ashore here and be done with it," he admitted. "Though what they would do then is beyond me."

He knew as well as anyone how hard it was to be cast ashore with no prospects. At least some of these men had families back in the Empire — it wouldn't surprise him if they tried to sneak back across the border, with all the peril that entailed.

"Many are still committed to the cause, though," Koenig pointed out. "They will want to sail back to Russian waters and take their vengeance."

"Do not mistake this for purely directionless rage, or a desire for vengeance," Baxter said. Those were both feelings he was familiar with, though he didn't say as much. "Yes, their captain and first officer were, by all accounts, atrocious. Matyushenko and a lot of the sailors' committee are truly committed, and their grievances are not unreasonable."

Koenig sighed, looking unhappy. "I know our service leaves a lot to be desired, compared to your Royal Navy and others. But there are — were — officers like Cristov Juneau, from whom I learned a lot. Things would have got better — if only the men had been more patient!"

"Action is always easier than patience," Baxter said, nodding to the red flag that snapped from the forward masthead. "It's a little late for 'if only', and this has gone far beyond sailors' grievances."

"I know — but to have risen while we're at war!"

Baxter made a shushing gesture with his hand as Koenig's voice rose. They couldn't be entirely sure no one in the vicinity had at least some French. He realised, with some surprise, that he hadn't even thought about the war with Japan for some time, except briefly in relation to the plot they were trying to foil. He had felt cut off from the wider world, somehow, in this steel castle. "What news of the war?"

"None of it good," Koenig said bluntly. "The reverses on land continue, and the Japanese Army stands ready to invade Russian lands. The naval situation is now unrecoverable, thanks to our failure. The Americans have offered themselves

261

as mediator for peace negotiations, but the Tsar drags his heels as more good men die needlessly."

Baxter raised an eyebrow, but looked away before Koenig could see his expression. It was small wonder the men of the Imperial Russian Navy, not to mention the Army, were angry. Koenig was certainly angry, and Baxter knew that if he really let himself think about it he would have more sympathy for the mutineers than he would like to admit.

None of this, however, was getting them anywhere. He was about to draw them back to the matter at hand when the Romanian officers reappeared, escorted cordially to the entry port by Matyushenko.

"Well, the discussions seem to have gone well," Koenig noted, his voice returning to its usual cheerfulness.

Matyushenko confirmed that after he'd seen the visitors over the side and back into their launch. "Brothers! Brothers!" he called out until he had everyone's attention. "I have spoken at length with our gracious hosts, who seem far more amicable than at our last port."

A ripple of laughter went through the crowd of men. "Good Captain Negru will cable Bucharest and seek agreement to our conducting trade with the people of this city."

"What if his Tsar says no?" a voice called out. "We are almost out of coal, and have had nothing but cabbage and potato soup for days. The bread is almost gone!"

"Only three days' water, at best!" someone else added.

"A good question! I do not think he will say no. King Carol, I am told, is a kind and just man. He is said to be liberal, as much as a head that wears a crown can be. In the meantime, Captain Negru has agreed that a party may go ashore to make arrangements for supply when we do have agreement."

Matyushenko held his hands up for calm as a nervous rustle went through the crowd. Baxter was struck again that so much energy could be contained in such a small frame, and how effectively he could rally his comrades and crush internal dissent purely through the force of his personality. "I know, brothers, this could be an ambush, like the one that bastard Karkhanov set for us. The Romanians have nothing to fear from us, and while the Tsar will no doubt apply pressure when he learns where we are, they are a proud people and not easily threatened. I shall go ashore, and will ask only for volunteers to come with me. Come, let us be about our business."

Baxter looked at the city again, at the shipping that crowded the harbour precisely because of the threat posed by the ship now anchored beyond the stone moles. He realised, with a startling clarity, that he was at a decision point — not unlike the one he had faced as the 2nd Pacific Squadron had approached Singapore and Hong Kong beyond it. It would take some doing, but he was confident he could get himself, Koenig and the two young folk ashore. He might even be able to extract the payment promised by Konstantin, or enough to get them on their way.

Safety, in a neutral country. A port city, no less! He could see the others set on a path back to Russia. Take Tommy by the scruff and escort him back to Edinburgh, and be done with this whole fiasco. Abandon his own mad scheme, hatched in the middle of the night and after a few drinks, to take a torpedo boat and go hunting across the Black Sea for his enemies.

Get back, instead, to his life of drifting between berths that never seemed to last long, and cheap drink that lasted even less time. Leave Arbuthnott and Bilyk and Ekaterina and everyone else who thought of themselves as his betters to their games, in which he was a very minor pawn.

Or he could smash up their game.

"Keep Tommy and Mashka close," Baxter said to Koenig, reaching a conclusion. "When it's time to move, we'll need to move fast."

"We are leaving the ship?" Koenig asked.

"You and I both know this will end in disaster," he replied. "So, yes, we're leaving the ship." Baxter straightened, rolled his shoulders. He still ached from the last few days, the minor injuries sustained during his incarceration and his escapades since then. "I need to go and talk to Konstantin Feldmann — it's about time I got paid."

CHAPTER 20

His decision made, Baxter prowled the battleship restlessly throughout the rest of the day and into the evening.

Getting even a meagre amount of roubles out of Konstantin, the Odessan revolutionary guarding the *Potemkin*'s safe, had taken some doing. The young man had protested that in reality Baxter had done very little for the cause, and had been so supercilious about it that he'd been in danger of going forcefully overboard. Only Kovalenko's intervention, drawn by the raised voices, had saved Konstantin and secured a modicum of payment.

"Surely you have been with us long enough," Konstantin spat. "Surely you know the justice of our cause? This money will buy coal, food, water…"

"I doubt you'll get it here," Baxter said, mastering his temper with an effort as Kovalenko handed him a satisfyingly heavy purse. "For what it's worth, I do see the justice. But this isn't my fight, unless I'm being paid to be a part of it. And given the way things are going, getting the money up front makes sense."

Even Kovalenko seemed taken aback at the ease with which Baxter slipped into the guise of a cold-blooded mercenary. He was a little surprised at it himself.

He spent the rest of the day trying to work out how to get off the battleship with the minimum of hassle. The main issue, he realised, was going to be the weather. A pretty dirty storm was brewing, the wind stiffening and bringing with it the smell of salt and rain; he reckoned it would come on hardest as night fell.

Just when he would make his move. He'd have to see what it came to, but he didn't fancy even a short journey in an open boat, particularly with Tommy and Mashka aboard.

He was so preoccupied with his thoughts that he almost walked into the young woman. She'd mostly been keeping to the stateroom, but seemed to have recovered some of her spirit.

"Mashka," he greeted her mildly, drawing her to one side of the quarterdeck where they would be out of the way. Look towards the harbour, he could see the crowds that had gathered to gawp at the battleship were finally starting to disperse, and it looked like the ship's boats were starting to return from the shopping expedition.

"You will abandon us?" she demanded. "You have been paid, and now you will desert us?"

That was a complicated question and he didn't want to go into it now — particularly as the only language he had in common with her was Russian, and her volume meant that they would be readily overheard.

Baxter sighed, rubbed his forehead, and wondered again why he particularly cared about her wellbeing — especially when she was such a difficult youth. Perhaps she reminded him of someone, perhaps there was just something about her spirit. "I'm getting a little tired of these accusations," he said, pitching his voice loud enough that nearby sailors could hear his side of the conversation. "I'm going nowhere, I'm just exercising sound business sense. Something my father drummed into me — always make sure you get paid."

Not that he'd ever taken much notice of his father, even when they'd been on speaking terms. He smiled slightly, realising that was the first time he'd thought of the old man — now comfortably retired outside Edinburgh — in a while.

"What about you, though?" he asked. "There's nothing keeping you here, and this is no place for a…" He saw the flare of anger in her eyes as she anticipated what he would say next. "Civilian," he finished. "You could go ashore, go anywhere from here. Back to Odessa, if that's what you want. I'm sure the sailors could spare a few roubles."

She crossed her arms over her chest. "I have nothing to go back to," she muttered, looking away.

"No family?"

"My father died in an accident in a factory," she said, voice filled with quiet bitterness. "My mother from consumption. My brother … he died in the riots."

She may have been small and thin, but Baxter was struck suddenly by her strength. Her voice didn't break, though he remembered seeing her weeping over a body scant days ago.

"The revolution will not be sparked in Odessa," she went on, dropping her voice. "I know this now. But I will stay with the ship, with Konstantin and Kirill, and we will find a way to kindle it elsewhere."

"This ship is going to be taken, or sunk," he pointed out.

"A risk I am willing to take," she said flatly. "Along with my comrades in the revolution."

Well, they'd see about that, he thought as she marched away. He crossed the quarterdeck and stood staring out to sea, arms crossed over his chest. "Foul weather indeed," he mused.

The gale came on in force not long after the shore party had returned. Matyushenko in particular seemed jumpy, but while they hadn't returned with supplies — no agreement being forthcoming from Bucharest as yet — their safe arrival lifted spirits aboard ship.

"There are rumours going around the ship," Kovalenko said as he, Baxter and Koenig shared vodka and the meagre soup the rest of the crew was eating. "They say one of the newer, faster destroyers is out looking for us, with orders to take us in hand or send us to the bottom."

Baxter raised an eyebrow. "They must have found some sailors whose loyalty they could guarantee."

The Ukrainian snorted in disdain. "She is crewed by officers, they say."

"It will be the *Stremitelny*," Koenig said quietly, smiling apologetically at Kovalenko as he acknowledged that this was not news to him. "Under a man called Yanovich. He will hunt you relentlessly, and is I suspect not much given to mercy."

"All hands turn against us, it seems," Kovalenko said unhappily. "Even the sea."

The storm was raging beyond the stateroom now, wind and rain battering the ships. Baxter thought of a few things he could point out to the young man, but there didn't seem much point in trying to crush his spirits further. The *Potemkin* had started to heave and roll at her anchor as the sea got up. Kovalenko, despite the fact he clearly had some experience, looked discomfited.

"I wouldn't worry about it," Baxter said, and called across to the other side of the cabin where Tommy sat sullenly, having been denied 'a wee dram of the vodka', and slurping noisily at his own ration of soup. "We've seen much worse and come through it, haven't we, Tommy?"

The lad just grunted in response. Koenig had sunk into a deep armchair, stretching his legs out in front as he nursed his glass of vodka. "The cyclone on the Indian Ocean, for instance," he said, sounding as calm as Baxter hoped he was. "That provided a challenging few days. Though we were in open water, of course, without a shore close by and no head of steam up."

Baxter couldn't disagree with that. He much preferred to be as far from a coastline as possible when a blow came on, not wanting to experience the horror of a lee shore, but in real terms this wasn't much to worry about. He tossed off the glass of vodka. "Gentlemen," he said. "I am done in and will, I think, turn in."

The gale had blown itself out by the time Baxter rose at his more usual time, not long after dawn had broken. Tommy was already up, but looking hangdog and more subdued than usual as he, Baxter, Mashka and Koenig took a simple breakfast of stale bread and tea.

"That's what happens when you go straight to the strong drink, lad," Baxter said, tousling Tommy's hair and receiving a glare in response.

The lad didn't have time for any further comment, however. Everyone's head snapped up as a loud *bang* echoed across the water.

"Is that thunder?" he asked.

"Unlikely," Baxter replied, then raised his hand for quiet. There was a second thump. "That's artillery."

Koenig nodded. "Who the devil would be shooting in this weather?" he demanded as they all leapt to their feet and headed for the hatch.

"Stay here!" Baxter ordered the two youths.

The wind pulled at them as they piled on deck. There were a few other men on deck, all of them peering out into the grey, early morning light. "Is it the squadron?" someone demanded, a note of panic creeping into his voice.

"I don't think so." Baxter tilted his head, listening hard.

"Where are the torpedo boats?" Kovalenko demanded, looking down into the battleship's lee where the smaller, fragile vessels had been seeking shelter.

"The *Ismail* went into port; it's too rough out here," Matyushenko said, joining them at the rail. He leaned far out, until Baxter caught his shoulder and pulled him back. "Have they opened fire on it?"

A gun fired again and Baxter's eye was drawn to a plume of water rising just beyond the harbour mouth. He picked out the low, sleek shape of a torpedo boat against the slate-grey waves; the shell had landed ahead of it and the boat was in the process of coming about.

"No, just warning shots from that old cruiser," Baxter said. "I don't think they want you in their port."

"Not a good omen," Matyushenko murmured. It was the first time Baxter had seen anything even approaching uncertainty in the mutiny's leader.

"That does leave the issue of the *Zataka*," Koenig pointed out. While he had not been in charge of the torpedo boat — in fact, it wasn't clear if anyone had been operating as its commander during the ill-fated attack on the *Potemkin* — he seemed to feel protective about the old boat.

"Its anchor was dragging," Kovalenko supplied. "The crew couldn't seem to find purchase, and by the time we realised, it was too far away for a line. They took it out into open waters, poor devils. I'm sure they'll be back soon."

The *Ismail* chugged back across the water, taking its time because of the heavy seas and the need to preserve her fuel supplies. Unlike the bigger ships, it was oil-fired so its engines weren't quite as hungry as the coal-burning monsters beneath Baxter's feet. She also had comparatively little space for storage.

Some while later, the little vessel huddled into the lee of the *Potemkin*, the helmsman carefully nudging it into place before they let go the anchor. The battleship's bulk wouldn't be much shelter, certainly not compared to the harbour that lay a short distance away. But it seemed it was the best they could hope for.

"I don't envy the crew of the *Zataka*," Koenig observed as, the emergency over, they returned to the shelter and relative quiet of the cabin and their scant breakfast. "Assuming they survived."

"They better bloody well have," Baxter commented, massaging his temples. He was restless, as was often the case when he'd come up with a plan but wasn't able to get started immediately. He refilled his tea and took to pacing the cabin.

"Do you want to take that outside, Mr B?" Tommy snapped from a recumbent position. "Yer makin' a hell of a racket."

"They grow up so quickly," Koenig said mildly. "I think I shall join you on deck."

"He's spent too much time around her," Baxter said darkly as he followed the Russian out of the stateroom.

"You haven't spoken of the countess at all," Koenig observed as they reached the quarterdeck at the rear of the vessel, coming up a companionway that brought them up between the big, twin 12-inch guns of the aft turret.

Baxter cursed himself for even mentioning Ekaterina in passing, as Koenig had taken it as an opening to bring up the recent past. "That's because there's nothing to be said," he growled, then nodded to starboard as a launch put off from the battleship and headed across the choppy water into the harbour. "Wonder what they're up to now? Another shopping expedition?"

Koenig accepted his abrupt change of subject. "I think they're going to get their answer from Captain Negru. He was aboard earlier, trying to encourage the men to surrender and promising them sanctuary here if they do."

Baxter looked along the length of the battleship, as much as he could see from this vantage point anyway. "Well, she'd be a fine acquisition for Romania, but I doubt they could afford to keep her afloat and fuelled."

Koenig nodded. "Nor would they want the conflict with His Serene Highness. This whole situation is bad for everyone in the Black Sea — it will stir up tensions whether these..." Koenig bit back on an epithet. "Whether the crew realise it or not. And it will make dissidents outside of Russia wonder whether they can gain by rising up, even under a relatively liberal monarch like King Carol."

Something about what Koenig had said niggled at Baxter, but he was tired and ill-tempered enough that he didn't try to follow it through. "You know what the trouble with young naval officers is, these days?" he said instead, but didn't wait for a response. "They think too much about things that don't concern them."

Koenig bowed with mock gravity. "I shall confine myself to considerations of more appropriate matters, like ensuring the brasswork is sufficiently shiny, in order to impress young ladies."

Baxter laughed, the tension that had fallen over him briefly easing. Koenig joined in the laughter, and they started to get dark looks from the sailors who were going about their daily chores in a slightly lacklustre fashion.

"It seems we are not welcome here, either," Koenig said. "I shall go below and see if Tommy's mood has improved."

Baxter glanced back out to sea, looking for the plume of smoke that would tell him other vessels were out there. "I think I'll take some glasses up to the lookout post and see if I can make out the *Zataka*. Hopefully the crew have at least a vague notion of how to handle the storm — I've got plans for that barky."

Koenig raised an eyebrow. "You have been remarkably quiet on the subject of what you plan to do next," he said.

"Well, what *we* plan to do next will depend a lot on whether that bloody torpedo boat is where we left it."

Baxter went up through the superstructure, past the batteries of 6-inch guns each in their individual barbettes and then up a companionway and behind the smaller 11-pounder guns mounted there, then up again from the dimness of the superstructure and onto the spar deck. He passed the steam launches hanging from their cranes and then moved up the foremast by a ladder located behind the enclosed bridge. The *Potemkin* was a modern vessel and didn't have the sort of sailing rig he'd experienced on older ships, or indeed the full-blown sailing rigs he'd had to train on after he'd joined the Royal Navy. This was a thick column of metal with crossyards from which dangled paraphernalia for the wireless telegraph, and it also supported an armoured fighting position just above the bridge which contained a handful of small guns.

He nodded a greeting to a handful of sailors enjoying a quiet card game in the compartment and continued up, moving with a comfortable familiarity past one platform and then up and up until he reached the top lookout platform. This was a flimsy and unprotected shelf with a railing, and the last place anyone would want to be in a blow. Right now it was perfectly pleasant with the comparatively gentle rocking of the vessel at anchor

— certainly not the hellish sway of the cyclone in the Indian Ocean.

Baxter had indeed acquired a set of glasses on his way up, but he hadn't really been intending to look for the torpedo boat. He swept the seas anyway, getting a magnificent view from this height. The sea, even here, was remarkably empty of shipping. He would expect to see a few civilian steamers and sailing vessels, but all he could really make out was the occasional flicker of white triangles that might have been local fishing vessels and once a smudge of smoke that might have been the funnel of a small vessel — perhaps the errant *Zataka*. He knew it wouldn't take long for the waters to fill with shipping again. Certainly once the *Potemkin* was brought to heel, assuming the Russians managed to get their act together and either corner her or starve her out.

More likely once the novelty of a rogue battleship being on the loose wore off — which it would do soon — and it became abundantly clear that the mutineers had no desire to engage in piracy, the merchantman would be hurrying back about their business. Time spent bottled up in ports or small harbours was time wasted, money lost in commerce and wages for sailors sitting idle. The ship owners would consider the risks against the benefits and try to guess which way Lloyds of London would jump, and soon enough they would decide it was worth the risk to other men's lives. Telegrams would fly and commerce in the Black Sea would begin again.

That smudge of smoke was working its way closer, and he could make out some sort of vessel beneath it. Low and sleek, without doubt a warship. Could it be the *Zataka* returning, having ridden out the storm; or was it the *Stremitelny*, under a command so committed to his cause that he would launch an attack in neutral waters?

Hearing calling from below, Baxter looked down to see Koenig waving up. He cupped his hand over his ear. "What's that?" he bellowed back.

"Matyushenko and the others are returning — it seems we have our answer from Bucharest!" Koenig shouted, exercising the sort of voice any experienced sailor required to be heard over wind and wave.

Lad will make a good officer one day, Baxter decided. *Assuming he survives this.*

He climbed back down, taking his time about it and casting the occasional glance out to sea. He paused on the lower watch platform and scanned the sea, once again picking out the approaching vessel. It was coming straight on, at least, with no attempt at subterfuge. That probably meant it was friendly, or at least neutral; that or this Yanovich was as unsubtle as Koenig had seemed to suggest.

Baxter was pretty sure, after a few moments' scrutiny, that it was the *Zataka*. The sailors were all gathering on the forecastle to hear what news Matyushenko had brought back, so there was no one to keep a close eye on it.

And if it was the destroyer on its suicide mission, well, they had time yet. The officers crewing it would be foolish indeed to try and attack during the day. As long as he had time to get Koenig, Tommy and Mashka into a boat, it wasn't really any of Baxter's business.

"So, you don't want to surrender, do you?" Matyushenko was shouting as Baxter got close enough to hear what was being said.

"They won't keep to their terms!" someone called out from the crowd. "Mark my words, as soon as we are ashore, away from our guns, we will be arrested and sent straight back to Mother Russia in chains!"

"And then it's the firing squad for you, and the noose for us!" Kirill called out, sounding oddly cheerful despite the dire predictions.

"We should go back to Russia, but not in chains and not to be shot!" Matyushenko declared. "We should go back in our good ship here, and strike such a blow to the Tsar that it will set his crown around his ears and send the fires of revolution sweeping across the country!"

"But we need bread and meat!" someone complained. "Coal and water."

"Leave that to the committee, brothers! We'll work something out, somewhere to take what we need from the Tsar's lackeys. Not from honest traders or other countries, you understand? We're not pirates, are we?"

"No!" came the roar.

"Then where do you want to go, brothers?"

"To Russia! To Russia!"

Baxter glanced across at Koenig, who was leaning nonchalantly against the forward turret. "Take it they didn't get what they wanted from the Romanians?" he asked after he moved close enough to be heard without having to yell.

"They've been promised all the food and drink they want, just as soon as they surrender the *Potemkin*," Koenig replied laconically. "Just as we thought. Sanctuary here in Romania if they want it. It seems they do not trust the offer, though."

"Are they wrong?"

Koenig gave one of his characteristic shrugs. "The Romanians are decent people, and their king is no monster. Whether he would end up having to succumb to pressure from the Tsar and his ministers is another matter. His Serene Highness is not a man to forgive or forget, I feel."

The ship's leaders, including Kirill and Feldmann, gathered and headed for the wardroom. Baxter was astonished to see Ensign Alekseyev amongst them. After their experience with Dr Golenko, he couldn't fathom why the mutineers continued to keep the young man in their confidence. Baxter had fully expected him to have been put ashore, or shot. Kovalenko at least had demonstrated his loyalty time and again, whereas, as far as he knew, the Ensign had done little but resist the revolution — albeit passively.

"Any sign of the *Zataka*?" Koenig asked as they watched the revolution's elite disappear towards the wardroom to plot their next move.

"Possibly. That, or it's your chum from Sevastopol come to cause an international incident."

Koenig sighed. "You joke, I think, but I have met Yanovich — just the once, you understand. I would not put it past him. I overheard him in the officer's mess at the base, you see, and he was already talking about putting together his 'suicide crew' of likeminded men. They cannot abide the affront to the Tsar and the service's honour, just as the young man who shot himself on the *St. George* couldn't."

"Well, hopefully we'll be away from here by then," Baxter said. Koenig looked to be about to enquire as to exactly what the plan was, but one of the crew finally spotted the approaching vessel.

"It's the *Zataka*!" the shout went up. "I think she's in trouble!"

Baxter glanced around, expecting to see Matyushenko's inner circle come racing back onto deck. They were nowhere to be seen, though, no doubt only just getting in to what would be a long debate.

He stirred himself. "Where are Tommy and Mashka two?" he asked, voice barely above a murmur.

Koenig looked quizzical. "In the stateroom. Why the conspiratorial tone — are we to act against the mutineers?"

"If we were, do you think I'd be discussing it openly?" Baxter asked, trying to keep the note of acid out of his tone and mostly failing. "Whether or not we end up acting against the mutineers depends a lot on whether they want to get in my way or not."

"Bilyk and Arbuthnott have truly angered you, haven't they?"

"Aye, they have. They should have left well enough alone." Baxter strode off before Koenig could press the point any further, looking for someone to browbeat into doing what he wanted.

In the end, he roped in Ivan Beshoff and a few of his mates. "Should we not wait for the committee?" Beshoff asked, once Baxter had ... well, not given him his orders, but made strong suggestions.

"You can see that the boat, your comrades, are in trouble!" Baxter said. "And I myself heard Matyushenko say this discussion was too important for them to be disturbed, unless the Tsar himself came to ask for their forgiveness and abdicate the throne. We need to get out to the *Zataka*, and both Koenig and I have experience of small boats like that."

That was true after a fashion, though Baxter *had* spent most of his brief career on cruisers. He certainly hoped that, in the heat of the moment, Beshoff and the others would forget that Koenig had recent experience on the *Zataka*, as he was part of the crew that had tried to sink them.

"I understand you, Marcus, and I trust you," Beshoff said, his expression torpedoing Baxter's hopes in the latter respect.

"But this *Lieutenant* Koenig must stay aboard until Matyushenko says he can be trusted."

Baxter stifled a sigh. Nothing ever went entirely according to plan at sea, he told himself. "Well, let's get a boat in the water before the *Zataka* sinks, eh?"

Half an hour later, Baxter was in one of the steam launches as it bobbed its way out towards the torpedo boat. Seeing them coming, the handful of crewmen gathered on the flat section of deck behind the conning tower, waving frantically.

"The engine is on the verge of dying!" one of them shouted as soon as they were within earshot.

"And we are taking on water!" another called out. "We have had a miserable night of it!"

Beshoff's face was glum. "There are only a few of them; we can easily take them aboard and let that cursed thing sink."

Baxter kept his face carefully neutral as the mutineer steered them towards the labouring boat. "That may be the most practical thing, but think of the morale of the crew. You've suffered a number of reverses, and while the *Zataka* cannot make up for the loss of the *St. George*, losing it now…"

Ivan considered that, then nodded reluctantly. "I see the wisdom in what you say," he said, though he also cast a slightly suspicious glance at Baxter. "You *do* seem to have a particular interest in this little antique."

"I have a fondness for relics, particularly those I've captured singlehandedly."

Ivan laughed. "Singlehandedly indeed! I heard you had a boarding party of at least three, and little Mashka counts for at least two."

Baxter smiled. It seemed the sailors had adopted the young Odessan as some sort of mascot, and that was fine by him.

Sailors went out of their way to look after their good luck charms, just as the crew of the *Yaroslavich* had with Tommy.

"We will go alongside — you bought it, so you can fix it."

Baxter shrugged. "That seems reasonable, but I'll need you to go back and bring me Kovalenko — I seem to recall he's an engineer."

The *Zataka*'s crew seemed to agree with Beshoff, that the damp little ship should just be allowed to sink beneath the waves. They therefore looked aghast as the launch was run alongside and Baxter jumped across. He stood with his feet spread wide to compensate for the swell, and clapped his hands together as other sailors came across from the smaller boat.

"Right lads," he boomed cheerfully. "Let's see if we can put this boat back into working order!"

He chivvied the crew before him purely through force of personality, assisted by his size. "This thing is sinking," the sailor who seemed to be in charge told him miserably. "The pumps have stopped and the bilges are now in the crew quarters. Such as they are. The engines will soon be submerged."

Baxter looked around at the dispirited men of the original crew. Their morose attitude was threatening to infect the five sailors who'd come across with him, and he couldn't have that. Not while Ivan took the launch back for Kovalenko, tools and supplies. He couldn't have that at all.

"What's your name?" he asked the spokesman, knowing he had to take control of the situation but knowing he couldn't just browbeat and threaten these men. They had mutinied, after all, to get away from exactly that treatment.

"Piotr," the man said sullenly.

"Well, Piotr, I can see you have buckets." Baxter gestured to the discarded vessels around the hatch in the deck. "And you must have bailed for your lives during the night. I'm going to ask you to do a bit more, with me and these fine lads, just to keep this old girl afloat and moving until the engineers can get here. Then there'll be vodka and tea for you as soon as we get it back to the *Potemkin*."

He very carefully didn't promise them anything more substantive than that. He wasn't even sure there would be soup for these haggard men.

CHAPTER 21

"My boys cannot guarantee the repairs," Aleksei Kovalenko said after he had finished conversing with the two machinists who had come across from the battleship with him. "But both the pump and the engines should last for a day or two more. What happens after that…"

Kovalenko made a gesture that expressed a lack of both surety and optimism in one wave of the hand.

Baxter nodded, rolling his sleeves back down and buttoning them. He'd worked with the Russian sailors through the morning, forming a bucket chain to empty out the torpedo boat. Well, not empty out — it had shipped so much water in the night they were never going to clear it. They'd made headway, at least, and kept her floating until Beshoff returned. The machinists had got the pumps working again, a simple enough task as they'd failed due to a lack of maintenance rather than actual breakage, and seawater had gone sluicing from the hoses over the side. Baxter could now move around the tiny crew cabin only ankle-deep in water and he didn't want to know what else. He didn't enjoy being down there anyway, as he had to crouch to get around.

"Where's next?" he asked, nodding to the *Potemkin*. She was underway again, the *Ismail* hovering on her lee side.

Kovalenko looked unhappy. "Theodosia, in the Crimea," he said. "Closer to Sevastopol than I would like, but also somewhere Yanovich is unlikely to hunt for us."

"Don't think I've been there," Baxter said, searching his memory.

"There is little there to bring anyone, these days, as they all go to Odessa. We should be able to resupply there, and not a moment too soon — they are going to have to put seawater in my boilers, and that will cause havoc in the pipes."

Baxter nodded slowly. He'd known things were getting desperate on the rogue ship — there had only been tepid distilled water for drinking and none for washing these last few days, and even that was dangerously close to the bottom of the barrel.

If things didn't go their way in Theodosia…

Well, no point brooding over it. It wouldn't be his concern much longer.

"Will they wait for us?" he asked. He knew there was some work still to be done, in the partly drowned engine room and also to close a seam that had opened in the torpedo boat's hull through which the water had come. The *Potemkin* already had a head of steam up and showed no sign of hanging around, putting her double-eagle prow to the east.

"I am afraid we cannot, our supply situation is now so desperate." Kovalenko had broken his usual habit and was speaking French in a quiet tone. "The crossing to Theodosia should be two days, and our supplies will only just get us there if we leave now. I will leave you Ippolit and Luka — indeed, they were happy to volunteer when they realised it would get them out of having to scrub the inside of the boilers and pipes — and you may even be able to catch up with us. Your oil tanks are half-full, which should get you there with some to spare."

If Baxter didn't have the three people on the *Potemkin* to worry about, the fuel situation would be more than adequate for him. He nodded judiciously. "Well," he said, as the launch pulled up alongside them again. "I'll see you in Theodosia, if not before."

"You know the way?" Kovalenko asked, shaking the hand Baxter proffered.

Baxter grinned. "East and north a bit, and don't go into any impressive and heavily guarded harbours I see along the way."

"Yes — this would be a bad idea."

Kovalenko exchanged a few words with the machinists, and then jumped across to the launch as it barely slowed down to sweep past them, the helmsman swapping good-natured abuse with the *Zataka*'s scratch crew as his wake rocked the boat.

Baxter watched the battleship recede into the distance. He thought back to the brief discussion he'd managed to have with Koenig just before he boarded the launch, the instructions he'd left about what to do with his pay and the two youths. Hopefully it wouldn't come to that.

"Right, you lot!" he called out to the tired-looking and soggy sailors. "Another hour and we'll be under way. I'm going to do my best to catch up with the *Potemkin*, and we should be able to manage it. If not, we'll meet her at her next destination, where there'll be beef and potatoes and not a few drams of vodka, I'm sure."

"Who put you in charge?" Piotr asked. His voice was truculent, but not so angry that he gave the impression he was ready to start a counter-mutiny.

"Do you want to be?" Baxter asked, with a smile that was not altogether friendly.

Piotr was a taller man, wiry and lean, and looked like he could handle himself. He obviously thought better about pressing any claim to command, though. "Where are we going?" he demanded instead.

"After that big bastard," was all Baxter offered, gesturing at the rapidly diminishing shape of the *Potemkin*.

As it happened, it was more like three hours before the machinists finished effecting repairs. The sailors chafed as their main protection disappeared over the horizon, but Baxter felt more relaxed as the oppressive presence disappeared. Concerned for this friends, yes, but he guessed they would be safe enough.

"And what if we run into this *Stremitelny*? Or some other patrolling warship?"

"Assuming the rumours are true that she's out here, she'll have more to worry about than a little minnow like us," Baxter said with as much bravado as he could muster. He got a few chuckles from the other sailors, but Piotr seemed unmoved by his attempt at humour. "Plus, with a crew this good we should be able to outrun her easily. As to any other ships we run into, well — as soon as we tell them we're part of the revolutionary squadron, I'm sure the crews will rise!"

That brought actual laughter, and an elbow in Piotr's ribs. One of the machinists — Baxter hadn't quite learned to tell them apart under the layer of oil and grease — emerged from belowdecks. "We can try the engine again," he said, blinking in the daylight as he threw himself down on some loose sacking.

"And not a moment too soon," Baxter said to himself as he got up and moved forward to what the sailors had taken to calling the 'bridge'. He knew from the occasional boat that emerged from the harbour and then dashed back in that the Romanians were deeply suspicious of their presence, anchored not far from where the *Potemkin* and consort spent the night. A single plume of smoke from within suggested that the old cruiser — the *Elisabeta*, he'd been told — was getting up steam. The sooner they were away, the better.

The 'bridge' was little more than the boat's wheel in a lightly armoured enclosure with enough space for the commander and quartermaster. Baxter couldn't fit comfortably behind it so didn't try, instead standing to one side as the sailor nominated to steer took his station. "Right, gentlemen. Stations for getting underway, if you please."

They didn't make top speed, not immediately. The other machinist emerged, pleading with them to slow to a crawl after they'd barely got moving, or better yet to stop entirely. While Baxter had presented a face of not being worried about being out from under the big guns of the battleship, that didn't mean he was happy about being left too far behind. "We will slow but cannot stop entirely," he growled. "We've more than outstayed our welcome here."

Baxter stood with one foot on the gunwale of the little vessel as they steamed slowly away from Constanza. While he'd joked to Kovalenko that he would steam east and north, having looked at the charts he'd found aboard he was dubious about taking this vessel straight across the Black Sea, certainly when not in company. He couldn't hug the coast around, as that would take forever and also bring them dangerously close to Odessa, where he guessed the *Stremitelny* would be heading if she wasn't there already. He'd ease them round, north by east before heading east. The *Zataka* was a small boat, and he knew from painful personal experience just how hard it was to pick out one of these vessels against the grey of the sea, particularly at night or in foul weather. They'd make it through.

Baxter looked around at the small, thrown-together crew. He knew only a few of these men, and had his doubts about leading them into any sort of action. He didn't doubt their courage, but he had no measure of their capability or their willingness to follow a complete stranger — a foreigner to boot — into battle. If his plan succeeded — and that was a big 'if', given the number of variables — he could very well be leading them into a firefight.

"Where are you, you bastards?" he murmured, staring out to sea, then snorted at his own foolishness. He doubted either of the men who had hatched this absurd plot would be aboard their Trojan horse — they would be leaving it to expendable underlings.

"What is this you say, Marcus Alexandrovich?" the helmsman asked, cocking his ear.

"Nothing, Sergei," he replied absently, looking to the sky. He sun was dipping towards the horizon, and they had been at anchor here for far too long. "Another point to the east, if you please, and see if the engine room can give us a few more revolutions."

Baxter slept on the deck of the little vessel, and then only fitfully. It was warm enough, the summer heat reasserting itself after the storm, and the crew quarters would be close and humid by now. A few of the men braved the damp bunks below, the others tucking themselves as securely as they could into crannies on the deck.

He wasn't sure what woke him, sometime in the middle of the night. He'd rapidly grown accustomed to the different, more pronounced movements of the little boat as it made its way across the water. It wasn't so unlike the motion of the pinnace he'd taken in pursuit of the traitor Yefimov, though the company on that jaunt had been considerably pleasanter.

His mind drifted as he lay in the dark, head resting on his rolled-up coat. He hadn't thought about Yefimov for a while. He was in the past, broken in their collective wake, the back of his head blown out by Cristov Juneau's pistol. The Russian nobleman had claimed he had fired in self-defence, as the captured spy had tried to break free, but it was clear that Juneau had murdered the man to prevent him remaining a threat to them.

Memories and recently learned facts swirled around in his head. He had at times wondered how Arbuthnott, who'd seemed to be Yefimov's controller, had even encountered the man, recruited him into his mad schemes. Baxter had been hoodwinked, lured in with the offer of decent pay. Yefimov hadn't seemed to be the type, but nor had he seemed to be the kind of man who would betray his country — no matter how bitter he might have felt at being perpetually passed over for promotion.

The involvement of the Okhrana in this, though — that changed things. Baxter realised Bilyk and Arbuthnott must have been in contact for some time, plotting and scheming together. It made far more sense for Bilyk to have brought Yefimov in, no doubt filling his head with stories of helping his beloved Tsar by stirring up trouble for hated enemies.

The secret policeman's attitude towards Baxter made far more sense in light of this realisation. No matter what he might have claimed during the interrogations, Bilyk would have known all along that Baxter had just been an unwilling dupe. All of his talk of ascertaining Baxter's guilt had been a smoke screen for his real intent. The occasional question he had thrown in about Ekaterina and Yefimov's fate, almost as asides, demonstrated his real interest.

The instinct that had woken him intruded into his mind again, wiping the meandering train of thought away as surely as Juneau's bullet had ended Yefimov. He rolled to his feet, staring around. It was dark, but the sort of darkness you only got at sea, with the moon and stars bright overhead and their cold light glinting on the waves.

Baxter cocked his head, closing his eyes so as not to be distracted by the false shapes night could create. There was something there, he was sure of it, but he couldn't quite make it out over the vibrations of their own engine. He went up to the conning tower, carefully stepping over sailors taking their well-earned rest. Piotr had the wheel, keeping the boat on the right heading despite the fact he was obviously tired to the bone and struggling to keep his eyes open.

"Take us down to one quarter," Baxter ordered softly as Piotr acknowledged his arrival with a nod. Reaching up, Baxter switched off the small light that provided a little pool of illumination.

The helmsman did as he was ordered without question, pulling the brass lever on the engine room telegraph to the slowest speed. A moment later, the lever showing the engine room's setting corresponded and both their speed and the noise of their engine dropped away.

Baxter stepped away from the conning tower, listening again. Piotr remained at his station, but his eyes were wide in the dimness.

There. Engines, somewhere not too distant. Not right on top of them either.

"Is it the *Potemkin*?" Piotr whispered urgently.

Baxter waved a hand behind him as he stared out to sea, trying to make out the source of the noise even though he knew it was futile. If it was close enough to be seen, then the mysterious ship was also close enough to see them.

"I don't think so," he said as he returned to the bridge. "Too small. Could be a merchant vessel, a small steamer."

The helmsman swallowed hard. "And if it's not?"

"Then it's a destroyer, and we've probably got a fight on our hands," Baxter said with a grin, then clapped the man on his shoulder. "Due east, I think, and up to one half."

He found his field glasses and went back to his station at the boat's side, just aft of the funnel. He swept the deceptively light seascape but couldn't make anything out. Baxter screwed his eyes up, trying to remember the charts and estimate their position. A bit to the east and south of Odessa, he thought, given their speed and how long they'd been travelling.

He caught a slick flicker of light, just out of the corner of his eye as he lowered the glasses. He brought them back up, breath catching in his throat. Probably just a flash of reflected moonlight.

Then he caught it again, properly this time, and realised it was a searchlight, flicking on and off. Maybe a mile away, or slightly more.

He managed to find the vessel with the glasses.

"All stop!" he ordered, his voice low. The destroyer — and it *was* a destroyer — was still some distance away, but Baxter knew how far sound could carry. Piotr complied immediately. The habit of obedience was hard to break, even for mutineers.

Baxter found the sleek little ship again. Koenig had said the *Stremitelny* was one of the newer ships in the Black Sea Fleet, with easily enough speed to overhaul the *Potemkin* or indeed his own little boat; her battery of quick-firing guns was also optimised for killing torpedo boats.

All in all, not a ship he wanted to tangle with.

Some of the other sailors were beginning to wake, disturbed by the change in the vessel's motion as they stopped. Piotr went about hushing them and sending them to the boat's two 1-pounder rotary barrel guns. Not that they would do much good if it came to a fight; their only hope was not to be spotted.

Baxter had the destroyer fixed in his glasses now. She was on a different heading, going south and west — he guessed on a course for Constanza — and using her searchlights intermittently, no doubt in some vain hope of catching a rogue vessel. Like, for instance, the *Zataka*. At least the officers of this 'suicide crew' were looking for a battleship, not the long sleek shape of a torpedo boat travelling by itself.

"Everyone stay low," Baxter said, keeping his voice low but pitching it to carry. "And keep quiet."

"You're not keeping quiet," some joker commented in the darkness. Baxter swept the deck with a stern gaze, but the sailor with an overdeveloped sense of humour realised he should probably clam up without being told.

Baxter looked back towards land again, managing to fix on the destroyer again thanks to the flicker of her searchlights. His heart started beating faster as she appeared to be turning. They had been pulling away, his change of course putting the *Zataka* at an almost perpendicular line to the *Stremitelny*'s heading. He watched the destroyer breathlessly, waiting to see if her turn was bringing her round onto a pursuit heading or...

She levelled out again, past the stern of the *Zataka*, a shallow angle and still at more than a thousand yards. The searchlight flickered, illuminating a patch of sea a few hundred yards astern.

"Come on, back on your course," Baxter whispered, urging Yanovich to be back about his business. He tried to put himself in the shoes of the keen officer on the bridge of the destroyer. Had the turn been occasioned by a slight suspicion that they weren't alone in this patch of sea, or was he just being cautious? Even if a lookout had thought he'd seen something, there was a calculation to be made — keep going for Constanza in the hopes of intercepting the rebellious battleship, perhaps with the opportunity to make a night attack, or chase shadows and ghosts in the night?

"Come on, friend," he whispered. "Nothing out here but ghosts."

After a few seconds more, the commander of the *Stremitelny* obviously came to the same conclusion, adjusting his course slightly to the west again. He disappeared into the night. Baxter breathed out hard, a release of tension that was echoed across the vessel.

"Bring us up to three-quarters speed," he ordered Piotr on the helm. "But slowly — no point making more noise about this than we have to."

"Shall we set more of a watch?" the helmsman asked. "In case he comes back, or there are more out there?"

Baxter took his cap off and scratched his head, then shook it. "No, I'm well awake now — I'll keep watch until morning. I don't think we'll run into any more ships before Theodosia anyway — I'm planning on giving Sevastopol a wide berth."

Baxter was almost right. While they didn't encounter any more ships as they made the rest of the crossing, they did happen across a boatload of mutineers.

The crew had been rattled by their close encounter in the night, and Baxter had to admit the near miss had concerned him more than he'd expected. He decided to circle wider round Sevastopol, the primary Russian naval base in the area, going further out into the Black Sea than he had otherwise intended. The machinists were still concerned about the state of the engine, and he had his own reasons for wanting the ship to remain operational without having to rely on the *Potemkin*'s resources, so they cruised along at an easy speed. The wind was fresh but not blowing a gale, and the *Zataka* was proving herself a more seaworthy boat than he'd previously expected, handling the long roll of the waves without shipping too much water.

The patched seam in the boat's iron hull was a further worry for him, and he inspected it regularly and organised bucket chains as well as keeping the pumps running. Bailing out by hand — first one man scooping a bucket full in the crew quarters, then passing it up into the light and the hands of a second man, and from there across the deck to a third man and into the sea — had the double benefit of giving the sailors something to do without overly exerting them on their short rations. While it was a pleasant enough day, Baxter knew exactly what this amount of isolation and uncertainty could do to a man.

"I feel like I should be keeping a ship's log," he commented to Piotr. After their initial clash when he had come aboard, he'd found the revolutionary sailor steady enough and easy to get on with. "I'm not sure I even know what the date is, though."

"It is sometime in June," Piotr said, with the peasant's phlegmatic lack of interest in such matters beyond when it was time to harvest and when it was time to plant. "Depending on which calendar you are using, of course. And who would you show the log to, Marcus Alexandrovich?"

Baxter chuckled, but his eye had been caught by something a few miles away. A flicker of white. A seabird, this far out?

After a second look, he decided it wasn't a bird but a shred of torn sail flapping in the wind. He brought his field glasses up without looking away, and a small boat jumped into view. "Lifeboat three points off the starboard bow, about two miles," he said, his tone neutral. Almost as though he was writing it down in a log.

Piotr shaded his eyes against the mid-afternoon light. "I think you are right. The poor devils look to be in distress." The mutineer paused. "Should we … go and help?"

Baxter rubbed his chin. He wanted nothing more than to be off the open sea, at least for now, and seeing to his friends' safety. Leaving a lifeboat in distress was something he knew he would never forgive himself for, even if these men would overlook such a transgression. And given the relative paucity of boats on the water — though they had seen a few in the distance — it wasn't unreasonable to think the boat had something to do with their current situation.

"You do not think it is from the *Potemkin*, do you?" someone else asked, a note of rising panic in his voice. "That she has been sunk?"

Baxter knew he had to put a stopper in that sort of talk pretty damn quickly. "Of course not," he said firmly. "If there'd been a battle, or even a torpedo attack, we would have heard it. And trust me when I say this, lads, you don't ever forget the sound a battleship makes as she sinks."

Baxter spoke with absolute conviction. It wasn't just a single sound, of course, but a cacophony. Tortured metal and doomed men screaming, the inrush of water turning to steam as it hit wrecked engines; the swirl and gurgle of the sea as the ship goes down. The only thing worse was the noise of a battleship blowing up, being wiped from existence by the magazines going up. The death of the *Borodino*, the ship that gave the name to her class, at Tsushima would stay with him to his dying day.

He shook the image off. "Well, there's only one way to find out — Piotr, steer us for the boat."

It took them another half an hour to reach the bobbing vessel. While it was clear even at a distance that the boat wasn't in good shape, it didn't appear to be sinking. Baxter didn't strain the *Zataka*'s engines by racing across, but did authorise half speed to get there.

The crew of the boat didn't spot them until they were only a hundred yards away, and if the situation hadn't been so desperate Baxter would have found their response comical. Panicking at the sudden appearance of an unknown vessel, but an obviously military one, they tried to get away. There was a flurry of activity and waving hands. Baxter saw the splash as one of the oars was lost overboard, and the ensuing struggle between exhausted and frustrated men threatened to topple the little boat.

"Brothers!" he yelled, following his instincts as to who these men were. "We are with the revolution — you have nothing to fear from us!"

The boat went very quiet, the figures that had been shoving each other disappearing below the line of the gunwale. A moment later, as Baxter had the *Zataka* slowed so their bow wave didn't topple the other boat, a head appeared.

"What proof do you have that you are revolutionaries?" a querulous voice demanded, as though its owner was in any position to make demands for evidence.

"Fuck the Tsar!" Baxter yelled back, almost without thinking and putting real feeling into the sentiment.

The head dropped out of sight, and Baxter could only imagine the whispered argument going on. Then a man in the uniform of a Russian sailor stood up. "Seems like sufficient proof to me!" he called out cheerfully. "Come ahead, brothers."

"As though they could stop us," Piotr muttered caustically, giving voice to what most of the crew was thinking.

The boat they drew alongside was clearly a smaller ship's boat, not one of the bigger launches that the *Potemkin* and others of her kind carried. It was an open boat, propelled by oars, and while it had a mast and sail, the eight men crammed into it had obviously made a hash of trying to set it.

"What ship?" Baxter called across as the *Zataka* finally came up to idle next to the boat.

"You first, brother!" the big, burly man who had either been nominated or nominated himself to be their spokesmen said cheerfully. Baxter suspected that he might be slightly drunk.

"The *Zataka* torpedo boat, attached to the *Potemkin*," he said, without adding any of the epithets that came to mind.

"What a coincidence! We're from the *Vekha*, formerly attached to the *Potemkin* as well."

"Traitors!" one of the men who had come across to the *Zataka* from the battleship shouted. "You abandoned us!"

"Not us, brother! We remained true to the revolution."

"And the others set you adrift rather than taking you back to Sevastopol as an offering for that dog Chukhnin?" Piotr demanded hotly.

"It's … a little more complicated than that, brother! Let us come across, and maybe give us a drink of water, and we can tell you more!"

Baxter was inclined to believe the story, but from the sullen expressions on some of the other sailors' faces, he guessed they would take some convincing. He also knew they wouldn't be able to get everyone on the little lifeboat onto their own vessel.

"We can't take you all aboard, but we can tow you to shore," he said. "Piotr here will get a line across to you while I consult the charts."

"We'd much rather come across." another sailor said, voice sounding more than a little shaky.

"Bah! Quit your bellyaching!" Piotr shouted. "All you'll have to do is lie back and enjoy the cruise while we do all the work. It's a beautiful day for it."

CHAPTER 22

In true revolutionary form, there had to be a discussion amongst the crew of the *Zataka*. Baxter chafed at the delay and had to fight down his urge to start barking orders. They ended up compromising and allowing two of the sailors to come across. This was achieved once a line had been passed between the two boats and the smaller one was drawn in far enough that the sickly-sounding man and the spokesman were able to step across.

"Fedotov, Petya N.," the larger, louder man declared, sticking his hand out to Baxter. "Gunner, formerly of the *Vekha*."

"That tub had guns?" Piotr said dismissively, saving Baxter the need to introduce himself.

"We're on our way to join back up with the *Potemkin*," Baxter said, carefully not mentioning where she actually was. He didn't think anyone would be in any doubt by now — the telegraph was everywhere these days — but there was no harm in being cautious. "If we tow you all the way we'll take forever, but I've identified somewhere we can put you ashore and then send someone back for you. We're not far from a formation called the Devil's Gate, which should be easy enough for the *Ismail* to find."

Fedotov looked unhappy, though it took Baxter a moment to realise that was because of the place rather than the idea of being left in general. "It is a bad place," he muttered from behind his enormous and somewhat shaggy beard.

Baxter knew better than to try to contradict the superstitions of sailors. "The Tsar and his admirals call you devils," he pointed out. "The name seems fitting."

That seemed to brighten the pair of them up slightly. They got back underway not long after that. The towed boat and her handful of passengers didn't slow the *Zataka* a great deal, but the extra strain on her engine and hull was noticeable. The sooner they could get them to safety and then be on their way, the better.

"You mentioned a more complex tale than just being cast adrift," Baxter said to Fedotov. The pair of rescued sailors were stretched out comfortably on the small section of empty deck, enjoying cups of tepid tea.

"Yes, yes, I did, though it's a strange tale indeed." Fedotov spoke with the cadence and aplomb of an accomplished spinner of tall stories, though when he saw Baxter's expression darken he straightened up somewhat. "Our erstwhile comrades and shipmates on the *Vekha* had us under arrest and destined for the noose," he went on in a more conversational tone. "They were making for Sevastopol to throw themselves on Chukhnin's slender mercy. Before we got there, though, we were intercepted by a gunboat and boarded. They claimed to be Turks and flew the Ottoman flag, though it was pretty clear right from the start that there was something not right about them."

Baxter had been half-listening to that point, but the mention of a mysterious gunboat got his attention. "Would you say they probably weren't Turks?" he asked, trying to hide his interest.

"They claimed we had strayed into their waters and must be inspected, but as soon as they were aboard it was clear they were agents of the Tsar. Sailors and policemen. We, of course, took the opportunity to slip away in the confusion. There was a fight and some shooting took place as we got the boat into the water, otherwise we would have taken the time to provision ourselves properly."

"It was not a fight," the other fellow, whose name was Onufri, muttered. "They murdered our brothers."

"Onufri is convinced he saw men being shot at the railing, so they fell overboard," Fedotov said. "I told him, the Turks may be barbarous, Onufri, but they do not just murder people out of hand. Not at a time of peace, anyway."

"You said they were not Turks!" Onufri protested, voice rising. "They were pirates, nothing more! Russian pirates!"

That was close enough, Baxter knew, but he kept his peace. No need to worry these men with what he knew, or at least suspected. And, more importantly, he wanted to avoid any questions about how he'd come by the information.

"There, there, Onufri," Fedotov said consolingly, patting the other man on the shoulder. "He has had a hard few days," the sailor explained to those around him.

"He'll have a nice relaxing stay on a beach shortly," Baxter said confidently, just before the line between the two vessels snapped with a twang. The rowing boat almost upended as the way came off it and it turned into the torpedo boat's wake.

Baxter sighed. "Get that line back and try to find one that isn't rotten through!" he barked. "We haven't got all bloody day."

They were in sight of the Crimean Peninsula before nightfall. The mountains had been a presence on the horizon for some time, and as the two boats drew closer the magnificent snow-capped peaks appeared, as though they were hovering above the sea rather than being enormous landmasses. Then, as the gloom descended, they seemed to fade away.

"Land ahead!" the fore lookout called.

"We've been able to see the mountains for hours, idiot!" came a mostly good-natured response.

"I mean, I see the Devil's Gate!" This was followed by a much quieter, "Idiot yourself," that Baxter only heard because he was making his way forward with his glasses. As the lookout had identified, they were indeed coming up on the feature.

Watching it in the gathering darkness, Baxter could see why it had such an ill-omened name. Set against a sheer cliff face, the Devil's Gate was a stone arch sitting a few hundred yards from a narrow strip of beach. He could well imagine how ancient mariners would have come to the conclusion that it couldn't possibly be a natural formation.

"There does not even appear to be any drinking water," Fedotov grumbled by his side. "We will not last long there."

Baxter was inclined to agree. "At least it's sheltered," he pointed out. "I swear, I've never seen a better beach for running a boat up onto."

Which, of course, was a lie. The sheltered bays along the coast of Africa that the 2nd Pacific Squadron had put into had been almost perfect for landing a small boat.

"Nothing to drink, and nothing to eat."

Baxter sighed. "I know — I was hoping for at least a stream."

Fedotov scratched at his enormous and, Baxter suspected, non-regulation beard. "Perhaps, now that we are at the shore, it will be easier for us to work our way to a village for supplies, maybe get inland and leave all this behind us."

There would be many amongst the mutineers who would be thinking just that. Getting home to their loved ones, if they had any. Or just getting away from the Navy, and the sea, and Russia itself.

"We'll keep going — I imagine there will be some fishing villages along the coast that haven't even heard of the *Potemkin*, let alone the mutiny. If we don't find anywhere, then we'll take you as far as Theodosia."

Fedotov regarded him solemnly. "The lads will thank you for it. But will this not divert you from your purpose? We will have to continue slowly, if you are towing the boat."

"Slightly," Baxter conceded. "Though if we have to, we can squeeze everyone onto the *Zataka*. And as to my purpose, well, I think you can help me with that."

They almost missed the little settlement, huddled right on the coast. Baxter and Fedotov, with occasional interruptions from the increasingly plaintive Onufri. Occasionally someone would call out from the towed boat, demanding to know if they could go just a little slower, but also hurry the hell up and get them back onto dry land.

"I think the gunboat had a forty-seven mil," the gunner was saying, as Baxter quizzed him in more detail. "And maybe a rotary gun."

Baxter screwed his eyes up, trying to remember the equivalence. A 3-pounder, a quick-firing weapon that wouldn't be a worry for anything much larger than a torpedo boat. The Gatling gun, likely a 1-pounder like the *Zataka*'s paltry battery, would be just as dangerous — more so, even, as it would spit out shells at a much higher rate than the 3-pounder.

"Marcus Alexandrovich!" the lookout called out. "I think I see lights to port."

Baxter brought his glasses up and swept them along the coast. They hadn't seen much during the journey, just scrubby land where the mountains didn't come down all the way to the sea in forbidding cliffs.

"I'm guessing it won't be garrisoned," Baxter mused, as he finally found the tiny collection of lights the lookout had spotted. "Just looks like a few houses."

Fedotov nodded eagerly. "As long as they have food and vodka I will be a happy man, but I would give anything for a jug of fresh water."

Baxter nodded. "Let's see if we can even get close enough to land you."

They got someone in the bows of the torpedo boat with a line. Baxter didn't know these waters at all, and no one else aboard had anything more than the vaguest idea of what to expect. He couldn't take any chances, with the leaking hull and suspect machinery, of running aground.

The linesman was calling out the depths in a steady cadence — he at least seemed to know what he was doing. Baxter listened to the numbers being called out in Russian and then ordered Piotr to bring the torpedo boat's engines to idle. He leant on the armoured shield around the wheel and stared at both the helmsman and Fedotov. "You don't use proper measurements, do you?" he said after a moment.

"He is calling the measurements in arshins, as we always have." Fedotov looked at Baxter curiously. "What system of measurements do you use?"

Baxter sighed. "A different one," he said shortly. He'd had enough of this, and didn't want to risk the boat any further. He didn't know the crew well enough to trust them to take the boat in, and the numbers being called out certainly sounded like they didn't have a lot of water under the keel. "Drop anchor," he said, before turning to the *Vekha* mutineer. "I think this is where we part company. We're only about a hundred feet from the shore, so you should be able to make it even with ... one oar."

Fedotov looked doubtful, then grinned hugely. "I am sure the tide will be coming in soon. Do you not need supplies as well?"

Baxter knew they desperately needed food and fresh water. The only thing they had in reasonable supply was oil for the engines. "Yes, but we don't have time to come further." He caught a few hard looks from the *Zataka*'s crew, and raised his voice. "Any man who wants to make this his port of call, he's welcome to," he said. He would be asking a lot of these men soon, and they owed him nothing. It wouldn't be such a bad thing to strip out those not completely committed to their mad cause. "This is a free ship, after all. Anyone who's got the guts to see this night through, we're not far from Theodosia and re-joining the squadron."

It was a gamble, of course. There were a few people, including the machinists, he couldn't afford to lose. As it was, only three men from his scratch crew of ten got up and went to the back of the torpedo boat to join Fedotov and Onufri in going across. They kept their eyes down as they went, ashamed of abandoning their crew. Baxter couldn't blame them — it wasn't much of a crew, and once they were ashore they would have a much higher chance of getting out of this mess alive.

Ten minutes later, they bid the boat a farewell, even if it wasn't a fond one.

The *Zataka* felt much more spacious with a few less men. Baxter sensed, though, that the men's morale had taken a hit with the departure of three of their number.

"Back us out gently," he ordered Piotr. "Back the way we came."

The helmsman nodded silently. Despite his initial bellyaching, he seemed to be the most competent and reliable member of the crew. Baxter went back round the single funnel and regarded the little circle of faces. The two machinists had come on deck for some fresh air and, apparently, to find out just what the devil was going on because no one told them *anything* down in the gloom of the cramped engine room.

Baxter wasn't too worried about those two. They were Kovalenko's people, and if the 'revolutionary rot' had reached the engine room's officers then he guessed the men themselves were committed. The others were evenly split, more or less, between men who had come across from the *Potemkin* and those who had elected to join the revolution from the small number of ratings ordered to accompany Koenig and the other officers on their suicidal attack.

"Lads," he said, keeping his voice calm and steady. Over the last few days — had it really only been a few days since he'd become embroiled in this? — he'd heard a lot of fire-breathing rhetoric. He was never going to be that kind of speaker, and now wasn't the time for that sort of leadership. "You're tired and hungry. I'm with you on that. Nobody knows what's going to happen yet, whether Afanasy and the others are going to manage to raise the red flag over Theodosia or any other city."

He made sure to make eye contact with each of them in turn, seeing the fear there, the fatigue, and in a lot of eyes also resolve.

He hadn't planned to tell them what his goal was, until this moment. He owed them the truth, though, or at least some of it. "What I do know is that someone is out pretending to be a Turkish man o' war, and that they've seized a vessel known to have been aligned with the *Potemkin*. Now, we all know the *Vekha* doesn't have a heavy armament, and we can only guess what sort of a crew she has now."

"Better than the one she did have," someone murmured, which led to a ripple of laughter. That was good.

"I don't know about that, Slava," Baxter said, causing the fellow to blink in surprise at the use of his name. It was a trick Baxter had picked up years ago, absorbing the names of the sailors under his command just by listening to the men. Something a lot of officers chose not to do. "Fedotov seemed to know what he was about. But that's all by the by. Even without the *Potemkin*'s fearsome batteries, those two ships can do a huge amount of harm to the cause."

"How?" someone else demanded. "They are nothing, compared to the old girl."

"Don't you see?" Slava demanded. "Few people will know that the *Vekha* left us, and no one will know she was captured by this freebooter. A ship known to have been in the hands of revolutionaries, being supported by what claims to be a Turkish gunboat, going around the Black Sea attacking shipping. It would destroy any sympathy for the revolution instantly!"

"It would lead to war with Turkey, when we are already losing a war against Japan!"

"They know they can beat the Ottomans," Slava responded smoothly. "Or they think they can, and there is nothing better to salve a people's wounded pride at losing a war than to start another one and win it. And never mind that it will be our blood that will be spilled to win it."

The sailor's voice was bitter, but Baxter had to admit he was right. He'd been overly focused on what Arbuthnott's original plan had been, to stir up trouble between Russia and Britain. The two countries, despite the fact their king and tsar were cousins, had a long and mutual enmity. But that bad blood was nothing compared to the seething hatred that existed between

Russia and the Ottoman Empire, sharing as they did enormous land and sea borders and a long history of warfare and religious tensions.

Not only that, but Britain had spent the last half century supporting the Ottomans as a counterbalance to Russia. Even if it didn't lead to war, between any of them, it would give Arbuthnott the naval panic he so desperately wanted.

It was playing with matches around an open case of propellant, but it was quite brilliant in its way. It would almost certainly lead to a conflagration that would tear the area apart, if not Europe, which was a prospect that did not bear thinking about.

"I assume you intend to do something about this?" Slava asked him.

He took a breath, looking back towards the forbidding, rocky coastline. By now, he thought, Fedotov and the others would have made it to shore. Piotr was easing them back out to sea and soon it would be time to be on their way towards Theodosia, to see how their revolutionary comrades had fared.

"I do — I intend to find the *Vekha* and this gunboat and sink them both."

It was a bold statement and caused a few raised eyebrows around the group. Before he could elaborate on it, though, or try to quell some of the objections the sailors were about to offer, a gunshot rang loud in the darkness.

Everyone scrambled to the port side of the *Zataka*. The shot had definitely come from shore. A second later there was another crack of noise, and this time Baxter made out the flash of fire. It was definitely coming from the village where they'd left the *Vekha* escapees.

Baxter got his glasses to his eyes, but in the darkness it was hard to make out what was happening. They were at least half a mile out and fights were chaotic things, but he caught enough to get a rough idea of what was going on.

"Cossacks," he snarled, then turned to Piotr. "Take us back in, close as you can!"

CHAPTER 23

Piotr, with Baxter's blessing, brought the *Zataka* back in towards the unnamed little settlement far faster than their previous approach. Faster than was safe, or than he was comfortable with.

Baxter was up in the bows, eyeballing the water in the vain hope of spotting any jutting rocks or sandbanks before they ran onto them and put an end to the mission before it had even begun. He looked up occasionally, raising the field glasses to scope the village. There was still shooting going on, the occasional crack of a rifle. It had the feel of a hunt rather than a skirmish, and certainly wasn't a full-on battle.

A muzzle flash, down by the shore, confirmed his suspicion. He caught sight of one of the *Vekha* mutineers, shot in the chest by a Cossack at close range. Baxter wasn't sure, but he thought the man had been trying to surrender — he'd certainly not seen any sign that any of the mutineers were armed.

His blood boiled. "Slava!" he barked, as that was the first name that came to mind.

"Your Honour?" the mutineer replied, almost automatically falling into the old ways of address and then coughing in an embarrassed fashion. "Yes?"

"Do we have ammunition for the cannon?"

"Plenty," Sava said with some satisfaction. "Shall we destroy the village?"

Baxter didn't quite like the note of savage glee in the sailor's voice. He clearly wasn't one who would argue against the shelling of Odessa. "No — fire over it, put some rounds onto the hillside above. Not too many, mind — we're going to need the shells in a day or so, I'd guess."

Sava hurried away happily. Baxter went back to his vigil on the water and the beach. A moment later he raised his voice. "All stop!" he roared. "Let go the anchor!"

Such was the note of command in his voice that the men jumped to obey immediately. Luckily, Piotr rung the telegraph before the anchor was let go, so the boat didn't rip itself apart by trying to keep going forward while the anchor was dragging in the shallow water.

"Hard a port!" Baxter yelled as the way came off it, but not fast enough to avoid the sandbank that was just becoming apparent. The combination of turning the vessel, the anchor and the engines switching off managed to stop it just before it ran aground.

"Sava, you may fire when ready!" Baxter barked. The sailors had mostly kept their footing as the boat stopped, and now there came a rattle as Sava started turning the handle of the Hotchkiss revolving gun facing the shore while his mate fed the fat shells individually into the ammunition hopper. They obviously knew what they were doing, keeping the rate of fire down. The five-barrelled gun coughed every few seconds, spitting out flame and smoke and sending the small HE shells arcing over the mean collection of houses to burst on the hillside above.

That raised some shouts of consternation amongst the troop of Cossacks, though how they hadn't noticed the boat coming in was beyond Baxter. More importantly, it got the attention of the sailors they were hunting. A few figures broke from cover and started splashing out until they were swimming towards the torpedo boat.

"Come on, brothers!" the sailors around Baxter started shouting, all sourness from earlier forgotten. The Cossacks were firing from the shore at the sailors as they thrashed towards the torpedo boat. Some at least were crawling or staggering along half-submerged sandbanks to reach safety.

Baxter saw a man go down, screaming piteously as he was shot through the guts. Only three remained, desperately struggling to safety. Baxter couldn't get the torpedo boat any closer and knew he couldn't go in after them. "Sava!" he shouted.

"I see them!" The gunner brought the Hotchkiss's muzzle down and started pumping shells at the cluster of men with their long, lethal rifles. The first few went overhead, and they were enough to send the Cossacks scattering. The next few were on target, and Baxter saw at least one horseman caught by the small bursting charge and sent flying through the air.

The first of the escapees reached the *Zataka*, his swimming style close to a panicking canine. Men reached down to help him aboard, and then Onufri was clambering over the side. Apparently Sava's shooting hadn't been enough to put the Cossacks' aim off entirely, though, and a round took him in the head just before he could drop below the gunwale. He fell like a sack of potatoes, sprawling across the deck. Baxter heard Fedotov's roar of grief and anger as he saw his friend shot, and reached down to pull the gunner bodily into the boat before he could turn round and charge back.

"Up anchor!" he yelled as he secured the furious gunner. "Sava, keep firing and keep their heads down! Piotr, slow astern!"

The torpedo boat started easing backwards as the powered winch drew up the anchor. The anchor chain was taut, the anchor obviously well stuck in the sand. More Cossacks were firing from other locations along the beach, bullets whistling overhead or sparking off the metalwork of the torpedo boat.

"You killed my friends, you bastards!" Fedotov yelled. "They didn't do anything to you!"

"Instead of shouting, would you like to do something about it?" Baxter asked him as he pulled the fellow to his feet. They were crouched on the far side of the funnel from the shore, as standing up in the open was an invitation to stop a bullet.

Fedotov nodded, his face ravaged by grief. "Then get on the other Hotchkiss and see if you can pot some of the bastards."

Baxter went aft behind the gunner as he ran for the rear Hotchkiss. It was still dangerous, but he had to show these men he was unafraid. He paused by one of the sailors who was lying flat while another fashioned a crude bandage for his arm.

"Just a flesh wound, Marcus Alexandrovich," the wounded man said with a forced smile. His face was white as a sheet, though, and Baxter suspected the bullet had broken his arm.

"That's the spirit, lads, we'll have you out of this in a moment."

Baxter got to the stern in time to see they were in danger of running into another sandbank. "All stop!" he barked. If the screw bit, they wouldn't be getting out of anything. Then, "Ahead slow and hard starboard!"

"Make up your bloody mind!" Piotr yelled from the conning tower, then yelped. Baxter held his breath, worried the helmsman had been killed. Then the torpedo boat went forward, its bows turning for the open sea again.

"Full ahead!"

Baxter had had more than enough of being shot at for one night. Or, he reflected, for the rest of his life. The *Zataka* was picking up speed, heading for the open darkness of the Black Sea. "Cease fire!" he ordered, as both Hotchkiss guns were still lobbing shells in the general direction of the land. "Cease fire, damn it!"

"All the back and forth," one of the machinists — Ippolit, Baxter thought — said, wiping his greasy hands. He squinted in the growing daylight.

"Not to mention the slewing around and the emergency stops," the other one, Luka, added.

Baxter held his hand up to forestall any further details. "Will the engines run?"

"Not forever," Luka, said.

"No engine runs forever," Ippolit supplied.

"Can you give me two or three days?" Baxter asked patiently. He knew from past experience that there was often little point in shouting at machinists and engineers.

"A day, maybe two," Luka said, then spat over the side. "If we are lucky."

"And you nurse the engine as much as possible," added Ippolit.

Baxter nodded, not pressing the point any further. A day, maybe two, translated into two days and maybe three, if they were very lucky. "Thank you, gentlemen. Piotr! Half ahead and east-north-east. Time to see what our brothers on the *Potemkin* are getting up to."

The *Zataka* had been unharmed during the brief skirmish the previous night, though this wasn't surprising given the best the Cossacks could muster was rifles. There were a couple of holes in the funnel and dents in the hull. The worst of it, in terms of the vessel, was the damage done to the engines as they had made the approach and then their escape. The crew had got off only slightly less well, with a few grazes from ricochets and one broken arm that would need a doctor soon.

Sava, Fedotov and the others were gathered on the main open section of the deck. Baxter was expecting to hear them debate, but they'd stood in silence for a few minutes with their heads bowed.

Sava looked up as the machinists disappeared into their murky kingdom again. "Some of us had our doubts yesterday, when you told us what you were planning on doing," he said. "But having seen our brothers shot down like dogs … we are with you, Marcus Alexandrovich, the rest of the way."

Baxter nodded, not sure if there was much to be said. He'd have preferred it if his words had carried them along, rather than seeing their brothers being murdered, but he'd take it.

"Though I would like someone to tell me what we are with you in doing," Fedotov said. "And what the plan is to achieve it."

"First, Theodosia," Baxter told them all. "Supplies, and pick up a friend or two. Then we'll work out how we go about finding these rogue ships, though I think I have an idea about that."

It had really only just come to him, the idea having been put in his mind when he'd noted Sava's eagerness to bombard civilian homes. He nodded. "I'll fill you in once we've resupplied."

"Here's hoping nobody shoots at us as we're doing it," Sava said.

As they drew in towards the crescent-shaped bay of Theodosia, Baxter got the feeling that the hope was a vain one. After a grey start it had blossomed into a beautiful, sunny day, and for the first time in what felt like a while Baxter actually started to feel like he was drying out.

There were a few steamers on the water now, suggesting that trade in this part of the Black Sea had either restarted or had never ground to a halt. It would take time, he guessed, for word of the rogue battleship's presence to spread amongst civilian shipping. Certainly those ships without wireless telegraphy, which would be most of them. Through his field glasses, Baxter could make out a disturbingly large number of ships making best possible speed away from Theodosia.

"What have you done now, Matyushenko?" Baxter wondered aloud as Piotr brought the torpedo boat round a headland and the sleepy little port town was spread out before them.

He was expecting to see the place in flames or shelled into devastation. Judging from the antlike figures of people moving up into the hills or towards the ancient fortress that overlooked the bay, that was certainly what the population thought. Peering through the field glasses, Baxter could make out the squat bulk of the *Potemkin*. The battleship's gleaming black 12-inch guns were uncovered and aimed at the city, certainly, but didn't appear to have been fired.

Sweeping the glasses round further, he finally made out the battleship's faithful shadow, the torpedo boat *Ismail*. She was further into the harbour, close to a wharf where there appeared to be coal barges. "Have they actually given you what you wanted?" Baxter wondered aloud. Looking beyond the barges, which already had tiny white figures crawling all over them, he saw a company of infantry moving at double time towards them. "No, no, they just set an ambush that you fell right into."

He couldn't blame the mutineers; they must be desperate for fuel at this point. Silence reigned on the torpedo boat as they ran in — although he had the only set of glasses aboard, the others could see that there was definitely something going on.

They could hear it a moment later as the soldiers opened fire on the mutineers. Baxter had the scene fixed in his field

315

glasses, and had seen the white-clothed figures going about their business apparently oblivious to the danger they were in. They had to have seen the soldiers, though, given they were making no attempt at a stealthy approach. They were just so sure that soldiers who came from the same stock as them, who had suffered the same as them, would not open fire.

The sudden fusillade had a dramatic effect on the men. They scattered like startled birds. Some fell into the water, obviously hit, or dived in, either to escape or rescue wounded comrades. Others took cover amongst the coal or on the deck of the barges, trying to return the shots but mostly keeping their heads down. The rifle shots almost sounded like a distant fire on a heathland.

"Why isn't the *Ismail* supporting them?" Sava asked, shading his eyes. The other torpedo boat had a stronger gun armament than their own and could easily have sent the soldiers packing — or at the very least forced them into cover. Perhaps that was why the mutineers hadn't appeared too concerned about the approaching infantry. That and the threat of the big ship, of course.

The *Ismail*, though, lay silently, barely a hundred yards from the wharf. Even as they watched, it got up steam, but instead of closing in to provide cover or at least rescue the men desperately swimming towards it, it turned away and slinked back towards the battleship.

Baxter and his crew were still too far away to hear much beyond the gunfire, but he could guess the men in the water were yelling furiously when they could, in between gasps of air and mouthfuls of water. They had no effect on the *Ismail*'s crew.

And that, Baxter knew in his gut, was that for the revolution.

"Are we going to help?" Fedotov demanded, voice full of anger and urgency.

"We'll try," Baxter said, even though he knew that was a lie. "With the engines the way they are…"

Fedotov nodded. "I will prepare the guns," he said, and hurried away eagerly.

"Ahead full, Marcus Alexandrovich?" Piotr asked.

Baxter made a show of considering that. "If what the machinists have said is true, we would risk blowing the boat up — ahead half, and steer a course for the *Potemkin*. We'll use her as cover as we come in, and try to inspire the crew of both ships to support your brothers!"

That brought a half-hearted cheer as the torpedo boat accelerated again, but the words left a bad taste in Baxter's mouth. It would all be over by the time they got there; it could very well be over even if they went in at full speed. And that wasn't why he was there, even if the mutineers thought he was.

The *Zataka* was slicing across the water now and raising a bit of a bow wave. Baxter switched his gaze to the *Potemkin* and could see a predictable confusion. The 6-inch and smaller guns along the superstructure broadsides appeared to be manned, but weren't thundering fire and death at the city yet. Men were running here and there and he could make out knots of arguing sailors.

"Come on, you buggers, do something," he muttered. He could see one of the steam launches, which had obviously taken the men across to the barges, on its way back to the battleship. They were close enough now that he thought he could recognise Matyushenko aboard, mostly from the energetic way he was moving about on the deck. Of course he would have led the expedition himself, no doubt Konstantin or Kirill along with him.

The firing was dying down on the wharf, now, and through the glasses Baxter could see sailors surrendering, others being pulled out of the water by boats obviously belonging to the garrison. Between them and the patches of white bobbing around in the water or sprawled out on the coal barge, it looked like most of the party had been taken or killed.

"We are too late," Fedotov growled from his position. "Should I fire on them anyway?"

Baxter gave that serious consideration. If nothing else, it would allow his crew to vent some of their frustration. "No," he said at last. "We probably don't want to inflame the situation any further, and we fired more than enough shells last night. House the gun — let's run alongside the *Potemkin* and see what they're planning to do next."

He had Piotr bring the torpedo boat alongside the big ship on the starboard side, away from the city, easing it near one of the entry ports. "Should we drop anchor?" Sava asked.

"No, I don't think we'll be here long. Just hold her steady here, and try not to scratch the paintwork." He raised his voice when it became apparent no one had seen their arrival. "Ahoy, the *Potemkin*! It's the *Zataka* — let down a ladder, would you?"

He'd hoped someone would have done that without encouragement and then forgotten about them, and he'd be able to creep aboard and do what he had to without too much fuss or having to explain himself. He might still get away with it in the confusion and discord aboard. Someone dropped a rope ladder to him, but he couldn't see who.

"Stay here and keep it down," Baxter ordered, before going up the ladder in a flash.

It wasn't complete chaos on deck, but it was definitely confused. Matyushenko was back aboard and making dispositions of his injured comrades; most of the rest of the crew's focus was on that. Men were chanting about bombarding the city for revenge, while others begged for moderation. Glancing around, he saw Koenig crouching by the ship's side, obviously trying to stay out of the way and remain unnoticed. He was also wearing a Nagant on his hip.

Baxter hurried over. "Thanks for dropping the ladder," he said gruffly, by way of a greeting. As was his habit when speaking with Koenig, he dropped into French. It was still quite rusty, even after just a few days of only speaking Russian.

Koenig gave him a tight smile. "Things have been very tense here," he said. "I am very glad to see you."

"Because I'm going to get you out of this?" Baxter asked with a grin.

"Well, yes. That and you brought my torpedo boat back."

Baxter had to restrain a laugh at Koenig's nonchalant tone. It didn't look like the *Potemkin*'s crew were in the mood for humour, and he remained convinced it was best not to draw too much attention to himself. "Mashka and Tommy still aboard?"

"Mashka wanted to go ashore here, but was … dissuaded from doing so. The crew had hoped to stir a revolution here, but while the mayor seemed willing to make compromises, the military governor has refused to."

"You locked her in, didn't you?"

Koenig smiled slightly. "I tried that, but she got out. Eventually I managed to reason with her. What is the plan?"

The arguments across the quarterdeck, where Baxter had come aboard, were getting more heated, and looked close to coming to a fight. Men were actually pulling their comrades away from the lighter, unshielded deck guns. Matyushenko was trying to restore calm, though the quick glance Baxter got of him through the press of men told him the mutineer was a beaten man.

"This is over, Yuriy, but we've still got work to do. I can't explain it all now. We'll get Tommy and Mashka, if she'll come, and we'll get out of here. With some food, if we can."

Koenig nodded and put his hand on the walnut grip of the pistol.

Baxter put his hand on Koenig's forearm. "These people aren't our enemies, and we don't want them to be. We do this quietly."

They moved through the ship as though it were the most natural thing in the world, as though they belonged there. Baxter had started to feel at home aboard, and almost accepted by the crew. He would always be an outsider to them, but he'd been a useful one. Like the mutiny itself, that was coming to an end.

"Don't get involved," he told Koenig as something between a debate and a brawl rolled past them before they headed down a companionway and back to the stateroom where the two teenagers were corralled.

Baxter started to open a hatch. "You had better be a revolutionary or a mutineer," Mashka shouted. "Because if you are a lapdog of the Tsar, I will shoot you."

"Usually best not to warn people before you open fire on them," Baxter said, before swinging the hatch open.

"She learned it from you, Mr B!" Tommy said, rising from behind the makeshift barricade the two of them had fashioned out of the dining table. Baxter was impressed they'd managed to upend it, given that it was normally bolted to the deck.

"Context, lad — I needed Pavel's attention so he didn't shoot Mashka in the head by accident. Now, get your things and let's get out of here."

"Where are we going?" Mashka demanded, stepping out from behind their barricade with the Luger self-loading pistol.

"We do not have time to discuss this!" he snapped. "Away from here, away from this ship, and back towards Odessa. I think the city is in terrible danger."

That got her moving, and as she was moving Tommy was grabbing his bits and pieces too.

"Yuriy, get your rank badges," Baxter said while they were busy. "Assuming they didn't go over the side. And my bloody money."

None of them had much, so they were done quickly — but not so quickly that the former Lieutenant Kovalenko didn't catch up to them as they hurried back up the companionway from the lower decks to the quarterdeck.

"I could not help but notice the *Zataka* has returned but has not anchored, and the crew has not come aboard," he called out from the far end of the passageway that the officer's cabins opened onto. He had a revolver but hadn't drawn it, and Ivan Beshoff was by his side, rifle in hand but not aimed. "I assume you will try and tell me it is standing ready to support our next action?"

Kovalenko drew his Nagant but held it with the muzzle pointed at the deck by his foot, to underline the implication that he would not believe any such story.

Baxter sighed, knowing any attempt at subterfuge was over. "No. We're leaving, and if you've got any sense you'll come with us, before the situation here turns ... ugly."

The mutineer seemed oddly mollified by his blunt honesty, and re-holstered his weapon. "It is precisely to prevent things turning ugly that I must stay, though I thank you for the offer."

"There is a sack of supplies by the ladder," Beshoff added with a grin. The two of them hurried away in the opposite direction, going to join the debates that were raging.

When Baxter and his little band got back to the quarterdeck, things seemed to have calmed down slightly. The red battle pennant that had been billowing in the breeze was being hauled down, though Baxter noted the main guns were now trained on the city. Unusually for such a situation, he didn't see anyone up on an impromptu stage, haranguing the sailors.

They skirted round the back of a growing group of sailors on the quarterdeck. While he couldn't see through the press of men, Baxter was pretty sure Matyushenko was at the centre of it, taking the council of his comrades. Some men were still shouting that the city should be bombarded in preparation for a landing, but more voices were shouting for a return to Romania.

They reached the top of the ladder, which was still in place along with the bag of food Beshoff had left for them. The *Zataka*, however, was nowhere to be seen.

"Hey, where are you going?" a sailor demanded, a rough hand landing on Baxter's shoulder as he peered over the side, looking for the torpedo boat. "Afanasy is speaking!"

Baxter turned to face the speaker. While discipline had been maintained to a high level amongst the mutineers, which was unusual enough, this one had obviously managed to get into the liquor stores. Fortunately, he was the only one who seemed to have noted the little group of escapees, though if he continued at that volume the others would soon notice.

Baxter stepped in to him, despite the reek of vodka, and lifted a knee hard into his midriff, driving the wind out of him and then supporting him as he folded up.

"It's alright, old man," he murmured. "You'll get your breath back in a moment. Just breathe through it."

A couple of sailors had turned from the debate, and Baxter grinned at them. "I think something he ate has disagreed with him," he told the other two, then supported the sailor to the side so he could vomit into the sea. "There we go," Baxter said, settling him down with his back to the side. The sailor stared balefully at him, gasping for breath.

"The torpedo boat has come back," Koenig hissed. Tommy and Mashka were huddled at the side by the entry port, both of them looking as uncertain as he'd ever seen them. Looking over the side, Baxter saw the *Zataka* coming back round the battleship's stern. Sava saw him, raised a hand in greeting, and steered for the side once more.

Baxter hoisted the bag of provisions. "Let's get out of here."

CHAPTER 24

There was no time to be lost, now, but Baxter was also acutely aware of the need to nurse the engines — not to mention conserve fuel. He therefore didn't race the *Zataka* back across the Black Sea at full speed, but kept them at three quarters speed for most of the way.

"Odessa is in danger?" Mashka demanded, a fierce glint in her eyes, once they were well clear of Theodosia and the coast of Crimea was little more than a dark blur.

"Hmm?" Baxter's attention was on the sea, but he was also listening for the distant thunder of heavy guns.

Nothing so far.

She hit him, none too gently, in the small of the back. "You said my city was in danger!" she repeated, voice rising.

The sailors, those of them who hadn't encountered the fiery young Odessan revolutionary before, didn't quite know what to make of her, and particularly of the way she spat fire and fury at pretty much everyone around her. They also seemed a little nervous about having a young woman aboard. They were only a few hours from Yalta, the next intended stop, where Baxter planned that she would stop being a problem.

"You have mentioned this a few times," Koenig pointed out mildly. If Mashka being back aboard was a cause for some discomfort for the sailors, the presence of an officer who had clearly not joined the revolution was certainly a sore point. Oddly enough, those who had been on the torpedo boat's crew when it had tried to sink the battleship seemed more comfortable with him.

"Oh, yes. Well, I have been known to do some thinking," Baxter said, turning back from his scanning of the sea. He'd seen some smoke plumes and a few masts, but nothing close and he suspected it was still the slew of ships fleeing Theodosia. Certainly no sign of the *Potemkin*, nor of the destroyer hunting her. "Matyushenko and the others made it very clear that they would consider bombarding Odessa. Made a lot of public proclamations to that effect, not to mention lobbing a few shells at the theatre. Now, we all know that sense and humanity prevailed, but the foreign press doesn't know that."

"Surely they must know we are not monsters?" Piotr demanded.

"You obviously don't know the press in the rest of the world — particularly those that tend to support governments and oppose things like civil disorder and mutiny," Baxter said drily. "I am sure there are some who support you, and Lord knows this will be exposing just how brutal your Tsar's autocracy can be. Bilyk, the secret policeman running this, knows this and knows it won't help his cause. The authorities will be desperate to destroy any public sympathy both at home and abroad, and what better way to do that than by the sustained shelling of a civilian population? Even by a couple of ships that have nothing like the firepower of the *Potemkin*."

There was silence aboard. The Russian sailors were all happily tucking into the supplies he'd brought abroad, mostly dried bread and hard cheese. He couldn't blame them, but he knew they'd need to resupply in Yalta at the rate they were eating.

"They could just harass or attack foreign shipping," Koenig pointed out. "Much less risky, and perhaps more chance of success."

Baxter nodded. "That did occur to me," he said. "But that'll take much longer, and wouldn't have the same impact as a city in flames. If they do take that approach, there's very little we'll be able to do about it. This isn't a huge sea — little more than a lake, really — but it's still big, and we'll never be able to find them."

Koenig smiled at the reminder of their conversation about Lake Baikal. "You caught up to Yefimov in the South China Sea. It does seem, with some evidence, that you have an instinct for such things."

Baxter snorted. "I knew where he was going and how quickly his boat would sail, that's all," he said. "And my instincts are telling me they'll go for Odessa. And it has to be Odessa. That's where this all started."

Koenig nodded placidly, apparently satisfied. The other sailors nodded their agreement, all but Fedotov, who just glowered at them.

"So what do we do about it? We are a little torpedo boat and the *Vekha* is a big ship, even if she has ... guns that are smaller than a battleship's."

Baxter reminded himself the barrel-shaped sailor had been a gunner aboard, and would likely be protective of his charges. He couldn't be *too* dismissive of her armament, even if Fedotov would not be happy about his next statement. "We're going to take on supplies at Yalta," he said, nodding to Koenig. "Seeing as we have a proper officer of His Serene Highness's navy, that shouldn't be too much of a problem — though I know it's a big ask, Yuriy."

Koenig dismissed it with a casual wave of his hand. "We have endured worse danger."

"We must be quick about the resupply, mind. The *Vekha* may not be fast, but we've already spent too long in these waters and she could be off Odessa as we speak. We'll keep a sharp lookout for her and her consort on the way, in case they do decide to indulge in some commerce raiding. We'll then patrol off Odessa for as long as we can, and if we find them — we sink them."

"And then what?" Sava asked.

Baxter frowned at him. "Let's tackle one problem at a time, shall we?"

It took them about five hours to reach Yalta, giving the coast a wide berth and not putting the boat under too much pressure. Baxter chafed at the delay, but he knew there was nothing for it. Many of the mutineers, with their bellies properly full for the first time in days and a ration of vodka in the offing, seemed to be treating it as a holiday, lounging about on deck when they didn't have the barest duties to perform.

"Could you even have imagined we would find ourselves in this position?" Koenig asked him. The two of them were stood side-by-side, watching the shoreline come closer after they'd made their turn towards the town. "It's been, what, barely a fortnight since we were on Lake Baikal and had that rather magnificent fight with the Cossacks."

Baxter glanced across at him, raising an eyebrow at the notion that it had been *their* fight. "Well, I suppose I did leave you one or two."

"It was very kind of you, though I must confess pugilism has never been my strong suits. I assume you learned such things on the playing fields of Eton?"

Baxter laughed. "Try going to school in Leith and spending most of my life at sea. And no, to answer your question, I couldn't have begun to imagine this madness. But then, two years ago I couldn't even imagine fighting alongside you and the others at Tsushima."

Koenig sighed. "Life is a funny thing, and can be a hard one."

"That attitude's for writers and playwrights," Baxter pointed out, trying not to sound too harsh. "We're sailors, Yuriy. We take events as they come."

Koenig seemed to shake off the introspective mood. "Indeed. We must be careful in Yalta — it is not so far from Sevastopol, and it is a popular resort. While most who stay there are your authors and playwrights, naval officers have been known to take their ease there."

"I know," Baxter said, voice dark. "It's a huge risk we're asking of you."

"I do this out of duty," Koenig said. "If the mutiny is discredited, that is not such a bad thing as far as I'm concerned. But to see Odessa damaged further, or worse, to see us drawn into another futile war... No, it does not bear thinking about. And it is not such a risk, really. They will be used to Russian warships popping in for resupply. I am more concerned about our, ah, crew."

Baxter glanced over his shoulder. "I'll keep 'em in line."

The seaside town of Yalta was drawing closer. The sun was starting to disappear behind the mountains that surrounded it and the streetlights were beginning to come on. Baxter raised his glasses and carefully examined the harbour, looking for the *Stremitelny* or, by some fluke, the *Vekha*. Neither were in evidence, and nor had the *Potemkin* somehow managed to beat them here.

He could see why the pretty little town was such a draw for Russia's elite and the intelligentsia. He could make out enormous *dacha* and more Western-style mansions dotted around the town and the hills overlooking it. There was more luxury here than any man on this boat, with the possible exception of Koenig, would experience in their entire life.

"Find us a berth as far out as possible," Baxter said. "Let's not draw too much attention to our presence."

Baxter was glad, for a number of reasons, that there didn't appear to be any warships or even a garrison here. There was no one to salute, no flags to dip, and there didn't even seem to be much need to report to the port authorities — particularly as they were coming in as night was falling.

"There may not be anyone awake to sell us supplies," Koenig pointed out, chewing his lip. He was, perhaps, more nervous than he had previously let on.

"Then wake them up. Sava and Fedotov will go with you. They still look like sailors."

The torpedo boat was easing up against a wooden wharf. It was quiet in this part of the town, but a couple of passers-by stopped to give them a curious look, and a handful of dock workers turned out to tie the boat up.

So far, so good. No one was running off to alert the authorities. "On your way," Baxter said to Koenig, having detailed the two sailors to accompany him and impressing upon them that they were there to protect and help the lieutenant, not keep him under guard. Koenig nodded, patted the pocket of his unit jacket to make sure he had the money Baxter had dispensed, and then jumped up onto the wharf.

Baxter watched the three of them head away, trying hard not to start feeling anxious already. He'd made it very clear to all of them that there was little time indeed, but he could not shake the feeling that there was less time than he'd previously guessed.

He wasn't looking forward to his next task, as it involved having an argument with two very strong-willed youths.

Despite his age, wisdom and size, he found he was usually on the losing side of these.

"This is where you two make your port," he told them bluntly, looming over them in the tiny crew cabin where he'd found them. "This next bit is going to be dangerous, and I'll be happier knowing you're both ashore."

"It won't be more dangerous than the battle!" Tommy protested.

"It will be considerably more dangerous," Baxter said flatly before this could devolve into a multi-part argument. "We're one small boat, taking on two larger and better armed vessels — assuming we can even find them. Not to mention the trouble that will come from being renegades. No — my mind is made up on this. I'm going to put money in your pocket, Mashka, and I'm trusting you to get Tomas'ka back to … well, the closest thing he has to family. He can explain it. And Tommy, when you get back to the countess, tell her that I said not to send you back if you don't want to go."

Not that Baxter expected his opinion to carry any weight with Ekaterina, but Tommy had said that was why she'd been trying to send him back to Scotland, why he had run away in the first place. It was therefore worth a try.

Something about his tone or his grim expression quelled Tommy. "What am I supposed to do, then?" Mashka asked, her voice bitter. "Off into God knows where in Russia, running errands, and then what becomes of Mashka?"

Baxter blinked. He wasn't used to hearing such uncertainty from the young woman. "Ekaterina is a good person," he said. "And a person of means. You're a smart young lady. I'm sure you two can work it out between you."

He left them sitting glumly below decks, not wanting to argue with them any further, and went back on deck. He paced the boat for the following couple of hours, until he realised he was making the crew nervous, then jumped up onto the wharf and stood staring into town.

"What ship?" a dock worker asked. He sounded tired, and probably a little put out that this unexpected arrival was keeping him and his mates here.

"*Zataka*, torpedo boat," Baxter replied, suddenly conscious of his civilian clothes. He tried to minimise conversation, knowing that while his Russian was good it wasn't perfect and his accent could give him away. "Detached service from Sevastopol," he added, hoping that would lend a sufficient air of mystery that they would leave him alone.

"You out looking for this rogue battleship, then?" the dock worker asked, smearing his dirty hands on the front of his tunic before taking out his pipe.

"Something like that," Baxter said. He could see a small cart approaching that appeared to have supplies on it. "You men don't have to hang around — our crew can take care of loading."

"Oh, we're not hanging around for you, friend, though if there are a few kopeks on offer, we can help," the dock worker said, as he lit up and then puffed on the tobacco with an evident air of satisfaction. "There's another boat due in, special service as well. Very quiet, we were told, but very clearly to do with this ship of rogues as well. Just like you."

And that was why it was impossible to keep a secret in a port. Baxter forced a smile, though a sudden cold certainty had gripped him. "Were you told anything about this ship — large, bringing in a lot of cargo?" He adopted a serious expression as the dock worker looked suspiciously at him, and he went on hurriedly. "It could be the ship I'm supposed to meet here.

You know how it is — they tell you to go somewhere and meet a ship, but don't give you the details."

The worker puffed a couple more times, surrounding himself with a haze of fragrant blue smoke. After a moment, he clearly decided that Baxter had an honest face. "Just a passenger boat, but the passenger will need a hand up onto the wharf and a carriage waiting for him."

Baxter nodded judiciously. "Sounds like just the man I'm waiting for," he said, feeling a stab of savage satisfaction as he guessed who was coming in. The cart had pulled up, the dray horse and driver both regarding him with a similar, solemn expression.

Fedotov jumped down from the back of the cart. "Butts of water and goods, your honour!" he declared. "His worshipfulness is arranging for an oiler as well."

Baxter was worried that the sailor was laying on the deference a little *too* thick, but the dock workers and driver all seemed to regard this as perfectly normal, and no doubt expected. He fished in his pocket and drew out some loose change. "I think we will take you up on the offer of assistance," he said as casually as he could manage. "We may be leaving in a hurry. When did you say this other ship is due?"

The dock worker shrugged, taking the coins and jangling them as he obviously decided whether the pay made it worth his time. Having inspected the relatively small amount of cargo, he clearly decided it was. "Any time now," he said eventually. "Running late, in fact."

Baxter paced a bit up the wharf. He'd been hoping for some more supplies, so they could continue to patrol for the *Vekha* as long as possible. And the old-fashioned casks of water would be a pain to stow. Better than nothing, though.

He looked back out to sea. It was fully dark now and the dim lighting along the wharf had killed his night vision, so he didn't see what was clearly a steam yacht closing in on the same wharf he stood on until it was almost too late.

It was the fact it was a yacht, rather than any kind of working boat or even a naval vessel, that confirmed for Baxter exactly who was on board.

He hurried to get out of sight before the sleek little vessel slid up to the wharf, about a hundred yards further in from the *Zataka*. He didn't sprint for cover, though every fibre of his being wanted to. That would have looked suspicious. He stepped across to the small warehouses that lined the land side of the wharf, hoping to give the impression that he was looking for somewhere to relieve himself

The yacht tied up after a few minutes of watching. She came in a bit faster than was sensible, and he winced as the polished woodwork crunched against the pier. "Typical bloody aristo," Baxter muttered, watching from the shadows of an alley. The dockworkers who had been assisting his crew left them to it, with a cheerful exchange of obscenities.

Baxter moved closer to the pier, keeping as much as possible to the shadows. He was still some way from the yacht, but he didn't want to make a mess of this. Not if it was who he thought it was. He was breathing fast, knowing this was absurdly dangerous and stupid. He should just walk away.

"Where's the bloody carriage then?" he heard someone yelling in English, in a nasal tone, when he was maybe five yards from the yacht, lurking in yet another alleyway that someone had clearly recently used to relieve himself.

"It is on its way, your honour," he heard another voice say, also speaking English but with a slight Russian accent. "As I said, the delays getting here…"

"Don't give me your bloody excuses! It's no wonder this country is going to the dogs, riven with revolution, if you can't even have a carriage here on time."

Baxter could see Arbuthnott now. The same, or a very similar, smart civilian suit he'd last seen the rogue agent in, and still on crutches. Still demanding and convinced of his own superiority.

"Bastard," Baxter growled, just as a smart carriage drawn by a pair of handsome chestnuts clattered along the wharf.

"About time!" he heard Arbuthnott snap. "Where's the chair to get me off this unpleasant conveyance?"

Baxter hesitated in the alleyway, hand on the grip of the revolver he still wore. He could just slip away, step back into the darkness and make his way back to the *Zataka*. It would be better and fairer for everyone if he did that.

Instead, heart in his throat, he stepped out from the shadows and crossed the wharf in a few quick strides, just as Arbuthnott was being assisted up the gangplank from the yacht, complaining bitterly that a bosun's chair hadn't been provided for him.

The coachman was watching the whole thing with an expression of wry amusement as Baxter flattened himself to the side of the carriage. He'd seen a few men who were clearly Okhrana officers, but they were all focused on their guest. The coachman had jumped down to open the door on the opposite side of the carriage to Baxter.

Now was the moment. Without giving himself time to pause or second-guess himself, Baxter opened the carriage door on his side and stepped lightly aboard, wincing as his weight caused the vehicle to shift slightly on its springs. Nobody noticed, though, distracted by Arbuthnott's constant whining.

Baxter settled as far back as possible, crossing his legs and pulling his cap brim down low enough that he gave the impression he'd always been in the carriage. Or that's what he hoped, anyway.

Arbuthnott finally made it into the conveyance. An Okhrana man barely glanced at Baxter and obviously assumed he was there as an additional escort. The Englishman barely spared him a glance as he finally settled in. "Get me to the *dacha* immediately!" he demanded.

Baxter had the briefest moment to examine the fellow, confirming his previous fleeting impression. The Naval Intelligence officer looked sallow and drawn. He guessed laudanum addiction would have that effect.

"The thing about a bosun's chair, old chap, is that it's no bloody use unless you're being lifted onto a higher vessel," Baxter said, bringing the Nagant up just as Arbuthnott opened his mouth to shout a warning. The carriage was moving now, the coachman expertly turning it on the wharf.

Baxter knew he only had seconds. He saw Arbuthnott's eyes widen in fear as he looked down the muzzle of the revolver. His mouth snapped shut with an audible clack.

"Quickly now," Baxter said, keeping his voice low. "The target is Odessa?"

Arbuthnott nodded, not taking his eyes off the weapon.

"When?"

"Dawn tomorrow."

Baxter scowled. That didn't give them a lot of time, but they might just make it. He lifted the curtain as the coachman managed to get them turned round, putting him on the harbour side of the vehicle. They needed to go now, but he had matters to attend to first. Matters that required Koenig to be back with them.

He banged on the roof of the carriage. "Hold on a moment," he called out in Russian.

"I thought he wanted to reach the *dacha* as soon as possible?" the coachman shouted back.

Baxter didn't bother replying as the coach came to a halt, and he turned his attention back to Arbuthnott. He guessed the Okhrana hadn't let the man have a weapon, and he wasn't going anywhere on his healing leg. If he had been armed, though, and fit, Baxter knew he wouldn't have the courage to try either.

"I assume a demonstration bombardment and then away?" he asked, seeking to confirm his previous analysis. "To make a point?"

Arbuthnott just stared at him, swallowing hard.

Baxter got a sick feeling in his guts. "What have you done?"

"Bilyk has arranged for incendiary shells, do not ask me how," the fellow quavered. "He's also made arrangements with a Cossack officer, a Captain Zubov, for his men to start setting fires in the slums once the bombardment has started. He will not just make a point, raise tensions between Turkey and Russia. He will burn the guts out of the revolution while he's at it."

It was Baxter's turn to stare wordlessly at Arbuthnott. He had never, in his worst dreams, imagined the conspirators would go that far. But, as he'd realised, Bilyk was a zealot. Fanatically devoted to his Tsar and maintaining his autocratic rule.

"I didn't want to go that far, of course," Arbuthnott started blithering, taking some comfort from Baxter's silence. "As you know, all I want is for our government to start taking our naval defences seriously. A bit of tension between the great nations of Europe is only healthy, isn't it? Particularly if it's only the

Turks and Russians who end up fighting; honestly, they're as bad as each other."

"You're a bloody idiot, you know that?" Baxter said. He could have gone on, explained just how horrendous the consequences of a war would be, whether it involved British soldiers and sailors or not. How brutal fires in the closely packed slums of Odessa would be.

Instead, he just levelled the big revolver at Arbuthnott's face, shutting the idiot up by pulling the hammer back. He held the heavy weapon there, the muzzle not wavering. He dearly wanted to pull the trigger. With the hammer all the way back, it would have taken the slightest squeeze to send a bullet through that high, sweating forehead.

He glanced out of the carriage's window, and could make out an oiler chugging towards his torpedo boat. Well, hopefully Koenig was on board or otherwise somewhere close.

"Why don't you stop all this foolishness?" Arbuthnott asked in a weak voice. "We could do great things together, you and I. For the good of the Crown!"

Baxter looked back at him, jaw set, willing himself to pull the trigger. Arbuthnott was a menace, but in person he was also pathetic. Baxter forced himself to breathe out, and dropped the muzzle. Arbuthnott actually sobbed as the threat of his extinction seemed to be lifting.

"I'm not sure if I've told you this," Baxter said, his calm tone surprising even himself. "But I don't give a shit about any of that."

He pulled the trigger. The pistol was loud in the confines of the carriage, the small space filling with smoke from the powder. Arbuthnott screamed as his hands flew to his shattered knee. Baxter was already moving, hurling the door of the carriage open and jumping down. People were yelling in confusion and fear. The nearest Okhrana man actually had his back to the carriage, staring down the wharf towards the suspicious torpedo boat. Baxter whipped the long barrel of the revolver across the back of his head, stunning him, then levelled in and fired twice in the direction of the policemen standing around on the wharf. They abandoned trying to draw their own weapons and dived for cover, though Baxter knew the couple of shots wouldn't keep their heads down for long.

He spun, bringing the weapon to bear on the coachman, but he was already jumping down on the other side of the carriage and running for it.

Baxter didn't hang around, and took off in a pounding sprint towards the *Zataka*. Men were shouting everywhere, from the torpedo boat and the wharf and the oiler that had been about to draw in next to the *Zataka*. Baxter ignored all of it, until he saw Fedotov and a couple of others running towards him.

"Get back to the boat!" he yelled breathlessly. They didn't need too much encouragement, and turned as one to spring back to their vessel. Baxter was only a few yards behind them when the policemen started shooting, the bullets whistling past him. There was nothing for it but to keep running, though, and hope the range kept him safe.

"Get us unmoored and get the engines running!" he bellowed. He was relieved, and slightly aggrieved, to see the crew had already done that and the *Zataka* was in fact a few feet from the wharf.

He took a running jump, landing untidily but quickly regaining his feet on the boat.

"What about the oil?" Koenig shouted from the tubby little vessel that he'd somehow procured to refuel them.

"We'll have to make do with what we've got!" he shouted back, then turned to Piotr. "Take us alongside that tub so the others can get across, and then get us the hell out of here."

"Where are we going, Marcus Alexandrovich?"

"Back to Odessa."

Back to Russia — the one place he'd never wanted to see again.

CHAPTER 25

The pre-dawn light found the *Zataka* idling a few miles off the coast of the Ukraine, not far from Odessa. Or that was what Marcus Baxter hoped. Navigation had never been his strong suit. Koenig agreed, at least.

It had been a close-run thing, getting him and Sava aboard and getting out of Yalta's harbour. Piotr, in his hurry, had damn near rammed the oiler, and that would have been the end for all of them. The sailor was still apologising to everyone for almost killing everyone in a fiery conflagration.

Negotiating their way past the oiler while recovering Koenig and Sava — who had got his feet wet, before Fedotov had pulled himself all the way aboard — had given the Okhrana men a chance to get closer, and a brief, furious and mostly inaccurate gun battle had ensued between sailors and policemen. Most of them agreed the only one of them to hit anything was Mashka, who had gleefully potted a policeman with her stolen Luger before they finally moved out of effective range.

Baxter had ordered a more sedate speed once they were away from the scene of their various crimes. The harbour was reasonably large, so while the gunfire would probably have alerted local police and any garrison, it would take a while for anyone to realise what was happening. A boat leaving at an unsafe speed, though, would have attracted immediate suspicion.

"It's just as well we did slow down," Koenig commented as they discussed the night's events over tea and bread. He was still a bit pale and shaken, not so much from those near misses but from the pressure that had then fallen on him. "The *Stremitelny* would certainly have come after us if we'd gone tearing past her without so much as a by your leave."

That, Baxter acknowledged, had probably been the most dangerous part of the night. They had cruised out past the destroyer, still no doubt on her mission to hunt down the rogue battleship, as she came into port. The two vessels had come so close in the darkness that there had been no way to avoid being seen. Instead, Koenig had managed to bluff their way past the destroyer without raising her captain's suspicions.

"I thought you'd been sunk!" Lieutenant Yanovich had called across, as the vessels had drawn apart.

"Not yet. Good hunting!" Koenig had replied cheerfully. "Let me know if you bag anything!"

Then the vessels had passed. Baxter was certain that if the destroyer commander hadn't been so focused on his hunt, he might have taken a bit more time to interrogate them further. Instead, the *Zataka* had been able to steam out into the night on her own hunt.

"Tommy said you planned to leave him and Mashka in Yalta," Koenig commented now, putting his tin teacup aside and taking up glasses to scour the gloom again.

"That was my plan, yes." Baxter couldn't deny feeling a certain amount of guilt about the situation. Once again, he'd been so focused on his own goals that he'd put a couple of youngsters at more risk. "I had thought of leaving you as well, but you'd just have found a way to sneak back aboard."

"And you think Tomas'ka wouldn't have?" Koenig asked with a laugh. His expression became still for a moment. "It's nothing. We could try and land them in Odessa before we go hunting?"

Baxter shook his head. "I don't think we have time. Arbuthnott told me the plan was to attack at dawn."

"You did the right thing," Koenig said. "We wouldn't have the intelligence we have now if you had not."

"I didn't have to shoot the bugger — that gave the game away."

"True, but someone would still have raised the alarm. Yes, we now have obstacles, but we have a good idea of where we need to be and just how vital our mission is. We will worry about the fuel later."

"And I'll just have to make damn sure we don't get sunk," Baxter added. "I just hope Arbuthnott is right and the Cossacks won't start burning anything if the shelling doesn't begin."

Koenig looked worried by the prospect. "With Cossacks, who can say? This Zubov will understand that the plan relies on the fires being set only with the excuse of the piratical mutineers — perhaps he will manage to maintain discipline."

"We met him, you know," Baxter said. "On Lake Baikal. I knocked him off his feet."

Koenig grinned at the memory. "I recall — he was the ringleader of the Cossack officers tormenting us."

"Ran into him again in Odessa a couple of times — we had a good go at killing each other. I put a samovar's worth of tea into his face."

"I think what you are telling me is that this man is not stable, and is probably quite angry?"

"That's more or less it, yes," Baxter said. "Once we've found and sunk the *Vekha*, and this gunboat if we can manage it, I think we will put into Odessa. We'll need to find a way to warn people at least, if we can't stop the Cossacks."

"It will be a death sentence for you and these men, if you are caught," Koenig said. "I will land and warn the authorities."

"If it's become known that you've been working with us…"

"I will tell them I was a prisoner," Koenig said placidly.

"Begging your pardon, Mr B," Tommy said, speaking in English. That was a sure sign that he wanted to speak in confidence. "Mr Koenig won't need to tell anyone anything. I can contact her nibs and she'll see it sorted, make sure nothing bad befalls him."

Baxter felt like he'd been kicked in the guts. Koenig had enough English to know that this wasn't a conversation he needed to be a part of, so took his glasses and stepped away a few feet. It was the closest to privacy they could manage without going below.

"She's in Odessa?" Baxter managed to get out, his voice sounding strangled. "Why in the…"

Tommy was nodding, wringing his hands unhappily. "She told me not to tell you," he said at last, looking on the verge of tears. "Made me promise, she did! We'd gone to that house to look for any evidence of where they'd taken you, an' then when you came in we were in separate rooms and I realised you could hear her, so I came out an'…"

"And since then I've been dragging you all over creation, putting you in danger, thinking it was the only way to keep you safe, when all I needed to do was put you ashore and off you'd pop!" Baxter's voice rose, and he struggled to master himself. "I should have known you wouldn't have been able to make it all the way there by yourself. Why in hell didn't she just talk to me?"

Tommy actually did start crying then, just a couple of tears before he choked them back and wiped his nose on his sleeve. "I dunnae ken, Mr B. She said it was better that you didn't know, for both of you, an' I think she thought you were angry with her for some reason. That you work best when nobody's trying to pull your strings, is what she said. An' she's staying away from the centre of town and it would have taken me ages to find the place, I swear, and I've been able to help you… Please don't be angry with me!"

Baxter was angry, yes, but it wasn't the red fury that sometimes came down on him. Perhaps he was just too drained by the last two days, and perhaps there was something to what Tommy said. It was too late to do anything about it now, anyway.

"I think she'll probably want to see you after this," the lad said cautiously.

"Maybe," Baxter grunted. "Assuming any of us survive it." He made himself reach out and ruffle Tommy's hair. The boy grinned at him. "You're getting pretty good at this lying business," Baxter said without rancour. "I think the intelligence services rather than the navy for you, my boy."

In truth, he didn't know what the future held for Tommy, or indeed any of them. They didn't have time to talk about it, though.

"Baxter, I think I have them," Koenig said quietly.

"Report it properly, Mr Koenig," Baxter said with mock sternness, trying to break the dark mood that had fallen over him.

"Unknown ships off the port quarter, Marcus Alexandrovich!"

"Thank you, Yuriy Makarovich." Baxter took up his own field glasses. "And yes, by God, I think we have them."

Baxter took the *Zataka* in slowly. There were rolling fog banks over the water, though he thought they would burn off quickly enough. He'd use what cover they and the twilight provided.

He watched the two vessels carefully as Piotr brought the torpedo boat closer. It was still too dark to glean much, though the *Vekha* was tall and well-lit enough that he could see the details. She was a transport, sure enough, and a known quantity. After some discussion with Fedotov and wracking his memory for comparisons, he'd worked out she mounted a 3-pounder on the forecastle and a couple of 1-pounders amidships. The gunboat, the false Turk, was of more concern to him. Fedotov had said it was lightly armed, and he couldn't imagine Bilyk, no matter his influence, had been able to source significant firepower for it, but until he could make her out he wouldn't take that for granted.

Right now, the gunboat was a low shape almost lost against the sea and the sky that seemed to blend together in the poor light. Even if it was lightly armed, it would be a problem — the *Zataka* had a truly pitiful gun armament, relying on her torpedoes for offensive power. The opposing vessel probably had too shallow a draft to torpedo, and he wanted both of those lethal items for the *Vekha*. They were notoriously unreliable and hard to aim, so he wanted to double his chances of a kill.

"We're between them and Odessa," Koenig said. The rogue ships were indeed coming in from the open sea. "And still some time until they're in range."

"Assuming the biggest thing they have is the three-pounder on the transport." Baxter lowered his glasses. There was something odd about that gunboat, but he couldn't quite put his finger on it. "Send the men to their stations, please, Yuriy, but quietly. And make sure Tommy and Mashka are below — tell them to pile up the food and water casks around them."

Baxter went back to the conning position. Piotr was at the wheel, and Sava joined him shortly, standing by to take over if anything should happen. Fedotov had gone to one of the gun positions, another sailor in tow, and the second weapon was manned shortly after two men Baxter knew to be torpedo technicians went into the bow compartment.

They were as ready as they could be. They had the element of surprise on their side, and the advantage that they were trained sailors, even if they hadn't worked together long as a crew. Baxter could only guess at who was running these ships — probably a mix of Okhrana men, sailors who could be trusted and Naval officers. Possibly some of the original crew of the *Vekha*, trying to win clemency from their superiors.

Baxter didn't let himself think about what they were about to do to those people. It was a necessity, to prevent the wholesale slaughter of innocent civilians.

"Ahead half, if you please, and starboard two points."

"We'll use the fog?" Koenig asked, joining him there.

"And the darkness, while both last," Baxter said. "The *Vekha* is the main target," he went on. "Unless positions change, on this approach we'll be able to run in perpendicular to her course. I don't know much about torpedoes, but firing that at the target's broadside seems to be the sensible approach. They're sailing line astern, so we should be some distance from the gunboat still. Fedotov can engage it on the way in, then we'll turn after we've launched and run out past her, give her everything we've got and hopefully do enough damage to put her off."

"Both torpedoes in one pass?"

"We're only going to get one pass," Baxter confirmed. "I'll need you on the tubes — launch only when I give the order."

Baxter yawned titanically after Koenig had acknowledged that and headed off. He'd been up a lot of the night, talking with the couple of crew members who actually understood torpedoes. As usual, he found the supposedly common sailor remarkably cogent on a subject they'd actually trained in.

"I'll fetch you some more tea," someone said, and it took him a moment to realise it was Tommy.

"I sent you below."

"Mr Koenig did pass that on," the lad called over his shoulder. "I know, I know, I'll go below once I've got you another mug."

"Your lad will grow into a fine young man soon," Piotr opined. Baxter was about to deny Tommy being his son, but realised he was beginning to think of him as one in a very real sense.

It would make what would come after they finished this, assuming they survived, even harder.

They crept closer to the hostile vessels, both to conserve their fuel and keep their noise down. The machinists had told him they could guarantee the engines for a few more hours, and Baxter guessed they had enough fuel for the attack and, hopefully, the escape. He wouldn't have been able to take the gamble of abandoning the oiler if he hadn't had a time and place for the attack.

Something kept nagging him about the gunboat. Now they were closer, and Bilyk's flotilla was coming in against the rising sun, he'd been able to get a better look at it. He was pretty certain they'd converted a small civilian vessel, a working boat rather than a pleasure craft. It was a time-honoured tradition, arming merchant vessels and disguising your own ships as those of the enemy or a neutral party in a time of war. And to Bilyk and men like him, Baxter knew, this was very much a war.

Her forecastle, he decided, was altogether too built-up for his liking. It would make her unseaworthy, thoroughly top heavy in fact, and only an idiot would have done that without purpose.

Something Arbuthnott said trickled through his mind. *Bilyk has arranged for incendiary shells.*

To the best of Baxter's knowledge, which was extensive after a year at sea with the Pacific Squadron, Russian naval artillery didn't really fire incendiary shells.

"They appear to be dropping anchor," Koenig called from the bows. "Or the *Vekha* is, anyway. They're well out of range still, unless…"

"That's not a bloody gunboat," Baxter said, then raised his voice. "They've improvised a monitor. Ahead full!"

There was nothing for it. They were still a mile out, give or take, and the torpedoes had a range of less than a thousand yards. He'd been working on an incorrect assumption that they had more time, that the course he'd plotted relative to the incoming vessels would bring them together without them having to go full speed until the last moment.

Baxter wasn't able to identify the weapon being uncovered on the gunboat; it looked to be more of a howitzer than a naval gun. It would almost certainly shake the vessel to pieces if not break her back after only a few rounds, but he guessed Bilyk hadn't cared or knew he only *needed* a few rounds and then for the ships to stay afloat long enough to be recognised and reported.

"Good God, they've put something heavy on the *Vekha* as well!" Koenig called out. "They are insane!"

It would explain why they had taken their time about launching this attack. It looked like the forward 3-pounder mounting had been replaced with an old 6-inch gun, a weapon with a considerably longer reach. It wouldn't do the transport ship any favours when it fired, of course.

Baxter knew they couldn't give either of the vessels the opportunity to open fire, of course. After even a single shell, the Cossacks would likely start their grim work in the streets of Odessa.

Raising his glasses, Baxter could see that the crews on the other ships were taking their time about this. He spotted men in both naval and army uniforms, and more than a few in civilian clothes. It was almost full daylight now, and he could see the improvised monitor was indeed flying the star and crescent of the Ottoman Empire. The *Vekha* had the red flag of revolution flying again.

They weren't in a hurry, he realised, because the *Zataka* hadn't been spotted yet. That, and they weren't a fully trained crew used to working together. Nonetheless, the *Vekha* at least looked like she was getting ready to fire the opening shell of the bombardment.

"Three points to starboard — aim our bows at her stern," Baxter rapped out. Piotr obeyed immediately. The *Zataka* was cracking along at a good eighteen or nineteen knots now, raising a fine bow wave, at a range of around a thousand yards. The manoeuvre brought their starboard Hotchkiss rotary gun to bear. "Fedotov! Fire on the *Vekha*'s forward gun!"

The mutineer didn't seem to have any problem firing at his own vessel, certainly not now that she had been chopped around. The 1-pounder started thumping as soon as the *Zataka* had steadied out.

The effect was almost comical. Although the first few shells whistled overhead rather than hitting anything, they distracted the crew serving the 6-inch gun. Then Fedotov managed to drop a few on target, although he was shooting at long range. He didn't manage to hit anything vital, but the small shells' detonations sent the crew diving for cover. One punched through the *Vekha*'s forward funnel and exploded inside, which made a hell of a noise even at this distance.

"Well, they know we're here now," Piotr said phlegmatically. Crews on both vessels were running to their smaller guns, and the *Zataka*'s easy run was over.

Although they'd distracted the crew of the *Vekha*, the gunners around the big beast of a weapon on the monitor were still working to load a fat shell. Baxter looked between the vessels, gauging the distances by eye. "Bring us three points back to port," he ordered Piotr. "Yuriy, stand by the torpedoes! Fedotov, hit that gunboat and hit it now!"

Both ships were firing at the *Zataka* now. The transport had single-barrel 1-pounders, and the gunboat at least one machine gun. Baxter held his nerve and made himself stand straight as bullets started slashing overhead and shells burst in the water around them. Fedotov was actually laughing now as he returned the monitor's fire, little flashes against her side and deck structures showing where he was managing to land hits. It was a much smaller target, though, and a lot of the shells seemed to be going overhead.

"Keep her steady!" Baxter ordered Piotr. The helmsman had, perhaps unconsciously, started to turn the wheel one way then the other, making them a harder target. That wouldn't do at all, not for a torpedo attack.

"Torpedoes ready!" Koenig called, then yelped and ducked as a machine gun round ricocheted off the top of the bow turtleback.

They were steady, steady... Then their bows were coming offline. Baxter turned back, a furious order on his lips, but saw that Piotr was slumped over with one side of his face covered in blood; a machine gun round had managed to tear a hole in the conning position's flimsy protection. Sava lunged forward, dragging his comrade out of the way unceremoniously, and righted the course without prompting.

Baxter spun back. They'd come dangerously close while they came off course and then corrected, into the hundreds of feet rather than yards, and the torpedoes would need time running in order to aim. "Launch torpedoes!" he yelled forward.

"Launching torpedoes!" Koenig confirmed. Baxter felt the vibrations through his boots, the satisfying *thwump* of compressed air hurling the 15-inch torpedoes forward and into the water.

"Hard starboard!" Baxter barked, staring intently until he saw the comforting tracks in the water that told him that both torpedoes were running true towards the target.

Remarkable, particularly given that a few days ago someone had sabotaged them before a similar attack could be launched on the *Potemkin*.

He didn't have time to worry about the torpedoes after that. "Bring us all the way round!" he ordered, ducking slightly as a shell from the *Vekha* whistled overhead. That would be just his luck, being killed by a ship he'd hopefully just sunk.

Fedotov kept firing until the last moment, until his gun could no longer bear on the monitor. Then he stepped away from the mount, disentangling himself from the padded rests that would have thumped the weapon back into his shoulders with each round, and dashed across to support on the port weapon as it came to bear. That saved his life, as the starboard mounting was torn away by a hit from the *Vekha*. The *Zataka* staggered as it was wounded but kept ploughing through the water. The monitor was moving away now, gunners running from the howitzer on her forecastle to pull the cover off a 3-pounder on the quarterdeck. That was good, but it would all be for nothing if they couldn't sink both these ships.

Baxter had been almost unconsciously counting down the moments until their torpedoes should detonate against the transport ship. He whirled to stare backwards, peering through the smoke of the recent detonation and the fire Fedotov was now struggling to put out. Nothing.

All of this for…

He staggered as the first weapon detonated against the *Vekha*'s side amidships. An enormous geyser of angry water rose, lifting the *Zataka* with it. A breath later, the second torpedo detonated astern of the first, tearing another great slash in the transport's essentially unarmoured side and shaking the torpedo boat again. Water rushed into those wounds and he could hear the scream of escaping steam mingling with the cries of terrified, dying men until he couldn't tell the difference.

Nothing to be done about that now. A 3-pound round from the monitor exploded on the water's surface a few yards off their port side and the port gunner went down, screaming and clutching his face. Fedotov stepped into the breach, heedless of the heavy machine gun bullets that hammered into the gun shield.

Sava crouched low at the wheel as they were raked with bullets that rattled off the funnel. Baxter had drawn his revolver without really noticing it. They were racing past the stern of the larger vessel at a range of about fifty feet, so he thought he may as well have a go. Koenig obviously had the same idea, and a couple of the sailors without other duties were firing rifles. Baxter realised, as he lowered the empty revolver, that Mashka was on deck and firing her Luger at the monitor. He doubted any of the small arms fire did any good, beyond throwing off the gunners.

They were racing away from it now. "Sava, bring us round her bows!" he ordered. They were a faster, more manoeuvrable vessel, and he could use that to keep them out of the firing arc of the 3-pounder.

The *Vekha* was out of it now, the holes in her side so extensive she was starting to capsize. Even if her deck wasn't already too canted to use the guns, her crew had better things to do with their time than shoot at the fast-moving torpedo boat — like trying to get the ship's boats away or just diving over the side and attempting to swim for the monitor.

Baxter wanted to shout to them not to do that, that he planned to kill that vessel as well, but it would be futile with the roar of the Hotchkiss firing and the rattle of machine gun and rifle fire. Fedotov was scoring hits all along the gunboat now, but she was more sturdily built than Baxter had previously thought and just ploughed on, trying to turn to bring her own anti-ship weapon to bear.

Baxter beckoned Koenig back to him. The lieutenant had lost his cap and was bleeding from a gash in his cheek, but otherwise he seemed to be in fine spirits. "Take over the con!" Baxter shouted in his ear. "Try to get us lined up on their forecastle!"

"Aye aye!" Koenig replied with a grin.

Baxter went aft, knowing he was leaving the steering in capable hands. The *Zataka* had cleared a little distance from the monitor, and he noticed the other vessel had stopped trying to bring her 3-pounder to bear. Instead, every man with a rifle was lined up along her side and was shooting at them, along with the two Maxim machine guns.

For the first time, Baxter saw that Bilyk was actually aboard the other vessel. He'd not expected the Okhrana official to be here at all, but rather supervising things from shore. He obviously wanted to make sure everything went to plan from this side, but it surprised Baxter he'd chosen the smaller vessel over the comfort of the *Vekha*.

Bilyk had got a proper grip on his crew now. While the small arms and machine guns rained lead on the torpedo boat and hopefully kept it at bay, he had ordered the main gun to be brought into action again. Baxter was pretty sure that was an old, obsolete piece, a fat-barrelled howitzer that looked absurdly out of place on the vessel. He dashed to Fedotov. "How many rounds do we have left?" he asked, ducking as another fusillade swept the decks.

"Last case," Fedotov said, nodding to the box of shells by the loader's feet.

"When I give the word, put all of them right onto that howitzer when she bears again," he ordered. "We might be able to damage the firing mechanism or kill enough of the crew."

The gunner nodded. The Hotchkiss gun just didn't seem to be up to the job. Baxter had no idea why anyone thought it would be effective against torpedo boats, aside from its comparatively prodigious rate of fire.

Koenig had Sava bring them round again. Baxter knew this was their last chance. Whoever had designed the monstrosity they were fighting obviously hadn't planned on it coming under attack, or not cared about the safety of the crew, and there wasn't any sort of protection around the gun at least.

"Hold her steady!" Baxter shouted as bullets snickered past him. He was reloading the Nagant with a handful of spare bullets, mostly just to give his hands something to do. Tommy and Mashka were flat on the deck, both staring at him with wide eyes. No time to worry about them now, no time for anything else really.

Baxter straightened up, put one foot on the gunwale. Bilyk was standing in plain view, still in his dark grey coat and little round fur hat, hands linked behind his back. Whatever else you could say about the man, he was no coward.

"Fire!" Baxter barked.

Fedotov did exactly as he was ordered, the Hotchkiss thudding faster than he would normally fire it. The loader went down, gut shot and writhing, and Baxter grabbed up the last few shells and fed them one after the other into the feeding box on top of the weapon.

Men were falling on the monitor, hit by rifle fire or caught in the explosions, while others were still scrambling to finish loading the gun, Okhrana men pitching in with the soldiers. Baxter marvelled at their dedication to duty. He dropped their last shell into the feed then looked across the water again. He locked eyes with Bilyk, just before Fedotov took his time over firing his last two rounds.

Baxter didn't see what those shells had hit. One second the Okhrana official was turning away contemptuously, raising his hand to order the shelling to begin despite this persistent gnat shooting at them. The next second, Bilyk was gone, and so was the rest of the vessel, disappearing into a fireball that dazzled them all.

The shock wave hit the *Zataka* a second later, knocking everyone from their feet and staggering the boat in the water. Baxter hated to think what Ippolit and Luka were experiencing below decks. That reminded him.

He raised his head. "I thought I told you two to stay below decks?" he shouted over the ringing in his ears.

Tommy mouthed something back, then raised his voice. All Baxter could really make out was 'flooding'.

EPILOGUE

Baxter staggered to his feet and shook his head, then smacked his palm against his temple. The ringing was starting to subside, though he had a suspicion there was blood leaking from at least one ear. He was just glad the young folk had been sheltered from some of the blast.

"Damn fine shooting, whatever you hit," he said to Fedotov, who was still leaning heavily against the double stock of the Hotchkiss.

"A shell, I think," said the burly sailor, before sinking to his knees. Baxter noticed the front of his grubby white tunic was stained red with blood. He raised his head, looking for someone to fetch a stretcher; but of course there was nowhere to take the wounded man.

All he could do was lie him back so he could see the sky while he died, which didn't take long. From the amount of blood down his front, he'd been hit a while ago but had somehow remained at his post.

"Tomas'ka say we floody," Mashka said, slowly and distinctly and in incredibly broken English. She no doubt thought his brain was sufficiently addled that he'd lost the ability to comprehend Russian.

Baxter got back to his feet. "Well, what the bloody hell do you want me to do about it?" he demanded, staring at the devastation they had wrought.

"Stop us flooding so we do not die?" Her acerbic tone reasserted itself as she switched back to Russian. "I like the sound of this Ekaterina and would like to meet her."

The monitor was gone, obliterated, reduced to a covering of splinters and scorched meat across a broad section of the sea. The *Vekha* had finished the painful process of sinking, though the water was shallow enough that her bows were just visible. A lot of the men in the water had been killed by the shock wave, but some clung to flotsam or were being gathered up by the boats that had got clear.

Koenig joined him, looking pasty. "Well, you did it," he said, offering his hand.

"Did what?" Baxter asked bitterly as he looked west, expecting to see the flicker of fires already.

"What you had to do," the lieutenant replied.

Baxter sighed and took the proffered hand. "I hope you don't take offense at this," he said. "But I think I'm done with Russia."

Koenig actually chuckled at that. "Well, given we are sinking, you may not ever have to set foot there again."

That shook Baxter out of his funk. "We're not sinking on my watch," he said. "The engines are still running, so the flooding can't be that bad, at least not in the engine room. Sava, get back on the helm. Yuriy, set a course for Odessa, best possible speed. The rest of you, let's get to bailing."

Not that there were a lot of them left. Piotr, from the look of things, was alive but knocked out. Fedotov was most certainly dead, as were the other gun crews. Baxter guessed the two machinists Ippolit and Luka had sealed themselves into the engine room so they could keep the boat moving, and would die if the rest of them couldn't keep it afloat.

"What about them?" Tommy asked, gesturing at the survivors from the *Vekha*. A few men shouted angrily at the torpedo boat that had visited such destruction on them, while others called out for help or just stared dumbly around themselves.

"There's nothing we can do for them." Baxter said, voice hard. "The battle and the explosion will have been heard in Odessa, and someone will have the guts to come out and check. They'll be fine. We have to worry about us now, lad."

They could only make one quarter speed thanks to the damage and the amount of water they continued to take on board. The helmsman was excused from bailing, but everyone else had to take a turn with the buckets — even Piotr when he came to.

"Thank God we're not too far from the coast," Koenig gasped as he upended another load of water, back where it belonged.

"I'm not sure we'll make it anyway," Baxter said. "I'll have to go below and see about plugging any holes."

"A ship! A big one!" Mashka shouted excitedly. She was taking a break in the stern. "We are saved."

"Well, that depends on a lot of things," Baxter growled under his breath. Straightening up, he could see more than one ship out there. A surprising number of vessels, in fact, given the fighting had only stopped an hour ago. He'd lost his glasses at some point in the action, and shaded his eyes. They mostly looked like civilian vessels, some flying flags other than Russian, but one or two could have been military.

"For instance, if one of those is the *Stremitelny* most of us are going to swing," he said, then turned in the direction Mashka was pointing. There was indeed just one ship visible out there, a big one. A three-funnelled modern battleship. One that started to look very familiar.

"Yes, I'm really not convinced we have been saved," Baxter commented sourly, as he spotted the *Ismail* sliding smoothly towards them, once again towing one of the battleship *Potemkin*'s boats. Baxter sighed. "All stop," he ordered. "Let's get Ippolit and Luka out of the engine room before the crew compartment is completely flooded."

It took some doing and everyone's efforts, but they managed to force the engine room hatch open and hold it against the water pressure long enough for Baxter to haul the two exhausted machinists out. He had to pull them against the flood water going in, drowning the engine they had nursed so effectively. By the time the *Ismail* arrived with the launch in tow, the water was lapping over the *Zataka*'s gunwales. The other rescue ships, seeing the suspicious torpedo boat, were giving them a wide berth and moving to help the survivors from the *Vekha*.

"It seems you have had a morning of it," Lieutenant Kovalenko called from the launch as it drew alongside.

"Ran into some old friends," Baxter told him, as he bodily lifted Mashka and then Tommy across the divide. The two machinists went next, then the other living members of the crew. They were all too exhausted to worry about the dead, who would go down with their vessel.

"I think I could get used to torpedo boats," Koenig said, before stepping lightly between the vessels. "Assuming I stay in the navy."

Baxter was the last one off. The *Zataka* gave a bit of a lurch and his step became a slightly less dignified jump into the launch before he could be pulled down with his command. "I think the Navy would be poorer for losing you," he said, as though nothing had happened.

"I am beginning to think I have seen enough of such things," Koenig decided, then threw himself down onto one of the bench seats.

Beshoff was at the wheel of the launch. The *Ismail* had cast them off and was hovering protectively nearby, its work of bringing salvation as quickly as possible done.

"I keep thinking I have seen the back of you, Marcus Alexandrovich," the cheerful young sailor said. "And you keep turning back up."

"Hopefully not for much longer," Baxter said. "No offense intended."

He turned to Kovalenko, shoving his hands into the pockets of his coat. "What's your plan?" he asked bluntly.

The Ukrainian looked despondent, but not necessarily beaten. "We are sailing back to Constanza, where we will take the Romanians up on their kind offer. This mutiny is over, even if the revolution will continue."

Baxter nodded. "Well, I was thinking of going that way anyway," he said. "I'll join you for the last stretch, if I may."

Kovalenko smiled. "Your account of this action will be an interesting diversion. And your friends?"

Baxter looked at Koenig, who was slouched with his head back, and Mashka and Tommy, both of whom looked exhausted and bedraggled. He remembered they still had work to do in Odessa, though — or at least, they needed to tell Ekaterina Juneau what work needed to be done.

"It seems I have one last favour to ask — while it will be a risk, it would be better if we could put them ashore in Odessa."

Kovalenko seemed to consider this, then glanced at Beshoff, who nodded uncertainly. "We can slip in somewhere close by," he said. "Worst comes to worst, there are only three of us aboard."

Koenig raised his head and blinked blearily at Baxter. "And what of you? It should be safe enough for you, so long as you don't run into Zubov, and I know there is someone who will want to see you."

Baxter took his hands from his pockets. There was an envelope in one of them, which he'd been absently toying with. It was damp and dirty, dog-eared from having been carried there since Vladivostok. He could just make out his name on the front of it, written in an elegant hand.

He folded the envelope carefully and tucked away again. He'd read it another time, maybe... "No. No, I think it's best if I go on to Constanza."

A NOTE TO THE READER

Dear Reader,

It is a tribute to Sergei Eisenstein's skill as a film-maker and propagandist that his 1925 film *Battleship Potemkin* has so permeated perception of the eleven days in Odessa in 1905, that even relatively recent history books have recounted some version of it. Details differ between accounts, over issues such as time of day or what triggered the violence, but the essential narrative remains the same — a line of Cossacks marching in step down the Richelieu Steps and delivering disciplined volleys into an unarmed crowd before it became a general rout and massacre. The image is so enduring and iconic, in fact, that to this day the magnificent stairs that run from Odessa's harbour up to the city are referred to as the 'Potemkin Steps'.

Modern scholarship, however, agrees that this particular incident probably didn't happen. Accounts continue to vary about the scope and scale of the violence and destruction. Some suggest thousands died in hails of machine-gun fire while the whole port burned down, while others indicate a more random and uncontrolled violence on the part of the state's forces and a more limited destruction.

Where does this leave the historical novelist? Once I had embarked on an account of the mutiny aboard the *Potemkin* and the civil unrest in Odessa, I found it hard not to include such an iconic scene. I tried to write it more in keeping with the picture of more random violence that current historical thinking has built, and hope I may be forgiven for taking some license with the facts.

I also could not have taken Baxter to Russia in 1905 and not find a way to involve him in such an important sequence of events in the first place. This presented its own challenges, as I feel a naval adventure should involve at least some form of naval action. The so-called 'silent battle' during which the mutineers faced down the combined battleships of the Black Sea Fleet offered a suitably dramatic and tense episode, yet with a distinct paucity of actual gunfire.

Much of Baxter's shenanigans are, therefore, entirely the product of my imagination. To the best of my knowledge, there was no secret police plot to launch a false flag attack in concert with rogue British intelligence agents. Tensions had certainly been high with the Ottoman Empire for much of this period, and relations between Russia and Great Britain were at a low point (though soon to improve), and history certainly offers some examples of similar plots, so I feel I have not strayed too far from the realm of the possible.

While Baxter, Koenig and the others are fictional, as is the *Zataka* torpedo boat (though I based it on an existing class of Black Sea Fleet vessels), I have otherwise tried to weave in as much history as possible. The *Potemkin* (or more accurately *Kniaz Potyomkin Tavricheskiy*) was, of course, entirely real and presented a significant if brief threat to the Romanoff regime. The *Ismail* torpedo boat and *Vekha* transport formed the bulk of the short-lived revolutionary squadron, though the fate that befalls the latter is again my own invention. The *Potemkin* was first surrendered to Romania, though the mutineers scuttled her in Constanza's harbour, and then returned to the Imperial Russian Navy. Renamed *Panteleimon*, she was repaired and returned to service and thereafter had a relatively unremarkable career.

Most of the mutineers and revolutionaries I featured existed. Afanasy Matyushenko leaps from the pages of history as a vibrant and fascinating figure, from what we know of his childhood to his eventual death by hanging in 1907. Ivan Beshoff is just as interesting, though less detail is available — the son of a middle-class Ukrainian family, his career veered wildly between sailor, revolutionary and finally chip shop owner in Dublin, Ireland where he died in 1987. Oleksander Kovalenko is a particularly interesting figure, who gave up a position of relative safety and privilege to fight for Ukrainian independence in 1905 and remained active in pursuit of that goal before turning to academia and eventual self-imposed exile in Geneva after the Second World War. Konstantin Feldmann survived the mutiny and actually went on to appear in Eisenstein's film before falling foul of one of Stalin's purges. Anatoly Berezovsky, better known as Kirill, suffered a similar fate.

One can only be struck by the passion and deep humanity of many of the mutineers and revolutionaries, though also repelled by the attitude of some to the idea of mass civilian casualties. The fact that the battleship alone could have levelled Odessa but the crew chose not to speaks volumes. In many ways they were ahead of their time — literally, in fact, as Matyushenko had been cautioned not to launch the mutiny until the whole fleet was assembled and could rise as one. The Russian Empire certainly simmered with discontent at the time, due to both the repressive policies of the government and its disastrous adventure in the east. It's hard to say whether the revolt could have spread if a few things had been different — if the mutineers had succeeded in shelling the military governor, if the wider revolutionary movement had been more coherent and organised, if… While it is incorrect to suggest, as

Eisenstein did, that the mutineers and revolutionaries were Marxists (they were predominantly Social Democrat), some of the groundwork for the coming revolution was certainly laid in those frenetic few days.

As for Marcus Baxter — I think it's pretty clear that he's done with Russia. Further adventures await in other troubled and war-torn parts of the world, though I suspect Russia is not quite done with him…

As before, I am greatly indebted to my good friends Dr Malcolm Kinnear and Paul Hurley, for their insights and wisdom. As always, the Edinburgh Schismatics writers group has been invaluable with their incisive criticism and boundless encouragement.

It goes without saying that none of this would have been possible without the team at Sapere.

Thank you for taking the time to read my novel — I hope you enjoyed reading it as much as I enjoyed researching and writing it. If you enjoyed it, it would be great if you could drop a review into **Amazon** and **Goodreads** — these can be a great help to authors. You can find me on **Twitter** and **Facebook** for short rambles about my hobbies, other interests and writing.

I'm also developing a blog, mostly about naval history and my great-grandfather's career in the Royal Navy, which can be found here: **timchantauthor.com**

Sapere Books is an exciting new publisher of brilliant fiction and popular history.

To find out more about our latest releases and our monthly bargain books visit our website: **saperebooks.com**